TRUSTING Cade

Custos Securities Series
Book 1
By
Luna David

Trusting Cade
Custos Securities Series Book 1
Copyright © 2016 and 2018 by Luna David
ALL RIGHTS RESERVED

Cover by Kellie Dennis at Book Cover by Design
Custos Securities Series symbol designed by Kellie Dennis, property of Luna David.
Editing by Miranda Vescio at V8 Editing and Proofreading
Proofreading by Allison Holzapfel at Allison's Author Services
Interior Design by Morningstar Ashley at Designs by Morningstar
Interior Design and Formatting by Flawless Touch Formatting

The unauthorized reproduction or distribution of this copyrighted work is illegal. No part of this book may be reproduced or transmitted in any form or by any means, including electronic or mechanical means, including photocopying, recording, or by any information storage and retrieval systems, without express written permission from the author, Luna David, author.luna.david@gmail.com. The only exception is in the case of brief quotations embodied in reviews.

This book is a work of fiction. While references may be made to actual places and events, the names, characters, places, and incidents are either products of the author's imagination or are used fictitiously. Any resemblance to actual persons, living or dead, events, or locales is entirely coincidental.

Licensed material is being used for illustrative purposes only and any person depicted in the licensed material is a model.

Intended for an adult audience. Contains explicit sexual content, violence, and elements of BDSM. **HFN Cliffhanger.**
Trigger warning: physical assault and recollections of past sexual assault.

Luna David acknowledges the trademark status of the following trademarks mentioned in this work of fiction:

Forrest Gump, Ford Edge, iPhone, iPad, Dropbox, Wikipedia, Google Maps, Google, Kool-Aid, Two Buck Chuck, Trader Joe's, West Point, House of Air, Hollywood Café, The Italian Homemade Company, The California Academy of Sciences, Walmart, Planet Granite, The Mission's Foreign Cinema Restaurant, The Maltese Falcon, Toyota Camry, Honda Civic, Green Beret, SEALs, Special Forces, LoJack, Wells Fargo Bank, Ambien, 7-Eleven, Krav Maga, Muy Thai, Jiu Jitsu, Pilates, Styrofoam, Jolly Green Giant, Hulk, Betty Boop, G. I. Joe

Dedication

To my Husband, the love of my life, and the man who makes me laugh like no other. Without you, this book wouldn't have been written. You make it possible for me to take time every single day to expel the voices in my head and get them on paper. I'm sorry I didn't title my first M/M Romance, The Adventures of Rod Steelcock: The Manhole Chronicles, as you suggested. I hope Trusting Cade will suffice.

CADE

Standing at parade rest—a habit ingrained in them from their early days in the Army—Cade and his best friend and business partner, Cooper, were four stories above their newest round of testing candidates, gathering first impressions by watching them pair up and run a timed obstacle course through Cade's office windows. Though Cooper was watching them diligently, Cade's mind was wandering. He'd been overworking himself to the point of mental exhaustion in an unsuccessful attempt at keeping his mind off the barren wasteland that was his personal life. And, unable to turn his mind off, sleep was scarce, causing the type of physical exhaustion he hadn't felt in years.

He used to be able to will himself to sleep in any given situation, but that particular skill had failed him as of late. He was getting old; he was doing it alone, and the fact that he'd never thought he'd be taking stock of his life at age thirty-eight and finding it wanting was just the icing on the proverbial cake, as far as he was concerned. He knew what the problem was, but not how to fix it, which just added fuel to the fire of this fucked up dilemma he found himself in because fixing problems was one of his greatest strengths.

Maybe a change of scene would help. He and Cooper were headed to San Francisco soon to do a job and visit their families. Maybe some downtime was exactly what he needed to get his head straight. He missed his family, which was one of the main reasons he was taking the trip to begin with. Maybe seeing his parents and his brothers and sister would combat this emptiness he couldn't seem to shake. Until then, at least he had Cooper by his side.

After fighting their way through the Special Forces training program together and years of combat fighting alongside each other, there was no one Cade trusted more than Cooper. Along with two of their closest friends, Jackson and Sawyer, they had agreed to get out of their Special Forces unit and go into business together. Custos Securities now enjoyed a reputation for providing unparalleled security for both civilians and businesses across the U.S., and they were searching for five to ten new security specialists, or guardians as they called them to honor the meaning of the Latin word custos, to meet their customers' demands.

The latest candidates seemed promising, but Cade knew from past testing sessions that looks could be deceiving. The group below them, seven men and one woman and all fit by military standards, stretched in preparation for the obstacle course as Jackson and Sawyer gave them the information they needed to get through the course.

The obstacle course was structured like the courses designed for Special Forces military groups to improve reaction times and physical stamina. None of the current group being tested had any clue of the amount of trust Cade and Cooper placed in their instructors, which was how they liked it. If the group saw Jackson and Sawyer as ordinary employees, they'd be more apt to be themselves and let their instructors see who they really were.

One of the biggest reasons for the strenuous testing of all candidates was to figure out exactly who they were at their core. The people they hired needed the correct temperament not only to do their jobs, but to deal with two alpha co-owners running the show.

"So, after this round of testing is done and we make our hiring decisions, we're headed to California next week to work on the Kensington job and to start looking at some real estate there."

Cade chuckled. "The Kensingtons. What do they need? Didn't we just put their system in last year?"

Cooper smirked. "Listen, I'll handle drumming up business, new equipment and security contracts, the press, and HR. All the details that you can't be bothered with. You focus on our security systems, planning security details, and the physical training programs."

Cade raised his hands in supplication. "Okay, okay. You get us the business, and I'll keep it. It's worked for us so far."

Cooper nodded, agreeing with Cade's assessment. They watched as the first two candidates took off in a race across the course. Cooper tilted his head and raised a brow. "We'll have enough time to see our families while we're in California. You're going to see yours, right?"

Cade was confused by the question. "Yeah, of course. Why?"

Cooper shrugged, not meeting his gaze. "There's no 'of course' about it, man. I've been struggling to read you lately. It's hard to read you on a good day, but there's just something... You've been off."

Cade was surprised that it had shown. He was adept at masking his emotions, and the fact that Cooper had seen his, or rather his lack of them, threw him off balance. He shook his head, but Cooper wasn't having it.

"Cade, I know you." He crossed his arms over his broad chest and raised a brow. "I've been with you on a daily basis for too many damn years. Something's going on. You're not exactly social, but lately, even going out for beers with the guys is such a rare occurrence I sometimes forget to ask you. Talk to me, man."

Cade knew Cooper wouldn't give up on this line of questioning. Once he dug in, he was pretty much set on a course, unless a bomb went off and caused a wrinkle in his plans. That wrinkle would only be a delay of the inevitable as he'd come back around again and dig until he got what he wanted. He could hardly be upset by it. It's exactly what got them contracts and made Cooper, well, Cooper. They were opposites in so many ways, which is why they'd become and remained best friends. Cade took the leap.

"I want to settle down. I've been dating with it in mind, but the guys I've dated aren't right. So, I stopped altogether. I don't really think I'm unusually picky, but none of the guys in my past have felt right."

Cooper's eyes popped wide. Cade quirked a brow at his friend. "You asked."

Cooper shrugged. "I'm just surprised you finally admitted it. I've known for a while, I was just waiting for you to talk to me."

Cade gave him a baleful stare. "Bullshit."

His friend chuckled. "Seriously, man. You've been wanting to settle down for a couple years. You're just going about it all wrong."

Exasperated, Cade turned away from the windows and crossed his arms over his chest. "Oh please, wise one, tell me why I haven't found the right guy."

"Look at your dating history. You've practically been dating yourself."

Cade threw up his hands in exasperation. "What the hell is that supposed to mean?"

"You've dated military and ex-military guys, other security guys, men you've met at the local fighters' gym." He continued ticking them off on his fingers. "There was a cop and what was that other guy, a firefighter, right? You're not going to settle down with someone like that."

"Why the fuck not?"

"Because they're all alphas and would resent you trying to take care of them. It's gotta be someone you feel protective of, someone that needs you."

"So I'm looking for someone that's helpless and needy?"

Cooper laughed. "I didn't say that. Don't turn my words around. I know you, Cade. You need someone who needs your strength and likes, or craves, your desire to protect and control. You don't need a top who turns bottom for you; you need a natural bottom. Opposites attract, man."

"How can something like that last?"

Cooper shook his head and chuckled. "It'll last because you'll be able to provide what he needs, and vice versa. You need to find someone to take care of and protect, someone who allows you to take control."

Cade narrowed his eyes. "You think I need someone weak?"

Cooper's brows drew together, and he scoffed. "Are you deliberately being obtuse? You wouldn't respect someone like that. Strength isn't always physical. The men you've dated won't need you, and you won't have any desire to protect them, not to mention they won't allow you any control. Oh, and we haven't even started talking about the kink."

Cade laughed, incredulously. "What the fuck, Coop?"

Cooper smirked. "You think I don't know you're skating the edge of the BDSM lifestyle?"

Cade shook his head, exasperated. "You act like I've got whips, chains, and a St. Andrew's Cross in my basement. I'm not some leather-wearing BDSM Master with a collar, handcuffs, and a tawse hanging from my belt."

It was Cooper's turn to look incredulous. "What the fuck is a St. Andrew's Cross and a tawse? No." Cooper held up his hand to stop Cade from answering, shaking his head. "I thought you just liked a bit of slap and tickle, maybe a bit of bondage. You're way more into this stuff than I could have imagined with that vocabulary. Just one more reason you and I could never be in a relationship."

Cade gave Cooper a sardonic look. "We could never be in a relationship because you're too damned ugly." They both kept their serious expressions for another second before laughing at the absurd response. Cooper's California surfer boy good looks were always prime fodder for jokes and teasing.

Cade continued after they settled down. "Not to mention, you swing both ways. I need someone who only swings my way... And, I don't have any BDSM equipment. I just know what most of it is. I've gone to a few fetish clubs, but I'd rather take someone to a club like that after we've established our relationship boundaries. I'm dominant, but I'm no Dom. If I was with someone that hated the idea, I'd be fine without it."

Cade paused, thoughtful. "You know, you're the last person I ever thought I'd be taking relationship advice from. I hate to admit it, but I think you're right. I think I've been looking for the wrong thing, or rather, for the wrong kind of person. But I don't know where the hell I'm gonna find the type of guy I need."

"I'm sure, now that you know what *not* to look for, it'll be easier."

Cade shook his head, unsure. "I'm used to dating men who are interested in the same things I am, so I'm not sure how to go about finding someone who isn't interested in those things. Seems the opposite of what one would try to do, but hell, what I've been doing isn't working, so I guess all I can do is try."

Cooper smiled. "Just keep yourself open to it. I think you'll find it when you least expect it and probably much sooner than you think." Cooper glanced down to the course. "It looks like they've long since cleared out. They should be done with the written portion of the testing in 30 minutes or so, giving us plenty of time to get down there and get ready for the ring."

Cade smirked. "Us, huh? All you'll be doing is running your mouth and looking pretty. I have to fight them all. See, this situation completely encapsulates our working relationship. You bullshit your way through while I do all the real work around here."

Cooper laughed. "It's been my master plan all along. Glad to see it's working."

Cade made a rude sound in the back of his throat and shook his head. As they walked, he thought more about their discussion. He had to admit to himself that Cooper was right. He probably did need someone who was completely different than him. Although he didn't share Cooper's belief he'd find his soulmate anytime soon. The perfect man wasn't just going to fall into his lap. He had no idea how the hell he'd find the type of guy Cooper had described, but he'd have to think on it and come up with a plan. He was good at making plans.

He walked into the locker room to change and get ready for the coming fights. He easily shifted gears, compartmentalizing his personal conversation with Cooper to get himself in the right mindset to take part in eight individual fights with the candidates. As Cade got dressed, Sawyer approached and began to wrap his hands in fighter's tape. He waited out Sawyer's silence. Cade knew his friend hated it when he did that. When Cade's hands were wrapped, and he was ready to head out to the ring, Sawyer looked up, and Cade raised a brow.

Sawyer huffed. "You've got a few possibles in this batch. Keep an eye out for candidate Thompson. He's been holding his cards close to his vest most of the day, but they'll pick up a bit on the mic later from a few conversations he had with one or two of the guys. I'm assuming he was mostly making sexually explicit and derogatory remarks regarding candidate Gardner."

Cade narrowed his eyes thinking he wanted to get a hand on the audio they recorded from all the testing sessions. Sawyer nodded. "Yeah. I know.

Anyway, my bet is, just from this upcoming fight, you're gonna count him out of the running. He didn't do anything overt to make me think he's truly a threat, but there's just something going on I can't get a bead on. When I talked about the upcoming fight, he looked just a little too happy to be able to try to best you. My advice, don't turn your back on him in the ring. I'm certain he won't be able to beat you, but I don't think the guy plays by the rules."

Cade knew advice from Sawyer should not be taken lightly. He made eye contact as he nodded, so his friend knew he'd taken every word seriously. He glanced behind Sawyer and watched as Jackson approached. "You're both good to go for the day. Thank you for your help. If either of you has something to report, besides what you just provided, you can do it tomorrow. Toss something on our calendar, and we'll talk. We won't be making any decisions until we've listened to all the audio and Cooper and I have been able to get through all the written tests."

Sawyer glanced at Jackson, who gave an almost imperceptible nod. Sawyer's eyebrow lifted. "Mind if we observe the fights, sir?"

Cade sighed. "Cooper is just as much your boss as I am, yet you don't call him sir."

Sawyer didn't smile as Cade had assumed he would. "Cooper wasn't ever our captain, sir."

"I'm no longer your captain. Knock it off."

They both nodded. Sawyer's response was automatic. "Yes, sir."

Cade rubbed his taped hands over his face and sighed once more. "Yeah, you can observe if you want."

Both men nodded, and they all left the locker room, Jackson and Sawyer heading out to the gym to observe while Cade hung back and watched from the alcove, taking in as much as he could before the fights began. He tuned back into Cooper's final remarks and made his way to the center ring. Once there, he put on his headgear and mouth guard and warmed up a bit, aware all eyes were on him. He kept his gaze on his partner and ignored those around him as Cooper wound down.

"As you all know, we've made it to the third and final round of today's testing. You'll be fighting Zavier McCade. A little bit of advice, use your brain in the ring. Keep your head and your wits about you. You need to understand going into this test this fight is not a challenge to see who can beat Cade. None of you can beat Cade. I know some of you will ignore this advice and look at this as an opportunity to prove your worth as a fighter, but as strange as it may seem, that's not what we're interested in seeing. We're much more interested in seeing your fighting style, your techniques, and how you adapt to the unexpected."

Cooper swept his gaze across the recruits, some of whom looked skeptical. "Cade will not be fighting at 100%. Knocking you out isn't his goal here. We want these matches to last. We want to see your skills in the ring, the breadth of your knowledge. Each of you will fight Cade for five minutes; if you're well versed in MMA, that's the length of one round. Because he will be fighting all eight of you, instead of the usual one minute between rounds, he will receive 90 seconds of recovery time. First up will be candidate Brown."

Cade kept his game face on as he tilted his head left then right to stretch it out and crack it. He rolled his shoulders and bounced on his feet a few times as he shook out his arms. Hand to hand combat was his forte. He fought two of the candidates without being impressed. They were both a bit unimaginative when it came to technique, neither of them using any creativity in their attacks. He didn't need the 90 seconds before the next rounds, and he knew just from fighting them Custos wouldn't be offering them a job.

While their guardians didn't need to be professional fighters, they did need to be quick on their feet and think outside the box. The third fighter was quite the scrapper. He was average height but very well built. He had a good floor game, and Cade was somewhat impressed with several of his attempts to get him in a hold. He was someone who would learn well but always put his own spin on things. Cade liked that.

Next up was candidate Gardner, and she had a wicked gleam in her eyes as she surveyed him. He liked her immediately. She was fairly tall with sleek and well-honed muscles. He soon found out she was lightning fast. As they tussled, he had to put more effort into their fight than he'd had to with the first two of the three men he'd fought. She wasn't trying to take him down which showed him she'd listened to Cooper and had taken his advice. With resourceful and creative moves, she kept him guessing.

When their five minutes were up, her breath sawed in and out and she had to bend over and rest her hands on her knees. His breathing was faster, and he'd finally broken a sweat. When she stood up, she was grinning from ear to ear.

"Damn, Mr. McCade, I haven't had so much fun in a ring in a long time. I look forward to you teaching me how to do the flip move that had me on my back in about two seconds flat. Thank you for the experience."

They shook hands, and he couldn't stop a smile from forming at her assurance she'd make it to the end and get the chance for some of the training. He nodded. "You did well. I look forward to training you if your other tests are as impressive as this one."

Her grin got even wider as she turned and hopped down out of the ring with more enthusiasm than she'd had getting into it, which was saying something. Cooper was just about to signal another fighter to enter when Cade heard a few uncomfortable chuckles and saw Thompson laugh and poke one of the other men in the side with his elbow, as he mock whispered, "I'd look forward to getting her on her back in two seconds flat, too."

Cade narrowed his eyes imperceptibly at the asshole and was about to speak up when Gardner made a choking noise while she laid a fluttering hand on her stomach and one over her mouth. "Sorry, I think I just threw up a little."

Everyone laughed with her at Thompson's expense, and he got red in the face, muttering, "Bitch," under his breath.

Cade was even more impressed when she looked the jerk in the eye and merely raised an eyebrow at Thompson as if to say, "Is that all you could come up with?" and stood her ground. She kept her shoulders straight and head held high and added insult to injury as she turned her back on him, letting him know she didn't feel he was any type of threat.

Cade made the decision right then and there to hire her and another decision not to waste any more of their time or resources on Thompson. He glanced at Cooper, raised a brow to see if his take was the same, and received a nod in response. Cade looked at Sawyer and spoke a few words in Dari, the Persian dialect some members of his team had learned while on deployment in Afghanistan. His words had Sawyer walking towards the locker room to gather Thompson's things. He didn't want the asshole in their building any longer than necessary. He made eye contact with Thompson. "You're dismissed."

The man's jaw dropped, and he narrowed his eyes. "The fuck? Why?"

Cade's perplexed expression spoke volumes to the onlookers. "Why? It's really not clear? I'd be willing to bet every single person in this room could answer that question, so why is it you can't?"

Thompson sneered and crossed his arms over his chest. "What? Can't you people take a joke?"

"Oh, everyone here can take a joke quite well, I believe. They all laughed when Gardner told everyone that your suggestion made her vomit in her mouth."

Done with the conversation, Cade turned to Cooper. "Who's next?"

Cooper looked at the roster in his hand and was about to answer when Thompson interrupted. "Whatever, you're just afraid to fight me."

Cade's only reaction was to raise a brow at the douchebag's audacity. His men didn't say a word, but Cade could see they were fighting hard to keep a straight face. The candidates collectively groaned which amused Cade no end. One of them spoke up, "Dude, you need to back off. Do you know who this guy is? He and his team are still the standard everyone is held to when being trained for Special Forces. You're gonna get messed up. Are you fucking crazy?"

"He's a fuckin' pussy, that's who he is."

"Come on then. You wanna fight me so badly, step into the ring."

It was obvious Thompson straight up believed he was a better fighter; he wasn't merely posturing. He got an excited gleam in his eyes, and Cade could see the adrenaline puffing him up as he hopped up into the ring. Cade centered himself and took a deep breath to reign in his annoyance. He'd need to dispatch this guy quickly and get on with the rest of the scheduled fights. He was frustrated he'd let the idiot talk him into this pissing contest to begin with. He'd never been one for public humiliation, but the truth was the asshole needed to be brought down a peg, and Cade wasn't one to let sexual harassment of any kind occur at his company.

Cooper rang the bell for the fight to begin. Cade's posture became fluid and his muscles loosened to prepare for the upcoming bout. To Thompson's credit, the joker wasn't a terrible fighter. He had some solid training under his belt, but he was sloppy with it. He took shortcuts that kept him unbalanced and slow on his feet. Cade parried several blows which would have been solid hits had he used his head and kept his feet moving as fast as his fists. Cade spent five minutes deflecting Thompson's blows and though his heart rate was up, he hadn't put forth much effort. Cooper rang the bell for the end of that round, and Cade backed off and waited him out.

Thompson was bouncing up and down and shaking out his arms. He looked like he had enough energy to go another round, so Cade kept his mouth shut and waited for the bell to begin the second round. He wasn't going to waste his breath on the guy. He wasn't worth it. He could tell his reticence was getting under the guy's skin because he started running his mouth. "You're supposed to be some big deal, you and your 'legendary' team. I don't see it."

He swung wild, distracted by his own diatribe. Cade sidestepped easily and ignored the chatter.

"So far, you haven't really even tried to hit anyone hard or take them down."

Thompson tried an uppercut, and Cade's eyes flashed as he caught his hand on the upswing, but he kept the momentum going and gave a twist causing his opponent to turn into him with his arm curled up towards the middle of his back. He tried to struggle out of Cade's grasp and didn't pay attention to his legs, which were swept out from under him. Cade followed him down to the ground and put his knee on his lower back and launched himself off him. He backed up, as Thompson, a look of pure hatred and embarrassment shadowing his features, lunged and tried, quite unsuccessfully, to tackle him back down to the mat. Cade waited him out as he got up, again.

Cooper rang the bell which was good because Thompson looked more than a little ragged at that point. Cade shook his head and finally spoke, "You can stop right now. Leave here, and you'll most likely never see anyone in this room ever again. This isn't going to end well for you if you continue pushing yourself past your limits."

Thompson's face was bright red from exertion and embarrassment. "Fuck you, asshole!"

He charged toward Cade with more determination than sense. His head was down, and Cade took advantage of his attack position, wrapping his upper arm around Thompson's neck, and grabbing Thompson's wrist with his free hand. He used the guy's momentum and fell with him into his guard position. Cade crossed his legs around Thompson's waist, and put pressure on his throat, putting him in a guillotine chokehold. Thompson struggled, and Cade pulled tighter around his neck, causing the man to whimper and finally submit by tapping out.

Cade immediately released his grip on Thompson's neck. The man pushed himself away, using Cade's chest as leverage, scrambling backward like a crab. Cade thought for sure he'd stand and try to come at him again until he realized the man had been so scared he'd pissed himself. Cade moved to help him up, regretting their sparring had deteriorated so quickly, but Thompson continued his backward momentum. He scooted himself down and out of the ring, successfully camouflaging his accident from the others if not from Cade.

On his way towards the exit, he hung his head in shame and embarrassment but shoved a couple of the other candidates out of the way, trying to gain back some of his lost pride. As he neared the back door, he almost attempted to push Sawyer but must have thought better of it. Sawyer held out Thompson's backpack, which he grabbed and ran.

Cade made eye contact with Sawyer and spoke again in Dari. "Make sure he's alright, and he leaves the premises. He's humiliated enough that he'll either hide or lash out. When we finish today, I want you to follow Gardner home and make sure Thompson isn't waiting around off site somewhere to do the same."

Sawyer nodded and left the building, followed quickly by Jackson. Cade settled his eyes on the rest of the group. "I'm sorry you had to witness that. Here at Custos, we don't tolerate the type of behavior he was displaying. Cooper, let's continue."

There was nothing to do but finish the remainder of the testing. Cooper called the next guy into the ring. That fight was more like the first couple, but the two after that impressed him greatly. He saw potential in both candidates and enjoyed their different fighting styles. Overall, he was happy with their take of possible recruits this round. He began to unravel the fighting tape on his hands.

Cooper looked over the remainder of the group. "We'll be in touch to let you know if you've made it to the next round of testing. Thank you for coming in to participate today."

As everyone made to leave the gym, Cade pointed to Gardner. "You watch yourself. He's not blaming his dismissal and embarrassment on himself. We both know people like that never own up to their shit."

Gardner nodded. "Yeah, I figured as much. I'll be vigilant. Thanks."

Cade shook her proffered hand, and she headed to the women's locker rooms to change and go home. Cooper let him know he was going up to finish some paperwork, and Cade assured him he'd stay and make sure everyone got out of there without issue. He hopped on a treadmill, turned the speed and incline up, and spent the better part of an hour burning off the remainder of his anger at Thompson and at himself for letting the situation get out of hand. When he was done, he showered and changed in the locker room and went home.

Chapter 2

BRADEN

Braden pricked his finger for the third time that day. He'd been testing out a new ginger scone recipe, so there was more sugar in his system than normal. He had to adjust his insulin injections with a correction dose. Ever since he'd woken up, he'd felt off. Hell, if he was honest with himself, he'd felt off for weeks now. He didn't want to think too much on the whys of it, so he dealt with his injection, pulled his blondish brown, shoulder length hair back in a leather thong, washed his hands, and headed back to his kitchen. He was at home there like nowhere else, and after a few deep breaths, he got back to it.

He was always testing new recipes and trying them out with the customers. Sometimes, he asked their regulars to taste test new muffins, scones, or other sweet treats and give their feedback on what was the best. He liked to change things up quite often. He updated his recipes with the seasons, of course, but in addition, he changed out the whole menu several times during any given season.

He had no formal training except the time that he spent at his grandmother's side while he was growing up. He learned everything he knew about baking from her. He knew from a very young age baking was her passion, and she was a natural at it. As soon as he was old enough to stand on a stool next to the kitchen counter, he was there by her side, proving he had the same natural talent.

His mother, newly graduated from high school, had died during childbirth from a brain aneurysm, so his grandparents raised him. His father had hightailed it out of town as soon as he heard the news he was going to have a kid; he was a lost cause. His grandparents were young when they had their daughter, and their daughter was young when she had him, resulting in his grandparents being the same age as some of his friends' parents which meant their makeshift family didn't feel too strange.

Several hours later, he was in the middle of making a batch of cranberry almond muffins and daydreaming about his past when his best friend and business partner, Maya, bustled into his kitchen with a cup of coffee she'd made for him. "Have you tested your levels in the last couple hours?"

"Yes, ma'am, I have, and thanks for the coffee."

She hopped up on his kitchen stool and crossed her legs. Balancing an elbow on her knee, she put her chin in her hand and studied him through long lashes. She wore her standard work attire, the cafe's t-shirt and her skinny white capris with an apron around her waist that she always managed to keep clean. She was a short little thing, but curvy with a peaches and cream complexion and cornflower blue eyes that missed nothing.

Their business, the Sugar n' Spice Café, which fit right into their cozy little neighborhood row of shops, was the culmination of both of their dreams. Maya had been a barista in college, and she'd always secretly wanted to open her own coffee shop once she was done with school. One night, while they were drinking entirely too much Two Buck Chuck from Trader Joe's, she'd let slip her little secret, thinking it was rather silly and she'd eventually get over it. But Braden had immediately latched onto her idea and told her he'd always wanted to become a pastry chef.

That had been the beginning of their combined dream which had inadvertently helped them both decide to become business majors. They spent freshman year getting to know each other, studying together, and making a business plan, solidifying it by senior year. Less than a year after graduation, they opened Sugar n' Spice, thanks to a lot of hard work, long days and nights, and a series of lucky breaks, including the café location opening up and their ability to put down a large down payment on the loan, expediting the approval. Word quickly spread in the neighborhood about Braden's decadent pastries and Maya's artistic espressos and specialty drinks, and before long, the café bustled with customers.

Braden put down the coffee she'd brought in and finished what he was working on. He set the timer for the muffins and cleaned up his workspace. After a while, he realized she wasn't going to give him back his privacy, and he lifted a brow in silent inquiry until she huffed out a breath and sat up.

"I'm worried about you, Bray."

"Worried enough to leave the floor to Lala?"

She snorted out a laugh. "It's Layla, and you damned well know it. She's getting better. More confident, less spacey, I swear. And it's 2 p.m., so it's dead right now…but yes, I'm that worried."

He gazed over at her and could see she was telling the truth. He knew the look in her eyes. If he didn't cut her off at the pass, she'd go full-fledged mama bear on his ass, and at this point, he was hanging on by a very thin thread and didn't have the energy for the whole routine.

"Look, I don't know…"

"Don't tell me you don't know what I'm talking about, Bray." She said it gently but with censure, a skill he'd yet to acquire.

"Baby girl, I was going to say I don't know what's going on with me. I'm in some sort of a funk, and I'm trying to wrap my mind around it."

She shrugged and held out her hands, palm up. "Well, we need to figure it out because I don't like seeing you like this, and I want to fix it."

"I don't like it much myself, but I'm not quite sure it's going to be an easy fix."

She sighed and slipped off the stool and into his arms. For a little thing, she could hug the stew out of him, and he loved her all the more for her concern and affection. She was the touchy feely type, and she brought that side out of him as well. So much so people had often commented they were a cute couple.

They would often stroll hand in hand when they were out in public or be caught hugging or touching in some other way. Obviously, that was not the case. He was gay, and she was straight, but none of those things ever stopped them from showing affection, almost from the beginning of their friendship. They'd met in Business 101 after she'd tripped on someone's bag in his row and landed nearly face first in his crotch.

He'd immediately taken to her when she snorted out a laugh while still face down in his denim. With an, "It's so nice to meet you," to his dick, and then an, "Oh, you too," to his face, he couldn't resist her playfulness. He remembered how rosy her cheeks had gotten in her embarrassment and how he'd immediately loved her sense of humor.

He'd responded with, "Well, you're not really our type if you catch my drift, but we're both still very happy to meet you, and we'd love for you to sit next to us and chat before class starts."

She'd laughed and taken him up on his offer. By the time the first class was over, he knew they'd be friends for years to come.

Coming back to the present, he squeezed her tight, kissed the top of her head, and shrugged. "I'll figure my shit out eventually. Until then, I'll probably be a bit broody, play loud music, and stay away from Lala as much as possible."

She rubbed his back then pulled away, chuckling. "That is why we kept the kitchen far enough away from the front, hmm?"

"What, my orneriness? Having it somewhat removed from the hustle and bustle of others probably keeps us both sane, don't you think? You no more want me talking to customers than I want you touching my whisks."

Smirking, she grabbed his face in her hands and placed a smacking kiss on his lips. "I think it's been far too long since someone touched your whisk. Not to mention, you just said more to me in the last ten minutes than you have in a week. If I didn't know better, I'd think you were trying to distract me from the reason I came back here to begin with. Maybe you need to get laid, Bray."

"Christ on a crutch, Maya, don't start with that shit." Just thinking about trying to start dating again made him feel a bit sick to his stomach. He'd resigned himself to being alone; perhaps not forever, but for the foreseeable future. He was utterly unlucky in love, and he had enough on his plate right now without adding anything else to the mix.

"No listen, I think it would be good…"

It was a soft entreaty, but he had to nip it in the bud before she went on.

"Don't, Maya. You know I'm no good with one-night stands. I'm not ready for anything romantic either." He'd escaped from an abusive relationship by the skin of his teeth a little over a year ago. That, coupled with the other short relationships he'd had in his life, warned him away from trying anything these days.

The problem was he was lonely. He might not feel ready for anything romantic, but he did miss it, the feeling of coupledom. He was a complete introvert, so he wasn't big on social situations, but he had always loved the feeling of being in a relationship even though he'd never really had a good one. He loved coming home to someone or someone coming home to him.

As much as he didn't like people in general, he loved taking care of the small group of people he did let into his inner circle. His grandmother had always called him a romantic though he wasn't sure the description fit. He just knew he preferred being with someone to being without, which was why this self-induced dry spell was hard in the first place. It didn't feel natural, his being alone, yet he didn't want to chance fate again, at least not for a little while longer. But, the abject sadness on his best friend's face was hard to ignore

"I think you're more ready than you think. I won't push anymore. I just hate seeing you like this. Most guys aren't like Eric. He was awful, and I know you didn't tell me half of what he did to you. I have a feeling if I knew the extent of what he did, I'd probably want to kill him, or at least have Cooper kill him."

He smiled at her protective streak. Her brother was a Green Beret in the Army. Braden had met Cooper several times over the years though he hadn't spent much time with the man one on one. He was just like his sister; gorgeous, kind, gregarious, loyal, and protective. They were both talkers, lookers, and go-getters. Maya was the face of the Sugar n' Spice Café while Cooper was the face of the security company he co-owned. They were charismatic and social, and they drew people in which was a very useful tool to have in your back pocket when owning or co-owning your own business.

Braden sighed. "There's no need for you, or your soldier-boy brother, to kill anyone. My relationship with Eric is over and has been for a long time. I'm over it." Okay, that wasn't true, but it felt good to say. The truth was he wanted to be over the relationship, desperately, and he was annoyed Maya could see the truth.

Maya shook her head. "Honey, you're not over it, because you haven't moved on. But not counting the last several weeks of funk, you've been more like your old self, your pre-Eric self, lately. I'm so grateful for that."

Braden rubbed the back of his hand across his forehead. "Yeah, I get it, I do. I know where you're coming from, but I'm not ready like you seem to think I am. I can't trust my judgment, not with my track record."

Maya grabbed his hand and held it, squeezing it gently. "Track record? You had no way of knowing what kind of guy Eric was. He fooled us both, for a long ass time. Only when you moved in together did things start changing. You were seeing him for several months before that happened, and he seemed great, even to me. You are not to blame, Braden."

"Maybe you're right, but the reality is before Eric there was Owen and before Owen there was Nick. Don't you see the pattern there? I see it clear as day, and it spells out my utter inability to pick someone suitable for me. I don't want the stress of it all. It just doesn't seem worth it." He didn't trust his judgment, that was completely true, but he also felt too paralyzed with the fear of disappointment and the possibility he might end up with another Eric to make any sort of move to find someone new.

In all of those relationships, he'd actually been the one to approach the men and hit on them. Sure, he was an introvert, but once he went to college, he made the decision he would go after what he wanted to get him where he wanted to be, even if it made him uncomfortable to put himself out there. He'd had the confidence back then to approach and flirt with men even though it was hard for him. Now, he no longer felt that confidence.

"Your happiness is worth it, Braden. Eric was a psycho, but Owen and Nick just weren't right for you. There was nothing wrong with them. They were both just macho dudes, and neither of them were ready for a serious relationship. That makes them idiots, not bad judgment calls."

"The fact is one of them cheated on me, the other completely lost interest and just up and left one day, and the last one nearly killed me; it doesn't speak well of my track record, okay? Can we just drop this discussion, please? My head is killing me, and I'm grumpy as fuck now, so I need you to back off before I blow a gasket."

He'd been pacing back and forth and finally stopped to look at her. She had tears in her eyes, a trembling hand covering her mouth. Fuck! He didn't think he was that harsh. What had he said?

She whispered, "Nearly killed you?"

A tear slid down her cheek as he grabbed her in a tight embrace. Oh fuck him sideways, he didn't mean for that to slip.

"I didn't mean that literally, Maya. I just meant he was sucking the life out of me. I'm not going to lie to you and tell you he never got violent, you already know. But, I didn't mean it like that, and I'm sorry I used those words. As soon as he began knocking me around and I understood that it wasn't going to stop, I got out of there as quickly as I could manage it. However, I'm still not confident in my ability to choose a guy who's good for me, so until then, I'd rather just steer clear of relationship entanglements."

There were a couple things he failed to mention. One was the only real reason Eric let him leave when and how he did was because he had filmed Eric attacking him that final day. He had an insurance policy which made it very hard for Eric to threaten his way back into Braden's life. Eric had a high-profile job, and he knew he had to step back or risk his livelihood with the truth coming out.

The other thing was what worried him the most. It terrified him that he was attracted to Eric's type. He was attracted to the macho, physically imposing, tough guy. It's just how he was built, both physically and mentally. He was 5'9" and slim, or what some might call slight. He had a runner's body because he was, in fact, a runner. Perhaps it was because he was small in stature he always sought out someone much bigger and stronger than he was. He wanted a partner who could protect him if needed —funny how it had royally backfired on him. He knew if he tried to begin a new relationship with the type he was actually attracted to, he would be facing the real possibility of getting himself into another Eric situation. Frankly, he'd had enough of that to last him a lifetime.

None of it really mattered, anyway. She didn't need to know the details of his insurance policy, and if she was smart, which she was, she already knew his type from his past relationships. It didn't take a genius to see all the men he'd dated were big, muscular, tough guys. One of them hadn't even been out of the closet for fuck's sake. Yeah, he sure knew how to pick 'em.

She watched him closely, and from the look on her face, she knew it was time to retreat and come around from the other side at a later date. He could see her planning her next sneak attack as they stared each other down. "Okay, I can see the headache written all over your face. I'm assuming ibuprofen will do because you don't look like you're gonna keel over with a migraine."

Maya walked over to a corner cabinet and proceeded to pour out a couple ibuprofen from the giant bottle he kept there. She walked back over to Braden, picked up the forgotten coffee and held them both out to him. He took them from her and kissed her on the forehead before tossing back the pills with the caffeine.

He was closing the oven and setting the timer for the batch of croissants he'd just started when Maya walked into the kitchen from the office hallway, a folder in her hand. Her skin was pasty white, her eyes full of tears yet to spill. He knew exactly what folder she held and his heart kicked up into panic mode, nearly beating out of his chest.

She dropped the offending file on the counter beside him, some of the letters spilling out. "What *is* this? Please tell me it's not what I think it is."

He saw the tears fall and watched as she quickly swiped them away. Goddammit. He'd never wanted her to see those and had no idea what to say to her. "Maya—"

"When were you going to tell me about these, Bray?" Her words were no more than a whisper, and she sat down on the stool next to him, opening the folder and pulling the last note out. She gaped up at him with eyes wide as saucers, her face devoid of color.

He took it out of her hand, glancing at the note. A chill swept through his body as recognition hit.

> **Braden, I saw you today while you were running. You took the long route, and I have to say I really love your new running shoes. I always like to watch you and imagine what's playing on your iPhone. What kind of music keeps you motivated? I know one day soon we'll be together, and I'll learn all these things about you that I'm unable to know from just watching you. I know you're looking forward to that day as well.**
> **All my love, Handsome Stranger**

He shuddered, and feeling the bile fill his mouth, swallowed reflexively and took a drink from his water bottle before he could do his best to change the subject, knowing it was futile but unable to think of another solution. He knew his voice was strained, both angry and defensive at once, but he couldn't help it. "Why were you going through my drawers, Maya?"

"Bray…" Her disappointed expression only made him feel worse. "I was looking for the invoice folder and couldn't find it anywhere, so I looked in your drawer. What's going on? Who's writing these letters? You have a stalker and you don't even mention it? How long has this been going on? Have you called the cops? Has this guy tried to hurt you? Is it Eric? Is he…"

"Maya, it's fine, it's nothing. It's not Eric. Really, it's just some guy that's trying to get under my skin. I don't know who it is, and it doesn't matter. It's not a big deal. I'm just ignoring it."

"Ignoring it? You can't ignore someone like this, Braden. They kidnap you and lock you in their dungeon. They lower your food down to you in a bucket on a string and cut off your skin to make a Braden suit. You can't ignore a psycho, Braden."

He forced a chuckle, uncomfortable with the truth of her words. "Calm down, Clarice."

His try at levity backfired, and he saw by her expression he'd gone too far by making light of it when she was genuinely scared to death for him. It lit a fire under her protective instincts. Face turning red, tears in her eyes, Maya lost it. "This isn't a fucking joke, Braden! We have to call the cops."

Chapter 3

CADE

Cade walked into the café behind Cooper and heard a little old lady say to the girl behind the counter, "If only I was forty years younger. I've never had a threesome!"

He raised his brows at the woman's cheekiness as she leered at them both and bit her lip. He gave her a flirtatious wink and chuckled when she put a hand to her chest and whispered, "Oh my!"

He gazed around the beautiful café and understood exactly why Cooper was so proud of his sister. There was a warmth about the place he liked immediately. Sugar n' Spice was both trendy and casual and would appeal to most everyone. The furniture looked comfortable and stylish, and the art on the rustic brick walls tied in the myriad colors splashed throughout the long, narrow room. But the smell, damn, it was like heaven. The best smells he could think of all melding together to create a heady aroma he'd gladly live on for the rest of his life.

He glanced at the cute girl behind the counter then over at Cooper who was grinning his most devilish grin and turning his flirt level to stun. The girl, whose name was Layla according to her nametag, muttered what Cade thought was "threesome" then slapped her hands over her mouth and turned beet red as the cute, little old flirt across the room choked on her coffee while inhaling what he supposed was a snort of laughter.

"Hmmm, what was that?" Copper asked her.

"OH MY GOD! Nothing! I didn't say that. I didn't."

Cade chuckled and couldn't help but tease her, just a little bit. "I think you did, sweetheart. I think you said threesome. Coop, didn't she just say threesome?"

Cooper grinned at him and nodded. "I think she did, McCade. I think…"

Shouting interrupted him, and before Cade could stop him, Cooper launched himself over the countertop and jogged into the back.

"You can't go back there, sir!" Flustered, Layla waved her hands in front of her face.

Cade did his best to placate her. "It's alright, sweetheart. Cooper is Maya's big brother. He's the protective sort, so he's just checking on her. Hold down the fort here while we go see what the problem is."

With a wink, he took the long way around the counter and ambled into the back towards the kitchen, leaving Layla wide eyed and mouth agape.

Braden

Braden glanced over Maya's shoulder as her brother Cooper raced into the kitchen, most likely to see what had caused his sister to lose her shit. Braden raised a brow when Maya ignored Cooper's arrival, but he did the same and met her narrowed eyes with his own. "You are not calling the cops, Maya."

"Braden, please. Please! We need to call them. This isn't a joke. You're being stalked."

He gritted his teeth, hating that he knew she was right but unwilling to bend, unwilling to give credence to the fact he was in danger. "There is no 'we' in this situation, Maya. This is my problem, and I'll deal with it."

Maya's brow creased in frustration. "You have a psycho calling himself Handsome Stranger stalking and harassing you wherever you go. Is he threatening you too? Calling you? Doing nothing shouldn't even be an option."

"What seems to be the problem here, Coop?"

Braden's head whipped around toward the sound of that deep gravelly voice. He did a double take when he laid wide, disbelieving eyes on the tallest, sexiest man he'd ever seen. He just about lost his train of thought until he looked back at Maya and remembered he'd been about to warn her against opening her big mouth. He narrowed his eyes at her. "Don't do it, Maya. Don't even think about it. This is my business."

"Let me tell them, Bray, they can help us. Braden, what if it was me?" She whispered it, and he could hear her voice shaking in an effort not to cry. "What if someone were sending me these notes, leaving these things for me, scaring me? What would you tell me to do?"

"It's not the same thing, Maya! I can take care of myself if I need to, but I won't need to. This is all just some silly prank. It's not a big deal. Don't make it out to be bigger than it is." He began to gather up all the nasty evidence and stuff it inside the folder when Maya's shaking hand rested on his. He looked into her pleading eyes and sighed, resigned.

Leaving everything where it was, he shrugged off his apron and tossed it on the floor. "Do what you want Maya, you're going to anyway. I'm going running."

Cade

They all watched him leave, and Cade spoke up, concerned for the beautiful man who'd just left in anger. "Does he need someone to run with him? Is he in immediate danger?"

Maya scrubbed her face in frustration and sighed. "I don't know. I don't think so. You probably couldn't keep up with him, so I think we just need to wait for him to get back."

Cade raised a brow at that, positive he could keep up with the smaller man. He tried not to be insulted by Cooper's sister's take on his physical stamina. Maya huffed out a laugh. "Your height alone has me betting that you're McCade."

She stepped forward, and he clasped her outstretched hand in his. "I am. Nice to finally meet you, Maya. It seems every time we've been scheduled to meet, something comes up to keep it from happening. I'm really happy we finally managed it. Now... What's this about me not being able to keep up with him?"

She smirked at him, and he saw a lot of Cooper in her expression. He couldn't help but grin as she looked him up and down, giving him an obvious and thorough once over. "I've heard a lot about you, and I can see for myself you're in great shape, but you're almost a foot taller than him and built like a brick shit house. You wouldn't be able to keep up with Braden. I don't know anyone that could."

Cade's brows rose in surprise. "He's that good?"

She smiled and nodded. "He runs marathons for fun and once signed up for an ultra-marathon on a whim just to see if he could do it, which he did and has a number of times since. You guys may be tough as shit, but he'd beat you both in distance running without breaking a sweat."

"Okay, I'll give you that, but if you think he needs someone with him, I can follow in our car."

"No. Not only would it piss him off, but he needs time right now to get over his anger. He has anxiety and stresses about everything. He runs twice a day just to relax. As much as I'm worried about him, I think he's okay to run in broad daylight."

Cooper gestured to the folder on the counter and asked, "So what's got you so worried?"

The fear returned to her face as she opened the file. "He's gotten dozens of letters, notes, receipts, paper clippings, just tons of crazy shit from some guy calling himself 'Handsome Stranger'. He says it's no big deal, but I know him, and he's worried. From the dates on some of the receipts, he's been getting these for months. He's been off lately, and I've been worried about him. Now that I've seen these, I think it's because he's scared and doesn't want to admit it."

Cooper wrapped an arm around her and rubbed her arm. "I'm glad we're here then."

She pulled way and crossed her arms over her chest. "Yeah, about that, what the hell, Coop? You walk into our kitchen as if you live down the block and are just stopping in. What are you doing here? Why didn't you tell me you were coming? I could have picked you up at the airport."

Cooper chuckled and shrugged. "I wanted to surprise you. Cade and I have a job over here that should be relatively quick and painless, and we both thought a nice little trip to San Francisco wouldn't be so bad. Cade is from here, so he'll be able to see his family, and I'll get to see you. Win, win."

She leaned into him and he wrapped his arms around her, pulling her into his chest for a quick hug as she said, "I'm glad you're here. Maybe I'll hire you to help figure out who this psycho is and protect Braden. I know he'll freak out even knowing I'm thinking about any sort of protection or investigation, but after you see what's here, I think you'll believe this is as serious as I do. I don't know if it's his asshole ex-boyfriend or what, but this stuff is creepy."

"Let's have a look, and we'll see what we think. If we decide to take the case, you know your money's no good with us," Cade responded as nonchalantly as he could. He didn't want either sibling to see his interest in the situation. All it had taken was one look at Maya's business partner, and he knew he'd have a hard time keeping himself from getting in too deep.

Braden wasn't anything like the men Cade had dated in the past. They hadn't even been properly introduced and he already couldn't get the image of the younger man out of his mind. As soon as he'd walked into the kitchen, his heart had started to race and he experienced tunnel vision.

He hadn't had an immediate attraction to anyone like this in a long time and never this strong. He was lean, long haired, green eyed, and beautiful. Cade was working mental gymnastics to try to reel in his reaction, slow down his protective instincts, and cool his jets. He had a feeling it was going to be a losing battle.

Maya moved aside to give them enough room to see everything. They began shuffling through the folder and looking at the notes and letters written to Braden. There was a lot to go through and it took quite a bit of time. But the more they looked at everything, the more he was convinced there was one deranged motherfucker after Braden.

It wasn't good, and with every written word, a calm came over Cade. It was the same calm that had saved his life and the lives of his unit many times in combat situations. In his mind, he was already on protection detail; it was only a matter of convincing Maya and Cooper it was necessary and he was the right one for the job.

It turned out he needn't have worried. Cooper took one look at him, nodded, and spoke his sister. "Sunshine, I'm not trying to scare you, but both Cade and I agree there's definitely a case here. This guy is unbalanced, and there's no telling how quickly he's going to escalate. It seems like the best course of action is for me to work on the Kensington case and get it ironed out then I can come back and help deal with this. Cade will be taking lead. We need to call the cops to at least alert them of the situation so it's all on record."

"Agreed. He needs to be guarded twenty-four-seven." Cade interjected, his gruff voice alerting Cooper to his personal involvement. Cooper peered up at his best friend with narrowed eyes for several long, drawn out seconds. Cooper's eyebrows popped up quickly in surprise then understanding dawned and there was no need for words. The case was important to him and that's all Cooper needed to know. Cade knew they might be having a conversation about this later, but for now, Cooper would leave it in his hands without further questions.

Cooper regarded him. "I'll get in contact with Mrs. Kensington first thing tomorrow morning to see if I can get in and out quickly. She said all they needed was a system upgrade, but she likes to spring things on me at the last minute."

Cade nodded, and Cooper glanced at his sister. "Do you think he'll be more likely to be cooperative about this after his run? We need him to be with us on this. It won't be possible for us to protect him and figure out what's going on if we don't have his involvement and agreement."

"I don't know. I hope so. Running usually gets him back into a good head space, so I think our best chance is to talk to him after he's been able to shower and eat someth…. Oh shit!" Cade watched, tension building as she frantically began to pat down her pockets and ran towards the phone attached to a wall mount by the door into the kitchen.

Cade watched in uneasy silence as she dialed a number and waited. "Come on, answer Braden!"

Cade didn't like the panicked look in her eyes. She hung up and dialed again—cursing under her breath. He gripped the countertop so hard his knuckles turned white.

"Oh, thank god, Braden! Are you alright? Where are you? I just saw your kit. When did you test last?" She paused and listened. "Okay, good. Do you need me to come and get you? I can get in the car right now if you're too far out. Oh, alright, that's close. See you soon. I'm so sorry, Braden. I know. I love you too, bye."

She took a shuddering breath then raised her eyes to theirs. This situation was taking a toll on her, and Cade watched as Cooper moved to her side, hugging her to him. "He hasn't eaten in a while. His blood sugar levels were fine when he last tested, but he should have eaten something before he ran. He turned around when he realized it. He should be here soon. I'm gonna put together a couple sandwiches for him, so if you guys are hungry, I can make you some as well."

"He's type 1? What the hell was he thinking?" Cade tried hard not to let his frustration with Braden show but knew he hadn't been successful. He reined in his emotions because he knew how he sounded, and he hadn't even officially met the guy yet. He looked up and saw the tiny flash of annoyance in Maya's eyes.

"Yes, he's type 1 and has a very good handle on it. He's actually just a few minutes out. Today is not the norm. He would usually never put himself in danger of having an insulin spike or drop for any reason. He's not prone to acting without thinking. In fact, just the opposite, he usually over analyzes everything."

Cooper shuffled the papers back into the folder and asked, "You think he's doing all right?"

She nodded. "Yeah. He's probably been thinking about this for several weeks and came to the same conclusions we did, but he didn't like me pushing it on him before he'd made his decision. I think he'll come around. He already sounded better on the phone."

Watching Maya as she washed her hands and pulled out sandwich fixings from the sub-zero walk-in, Cade realized he'd jumped to conclusions. He was glad Braden had such a good friend. Stepping over to the counter, Cade helped her assemble enough sandwiches for everyone. Maya checked in with Layla up front and was back with them in moments, waiting for Braden to return.

Braden

Braden walked into the back of the café and took in the scene before him with resignation. Cooper and his friend sat eating sandwiches at his workstation in front of the pile of what he had been sarcastically thinking of as fan mail, mostly to keep himself from losing his shit every time he got a new note. Maya ran to him and told him how sorry she was. He grabbed her to him and kissed her cheek as he murmured his own apology, upset with himself for his reaction when she was just trying to help.

"It's all right. I'm sorry I yelled. It's not your fault, and everything you said is right. I just don't like it and find myself at a loss as to how I got myself into this situation."

"You didn't get yourself into anything, Braden. This isn't something that you can blame on yourself. Here, come on, let me pour you some juice. Go test your levels, and we'll see if you need anything besides what I've already made."

He grabbed his testing kit and headed off to the bathroom to test his blood away from the kitchen, not to mention the prying eyes of the gorgeous man he'd yet to meet. He gathered himself, pricked his finger, tested the strip, and let out a relieved sigh when his levels weren't too far off track. He prepped the needle. After a small injection, some juice, and a sandwich or two, he'd be back on track.

He suddenly felt exhausted and knew the stress of the fan mail had finally caught up with him. He'd known he couldn't go much longer without talking to Maya and probably the cops as well, but he wasn't looking forward to dealing with any of it. He yanked his hair out of its leather thong, ran his hands through it, and tucked it behind his ears.

Maya was sitting on his stool and picking at her food when he walked back into the kitchen. She hopped down and brought him his food and juice, a worried look in her eyes.

"Just a small injection, My, I'm okay. Thanks for the food." He guided her back to her seat and stood next to her which just happened to be right in front of the file folder. He grunted as he took his first bite, his mouth full. "So, what's the consensus on the fan mail?"

He watched Maya and Cooper glance up at the tall guy who held his hand out for Braden to shake. "Braden, right? My name is Zavier McCade. I go by Cade most of the time."

Braden met Gigantor's eyes—*Christ, the man was huge*—and found his face heating at the heated look he got from him. He liked his name; it suited him and had a distinctly sexy ring to it. "Braden Cross. It's nice to meet you, Zavier, though I wish it was under better circumstances."

Braden smiled to himself as Cade raised a brow at his choice to call him by his first name rather than his proffered nickname. Cade's soft smile of approval had Braden's cheeks burning even hotter and his heart beating a bit faster.

His eyes slid down to Cade's soft, full lips when the huge man spoke. "So, Braden, this 'fan mail', as you call it, is more than just a mild annoyance. I think you know that deep down if you've been paying attention to the words he's written to you. The guy seems to be quite prolific, in addition to being batshit crazy."

Braden nodded. "It's gotten worse as time passes. More volatile I guess."

"Exactly. We're all assuming you'd like this harassment to stop, so I guess my question is are you going to let us do what needs to be done to make sure you're safe and this psycho—and I don't say that word lightly—is caught and dealt with?"

Braden was mildly taken aback by Cade's vehemence. He'd begun to take the notes more seriously in the last several weeks as the quantity of the notes increased and the implied threats worsened. However, Cade seemed to think he was in imminent danger which gave him pause.

He would admit he'd been a bit of a wreck as a result of the messages, and he'd been in denial for too long. He'd internalized most of it in the hopes it would just go away, but it wasn't happening. He rubbed both hands over his eyes and ran his fingers through his hair.

"Well, it's obviously not going away on its own." Feeling suddenly exhausted, he continued, "I get the feeling I'm not going to like whatever it is you guys have planned, but I'll admit it's not exactly my area of expertise. I'm having a hard time understanding exactly why this guy has latched onto me."

Cade shook his head. "Things like this are rarely logical."

Frustrated, Braden sighed. "But, I'm nobody. I'm just a pastry chef. My daily life pretty much consists of waking up, eating, baking, running, showering, baking, eating, baking, eating, running, showering, and sleeping. As pathetic as that sounds, it's as close to the truth as an oversimplification can get."

Maya clasped his hand and looked at him pointedly. "Bray, you're not just a pastry chef; you're the best pastry chef in town, and your desserts have won awards. You run marathons and ultra-marathons. You volunteer for the local Diabetes Advocacy and Awareness Group. You bake cookies for our neighbors and help the little old ladies in the neighborhood. This guy, though a total and absolute nutter, sees what others have seen in you. Not to mention Braden, you're friggin beautiful, that alone could get someone hooked."

Braden huffed out a laugh. "If I ever need a pep talk, I know where to go, but that's not what I meant. All I'm saying is I'm not in the public eye much. My daily life is boring and routine. I'm having a hard time grasping the fact that someone has latched onto me like this. I haven't been in a relationship in over a year, and I don't go out to the clubs. I just don't get it."

Cade stepped close to Braden, placed a gentle hand on his shoulder, and slowly caressed his collarbone with his thumb. The casual, yet tender touch puzzled and soothed him. He lifted his gaze to Cade's. "Be that as it may, something triggered this guy. He may or may not be someone you know. We'll be looking at all the possibilities. We'll also be calling the cops to report the situation so we're keeping everything on the up and up."

"I was afraid you'd say that."

Cade gave him an apologetic look. "In order to keep you safe, I'll need to guard you twenty-four-seven. I want you to be as comfortable with my presence as possible so you can go about your normal routines."

"With you as my shadow."

Cade spread his hands wide and shrugged. "Basically, yeah. So, when you wake up, eat, bake, run, shower, bake, eat, bake, eat, run, shower, and sleep, I'm going to be doing those things with you." He gave Braden a flirtatious wink. "For now, a few of those things you'll get to do on your own with me not too far away. However, that's negotiable, but we can get back to that later."

Utter shock followed by a lightning bolt of heated desire flashed through him. Those feelings warred with disbelief and embarrassment that Cade was flirting and teasing him in the midst of everything. Such a range of emotions in the span of a few seconds threw him off his stride and he found himself completely without words.

Cooper cleared his throat, a mischievous look in his eyes. "On that note, I think I'll call the local PD and see who they can send out to look at your fan mail. I'll make the call from the office."

Maya had a huge smile on her face and looked back and forth between him and Cade. To Braden, it seemed misplaced and ill timed, but at this point, he was flat out of energy and just wanted to finish his meal and get this day over with. He took the last half of his sandwich in hand, stood up, and went to the back door. "I'm going home to finish eating, get a shower, and change. I'll be back to deal with the cops in 30 minutes."

Cade made a move to follow him which snapped the tenuous hold Braden had on his temper. "Listen Gigantor, stay right where you are. I haven't agreed to all of this yet. I know I'll eventually have to give in but for right now, give me the illusion that my life is fucking normal. I'm going home for 30 minutes, alone. If anyone follows me, I swear to Christ, I'll lose my shit. Got it?"

A broad, sexy as sin grin flashed across Cade's face as he gave a two-fingered salute to Braden and a deep rumble came from his chest. "Mmhmm. Got it, boss."

Braden rolled his eyes and threw his hands in the air, muttering about sexy giants that thought they could control everything and cursing himself internally for his physical reaction to the huge man. His hands were sweating, and he had goosebumps all over his body from that deep sexy voice. He walked out of his kitchen to cross the street to his and Maya's split row house, all the while trying desperately not to think about the man's alluring smile, his beautiful body, and his stupid gorgeous face.

Cade

Maya had a speculative gleam in her eyes, and Cade guessed it would be less than ten seconds before she started talking about what was on her mind, so he jumped in first. "Hit me with it, gorgeous. What you got brewing in that brain of yours? I can see the hamsters spinning their wheels."

She smirked but crossed her arms over her chest. "So, you seem really confident, but I guess that makes me worried you're arrogant. You're really good looking, I'm sure you know that. And, you're so macho I never would have guessed you're gay, but I guess the same could be said about Cooper being bisexual. And now I'm stereotyping, which I hate. I'm just surprised Cooper never mentioned it."

"It's never been a secret which is probably what made it a non-issue. I didn't talk about it when I was in the military because it's not something I feel the need to justify. My closest friends in my unit all knew and when others found out, it wasn't an issue."

"I'm surprised with all those macho guys beating their chests."

Cade chuckled. "Yeah, for the most part it's not like that. But, it probably didn't hurt that, even by military standards, my height and size make people think twice before messing with me. And the good looking bit?

Meh, you're not really seeing me; you're just seeing my appearance and I'm not responsible for that. It was the luck of the gene pool."

Maya tilted her head as if contemplating his response. "So, are you truly interested in Braden or were you just teasing him to get a reaction?"

Cade knew she wasn't going to give up this line of questioning. He also knew she was Braden's best friend, and it was reason enough to lay his cards on the table, such as they were. He took a deep breath and put it all out there.

"Very interested. I've never believed in love at first sight. To be completely honest, I'm still not sure I do. But when I walked back here, all I saw was him. When I learned he was in trouble, I wanted to fix it. Granted, I'm a fixer by nature, but this feels different to me. This feels... more. I don't know if that's what you want to hear or not, but it's the truth."

Maya gave him a smile and patted his arm. "I think I'm going to like you, Cade. It probably helps that I trust my brother's judgment. Braden is one of the most important people in my life and he's had some really shit luck with men. It might be hard to gain his trust, but it will be worth it in the end. He deserves to be treated well." She narrowed her eyes at him when she continued, "I know you'll appreciate the sentiment when I say if you hurt him, I'll kill you in your sleep."

Cade laughed and winked at her. "I think we'll get along just fine, Maya. However, I think I'll sleep with one eye open for a bit."

Chapter 4

BRADEN

Braden headed back across the street, realizing by the oncoming darkness it was later than he'd thought and the café had already closed. Earlier, on the walk from the café to his place, he'd felt the beginning of one of his migraines and the telltale blurring around the edges of his vision hit at the same time. The vision issues usually came thirty minutes before the pain, allowing him enough time to get his migraine meds down and working before the pain became debilitating. But, just like the rest of his shit day, his body didn't feel the need for that early warning.

He only had himself to blame, and he could only hope that the meds would kick in and work so he could get through the discussion with the cops. With all the drama, he'd taken off on a run and skipped his scheduled meal. Any change in his insulin routine was a strain on his system. His glucose levels spiked and a migraine usually followed.

He maintained a strict schedule for eating and exercise. Any undue stressors, and there'd been a shit ton of them lately, always caused unwelcome responses in his body. Sometimes he'd have anxiety attacks, come down with a cold, or have flu-like symptoms, including nausea and vomiting; other times, he was hit with one of his migraines.

He'd gotten pretty adept at keeping himself regimented and therefore free of strange bouts of sickness, but when he didn't, he was usually able to ignore most of the symptoms and push through. However, when it came to migraines, if he didn't get fair warning, they hit hard and were completely debilitating. It was one of the many reasons he was always so careful and disciplined about everything in his life.

Stepping into his kitchen, he struggled to compose his features so Maya wouldn't realize he was in pain. The bright lights did a number on his vision though, and he had to blink a number of times before the spots lessened enough for him to continue forward. Conversation stopped when the others realized he had returned. He stuck his hands in his jeans pockets and curled a bit more into himself. He hated being the center of attention.

Maya was next to him in a second. "You don't look that great, Braden. Do you want to do this another time? I'm sure Detective Miller can take your statement tomorrow."

"No, I'm fine. Let's just get this over with now." God knows he didn't want to have to psych himself up for this a second time. Sheepishly, he noticed a man with a badge standing with Cooper and Cade.

"Detective Miller, I presume?" Braden extended his hand as he sat on his kitchen stool. "I'm Braden Cross. Thanks for coming out."

"You're welcome. Seems you've been having some trouble with a stalker. Care to tell me when this all started?"

"Just shy of three months ago. At first, the notes were friendly, almost like a secret admirer, and didn't worry me in the least. For the first month, I honestly thought it was some kind of joke and one of my friends was going to fess up any second. Then he started to say some stuff that made me realize there really was someone watching me. He would comment on what I was wearing on a specific day. He'd include receipts from a place on my running route, receipts with dates and time stamps."

"I'd like to take all the notes with me today, if I could."

Cade cut into the conversation. "Sorry, Detective, we can make copies for you, but we're keeping the originals. We'll be launching our own investigation into the situation and providing Mr. Cross with protection, as we discussed several minutes ago."

The detective was about to argue when Cooper interrupted, "Detective Miller, we know how these things work. You don't have the manpower really to do anything more than take a cursory glance at the letters and keep an open file. We wanted it on record with you in case things escalate."

"But–"

Cooper's voice oozed charm when he interrupted, "I've already made copies of all the notes and receipts; anything the stalker has left Braden. You can take them with you to keep on file. We know your hands are tied unless there's a direct threat and even then, with no clue who is threatening him there's not much you can do. We'll be providing protection for Braden and investigating this situation ourselves. If we come up with anything, we'll keep you informed."

The detective sighed but didn't argue as he took the proffered file. He asked several more questions, but Braden didn't have many answers to provide, so the conversation wound down pretty quickly. He was feeling worse by the minute, and it was obvious he wasn't really needed any longer. "I think you have what you need. If you'll excuse me, I need to get home."

He stood up slowly and was hit by a wave of dizziness and nausea. He gripped the countertop with both hands to steady himself, his knuckles white on the edge. He heard Maya whispering to Cooper who quickly ushered the police detective out the door.

Her voice, though a whisper, was full of admonishment. "Braden, why didn't you tell us about the migraine?"

"Migraine? What's he even doing h…" Cade's voice was cut off mid-tirade by Maya's shaking head and raised hand.

"You should have said something, Bray. When did the symptoms start? How bad is it? Let's get you home."

"About an hour ago. I'll be okay. I took all my migraine meds thinking they'd do the trick, but with my schedule being all sorts of fucked today, I don't think they're going to do more than dull the ache. The worst of it hasn't hit yet. I'll go home now," he whispered while his eyes were nearly closed against the dizziness and bright lights.

Maya put her arm around his waist and began to help him to the door which Cade held open for them. Braden gripped the hand Maya placed on his waist and squeezed. "Thanks, My. Sorry about all this. What a disaster of a day."

Dizziness engulfed him, and he realized he was going to be sick. His steps faltered as he bent at the waist, clutching his stomach. Cade was at his other side immediately, but he pushed them both away as he lurched to the gutter and fell to his knees, losing the contents of his stomach. He felt Maya's hands rubbing his back and what must have been Cade's hands holding his hair out of the way.

Because this whole situation wasn't embarrassing enough, he needed every weakness he had to be displayed for mister macho who'd probably never been sick a day in his life and would never be remotely intimidated by some fan mail.

Thoroughly humiliated, Braden's voice shook. "God, I'm so sorry, you guys. Gimme a second and I'll be ready to get up."

He thought he heard Cade whisper, "Fuck that," before he was lifted gently from his knees, picked up, and carried against a huge, solid chest. He heard Cade whisper, "If you need to be sick again tell me and I'll stop."

Cade

Braden began to shake in his arms. Cade looked down at him and swore under his breath. What color he did have was slightly tinged green, and his eyes were shut against the light. Cade knew he must be in awful shape to allow himself to be carried. He hadn't known Braden long, but he knew he almost never asked for help and would have done anything to avoid being in this situation.

Cade followed as Maya took out her keys and unlocked their front door, turned to the interior door on the left, and unlocked Braden's door. All the lights were on in his house. As Maya led him through Braden's home, she turned off most of them to lessen his discomfort. In the bedroom, she turned the dimmer light on as low as it could go so he could still see to put Braden down on his bed. Braden moaned a bit and curled up in a ball facing away from them.

Cade watched as Maya pulled Braden's shoes off, covered him with a blue fleece blanket from the foot of the bed, and led Cade out of Braden's room and into his kitchen. "I'm gonna get him a cold compress and stay with him until he sleeps. Thanks for your help."

"How bad does it get?"

She shrugged. "Pretty bad if the meds don't work. He could be awake for thirty minutes or as long as six hours with pain. He never knows how bad they'll be, but I think this one's been brewing, and he's just been too distracted to catch the signs. Stress makes his blood sugar spike and he's probably been compensating by increasing his doses, but in doing so, he probably triggered the migraine."

Cade shook his head. "I'm not leaving. I'm his protection detail and I want to help him, regardless. Go spend time with Cooper. Check in if you want, but I'm not going anywhere. Not when he's in danger, and especially not when he's in this much pain."

"You're sure?"

"Yeah. Tell me what he needs, and I'll take care of it. Cold compress and what else?"

Cade's mind was reeling. He'd barely met the man yet there he was, offering to take care of him. It was a first for him, but like he'd told Maya, everything within him was aching to help Braden and take the utmost care with him. He wasn't one to ignore his instincts. He felt an innate sense of responsibility for him, and as strange as those feelings were, they also felt right.

The thought of Braden enduring six solid hours of pain made him sick. He wondered how often it happened and what other symptoms he would have normally caught but didn't because of this fan mail bullshit. He wanted to pummel someone, namely the stalker, but he also wanted to shake Braden for not taking better care of himself even though he knew it wasn't fair. He hated feeling helpless.

They walked into the kitchen. Maya scrutinized him closely, looking for what he could only imagine. But she must have found it because she nodded and said, "I'll go get Cooper settled into my place and come and check in on you guys in a bit. He won't be able to work for a day or two, so I need to run across the street and take our emergency pastry stash out of the freezer so we have enough to tide us over for a couple days."

She pulled out a cold compress, wrapped a tea towel around it, and handed it over. "Take this in to him and he'll put it where he needs it most. When it's bad like this, he rubs his temples to relieve the pain. The pressure helps him fall asleep. That and keeping the room dark and quiet is the best we can do. He'll probably get a migraine hangover, so he won't feel good for about twenty-four hours after the pain subsides."

Cade's eyebrows lifted in surprise. "Fuck, I wish I could take his pain away." He held up the cold compress. "Hopefully this helps. I promise to take good care of him."

When he went back into Braden's room, he shut off all the lights completely, sat down beside him and put the cold compress on his head. Braden reached up weakly and murmured a thank you when he grabbed it and moved it slightly to a more comfortable spot.

Braden began to put pressure on his right temple with his other hand, but he couldn't imagine he could keep it up on his own for very long. Cade was at war with himself for several minutes, finally lying back against the pillows so he could hold the compress for him. He grabbed a pillow, helped Braden wrap his arms around it, and began to rub the man's temples. After a few seconds, Braden pulled the pillow tightly to his chest and sighed. Feeling better once he watched Braden get more comfortable, Cade was able to relax as well. He stilled when he heard Braden's voice. "Thanks, My. I'm sorry for everything."

The fact that Braden thought it was Maya helping him was probably for the best though a selfish part of him wished Braden knew it was him. He moved around a little trying to get more comfortable until Cade adjusted him so he was lying on Cade's chest. He set the cold compress aside, freeing his arm, so he was able to run his fingers soothingly through Braden's silky hair and continue massaging his temple and the rest of his head.

Cade knew he was in too deep already when he realized there was nowhere on earth he'd rather be. With Braden in his arms, he was feeling more protective than he'd ever felt towards anyone in his life. He knew Braden was finally asleep when he turned towards Cade, his head resting high on Cade's chest, and snuggled up against him. He continued to massage Braden's head as he slept, laying a gentle kiss on Braden's hair, breathing him in, and closing his eyes in contentment.

A little while later, Cade felt someone watching him and opened his eyes just enough to see Maya in the doorway. She looked a bit surprised to see them cuddled up close to one another, but Cade relaxed a bit when she smiled at them. He was glad she didn't seem upset he was holding Braden so close because he didn't have any intention of letting him go. He was feeling more possessive by the minute as Braden lay cuddled in his arms, all soft and warm.

Maya approached them, grabbed the blanket that had come off of Braden's lower legs, and went about covering them both with it. He kept silent, not wanting to disturb Braden or let Maya know he'd been observing her. Cade watched her walk from the room and found himself getting drowsy. He was out moments later, more relaxed and more at peace than he'd been in a long time.

Braden

Braden woke to the feeling of being in someone's arms. Thinking Maya must have stayed with him the night before, he opened his eyes only to realize the expanse of muscular chest he was lying on was *definitely* not Maya's. Humiliation rushed through him when he thought about the previous night. He waited for the panic to come after being in close proximity to such a big man, but strangely, it didn't. He made to get up off the bed, but Cade grasped him gently by the wrist. Braden looked down into groggy, heavy-lidded, sexy blue eyes and wondered how in the hell he'd missed them the day before.

Cade gazed at him and asked in a quiet, sleepy whisper, "Hey, how are you feeling this morning?"

The concern in Cade's voice, hell, in his eyes, was real and just made

Braden feel worse. He was so far removed from making a good impression on this man it was almost comical. He didn't quite understand why the guy hadn't run in the opposite direction once all the drama started the day before then he realized with chagrin Cade had promised to provide protection detail, so he was stuck.

"I'm fine, Zavier. I don't remember much after humiliating myself all over the gutter last night and you picking me up. I'm so sorry you felt you had to sleep here. You didn't have to put yourself out."

"No, Maya just told me what she thought would help. She was going to do it, but I told her to get her brother settled in at her place, and I'd take care of you."

Braden, still exhausted, felt the echo of pain still reverberating through his body. Sometimes the hangover was just as bad as the migraine itself. He rubbed his forehead, more than a little confused. "But, why? You don't even know me. And, contrary to what you saw yesterday, I am very adept at taking care of myself and my health. I have to be. I guess I just finally hit a wall yesterday, and everything went to shit. I'm really sorry you felt like you had to stay with me."

Cade tilted his head, his gaze intense when he responded, "Do I look like the type of person that does anything he doesn't want to do? You were hurting last night, and I wanted to help you. I don't want your apologies, and I won't apologize for doing what was right or for doing what I wanted and what you needed. You gonna be okay with that?"

Was this guy for real? Who said those kinds of things? Not to mention, he just met the man yesterday. Braden gazed down at Cade, who was still lying back on his pillows. He was gorgeous, and so huge he made Braden's king sized bed seem small. He had dark hair cropped close to his head and a very short beard, making him look scruffy and rugged. He was in a fitted, gray t-shirt and dark washed jeans, which he'd unbuttoned sometime during the night, rode low on his hips. He realized he never responded to Cade's question because he'd been too busy giving him a thorough once over. He felt his cheeks heat when he finally did respond.

"I don't know if I will be, to tell you the truth. I don't know you, and you don't know me, not really. We met each other yesterday afternoon, and I just woke up in my bed with you wrapped around me. That's a lot to take in, Zavier. You've come at a time when the shit has hit the fan, and things are falling down around me, and my life is so far from my norm I'd be crazy if I didn't feel a bit overwhelmed."

Cade sat up, bringing him even closer to Braden. Braden couldn't help but breathe in his scent. Even after sleep, Cade smelled so good, like some kind of sandalwood cologne along with a natural manly scent that was an aphrodisiac in itself. Braden had never seen such a broad chest, huge shoulders, thick, muscular arms, and massive hands. Those arms were works of art all by themselves, but add in the fact both of them were sleeved with black ink, and Braden could barely look away.

At five feet nine inches and no more than a hundred and fifty pounds, Braden had always felt slight, but Cade's sheer size made him feel so small, it was almost ridiculous. One of those arms he had just been admiring reached towards him. Cade caressed the side of Braden's face with his thumb while his fingers combed into his hair. Braden's eyes were drawn to Cade's, and what he saw there was both tenderness and hunger. The combination about did Braden in.

When Cade pulled his hand away, Braden nearly groaned at the loss. He glanced up as Cade spoke, his deep, rough voice buzzing along Braden's nerve endings. "I can handle overwhelmed. We can work with that. I'm interested in getting to know you. Maya mentioned you've had some shitty relationships in the past."

Braden was about to grill him about what Maya had said but Cade held up his hands. "I don't know the details; she didn't share them with me, and I'd much rather hear them from you. Just know I'm going to be straightforward with you from the get go because I don't want there to be any confusion."

Cade reached over and trailed a finger down Braden's arm and gently clasped his hand in his own much bigger one. "When I walked into your kitchen yesterday all I could see was you: your silky, long hair; your strong, smooth jawline; your gorgeous green eyes; and your beautiful lips. You take great care of yourself, and I'm *very* attracted to you, Braden. Something in me recognized something in you."

Braden eyes popped wide at Cade's honesty. "Wow, you really put it all out there, don't you?"

"For you? Yeah, I will. You're worth it. I have no idea what will happen with us. I don't know if we'll even get along, frankly, but I really want to find out because this attraction I feel for you is so strong I'm having a hard time keeping my hands off of you."

Braden looked down at his lap. "I don't know what to say."

He was too tired to figure it out and was starting to feel the effects of the hangover more strongly, which Cade must have seen because he continued, "You don't have to say anything. I can see you're still in pain and exhausted from your migraine; I'm gonna go find my bag, take a shower, and give you some time to yourself. We'll talk more over breakfast."

Cade placed his other hand gently on Braden's neck, his thumb lightly caressing his jaw. He leaned forward, kissed Braden's forehead, and was on his way out of the room before Braden could react.

Braden sighed in relief. No one had ever spoken to him that way. He was glad Cade left because he couldn't have responded to him if he tried. Feeling like shit but knowing he needed to get up and check his glucose levels, he pushed to his feet, ignored the residual dizziness, and trudged to the bathroom to the testing kit he kept at home. After giving himself an injection, he realized he needed to eat something quick to get himself back in line.

Hearing the shower running, he knew he'd be missing breakfast with Cade. He was half relieved and half disappointed by the fact, but he knew he couldn't wait. He grabbed several breakfast-on-the-go snacks he kept for mornings where he needed to recover from a migraine and trudged back to his bed. He ate quickly, not feeling like eating at all but knowing he had to, and was thinking about getting up to shower when he decided to rest for a couple minutes instead. Maybe if he did, the migraine hangover would go away.

Chapter 5

CADE

After his shower, Cade headed toward the kitchen. He had just made some coffee when Maya walked in. He raised the cup in his hand and she shook her head. "No, I'm good thanks; I'll have some at the café. I'm going over there to get things ready to open up but wanted to check on Braden. I have some extra help coming in today, so I can be available to Braden if he needs it. Most likely, he'll sleep a lot today."

Cade nodded. "He looked a little wrung out, but I think he's probably showering and getting ready to come eat."

"When did he wake up?"

"About 35-40 minutes ago. We talked for a bit then I came out to get my bag and a shower before starting coffee."

She shook her head and started towards Braden's bedroom. "He's already eaten something because of the diabetes, and after chatting with you and grabbing something to eat, he most likely ran out of steam. My guess is he's asleep again."

"Shit, I wasn't thinking about the diabetes. Fuck, he has a lot to handle to keep his body functioning properly. I'm sure it's hard enough with the diabetes, but to add migraines to the mix if anything gets out of whack, it must be stressful."

They both peeked in on him. Cade approached Braden, took the remnants of his breakfast off of the bed, and pulled the covers over his sleeping form. Maya came to his side. "Here, give me that stuff. I'll take it to the kitchen."

Cade crouched down next to the bed and gently brushed Braden's hair away from his face, careful not to wake him. He leaned in to kiss his soft cheek as Maya stepped back into the room.

"I think you're gonna be good for him, Cade. I hope he lets you in. If anyone deserves to be happy, it's Braden."

Cade followed her out of Braden's room. "Do I need to wake him up to make sure he checks his glucose?"

"He should be good for three to four hours. If he doesn't wake up by then, wake him up and ask him what he wants to eat. His test kit is in his bathroom. I got your number from Cooper, so I'll text you in the next several hours to check in. Thanks for taking care of him, Cade."

After Maya left, Cade asked Cooper to come over. They reviewed each and every note and letter the stalker had sent to Braden. The guy was all over the place, almost manic with some of his notes, which worried Cade the most. There were some love letters with sappy, sweet words; some just listing dates, times, and locations where Braden had been watched; and others were angry and threatening.

One missive mentioned he'd been watching Braden run in the park and had seen another man join him for part of his run. He'd gone on and on about how unacceptable Braden's behavior was and how he was not to flirt with other men and give other men the impression he was free. There were receipts from shops, restaurants, and bookstores on Braden's running route.

Almost everything was focused on when he was running, most likely because it was when he was alone and out in the open on a fairly regular schedule. They came up with a list of questions to ask Braden to help clarify a few things. However, it had become quite clear it was a serious issue, and the person who was stalking him was becoming unhinged.

Cooper left to meet with the Kensingtons to get their job under way, and Cade set about making lunch for both himself and Braden. Putting the lunch tray down on the nightstand beside Braden's bed, Cade went in search of Braden's test kit. Once he'd found it, he sat by Braden's side, brushed back the hair from his face, and gently rubbed his thumb over the dark circles under Braden's eyes. He didn't know how it happened in less than twenty-four hours, but he cared about Braden more than made sense. He didn't even know the guy, not really, yet he felt they were tied together in some inexplicable way.

Braden's eyes blinked groggily open, peered up at him, and he smiled such a sweet, bewildered smile it melted Cade's heart. He couldn't seem to stop touching him, so he moved his thumb over to Braden's temple and gently rubbed there, hoping to ease any residual ache left in the migraine's wake.

"Hey, I wanted to get you up because it's been four hours, and you need to test your blood and eat some food. Let me help you get propped up against some pillows; I've got your kit right here."

Braden

Braden still felt exhausted, so he allowed Cade to help him sit up. "Thanks, Zavier," he managed as he rubbed his face and tucked his hair behind his ears.

His movements were a bit slow, and he didn't feel like he had much strength. He hated this part of the migraine. The hangover sometimes felt just as bad as the migraine itself and made the whole episode last so much longer. He was able to open his test kit, prick his finger, and test the blood, but afterward, he had to sit for a minute. He glanced over at the nightstand to check the time and saw the lunch tray containing two plates with big sandwiches, a bowl filled with carrots and celery and another bowl of grapes. There were a couple glasses of milk and even folded napkins.

He smiled shyly over at Cade and joked, "Maybe I need to keep you around to help every time I have a migraine. I get door-to-door transportation, personal nursing through the night, and now meal service. That's not even taking into account the personal protection detail to come, along with an investigation. I'm gonna be indebted to you big time."

Instead of laughing as Braden had intended, Cade looked at him as if he was carefully weighing his words. "You want to keep me around? Just say the word and consider it done. But you're not, and never will be, indebted to me. Understand?"

Braden's mouth dropped open, and his eyes widened. "I understand. And I appreciate all you've done, I really do. I just wish I was meeting you at a time when things were normal for me. Having you swoop in to save the day when I get myself in a bind with some crazy stalker then manage to give myself a migraine is a little unsettling."

"Stop blaming yourself for shit that's out of your control. Now, eat your lunch."

He tried to hide his smile because good lord, grumpy Cade was really cute. He nodded his head but bent over his kit again. He mustered up the energy to measure out the correct amount of insulin and looked at Cade. "If this is going to bother you, you can look away."

"Do you mind if I watch?"

Braden blushed a little and felt as if the act of giving himself insulin with this virile man watching was somehow very intimate, but he shrugged. "No, I don't mind."

He lifted his shirt and injected himself in the stomach, rubbing at the spot afterwards, he was surprised Cade scooted closer and caressed the back of his hand. Braden shivered at the contact; Cade's large, roughened hand felt foreign, yet soothing. His eyes flitted up to Cade's, and his breath caught in his throat. They stared at each other for several long moments until Cade smiled devastatingly and Braden had to blink several times to break whatever spell he'd cast.

Cade let go of Braden's hand and placed the tray of food on the bed. "Maya stopped by several times today while you were sleeping. She's worried about you. Let's eat so you'll feel better. I pulled all of this from your own supplies, so I'm assuming it's all okay, but if it's not right, tell me and I'll make you something else."

Braden touched Cade's knee. His voice caught in his throat so it came out as a whisper. "It's perfect. Thank you. Tell Maya, if I miss her again when she stops in, I love her."

Cade agreed, and they ate the meal in companionable silence. After

Braden had eaten what he needed to keep his levels healthy, he set the plate aside, reclined back, and thanked Cade again. He watched in amused silence as Cade picked up the remains of his food and demolished it.

Cade grinned, his voice sheepish. "I'm pretty much a bottomless pit. I ate another sandwich while I was making these. And I found a stash of chocolate candy which surprised me. I ate some of that too."

"Oh no." Braden's burst of laughter surprised him. "Zavier, it was sugar free candy I get from a local chocolatier for when I need something sweet but don't want to mess with my glucose levels or bake myself something. If you're not used to the stuff, your stomach might not be too happy with you."

"Well, shit."

"Yes, precisely."

They looked at each other and laughed. After they caught their breath, Cade loaded everything back up on the tray and leaned in and kissed Braden on the temple. "You look like you're about to keel over. Rest some more. If I need to wake you for dinner, I will."

Braden couldn't remember a time in his adult life when he'd been so thoroughly taken care of by another man. For the life of him, he couldn't figure out why he was letting Cade help him in the first place. It was completely uncharacteristic without even taking into account the fact he'd just met the man. Not only was he allowing himself to be helped, he was allowing Cade to take control and tell him what to do.

He felt a pull towards Cade he couldn't explain, and while a part of him wanted to push back and tell him to back off and mind his own business, he had to admit another part of him, a part which obviously edged out the other, was telling him to do what Cade asked of him because so far, Cade was taking better care of him than he had been of himself.

He let that boggle his mind for quite a while, flipped it over and over in his head and tried to dissect it or prove himself wrong, before he gave up and felt himself let it all go. Just as he fell asleep, he once again thought about how much trouble he was in with this man.

Braden found himself being woken up a second time by Cade who was bearing dinner and his testing kit. He felt better but still a little out of it. What he did know was being woken up by a gentle hand caressing his forehead and running through his hair felt really nice. He felt a bit off kilter every time he was near Cade. He needed to get a grip.

"We gotta quit meeting like this, Zavier."

Cade chuckled and helped him sit up. "You've been out for another four hours. It's time for some dinner and a blood test. How are you feeling?"

Wiggling his hand back and forth, he grumbled, "meh," while he reached for the kit. He tested his blood, got his dose ready, and injected it into his stomach, rubbing the area afterwards. "I usually don't feel one hundred percent for several days after a migraine, but I'm a bit better than I was at lunch. Thanks for waking me."

"Do you need to eat and sleep again right away, or do you want to be up for a bit?"

"I feel like I could sleep again right now, but I'd probably be up at 3 a.m. and not be able to fall back to sleep, so I think I'll try to stay up a bit after we eat."

"You want company or would you prefer to be alone?" Cade gave Braden his most charming yet hopeful smile.

Braden chuckled and shook his head. "You don't fight fair, do you?"

"What? I don't know what you're insinuating."

"Yes, you do. You with the innocent look on your face; I'm hip to your games," Braden teased.

Cade's smile faded. "I'll tease you and joke around with you, Braden; you can be sure of it. But I'll never play games with you. That's a promise, okay?"

Braden looked down at his hands still holding his testing kit, glanced back up at Cade and shrugged. "Okay."

"In that vein, I'll just say I find myself in a situation I've never been in before. I'm crazy attracted to you. And I find myself wanting to share things with you I'd normally keep to myself so you can get to know me. But I guess the real question is, will you allow *me* to get to know *you*?"

Braden blushed, glanced down at his hands and looked backup with a shy smile. "How about we eat dinner together at the table, and we'll see how things go?"

"That's a good start. I baked some chicken and steamed some veggies. Made a bit of quinoa and cut up some apples."

"You made it yourself? It smells really good, and I'm actually pretty hungry. You didn't have to do all this, but thank you."

"I don't mind cooking. Once we were teens, Mom and Dad made us each take a day a week to cook meals for the family, so we all got rather proficient at cooking."

Cade picked up the dinner tray and led Braden out to the dining table. Once they got there, they kept conversation to a minimum in favor of eating the delicious meal Cade prepared. After dinner, Cade led them out to Braden's living room so they could start getting to know each other. Braden asked how many siblings Cade had and learned he had an older brother, two younger brothers, and a younger sister. He regaled Braden with stories about his siblings, and they talked for a couple hours, learning a lot about each other's childhood and teenage years.

Braden loved listening to Cade's deep voice. He found it so sexy he could listen to him read the phone book and never tire of it. He also learned Cade had a really great sense of humor and an enormous love for his large family. When he spoke of them, his face lit up and his laugh was infectious. One story in particular, regarding his siblings playing a prank on their mother, had Braden laughing harder than he could remember laughing in quite some time. He felt tears form at the corners of his eyes and wiped them away. "Did she kill you? How long was her hair purple?"

Cade chuckled. "Not long, it was only Kool-Aid, but yeah, she was pissed when she thought it was permanent. I also came out to them when I was 16 with a prank."

"What? How did you do that?"

"One of my best friends and I came up with this whole story and I used her as an accomplice. We told them she was pregnant, even showed them a copy of an ultrasound we found in the school library and photocopied. Said we needed their signatures so we could get married, had a marriage license and everything."

Braden slapped both hands over his mouth, stifling a gasp. "You didn't!"

Cade threw back his head and laughed so hard it made Braden grin. "We really did. Oh my god, Braden, they lost their shit! Both of them yelling at us, telling us we were too young to get married, on and on. I finally settled them down enough to listen to me and told them I was kidding. I was just gay."

Braden was on the edge of his seat. "What did they say?"

"My mom burst into tears, hand to her chest like we'd given her a heart attack, and my dad cussed a blue streak telling both of us we were grounded until we were thirty. Turns out they didn't care so much I was gay as long as Jen wasn't pregnant. They asked Jen if she was staying for dinner, and that was that."

"Your parents sound great."

Cade smiled. "They're pretty amazing."

That story prompted Braden's telling of his coming out story. How he grew up with his grandparents and finally got up the courage to tell his Nana when he was fourteen. He sat her down and told her he had a crush on someone. Just as he was about to take the plunge and tell her, she asked, "What's his name?" He'd been so scared and stressed to say it, he just stared at her shocked and started crying. Then they were both crying, and she told him she had known for some time and was waiting for him to come to her.

"She sounds pretty great, too. Are your grandparents still alive?"

A sad smile flitted across Braden's face. "Papa passed my senior year of high school. That was a tough year for us. Nana is still alive, and she's quite the character. Lives in a retirement home, and I swear she has half the men there following her around. She's a flirt, and she has more dates than a single woman half her age."

Cade grinned. "She sounds like a kick in the pants."

Braden nodded. "She's the best."

Cade sat silently for a couple minutes, watching Braden closely. They sat together on the sofa, near enough to touch. Braden felt shy and blushed a little at the attention, but the silence felt comfortable. Cade leaned forward and tucked a silky thread of Braden's hair behind his ear. "You look tired. Are you ready to go back to sleep?"

Braden blinked. "Sorry, yeah, I'm still feeling a bit off. I think I'd like to take a shower before getting back in bed since I didn't have the energy this morning."

"Don't apologize." Cade gave Braden a patient smile, eyebrows raised. "Are you sure you have the energy now?"

"I'll take a quick one, but I think it will make me feel better."

Cade stood and helped Braden to his feet. "Okay, I'll clean up the mess from dinner, you go take your shower, and I'll come and check on you in a bit."

"I'll be fine, you don't have to..."

Cade gave Braden's hand a gentle squeeze. "I want to."

Braden ducked his head shyly and went back to his bedroom. With a fresh change of clothes, he walked into his bathroom and looked at himself in the mirror, surprised to see a smile on his face and flushed cheeks. He was in and out of the shower in less than ten minutes. When he was finished with his night time routine, he headed back into his bedroom and got himself back under the covers.

He sat for a few minutes, thinking about the man who was now sharing his living space for the foreseeable future. Cade was the epitome of everything Braden had ever been attracted to. The thought scared him, but it also intrigued him. He hadn't had feelings like this in more than a year and a half. In fact, he wasn't sure he'd ever felt this pull, this energy, around anyone. Sure, there'd been attraction before, but this, this was altogether different. It was like he had an internal hum resonating through his body when he was near Cade. When Cade touched him, even if it was just briefly, he felt electricity whirring through his veins.

He wasn't used to being pursued. When he was attracted to someone, he usually forced his shy nature aside in order to make the first move. He thought it was because he didn't like being alone, so he took matters into his own hands, but he knew it was also because he needed a measure of control in making the choice of whom to approach. Cade being the one essentially hitting on him and pursuing him had him off kilter. However, Braden wasn't feeling the stress of making any moves, and it felt good letting Cade take the lead. He felt some measure of control because he knew he could say no whenever he wanted to, and Cade would back off. He had no idea why he felt like he could trust him, but he felt sure he could.

From what Cade said, if he could be believed, he was feeling something similar. No matter how many ways he looked at it, Braden couldn't figure out any reason at all Cade would lie to him about it. He wouldn't gain anything. He was best friends with Cooper, not to mention business partners. He was gay and out. He was going to protect and investigate the stalker situation for free. Cooper and Maya were remarkably alike, and Maya was a great judge of character, so he already felt he could trust Cade to be truthful about most anything because Cooper trusted him implicitly. If anything, lying would not only be illogical, but it would risk his relationship with Cooper if he ended up hurting Braden because Maya would be out for blood, and Cooper was an extremely protective older brother.

While it didn't make sense to Braden someone like Cade could be interested in someone like him, it made even less sense he'd lie about it. In fact, he had been so completely forthright about everything so far Braden could do nothing but admire him and believe him. Doing anything else seemed disrespectful. The things Cade had said took an amazing amount of courage to tell someone you've known for months, let alone someone you've known for less than forty-eight hours.

Feeling this level of trust towards a man this early was so completely foreign and utterly inexplicable he felt overwhelmed and yet strangely euphoric about it, which put a huge smile on his face. He jumped when Cade knocked on the door frame before walking in. He'd changed into some plaid pajama bottoms and a tight white t-shirt. He looked delicious, and Braden caught himself before he said it out loud, licked his lips, or did something equally ridiculous and embarrassing.

Cade stopped in the middle of Braden's room as if dumbfounded. He shook his head and grinned broadly. "God, that smile. I could look at that smile every day and still never get enough of it. I don't even…. What was I…. Oh, I brought you some water. Do you need to take pain pills?"

Braden blushed and tried not to smile even wider as a result of Cade's compliment. "No, thanks. I'm just a bit groggy and really exhausted still, but I don't have any pain right now. I'll take the water though. Thank you."

"Okay. So you don't need me to rub your temples or hold an ice pack to your head. I'm trying to figure out any other reason you might need me to sleep in here with you again. Zombie apocalypse? Killer bees?"

That surprised a laugh out of Braden, and he felt comfortable enough to flirt back in response. "Sadly, I don't remember much of last night, but I'm almost one-hundred percent positive I would have thoroughly enjoyed being held in your arms all night even without the imminent threat of zombies or killer bees."

Cade, eyes wide, lifted both arms, looking at them like he'd never seen them before. "Yeah? These arms?"

Braden chuckled. "Yeah, those are the ones."

"So, that means I can stay, right?"

Braden smiled flirtatiously and shook his head. "Nope."

"Damn."

Braden smirked. "I think you'll live. My guest bedroom has a pretty nice bed in it."

"Right, but it doesn't have you in it." Cade sighed dramatically. "I suppose I'll muddle through." He leaned forward, caressed Braden's cheek, kissed the top of his head, and whispered softly in his ear. "Sleep well, Braden."

Braden shivered from the touch, the kiss, and the sexy whispered words and couldn't help but watch as Cade left, giving him a fantastic view of his tight round ass. Jesus, those glutes. Braden sighed as he lay down and got comfortable. There was no stopping it; he was going to have dreams, really good dreams, of Cade's perfect ass, among other things.

Chapter 6

CADE

Cade woke up around five the next morning, headed to the electric kettle to heat up some water for his coffee and heard a noise in Braden's room. Curious, as he hadn't expected Braden to be awake, he walked in there and caught Braden doing yoga or some sort of sexy, flexible…something. He propped his shoulder on the doorjamb, crossed his arms over his chest, and rested one ankle over the other, getting comfortable as he watched Braden do…whatever it was he was doing.

He was already in full running gear which seemed so incongruous with what Cade thought of as Braden's hipster, metrosexual vibe he could do nothing but grin and watch him while he contorted his body into positions that really shouldn't be physically possible. Frankly, it was giving him a semi. A couple more downward dog, upward dog combos and Cade was going to embarrass himself. He must have made some sort of noise, his guess was a whimper, because Braden jumped and swung around towards him.

"Jesus, Zavier, you scared the shit out of me!"

Cade stood from his position against the jam. "Sorry, I…" He rubbed a hand over the back of his neck and smiled. "You're really bendy."

Braden huffed out a laugh. "Bendy? Well, in order to be able to run as much as I need to, I have to make sure my muscles stay loose, so there's an enormous amount of stretching. Yoga and Pilates, those sorts of things."

"Pilates? I don't know what it is, but I can see it's helpful, you know, with being... bendy. So, I take it we're running today? I guess a little stretching is in order for me as well. Are you going to take it easy on me?"

"So, you weren't exaggerating when you said you'd be my shadow? You're really going running with me?"

"Exaggerating? No. We're taking this seriously. I'll do my best to stay out of your way, I can even run behind you if you'd prefer. I want to get to know you, but I wouldn't use this as an excuse to get close to you."

"I know that." Braden grinned at him." I suppose I can take it easy on you. I don't really have the energy after the migraine to go full tilt, anyway."

"Alright, do you want to eat first? If not, let me go get ready."

"I was gonna make some breakfast first, so you can get ready, and I'll fix us something. We won't be running until around seven. I need to get over to the café and start baking. I run while the croissant dough is rising, then I come back for my second round of baking."

"Sounds good. You do what you'd normally do, and I'll do my best to stay out of your way.

Braden gazed up at him, a blush tinting his cheeks. "You can run beside me, but I need the time to empty my head and relieve my stress, so I usually don't talk much and most of the time I have my buds in. Sorry."

"Don't apologize. Whatever works best for you. We'll need to talk later today about the stalker, but if you're willing to do it while you're baking, that'll work for me."

Braden nodded. "Can we have that talk after we run?"

"Yeah, of course."

"Thanks. Do you like eggs?"

Cade smiled. "You'd be hard pressed to find food I don't like. Now, MREs I will gladly do without for the rest of my days, but real food? I'm a glutton."

"All right, eggs it is."

Cade changed into a pair of compression shorts, a long loose pair of basketball shorts, and tugged on a fitted wicking tee. When he walked into the kitchen, his body tightened at the awareness he saw in Braden's eyes as he gave Cade a thorough once over. He willed his dick to behave when he saw Braden lick his lips. Jesus, the guy was gonna be his undoing.

After eating breakfast, Cade stopped Braden before he walked out the door. "I'll always need to be on your right side so my right hand is free to draw my weapon. There's no reason for you to remember that, I just wanted you to understand why I may sometimes reposition you or myself."

Cade could see the surprise on Braden's face and berated himself for forgetting to tell him he'd be carrying. He knew some people had an aversion to guns, but he'd been handling guns since he was a kid and had carried one for too many years to count. Carrying a gun was like putting on his clothes in the morning. He'd tuck his gun in one of his concealed holsters without even thinking about it. Even when he wasn't working, he sometimes carried a concealed weapon depending on where he was going and what he was doing. It was a habit that was hard to break.

Once they were at the café, he watched as Braden prepped his work area. He got out his iPad and got some work done while Braden, buds in his ears, made several batches of scones and muffins and put them in the ovens to bake. After that, he started on some other batters and bread dough and set them aside as he took his first batches out of the oven.

He loved watching the smaller man work. His movements were fluid and confident. When he couldn't take the smells a minute longer, he cleared his throat loudly and watched as Braden took his buds out. The look of yearning on his face must have given him away.

Braden chuckled. "Give them a couple minutes to set and cool so you don't burn your mouth then take whatever you want."

Right around that time, Cade heard a loud bell ring and watched Braden pick up a cloth from the counter to wipe his hands. He walked towards the back door, but Cade stopped him with a gentle hand on his shoulder. "Is it the back doorbell?"

"Yes, Layla is here. She comes in to get the café set up with the baked goods and gets the coffee started, and in another few minutes, Zoe will arrive to get the register drawers in so they can open the doors at seven."

Cade assured him, "Go ahead and keep working, I'll let her in."

Layla looked surprised to see him and took a step back. "Sorry to surprise you, Layla. I'm here with Braden, come on in."

"Okay," Layla practically squeaked as she slid past him as quickly as her little feet would carry her to the break room. She came out wearing an apron and grabbed one of the trays Braden had filled with the fresh baked goods. She was about to make her escape when Cade reached out and snagged one of the scones from the tray and gave her a wink and a lazy, flirtatious smile. She raised eyes that were now wide in shock to Cade and let out a startled little meep before practically running to the front of the café.

Cade chuckled and took a bite of the scone and stopped in the middle of the kitchen in bliss, making a deep rumbling sound of sheer happiness when the flavors burst on his tongue. He looked over at Braden, who was pulling out a few more pans of baked goods from the oven and shaking his head in exasperation.

"You're gonna scare the girl to death. She's already a little jumpy around me, now she's got Gigantor to contend with too? She'll expire on the spot if you keep flirting with her."

Cade laughed and lied through his teeth. "I'm harmless, and I wasn't flirting. She was taking my scone!"

"I saved you a scone and a muffin, right by your iPad."

"Oh good, this one won't be enough and don't think you're gonna get away with calling me Gigantor without some retribution."

"Retribution? Like what? And, would you prefer Gladiator, the Jolly Green Giant?"

Cade's deadpan face and raised eyebrow had Braden chuckling. And goddamn, he'd do just about anything to hear more of his laughter and see more of his smile. "If I was green, I'd be the Hulk, thank you very much. I'll think of something for retribution, and yeah, Gladiator is better and much more accurate."

Braden threw up his hands in surrender and went back to work, mumbling about hot giants with huge egos. Pretty soon, Braden was taking the last tray out of the oven, and the back doorbell rang again. Looking through the peephole, Cade glanced back in surprise, Braden grinned. "Tattooed, pin-up knockout. Remind you of anyone?"

Cade raised his eyebrows when Braden laughed at the look on his face, shrugged and opened the door to the woman who could only be Zoe. They took stock of each other for several moments then both of them grinned like loons, each apparently didn't quite believe they were looking at the other.

"Well, aren't you something, Miss Boop."

"Not so bad yourself, G.I. Joe."

"What gave me away?"

She sauntered by him and poked his left arm, directly on the spot where he had his Special Forces tattoo even though it was somewhat obscured within a bigger tattoo. Impressed, and liking her sassy attitude, he followed her in and admired the gorgeous and vividly colorful tattoos she sported on her arms. He made a mental note to ask her who the artist was. He'd need a local tattooist.

He watched her approach Braden, who smiled and tilted his face down for her to kiss. "Hey, Boop."

Zoe hugged Braden around the waist. "Hi, Sweets. This big lug here to take care of you?"

"That's the plan."

"Good. Can't have anything happen to our boy." She smiled coyly at Cade and leaned over to his plate and stole the scone.

"Hey!"

"Oh stop, there's more where that came from, big guy. Try the chocolate ones."

"You guys are going to give me a complex. Between being called Gigantor, big guy, and a big lug, I'm feeling rather self-conscious."

"Gigantor? Love it! Braden, you slay me." Still laughing, Zoe bit into the scone, winked at him cheekily, and swished her hips into the office.

Braden smiled as he loaded up the last of the trays, and Layla came back in to grab another one to take to the front, avoiding Cade's eyes. Braden pulled off his apron and once again looked like a distance runner. Braden asked Cade if he was ready, and they both headed out of the café. They stretched for a few minutes in silence then strapped on their iPhones and earbuds and went for a run.

After a couple miles, Cade caught Braden watching him, maybe even assessing him. He took out an ear bud and asked, "What's up?"

Surprise seemed to put a hitch in Braden's stride. Looking distinctly uncomfortable, Braden shook his head. "Nothing."

"Braden, you've been watching every move I make for the last quarter mile. Am I making you uncomfortable? I can run behind you if you'd prefer."

"You're fine."

"Talk to me, Braden."

"It's nothing. It's not a big deal."

Braden's response seemed stilted as if he was scared to talk to him. Cade didn't like it at all, but he didn't think forcing it was the answer. "All right. I won't push, but I think I'll give you your space, anyway."

Cade slowed down so Braden could take the lead. Something was up, but this was Braden's time to run off the stress and he didn't want to take that from him. Cade was settling in behind him when Braden turned. "Your shoulders are hunched in too much."

Well *that* wasn't what he'd expected to hear. "I... What now?"

Braden slowed his stride so they were next to each other again. "When you're running, your shoulders–" He cut himself off and shook his head. "Nevermind, I'm sorry. I don't want to make you mad."

Mad? "Why would I be mad?"

"Because I'm correcting you."

Cade kept an eye on their surroundings as he answered, "Braden, you're the expert here, not me. If I can improve my stride, please tell me what I'm doing wrong."

"Really?"

Why would Braden be afraid to tell him something as simple as that? "Yeah, really. Why wouldn't I want to know?"

"Well, usually guys don't like anyone pointing out they're doing something wrong."

"Okay, well how about this; when we're running, if something's wrong with my stride, you tell me so I can fix it. And if, say, you're field stripping a weapon, I'll tell you what *you're* doing wrong, so you can fix it. Sound fair?"

"I don't know what that is."

Cade shrugged, thinking their conversation had gotten very convoluted. "Okay, well I can teach you."

"No thank you?"

Cade couldn't help but grin at his confusion. "Is that a question?"

Braden shook his head. "No."

They glanced quickly at each other and laughed, dispelling the tension. Cade focused back on their surroundings as he explained, "All I'm saying is I would consider you an expert at the proper running form. And I could be considered an expert at proper weapon handling. I'm okay with you correcting me in this because *you're* the expert."

"Oh. Okay."

"Okay. So?"

"Your shoulders." Cade watched Braden hunch his shoulders. "They're hunched. Open them up."

Cade did what he suggested and Braden nodded. "Yeah, like that. And your elbows should be at a ninety-degree angle, there you go. It'll feel off at first but it will help in the long run. Less shoulder and back strain, more fluid stride."

"Yeah?"

Braden's grin was infectious as he nodded. "Yeah."

"Thanks. Now, about that field stripping…"

Braden laughed. "No."

The farther they ran, the more he realized Braden was really taking it easy on him. Even not feeling his best, he could have probably gone much faster than they were going. And while Cade could run much faster as well, the more effort he put into it, the less he was paying attention to what was going on around them. He couldn't do his job if he was putting all of his energy into keeping up. They'd have to run relay to keep from burning out or something.

He was bothered by Braden's reluctance to tell him what he was thinking. He seemed afraid to give his opinion, thinking Cade would be angry with him for voicing his thoughts. He had a feeling the past relationship Maya had warned him about was what made Braden so cautious to voice his opinion.

Without blatantly coming out and asking Braden point blank Cade had to be sure he let Braden know with his actions he felt his opinions and feelings were important. He never wanted him to feel like he had to hesitate to tell him anything. He wanted Braden to lighten up a little and feel more relaxed around him.

They both showered after their run and met up in the kitchen. Braden had put on a pair of black rectangular glasses and tied his hair up in some kind of messy bun. He wore brown leather, well-worn ankle boots with dark wash, fitted and cuffed jeans and an old and very faded Beatles t-shirt with a plaid cotton button-up shirt layered on top. He was gorgeous.

His rolled-up sleeves showed off a very wide, leather, cuff-like bracelet that Cade realized was actually a McCade Watch. He smiled wide, surprised he hadn't noticed it before, and tucked the information away for later, not to mention, he needed to have a discussion with his family regarding offering a new type of band.

Braden had a really sexy style he never knew he'd be so utterly enamored with. His own sense of style was practically non-existent. His mother called it "military chic" as most of the men in the family were soldiers or sailors and shared the same exact military palette. Not to mention, most of the men were over six foot four, so a lot of their clothing had to be tailored.

More often than not, he was wearing a pair of tactical pants with a comfortable cotton shirt. He'd never cared one way or another about clothing and wore what was comfortable and practical. In fact, he'd never been interested in fashion as it related to his past partners either, but he could see Braden was very fashion forward, while still maintaining a completely relaxed feel about it all.

He knew if he commented about Braden's appearance, he would blush and get uncomfortable, so he merely gave Braden a very admiring look which no one could misinterpret. "Glasses?"

He'd done his best not to embarrass him, but Cade still noticed the telltale blush suffusing his skin. Braden touched the side of his glasses shyly. "Yeah, I've been wearing my contacts for a few days too long. I forgot to change them out because of the migraine, and my eyes are getting tired, so I'm giving them a break."

Cade smiled. "They suit you."

Braden avoided eye contact and stammered. "Uh, thanks. Ready to go back over to the café?"

"Yep, ready when you are."

Leaving the apartment, they crossed the street to the café, and once he got Braden safely ensconced in the kitchen, Cade went back to his seat at the counter to check emails. Maya came back from the front and hugged Braden tight. The smile on both their faces was infectious. He loved that Braden had her in his life and she so obviously loved Braden just as much as he did her. They talked for several minutes in the corner of the kitchen. Maya peeked around Braden several times, checking out Cade and smiling knowingly.

God knows what Braden was telling her, but he kept a smile on his face because it couldn't be bad when she had that devilish look in her eyes. After their conversation died down, she admitted she had to get back up to the front. They hugged again, and Cade heard Braden murmur, "I love you too, My."

Braden got to work right away, and Cade could tell he was in his element. Wanting to get the lay of the land, he verified with Braden he wouldn't leave the kitchen. He locked the outer door and asked Braden not to open it for any reason, assuring him if deliveries came through that door going forward, he would be the one to answer it.

He left Braden to his baking while he looked around the café to figure out what security issues there might be. They had a shitty, outdated security system which would need to go right away. He placed a call to his team and got Sawyer and Jackson to make the trip out with the right systems and equipment to arm the place properly as well as Braden and Maya's places since it didn't look like they had any security at all. He also asked them to bring several tracers for Braden, should they be needed.

Feeling more at ease now help was on the way, he went back into the kitchen and asked Braden if he was doing all right. Braden didn't respond, and Cade realized he had his buds in. He approached Braden from the side so he didn't spook him. Braden noticed him, pulled out a bud, and smiled. "Hey, sorry, were you talking to me? I tend to zone out."

Cade borrowed the bud to listen in and smiled when he realized it was Ray LaMontagne, one of his favorites. Handing the bud back, he ran a gentle hand up Braden's back as he leaned his hip against the counter. "Just checking on you. Do you need anything to eat or to check your blood?"

Braden looked at him, a little surprised. He smiled, pointing to his watch that was sitting on the counter next to the sink. "What you saw a couple days ago was an aberration, I promise you. I have timers set up at regular intervals so I don't forget anything. I'm very good at taking care of my health, Cade. I have to be, you've seen what happens if I don't."

Cade nodded his head sheepishly. "Of course, you're right, sorry."

"I'm not. You can ask me anything, it won't upset me."

"Okay, then one more question?"

"Yeah. Of course."

"I know they have those pumps you can get that deliver insulin automatically. Why don't you use one?"

Braden's nose scrunched up, and Cade just wanted to kiss it. "I tried a pump, years ago. Hated it. I need to feel like I'm controlling my diabetes, not like it's controlling me. The pump is connected to you with tubing like a catheter, and I hated how it felt, how it was connected to me, and how I couldn't get away from it."

"Like you were trapped?"

"Yeah. I also had some bad readings and some other issues with it. My Endo took me off of it after less than a month, and I was happy to see it go. I manage my diabetes with MDI, which means I have to have at least four injections a day, sometimes more if needed."

"What's MDI?"

"Multiple daily injections, some of them slow acting to last all day, others fast acting around meal times. To some, it seems like a reason to get on the pump, but not for me because I'm very regimented. It gives me full control."

"I didn't know it was so complicated. Will you share your schedule with me, so I can understand it?"

Braden's brows rose. "You want to know my insulin schedule?"

"Yeah, I do. I think it would be good for me to have it if it doesn't bother you."

"No, it's fine. I don't know why you'd want or need it, but it doesn't bother me at all to give it to you."

"Okay, good, thanks. I hate to bring it up, but we need to talk about the notes. I need to get information from you if we want any hope of getting this guy. I don't want to get in your way here, but since it's been a couple days, we can't put it off any longer. Are you okay to keep working while I ask the questions?"

"Yes, go ahead."

For the next few hours, Braden baked and Cade asked questions. When Braden told him all the places he'd found notes, Cade's insides tightened. The fact that they arrived in his mailbox, on his car windshield, in the business mail slot, and taped to the back door of the café made it so much worse. He knew Braden felt like he couldn't get away from them and never knew when or where they'd show up. Some weeks, he would receive three, some none, with no discernible pattern in their delivery.

The only common thread Cade could find was they all seemed to revolve around Braden's running schedule. And it absolutely wasn't an option for him to stop running. It wouldn't make the stalker go away, would probably only anger and escalate him sooner, but it would also serve as just one more way to fuck with Braden. His life had been turned upside down enough without taking his one stress relieving outlet away.

As much as he liked to hear that Braden hadn't dated in a little over a year which meant no recently scorned lovers, he hated seeing embarrassment and shame accompanying the admission. He moved on to another line of questions to give Braden a break.

Braden had received several hang-ups over the last several months, but there'd been no break-ins. Knowing he needed to focus on the last five years of relationships, he asked Braden to tell him the names of the men he'd been involved with. When he mentioned Nick Stevens and Owen Hoffman, he seemed perfectly at ease. But when he mentioned Eric Pollard, the color drained from his face, his movements became stilted, and his hands started to shake.

Cade tread lightly, seeing it was taking its toll on Braden. And he was nearly as relieved as Braden was when his watch alarm beeped. It felt like a saved-by-the-bell moment for both of them, he was sure. He approached Braden, knowing he needed something but unsure what he'd accept. He slid a hand up his back and gripped his neck, massaging a bit as he suggested Braden get his insulin dose while he grabbed them some lunch at the deli down the street. The shaking of Braden's small frame diminished a bit, and he smiled at Cade in relief, knowing he had a small reprieve.

After getting Braden's order and his promise not to leave the kitchen for any reason, Cade ran up to the front, surprised to see how busy the place was. He asked Maya and Layla if they wanted him to pick them up anything. He took his time walking down to the deli and called Cooper on the way. "Hey, how's the Kensington job?"

"Boring and easy, but the place is a palace, so it's time consuming. They just want us to upgrade the system and cameras, but they want to stick with their own security people at their gate. Mrs. Kensington looked decidedly uncomfortable after I asked if she felt she had the right people for the job. Blushed down to her roots and admitted the owner of that security firm was a cousin of her husband's. Guess we'll hear from them if they have issues there. I should be done at the end of the day tomorrow."

"Good. I'm going to need you on this once you're free. Jackson and Sawyer will be here with full systems for the café, Braden's place, and Maya's along with tracers for Braden tomorrow. They're also bringing other supplies and firearms we might need. They have a shit system at the café a twelve-year-old could bypass, and as far as I can see, the only thing they've each got in their homes is a deadbolt on their front doors."

"Yeah, I read Maya the riot act about it yesterday. She didn't want my interference, but she promised me she'd get a system set up for herself back when they opened the café. She thought the crap system they had installed there was enough to feel like she was keeping her word. I need my little sister safe, and I get the feeling you need your boy to be safe as well."

Cade grumbled at that. "He's a man, Coop. Don't piss me off."

"Yeah, he's a man, but he's *your* boy. You're all growly and protective around him, and from what Maya has said, he's not used to it, but he likes it a lot. Admit it, you're already thinking of him as yours, aren't you? I told you it would happen sooner than you expected. Shit, I'm good."

"It's too soon to know, but if you're asking if I'm protective of him, fuck yes, so keep the jokes to a minimum."

"See? Growly. Too soon to know my ass, Cade, you've never acted like this with anyone before. Not to mention, he seems to be exactly the type you need. He's your boy, and you know I won't disrespect that."

Cade sighed. He couldn't help but admit it. "Yeah. Okay, so I haven't gotten much we can use so far. He was more forthcoming with me than he was with the cop, but there's not much there. When I began to steer the conversation towards his past relationships, he tensed up like crazy, so I think that's where we're gonna get what we need, but I have to be careful with him."

"You'll do fine. Let me know how it goes."

"I will. I'm going into the deli to buy everyone lunch, so let me get to it, and I'll talk to you tonight once I've got more info regarding suspects. My gut says the shitty relationship Maya mentioned to us is going to be where the goods are, but we'll see."

"Agreed. Talk to you later."

Cade placed his order and waited, responding to a few work inquiries on his phone. He grabbed the food when it was ready and went back to the café, already feeling uneasy about Braden being without his protection for so long. He needed to get someone else to run out for lunch going forward.

Chapter 7

BRADEN

Braden checked the muffins in one of the ovens, ignoring his growling stomach. He was hungry for lunch but nervous to tell Cade about his past mistakes—and that's what the last five years' worth of relationships were. He'd have to share a lot of information he'd much rather keep to himself. Cade was obviously aware of his unease. He seemed to be able to read him like a book which made no sense but was true, nonetheless. Cade knew exactly when he needed a break, so he'd come up with an excuse to give Braden a few minutes to get his shit together.

He'd just removed the muffins from the oven and was about to start a batch of cookies when Cade arrived with lunch. They spent a relaxing thirty minutes eating and chatting about music and other non-threatening things. Braden got up to walk back to the kitchen to begin baking the cookies and told Cade he was ready to talk.

Braden figured he needed to metaphorically pull on his big boy shorts and get this awful conversation over with. Cade needed the info, and at this point, Braden just needed to get it off his chest. He started by discussing his relationship with Nick. He gave him Nick's full name, occupation, and the information he had about his last known address and phone number.

They'd been seeing each other for about six months and Braden thought it was going really well until the night he and Maya had gone to their favorite dance club to have some fun and blow off some steam. Instead of working late, Braden caught Nick on the dance floor plastered all over some bear. After Braden broke it off, Nick tried to call him repeatedly, but he never answered his phone and tossed out the flowers he'd had delivered to the café. There were around five phone calls and messages and numerous texts, but after receiving no response, Nick gave up, and they'd never spoken again.

What he didn't tell Cade was Maya had wanted to hightail it out of the club that night immediately, but he'd insisted on staying and waiting until Nick saw him there. He'd ordered a beer, which he never did, chatted with Maya like nothing was amiss, and when a startled Nick looked up from his make-out session into Braden's eyes, Braden had saluted him with his bottle, tossed the rest of it back, grabbed Maya's hand, and walked casually out of there like he hadn't been heartbroken. Of course, he also didn't mention he'd cried the whole cab ride home in Maya's arms and was depressed for several months after that.

Next, he told Cade the story of Owen, the guy following Nick. He dated Owen for only about four months. They'd agreed to be exclusive, something Braden had wanted discussed prior to going very far in the relationship in response to the Nick disaster. Braden really liked Owen and had a lot of fun with him. He thought things were getting pretty serious until Owen took him out on a date one night. After they spent the night at Braden's apartment, he woke up alone to a note saying it had been fun while it lasted, but Owen was moving to LA for a new job opportunity. He'd never contacted Owen after that, and Owen had never contacted him.

At that point, he'd rather not think about how pathetic he seemed to Cade. He hadn't even begun to talk about Eric, and he already felt humiliated. He knew he needed to get it over with, but damned if he wanted to discuss the pain with a near stranger. The truth of it was, Cade didn't feel like a stranger at all, and that was probably the biggest issue right there.

He didn't want to appear weak to Cade, or perhaps more accurately, he didn't want to appear any weaker to him than he already did. Cade was going to know every single skeleton in his closet, and as much as he prided himself on being an honest man, there was quite a difference between being honest and completely baring your every secret to a man you were not only interested in but had only met a handful of days ago. He could feel the stress building, and he knew he had only one option open to him right now. He needed to get it out, get it done, and run.

Cade

Cade could see the wheels turning in Braden's head. He had a feeling he was about to hear about the abusive ex-boyfriend, and as much as he knew he needed to hear it, he hated it as well. He hated the look of dread and embarrassment on Braden's face. He hated having to put Braden through the retelling. He hated that someone was scaring Braden, causing him to have to bare his soul to Cade before he was ready. God, his respect and admiration for Braden was growing every minute. He'd had to ask a lot of questions and have Braden tell him everything multiple times to be sure he learned all he needed to learn about his relationships. Throughout everything, Braden answered every single question without complaint.

Cade was used to people getting pissed off when he had to ask probing questions about their past. He'd had people run the gamut of emotions; from anger and sorrow to embarrassment and lashing out. He was used to cataloging peoples' reactions, and thanks to his military training, he excelled at discerning facial micro expressions. Braden had yet to rehash his abusive relationship with him, but already Cade could tell he would get it done. Braden was brave as hell but Cade could see the exhaustion just waiting to take hold. He was about to suggest a break when Braden spoke up, cementing Cade's utter respect for him.

"So, I know you need to hear about Eric next. I have to be honest with you and say it's going to fucking suck for me."

"If you need to take a break and tell me later or after a run, it's all right. You tell me how it's going to go, and I'll work around your needs."

"I want to get this over with as fast as possible. I'm already on edge and stressed about it. I'll tell you what you need to know, and you can ask what you need to ask, but first, I'm going to grab a snack so I can keep working. The more I keep busy, the easier it will be for me to get through it."

He looked up, embarrassment clear on his features. "Whatever you need to do is okay."

Braden nodded. "Afterward, I'm going to have to get the hell out of here and run. I don't know how many miles I'll need to run it off, but the four miles we ran this morning will be a drop in the bucket. So, do what you need to do to be able to protect me, but this time I *will* ask you to run behind me so I can at least have the illusion of privacy."

"Are you going to grab your snack here? I need to place a call but want to be sure you're not leaving."

"I'm not leaving."

"Okay, I'll be back in a few."

Cade walked to the office and placed his call to Cooper.

"Where are you?"

"Just parking outside of Maya's house. Was gonna change into some gear and visit Vaughn's."

"I'm gonna need you here instead. You ready to get a good, long run in?"

"Uh, sure, I could stand a run. You need me right now? What's going on?"

"Braden said he's going to want to run to help get through everything he's going to tell me. So, he'll want to go right away. We ran four miles this morning which he said will be a cakewalk compared to what he'll need to run tonight."

"It must be pretty bad for him to need that."

Cade ran his hand over his hair. "Yeah. My guess is he'll need more than ten miles, but it's just a guess. He runs ultra marathons so who the fuck knows. I actually had to look them up and they range from thirty to a hundred miles."

"So we're fucked six ways from Sunday, and Maya wasn't joking when she said he could run circles around us."

"Pretty much. But we'll do what we gotta do to keep him safe tonight. I could push myself, but I won't be at my best to protect him if I'm exhausted."

"No. We'll need to relay it. Since you ran this morning already, why don't you let me run a big chunk of it tonight? I'll call you when I've got about a mile or two left in me before I'm done, so you can take over from where I leave off. I'll skip the gym and just wait around until he's ready to go."

"Sounds good. Make sure you're well-armed though. I don't expect the guy will make a move today, out in broad daylight in public, but I want him covered."

"Goes without saying. Do you want me to come over and help with the questioning?"

"No, this is hard enough for him to do without having someone else here. I'll call you when he's headed over to change for a run."

Braden

Braden was finishing up with a big pan of coffee cake when Cade came back in eating a banana and drinking a coffee.

His brows rose in interest. "Is that coffee cake?"

Smiling slightly at Cade's hopeful question, he held a knife to one side of the pan. "Yeah, tell me how big of a slice you want."

As he moved the knife further and further out, he started laughing. "You're gonna eat this much cake?"

Cade looked at him as if his question was ridiculous. "Braden, coffee cake is my favorite, and I'd be willing to bet from just smelling it yours is going to be the best I've ever eaten. I could eat the whole damn thing, so whatever you're willing to give me is what I'll take."

Chuckling, despite his shitty mood, he cut off a gigantic portion of the cake and set it on a plate in front of Cade. Thinking he'd be told it was too much, he laughed harder when Cade looked at him with wonder in his eyes and a huge grin. "Will you marry me?"

Braden smirked and raised his eyebrows. "How about we wait until we get to know each other a bit better before I agree to marriage? I will, however, bake another coffee cake for the front and bring the rest of this one home for you. If I'd known it was your favorite, I would have done it from the get go. You gotta keep me informed of your preferences, so I can make you what you want."

Cade's mouth dropped open. "What? You mean I can make requests? Are you kidding me right now?"

Braden chuckled. "Nope, not kidding. I love baking for people. I'm happiest when I know I'm baking something specific for someone who really loves it, so all you really gotta do is tell me what you like, and I'll get to work. Keep in mind, you may gain fifty pounds while you're protecting me."

Cade shook his head. "Nah, I eat anything and everything and don't gain a pound. Pisses my mom and sister right off."

"I don't doubt it."

Cade, foregoing the use of utensils, lifted the enormous piece of coffee cake to his lips and took a massive bite. His eyes closed as if in bliss and he moaned, loud and long. "Oh god, Bray, this is one of the best things I've ever tasted."

He took another bite and mumbled incoherently. Sexy noises that sounded suspiciously like the type he'd make in bed, tumbled from his lips. "Mmmm. This is better than my mom's, but if you tell her, I'll deny it." Cade grinned then saw Braden's expression. "Sorry, is it okay that I called you Bray? I know it's Maya's nickname for you, but it suits you."

Braden blushed. He was glad Cade thought the expression on his face was because of his use of the nickname, and not because Braden was half hard and very close to jumping over the kitchen island to feast on Cade's lips. He cleared his throat. "No, I don't mind, and your secret is safe with me."

Cade looked up and his face went from pure enjoyment to very serious. "You know your secrets are safe with me too, right, Braden? I'm running your investigation and will be the one closest to you at all times. I'll be sharing some of your info with Cooper, but I won't be sharing it all. I'll make sure he knows enough to be informed, but the rest I will keep to myself if that's what you would prefer."

Braden's breath caught in relief. "Yeah, I would really appreciate it. I know you guys need the info, but I'd prefer it if all of my personal history wasn't being shared with others. I guess, on that note, we should probably get down to it, right?"

"At your pace, Braden."

Braden shook his head. "My pace is warp speed at this point. I don't like talking about it, and I want to get it over with."

Braden began the painful task of telling Cade about Eric. He began with all the contact info he had and all the other pertinent data Cade would need for what Braden assumed would be ridiculously thorough background checks if Cade's professional behavior was anything to go by.

He talked about the length of their relationship and the timing at which it went from bad to worse and what exactly worse meant for him all those months. Cade took him through everything several more times, asking several questions and coming at it from different angles.

Braden knew he was holding back on Cade, the minor details, the emotional abuse portion of the relationship, even some of the worst of the physical abuse, but he couldn't help it. He had to keep some of it in, or he'd fall apart. He didn't really feel it was necessary to tell Cade every single detail because Eric wasn't really a suspect.

Braden leaned his weight on the counter. "Look, Zavier, I know you think he's a great suspect for being the stalker, but I need you to know it's extremely unlikely that it's him."

Cade tilted his head, his expression quizzical. "Why do you think that?"

Braden shrugged. "Because all the notes sound as if I've never actually met the guy. And because I kind of have an insurance policy."

Cade drew his head back, and his brows furrowed. "What the fuck does that mean, Braden?"

Braden broke eye contact and stared at his hands. "I knew when I told him I wanted to leave him, he'd beat the shit out of me, so I..."

"You what?" Cade stood and planted his hands on the countertop, leaning towards Braden, anger etched across his features.

Braden bit his lip and crossed his hands over his chest. "I, uh, video-taped it."

Cade's hands fisted on the countertop, knuckles going white. "You knew he'd beat you, yet you stayed and told him you were leaving him, so you could videotape it?"

Braden had never seen him angry and didn't like it at all. He took an instinctive step back. The anger pulsed off him in waves, but he realized immediately Cade would never hurt him, so he took a deep breath stepped forward again, met his gaze, and answered him. "Yes. I knew if I ran, he'd find me, and I'd have to keep running. I wasn't going to do that. My life is here and fuck if he was gonna run me off."

He watched, transfixed, as the color drained from Cade's face, and hanging his head, Cade whispered, "Jesus fucking Christ."

Knowing he couldn't stop, Braden took a deep breath and continued, "I knew I'd need something to bring him down, so I taped it and sent him a copy. I told him there were more where that came from, and if he ever came near me again, I'd bring up charges against him and he'd lose not only his job but his reputation in the community."

Cade sat back down and scrubbed his hands over his face. "God-dammit, Braden."

Braden shrugged. "Well, his job and reputation mean everything to him. When it comes down to it, he ties his self-worth and his identity directly to his job as a CEO. Anyway, now you know why it can't be him."

Cade stared at Braden for several long moments as if trying to get himself under control. Braden watched as he took several deep breaths, clenched and unclenched his fists, and rubbed a hand over his head in what Braden assumed was frustration or anger. The more he watched Cade, the more uneasy Braden felt. He hadn't meant to make Cade mad, but he was positive that's what he'd done.

Cade shook his head, picked up his phone, dialed, and lifted it to his ear. "Get ready to run. We'll be over at Braden's in ten minutes."

Cade hung up the phone and met his gaze again but there was no warmth or emotion in his eyes. "Cooper will be ready to run with you when you can get your kitchen shut down for the night. Do you need help?"

Braden was a little taken aback by Cade's detached tone. He didn't know what he expected, but the seething anger that morphed into this sudden wall of eerie calm was very unsettling. "No. I'll be done in a few minutes."

"I'll be just on the other side of the door when you come out."

Braden watched as Cade left the kitchen with quiet measured steps and went out the back door. Braden worked fast at getting everything cleaned up and put away. He called up to the front and told Maya he was leaving to take a run and he'd talk to her later. He walked out the back door and found Cade there, arms crossed over his chest as he waited calmly.

Braden's brows drew together. "Cooper is going to run with me?"

"You said you'd need to run for a long time tonight, so he's going to take the first leg and call me when he's got only a few miles left in him, so I can meet you and handle the final leg."

They walked together across the street to Braden's house. He was watching Cade who was in turn watching the street around them, keeping his eyes attentive for anything that might cause Braden harm. It was humbling in a way, seeing what type of diligence it took to always be on guard for someone else. Knowing Cade was pissed off, despite his ability to mask the anger and remain so laser focused on protecting him, made him respect Cade all the more.

Funny, his own anger and humiliation at having to recount everything had dissipated with the knowledge something he'd said had set Cade off. Sure, Cade had covered up his reaction, using his calm façade to gloss over his response, but Braden knew deep down the anger festered.

They reached Braden's door where Cooper stood in his running gear, waiting patiently. He smiled at Braden then looked at Cade and the smile disappeared. That same sort of calm that came over Cade, slid over Cooper's features. What the fuck was with these guys?

Cooper glanced at Braden then back at Cade again. "Vaughn's?"

"Yeah. Call me when you need me to take over the last leg, and I'll be there."

Cade turned to Braden and though their eyes met, his were devoid of emotion and their usual warmth. "Cooper will be running the first leg with you. You'll be safe with him. He'll run behind you, as you asked, not beside you. You can run as long as you need to run, we'll make do with the relay system, until you feel like you're ready to stop. I'll see you later."

Then Cade was gone, and Braden was left speechless in the hallway outside his door. He turned to Cooper, not quite knowing what to say, so he went with the truth. "I think something I told him really, really pissed him off. He looked angrier than I've ever seen anyone look then he turned emotionless, and he's been like that ever since."

Cooper frowned. "Cade's fine, Braden, you don't need to worry about him at all. You'll see him later. Now, let's get you inside so you can change and get ready to run."

Braden let Cooper into his place and left him to his own devices while he got himself another quick snack, tested his blood, and changed for his run. He stretched as much as he could stand before he had to get the hell outside to run off the stress.

Six miles in, he motioned to Cooper to come up and join him. "I'm ready to head back; I'm not going to go as far as I thought I'd need to tonight. Do you have about three miles left in you, or do you need to call Cade?"

Cooper wiped sweat from his brow. "We've been running for over six miles; it won't take that long to return?"

Braden shook his head. "Not going the route I'll take us to get back. It's a shortcut. Can you stick it out?"

"Yeah, I'm doing fine. It's not that we can't go for lengthy runs without issues; it's more if we get fatigued, we aren't at our best to be able to protect you. We won't allow ourselves to be impaired at all while we're covering you."

Braden nodded. "That makes sense. I'm glad you won't need to call Cade. I have a feeling he needs the time to let out his anger. I don't want to interrupt that."

"You don't need to be worried about him, Braden, if that's the reason you're not going to run farther. He wouldn't be happy knowing you were cutting your run short because you feel he needs time to get control of himself. In fact, he'll be pretty damn pissed off you aren't taking care of your needs if that's the case. For Cade, your needs come first, his are secondary."

Braden frowned. "But that's ridiculous, everyone's needs are equally important. I thought I'd need to run around fifteen miles to get today out of my mind. Seeing Cade's reaction kind of took the wind out of my sails."

Cooper raised a sardonic brow. "Yeah, funny how caring for someone kind of makes you worry more about their needs over yours."

Braden expelled a breath and shook his head. "It's not like that."

Cooper huffed out a laugh. "It's exactly like that, Braden. I've never seen Cade act the way he does around you. This is much more than him just protecting you."

Braden didn't know what to say, so he kept silent. Cooper must have gotten the hint because he changed the subject fairly quickly. "So, Cade mentioned earlier you helped him with his form. You gonna do the same for me?"

Braden smirked. "You're leaning forward too far over your feet. You need to stay more upright. Yep, like that."

"It feels awkward."

"Yeah, it'll take getting used to, but your stride will be stronger, and in the end, it'll lengthen it so you can get more out of your runs. Also, when you run long distances, you probably end up with a bit of achiness in your joints, possibly your lower back, the next day. This will get rid of that for you."

Braden watched as surprise washed over Cooper's face. Cooper thanked him, and they ran in companionable silence for the remaining miles.

Chapter 8

CADE

At Vaughn's gym, there were no aerobics classes or juice bars, no mirrored walls or techno music. This was where people came when they were either serious about learning the best MMA fighting techniques or wanted to learn how to defend themselves. Cade and Cooper had recovered someone very important to the owner, Vaughn Bowman, an ex-MMA fighter. In return, they enjoyed free use of Vaughn's facilities any time they were in town and tickets to any MMA fight they wanted to attend.

Cade entered the gym and walked straight to the security guard. Vaughn didn't allow weapons of any kind into the gym itself, and everyone had to pass through the security metal detector before entering. It was a precaution he instigated after one of the gym's members brought a knife into one of the rings and cut the guy he had been sparring with after losing the match. After that, he wasn't taking any chances. However, for a select few, Vaughn would personally lock up weapons and firearms in his own office. The security guard was a new one, so Cade wasted no time with small talk. "Vaughn."

"Who should I say is asking, sir?"

"Cade."

The security guard straightened, obviously having heard this name before, most likely from his new boss. "Right away, sir." He picked up his phone and dialed. "Cade is here to see you... Yes, sir."

"He'll be right down, Mr. McCade."

Cade removed his two guns and a knife and placed them on the counter. The security guard's eyes went wide at the weapons, but he refrained from comment. Vaughn came out from the gym and his smile of greeting fell when his eyes landed on Cade. He glanced down at the weapons and gathered them up into a small fireproof lock box he stored under the counter. "Go ahead and get changed and go out to the heavy bags. I'll lock these up and get changed myself, and we can go a few rounds when you're done on the bag."

Cade walked toward the gym but heard Vaughn's discussion with his new guard on his way out. "The list of people I allow to do this is extremely short and kept here by the monitor. Next time, check the list, grab the weapons, and put them in the lock box immediately if I'm unable to come up here right away."

He missed the guard's murmured response as he made his way to the locker room. Dressing in only a pair of loose fighter's shorts, he emerged from the locker room. Approaching the heavy bags, a guy took one look at him and moved aside to the speed bags. Cade stepped up to the bag he'd vacated and was finally able to let shit fly. He pounded the bag with fists, elbows, knees, and feet.

Nearly an hour went by and he would have kept going, but Vaughn intercepted the swinging bag and made eye contact, slowing Cade down. He bounced in place and shook out his arms, loosening his neck and shoulders while Vaughn called over the same kid who'd moved over to the speed bags for him earlier. "Mark, bring some tape and gauze. Get Cade's hands wrapped so he and I can go a few rounds, and wipe down the bag too, please. Thanks."

"I'm fine."

"You're bleeding all over my bag, Cade. You'll get wrapped before we dance."

Cade shrugged and set the timer on his phone so he'd be able to get to Braden when it was time to run. He donned his headgear and mouth guard and let the kid wrap his hands. He was already feeling some of his anger dissipate. A little sparring with Vaughn would probably be exactly what he needed.

He made his way over to one of the boxing rings and stepped inside to bump both fists with Vaughn. He zoned in on his sparring which he was happy to learn was more full contact than he thought Vaughn would give him. He took Vaughn down with a series of front and straight kicks and backed off immediately. Vaughn hopped to his feet with a huge grin splitting his face. "I forgot you're more than just a pretty face."

They went on for another twenty minutes, Cade keeping up with his friend. Sometimes he'd beat Vaughn and sometimes not. They'd drawn quite a crowd, but Cade barely noticed. He'd set his phone on the edge of the mat, and it dinged at him, letting him know he needed to wrap things up. Vaughn heard it too and backed off immediately. Cade gave him a two-fingered salute, grabbed the phone, and hopped over the ropes. "Thanks, man. See you out front in ten minutes."

He grabbed a small towel from one of the bins and wiped the sweat from his face, head, chest and arms. Cade heard Mark, who sounded both excited and in awe, ask, "Does he train people? He's amazing, boss. Was that Krav Maga?"

As he made his way to the locker room, Cade heard Vaughn laugh. "That was a mix of Krav Maga, Brazilian Jiu-Jitsu, and Muay Thai; and no, he doesn't use his skills for evil like us MMA junkies, fighting for money, he uses them only for good."

Cade shook his head in amusement as he entered the locker room. He stood under a cold shower spray for a couple seconds to wash away the worst of the sweat, figuring he'd take a real shower after he finished his run with Braden. He dried off, threw his clothes back on, and met Vaughn up front to gather his weapons. "Thanks, man. This is exactly what I needed today. I'm here on an extended assignment, so I'm sure I'll be back."

"You're welcome any time, you know. I've got a couple pro bono self-defense classes a few times a week. I'd love to have you teach any of them if you're free."

"We'll see. I might be able to help you with a few of them. I didn't know you offered pro bono classes."

"Ever since you brought Mikayla back to me, I've been offering free classes for women, along with a few men and kids, a couple nights a week. I know you're in the middle of an assignment, but give me a ring and we can discuss the schedule if you're up to it. It would be a great help."

"I'll let you know. Coop will be here as well, so between the two of us, I'm sure we can work something out."

"Sounds like a plan. Hope today did some good. You looked like you needed it. Take the tape off when you get home and wrap your hands properly."

Cade chuckled and agreed. He got into the car and let out a pent up breath. He was feeling remarkably better, but he still had Braden to contend with when he got home. He'd have to apologize after they were done with the run and talk to him about his reaction to put Braden back at ease.

Cade was just unlocking Braden's door when he heard Cooper and Braden come in behind him. "What are you doing back already? I was expecting a call to come meet you guys. Everything all right?"

Cade watched as Braden scrutinized him then saw his shoulders relax as he let out a relieved breath. His boy smiled at him and he felt like a complete shit for worrying him. "Everything's fine. I just didn't need to run as long as I thought I would. How are… What the fuck? Zavier, what the hell did you do to your hands?"

Braden rushed to Cade and grabbed his hands, pulling him through his front door. Cooper took a look at them as well. "I've got my kit over at Maya's. You okay for a few while I go take a quick shower then I'll bring it over so you can wrap them?"

Braden huffed. "No, we need to take care of this right away."

"Braden, look at me. I'm fine, this is nothing but heavy bag hands." To Cooper, "Yeah, it'll take me that long to get myself free of this fighting tape and washed up."

Cooper left, and Braden grabbed Cade's wrist and pulled him into the kitchen. "Here, sit."

"Braden, I'll take care of this myself when Coop brings his supplies, don't worry about it."

"Zavier, so help me god, if you don't sit your fine ass in the chair right now, I'm gonna lose my shit."

Cade grinned at Braden and sat. "Has anyone ever told you that you're absolutely adorable when you're angry?"

Braden laughed and shook his head. "Shut up, you jackass. Let me fix this. It's my fault your hands are messed up in the first place. Don't think I don't know how pissed off at me you were, despite your automaton act earlier."

Braden pulled another chair up, sat in front of Cade, and gently held one of his damaged hands in his own. He began to unravel the bloodied tape over Cade's fingers. Cade watched Braden closely. He didn't feel any pain, Braden's touch was so light. At Braden's concerned noise, Cade looked down at his battered hands and tried to pull them away. "Braden, really, I can take care of them."

Braden's eyes widened, his head tilted to one side. His mouth formed a sexy pout. "Please, let me help you."

Cade smiled and sighed. "All right." He leaned down to put his forehead to Braden's. "We're fine, you and me. I wasn't mad at you."

Cooper walked in and cleared his throat. "Ah, sorry guys. Want me to come back?"

Braden moved back. "No, set it all right there. Zavier, wash your hands in warm water with soap, please. Why you guys have stuff for after the fact when you should very well be protecting your hands before you use a big bag is beyond me."

"Heavy bag," both men retorted.

"Whatever the fuck. Use your heads and wrap your hands first, not last. Imbeciles."

Both men snickered and tried to hide it. It didn't work from the glare they received from Braden. Once Cade sat down, Cooper handed over his kit and Braden wrapped Cade's bloodied hands up with fresh gauze and tape after putting on some ointment. Cade hoped it wouldn't be the last time Braden wrapped his hands and smiled at how happy that thought made him.

Cooper gathered his kit together and went back to Maya's after Braden said he was going to get cleaned up from his run. While Braden took a shower, Cade fixed dinner. He wanted to talk to Braden about that afternoon. He was usually much better at masking his emotions, and the fact Braden thought it was his fault Cade's hands were messed up was making Cade more and more frustrated with himself for how he handled the situation.

Braden came out of his bedroom in loose sweatpants and a long sleeved t-shirt. His hair was still damp and though he looked tired, he didn't look as haunted as Cade feared he might after their conversation earlier in the day. Cade pulled out a chair at the head of the table and sat next to him. "Go ahead, dig in before it gets cold."

Braden rested a hand on Cade's wrist and squeezed. "Thanks for making dinner again. You didn't have to. Are you trying to take care of me, Zavier?"

Cade turned his wrist over and clasped Braden's hand in his own. "Would that be such an awful thing?"

Braden blushed. "You know I can take care of myself, right?"

Cade nodded. "Yeah. I'm very aware of it. Does it feel so bad, having me take care of your needs?"

Braden's brows drew down. "Bad? No, it doesn't feel bad. I just don't want you to feel obligated when I'm perfectly capable of doing it myself."

"But, does it feel good?"

Braden paused as if he wasn't expecting the question and he really had to think about how it made him feel. Cade watched as a myriad of emotions flitted across Braden's expressive face. Finally, he blushed but surprised Cade when he shook his head. "No, it doesn't feel good."

Cade tried but obviously couldn't keep the disappointment from showing because Braden clasped his arm when he made to pull away and whispered, "It feels great."

Cade smiled so big he thought his face might split in two. "Yeah?"

Braden, looking dumbfounded only nodded in response.

Cade let out a relieved breath. "Good. That's what I want."

They looked at each other for several moments until Cade finally broke the silence. "So, we should talk about today."

Braden glanced up and nodded. "I'm sorry. I know the way I handled Eric made you angry, but I didn't know what else to do."

Cade leaned toward Braden, who set down his fork, and took the opportunity to take Braden's hand in his bigger one. "I handled today poorly. None of what happened was your fault, and if I made you feel to blame for any of it, I can't apologize enough. Bray, I wasn't pissed at you; I was angry you were in such a dangerous situation and had to go through it at all. The last thing I wanted to do was scare you."

Braden shook his head. "You didn't."

"I did. You stepped back from me and–"

"That was instinct, but I knew immediately you'd never hurt me, and I stepped forward again."

Cade sighed, "You did, but I knew I needed to get away from you, calm myself down, and find an outlet for the anger. I obviously didn't hide my feelings from you at all, and I guess that's good because I want you to see the real me, even if it means I can't ever hide behind my calm façade with you."

Braden caressed his thumb over the back of Cade's hand. "I want to see the real you as well, Zavier. I didn't know who Eric was until it was too late. If this friendship of ours turns into something, I have to know I get to see the real you from the beginning."

Cade nodded. "I'll do my best to share my thoughts and feelings. Though I gotta be honest, it does make me a bit uneasy. I'm not used to being so transparent this early on. But I know in the long run it's worth it."

"I feel a bit uneasy as well. Things with us are moving pretty fast. Not only are we together twenty-four-seven, but you've set a precedent from the beginning by telling me exactly how you feel. I'll do my best to be as open as you are with me."

"So, we'll continue to be uneasy with the situation because we both agree that it's worth it in the end."

Braden nodded. "I think that about sums it up."

While Braden spent some time with Maya, Cade focused on getting some work done. He placed a call to Brody, their resident computer hacker, with the info Braden had supplied him with earlier in the day. No matter what insurance Braden had, something in Cade's gut still pegged Eric as the stalker, but he knew the sooner they had the information on all three of the guys, the better. He must have let the emotion come through over the phone because Brody said it sounded like it was personal so he'd make it his main priority.

Just as he was ending the call, Maya came out of Braden's room. "He's pretty wiped out. Nearly fell asleep while we were talking. This is taking a toll on him. When I left him, he was just starting to get ready for bed."

Cade gave her a hug. "Thanks for coming, he needed some time with you, I think. I'll check on him in a bit."

He let her out, locked up, and made a couple notes from his call with Brody. Cooper would be over any minute to iron out their plans for Braden's protection detail. Wanting to catch him before he fell asleep, he headed back to Braden's bedroom to check on him and tell him goodnight. The lights were already off and he was disappointed to find he was too late. But even though Braden was asleep, he couldn't resist leaning down to kiss his forehead.

He turned to go when Braden reached out and touched his hand. That simple touch seemed poignant in some way. Braden reaching out first thrilled him. Cade crouched down, brushing his hair aside, and resting his hand at the nape of his neck. "Hey, I didn't mean to wake you. I just wanted to come check on you and tell you goodnight. Was it good seeing your girl?"

Braden smiled. "You didn't wake me. And yeah, it's always good seeing her."

He couldn't help but run his fingers through Braden's soft hair. "I'm glad. You all right? Do you need anything?"

Braden shook his head. "I'm good, thanks."

"Okay, I'll be in the living room with Cooper. We'll try to keep it down. If you need anything, just let me know." Cade stood and was about to walk away when Braden's hand stopped him again.

Braden whispered, "Zavier?"

He crouched down and placed his hand on the side of Braden's face, rubbing his thumb across his cheek. "Yeah, baby?"

He heard Braden's breath catch at the endearment, and Cade watched as he bit his lip. Cade's dick shifted in his pants at the needy look in Braden's eyes and he nearly missed what Braden whispered. "I'm glad you came to tell me goodnight. Thank you."

He rubbed his thumb over Braden's plump lower lip and watched his eyes fall to half-mast. Braden hummed and leaned into his touch. "You had to know I'd come check on you, right?"

Braden bit his lower lip again and looked at Cade with longing. "I had hoped."

Cade groaned, bringing his forehead down to Braden's temple and whispered in his ear, "You're killing me, baby. I promise you, until I'm in this bed with you, I'll come and tell you goodnight every night. All right?"

Braden shuddered, and Cade pulled away to see his boy's grateful smile. "Yeah. I'd like that."

Cade kissed his forehead. "Good. I'll always do my best to take care of your needs, Braden. Get some sleep, you're exhausted. I'll see you in the morning."

"Okay, goodnight, Zavier."

Cade watched as Braden licked his lips and just barely lifted his chin in invitation. Cade smiled, the blood in his veins thrumming, as he leaned forward and captured Braden's lips in a soft, languid kiss. With regret, he stood while brushing his hand down Braden's arm. "Night."

By the time Cade got back to the living room, Cooper had arrived. They stayed up well after midnight hashing out their protection detail for Braden. Cooper would be done with the Kensington job by the end of the next day, and Cade was going to need his help, so the timing was perfect.

Cooper had jumped to the same conclusion as Cade, thinking the abusive ex needed very close scrutiny. The video insurance Braden had was actually a good safety net, but something still felt off about it all. In the end, as a result of that video, the situation didn't feel as cut and dried as it had only a day before which made both Cade and Cooper uncomfortable.

If it wasn't one of Braden's exes but a stranger, it was going to be much more difficult to find the stalker. They'd have to keep him in sight at all times and wait for the stalker to make a mistake. It would happen eventually but might take more time than Cooper and Cade were comfortable with. Once they got what was sure to be an extremely thorough report from Brody, Cooper would be free to follow up on any and all leads while Cade watched over Braden.

In the end, both Cooper and Cade decided the best way to go about covering Braden without making it obvious was to feign a relationship between Cade and Braden. Cade knew he wouldn't have to be pretending much of anything since he already felt like they were in a relationship.

He knew he'd have to show some outward affection towards Braden to make it appear to outsiders they were a bit deeper into a relationship than they actually were. He'd have to explain everything to Braden in the morning and make sure he was all right with it. He didn't think there would be an issue, but he wasn't about to start making moves physically with Braden in public without discussing things with him first.

Chapter 9

CADE

Braden was plating their breakfast when Cade walked into the kitchen. He grabbed the carafe of coffee and ran his wide palm up Braden's back, gently squeezing his neck before reaching above him to grab a coffee cup from the cabinet. "Omelet smells great. Sleep okay?"

Braden turned and smiled. "Slept great. You?"

"Yeah. Coop was here till about twelve thirty or so. I conked out pretty quick after he left."

"Everything go all right with Cooper?"

Cade decided not to delay telling Braden, so he replied, "Yeah. We decided the best way for me to protect you, without it looking too obvious, is for us to act like we're in a relationship."

Braden's mouth dropped open. "Uh...."

"We think it's best if I'm seen out in public with you holding your hand and being affectionate. We can do it another way if you're adamant you don't want to do that, but we think it's the best way to go about it, so I wanted to ask you for your thoughts."

"Am...am I bait?"

Horrified Braden would think such a thing, he rushed to explain. "Jesus, Braden, no! The last thing I want is for you to be in danger, but the fact is, you *are* in danger. Right now, this guy is escalating, and I need to be on you twenty-four-seven. We want to avoid questions about why I'm protecting you and who I am, so we figured a relationship would be the best option. Look, frankly, we don't know what will set the guy off."

Cade stepped into Braden's personal space, cupped the back of his neck in his large palm, and drew them even closer. "You think of yourself as someone who only sleeps, runs, and bakes, but people know you and gravitate towards you because you're kind and genuine. If they know you're being protected, they're gonna ask questions. At least this way, they're talking about a relationship, rather than some kind of trouble you're in, that's all."

Cade felt like shit he'd made him so nervous when his shoulders sagged in what was obviously relief after he explained himself. Finally, Braden nodded. "It makes sense. I'm sorry, I just thought you were trying to manipulate him into making mistakes. I didn't think about the fact having you near me might get others talking or set him over the edge."

Cade kissed him on the forehead. "We want to figure out who it is and put a stop to it without any impact to you at all. I really won't be doing anything differently than I do now. I might hold your hand and touch you, but I touch you now, I can't help myself. I just didn't want you to be upset or confused when I started to do it in public."

Braden looked uneasy. "That's fine."

"Braden, will you look at me?"

Braden glanced up at him. "You're upset."

"I'm not upset; I'm fine."

Cade slid his hands gently down Braden's arms and clasped his hands. "I think we've both become pretty good at reading each other. You're anything but fine."

Braden sighed as if resigned. "I don't know. I guess with you here, I've been feeling pretty secure. Hearing you talk about him lashing out just made reality come and bite me in the ass. The way you're handling everything is fine. I guess I'm just feeling vulnerable and scared suddenly, and I hate it."

Cade pulled Braden into his arms and rocked him, leaning down to kiss the top of his head, he breathed in the tantalizing smell of his hair. "I will do everything in my power to keep you safe. Please trust that I know what

I'm doing. You mean so much to me already, Braden. I'd protect you with my life, and if it came to it, I wouldn't regret a single thing."

Braden shook his head and laid it on Cade's chest, clutching his shirt in his fists. "Don't say stuff like that. I don't want anything to happen to you."

Cade pushed his fingers through Braden's hair and tilted his head up, forcing Braden to look at him. "I know, baby. Hopefully, it won't come to that. But, if there's ever a choice between me and you getting hurt, it's going to be me every single time." He stepped back and rubbed his hands up and down Braden's arms. "It's getting late. Let's get out of here so you can bake me something then kick my ass for four or five miles."

Later that day, Jackson and Sawyer arrived and began the process of removing all remnants of the old security system from the café and installing their own state-of-the-art security hardware. Cade kept his eye on the work being done, but mostly stayed with Braden in the kitchen. He could tell Braden was feeling tense, so he didn't want to go far. Both Jackson and Sawyer were always his first choice of installation guys for this system as they'd had a part in creating it, so he knew the job would be done right.

Jackson and Sawyer worked incredibly well as a team, communicating very little with others or between themselves. The two men had grown up together and served for years with Cooper and Cade. They had a strange bond he'd probably never understand. They weren't related, but they almost had their own language like siblings might have. He was always curious about them, but they never shared their past with anyone, and everyone knew not to ask questions.

They were both very good men to have in your corner, and Cade trusted them implicitly. Most of that was simply because they'd always had his back, but some of it was a result of Sawyer's hunches which were always eerily accurate. After several of those hunches saved the lives of men in their unit, Cade learned to never doubt them. So, when Sawyer caught his attention and summoned him over to talk to them with a concerned look on his face, he went immediately.

He recalled when Sawyer had confided the hunches were a lot like what others described as someone walking on your grave or the feeling when you knew you were being watched. Cade had listened with rapt attention when Sawyer explained he got goosebumps, the hair on the back of his neck would stand up, and he'd feel like he was being nudged into action.

Cade remembered the haunted look in Sawyer's eyes when he'd said the few times he ignored the instinct when they were kids things ended in disaster. Now, he always listened when Sawyer had a premonition—and was always happy he did. He saw Sawyer rubbing the back of his neck, and he knew, without a doubt, he'd be listening to his friend's suggestion.

"Cade, if you don't mind, I think we need to go to Braden's house and get started on the security there. Can you get a key from him?"

"Do you need me with you? We can call Cooper back."

"Jackson and I will be fine, but I think it's important we finish the system here later and work on his house right now."

"Okay, let me get his keys."

Jackson and Sawyer gathered their tools and set aside anything they had yet to finish at the café. Cade approached Braden, caressing his fingers over the back of Braden's hand, he waited until he'd pulled out his buds and cocked his head in inquiry.

"Hey, the guys want to start getting your place wired. Can I grab your keys?"

Braden dug in his pocket, produced the keys, and gave him a worried frown. "Hey, you okay?"

Cade smiled, brought his hand up to the back of Braden's neck and squeezed gently. "I'm good. Keep working, I'll be here with you."

Braden smiled, reassured, washed his hands and put his buds back in, getting back to work as Cade headed back over to his men.

Cade handed the keys over to Sawyer. "Call me immediately if there are any issues. Coop texted about an hour ago and said he'd be wrapping up the Kensington job before the hour was up, so he should be here any minute."

"We'll be in touch. In the meantime, stay on him like a rash. My skin is crawling."

"That goes without saying. You're both armed, correct?"

"To the teeth." A slight grin passed over Sawyer's lips, and Cade saw him giving Braden a very long, intense look which made Cade clench his jaw. "And sir, that man right there?"

Cade's eyes glittered dangerously, and he growled. "What about him?"

"He's meant to be yours, so take good care of him."

Cade's shoulders relaxed somewhat, but his tension remained as he gritted his teeth. "I intend to. Now get outta here and call me with news."

The call came less than five minutes later. Cade wandered slowly down the hall towards the office but kept Braden in his sight. He answered tersely. "Tell me."

"He was here, Cade. Braden's bedroom was broken into. His window facing the back of the house is busted in."

"What aren't you telling me?"

"His bedding is slashed, his room is a bit trashed, and there's a note. We haven't touched anything, only looked through the house to make sure it was empty."

"What does it say?"

"'You better be sleeping alone.' Someone very fucked up wrote that note Cade, and he's pissed you're in the picture."

"Call Vaughn and ask him if he can help find a good local window installer, someone who will get a new window in that wall within the next two hours. I don't care what it costs. I won't have Braden coming home to a smashed window."

"No problem. Anything else?"

"Yeah, call Detective Miller and get him over there to get this on record, dust for prints, whatever they have to do. Braden will be working for at least two hours. I want a new mattress, new bedding, and any trace of this shit gone."

"On it, Cap. You gonna tell him?"

"I will, but not until you assure me his room looks like new."

"Consider it done. Coop just walked in. Do you want him to come relieve you so you can come check this out?"

"I'm not leaving his side for anything. This can be handled by the three of you. Get working on the security so he can sleep tonight knowing this won't happen again."

"Will do. We'll finish up the café tonight as well, and Maya's place tomorrow."

"Thanks, Sawyer. I need every single place he spends any real amount of time wired up with all the bells and whistles."

"We're on it, sir."

Cade hung up, texted him Vaughn and Detective Miller's numbers, and walked back into the kitchen. Braden was completely immersed in his work, but he'd set out a big piece of coffee cake for him. Though he would normally never eat at a time like this, he found he couldn't resist. He grabbed a fresh cup of coffee and dug in while getting some work done.

Over the next couple hours, Cade kept in contact with his team. Vaughn had apparently offered to deal with the bed and new bedding for them, so he made a mental note to reimburse his friend and thank him for the help.

He received a file from Brody on both Nick and Owen. As he suspected, those two were clean. If the stalker was an ex-boyfriend of Braden's, sure as shit it would be Eric. No matter what Braden said about the evidence he had on the guy, Cade felt like he was still their best lead. He knew Brody would have a file on Eric as soon as it was possible, but he was getting impatient and edgy. The break-in today had crossed a line.

Just shy of three hours later, Cade received a text saying everything at Braden's was better than he'd left it that morning, which was a good thing since Braden was cleaning up the kitchen and shutting things down. Sawyer and Jackson were still working on the security system over there but would be done in the next hour. When Braden took off his apron and tossed it in the laundry bin in the break room, Cade met him back there and placed a hand on his shoulder.

"Hey, can you sit down for a minute with me? We need to talk."

Braden looked up at him, panic in his eyes, and Cade hated like hell that he had to tell him everything. Once Braden sat, Cade crouched in front of him and looked up into Braden's eyes as he held on to his hands. "When Sawyer and Jackson got over to your place today to begin working on your security system, they found your stalker had broken into your house."

Braden gasped then yanked his hands from Cade's, pushed the chair back, and got up and started pacing. Cade stood but gave him the space he needed. Braden's breathing got faster, more shallow and he began to get agitated. He'd seen enough panic attacks in his lifetime to be able to see the signs. Cade crowded him and brought him to a halt by sifting his fingers into his hair and tilting his head up so he had to meet Cade's eyes. "Baby, keep your eyes on me. That's it. Take one big, deep breath for me."

Braden shook his head and tried to get away, his breathing labored, but Cade held on, walked him backwards to the wall, and pushed his body against Braden's. "I'm here with you. You're safe. Feel me with you, you're not alone. Nothing is going to happen to you. Keep your eyes on mine and take a deep breath, just one deep breath. That's it, now another. Good, Braden, one more."

After several minutes of breathing and calming himself, his forehead on Cade's chest, Braden asked when Cade had found out about it. Cade told him the truth and felt him stiffen up in his arms. He stroked Braden's sides and asked him if he was able to listen to the rest of it. His heart squeezed in his chest when Braden wrapped his arms around Cade's waist as if he was a lifeline and whispered a yes.

Cade walked him through everything he'd missed, from the window being broken and the room being trashed to what the note said. He told him about the cops coming by and the window being fixed. "Sawyer and Jackson are finishing up the security system installation. There will be cameras and sensors on every egress of your home. We'll make it safe for you, Bray."

In the end, Cade needed to know how Braden wanted to handle it. "I need you to tell me what you need. Whatever you need, you'll get. We can stay in a hotel tonight, a reservation has already been made; you can sleep in your guest bedroom and I can sleep on the couch; or you can sleep in your room, it's better than new, Braden. You have a new window, like I said, but you've also got all new bedding and a new bed."

Braden looked up, confusion in his eyes. "A new bed? Why? Did he destroy more than just the bedding?"

"No, just the bedding, but I wasn't going to have you sleeping on a bed that bastard touched, so I told the guys to get you a new mattress and they did. I hope I didn't overstep."

Braden's eyes widened in shock and he shook his head, gripping onto Cade's biceps. "Overstep? Zavier, why would you think that? You kept this whole thing quiet all day until every trace of it was gone. The cops came and went, I have a new window, and the brand new security system is getting finished as we speak. You fixed it so I didn't have to feel him in my home. If you had asked me what I'd want done, I don't think I would have even thought of everything you did. Thank you."

"It's my fault. I didn't act fast enough. I should have had the security system in your house and the café the day after we met. I'm so sorry. I didn't think he'd escalate as fast as he did, and all I can do is apologize and work to fix my mistakes."

Braden shook his head, his brows drawn together in frustration. "Don't blame yourself. Because of you, I'm going to stay in my own home tonight, and after I see if I feel comfortable in my room, I'm hoping to sleep in my own bed tonight, as well."

Cade knew he was responsible for what had happened, no matter what Braden said, but if what he said was true, Cade would owe his friends big. "I hope so, too. I asked them to fix everything I could think of that might bother you."

Braden gripped him tighter and nodded. "You did. The first thing I thought of when you told me what happened was, 'How the hell am I going to be able to sleep tonight?' but you thought of everything I might need. Like you always seem to do, you took care of me, Zavier."

Reaching up, Braden hooked his hand behind Cade's head and drew him down into a gentle kiss. Cade's hands tightened around Braden's lower back and drew him closer for another kiss. Braden pulled away slowly and smiled shyly up at Cade, who felt a little dazed. They looked at each other for several long moments then Braden pulled out of Cade's arms. Cade watched as Braden pulled out his phone and sent a text.

Braden

Shoving his phone back into his pocket, Braden explained, "I asked Maya to come back here when she can get free. I need to tell her what happened. She's gonna freak out, and I don't want her finishing up here then coming over with no idea what happened."

After he broke the news to Maya and weathered the storm of her reaction, they went across the street to his place. The front door was open and Jackson was standing just inside affixing the security panel beside the door. Cade looked surprised to see someone across the room and walked over to him immediately with an outstretched hand, thanking him for helping out. They had a quick whispered conversation, which ended in Cade hugging him, stepping back, and beckoning Braden forward.

"Braden, this is my friend Vaughn. He's a former MMA fighter, who now owns a fighters' gym called The Knockout which isn't too far from here. He helped find us someone that could fix your window today, and he personally purchased your new bed and several other things for your room and made sure it was delivered and set up for you."

Braden shook Vaughn's hand and thanked him profusely, but then smiled when he remembered, "So, it was your heavy bag that beat the hell out of Zavier's knuckles?"

Vaughn laughed and thumped Cade on the shoulder. Braden felt that thump all the way through his body and couldn't believe Cade didn't even budge. Vaughn's smile was infectious though. "Yeah, then I did my best to take him down with some full contact sparring and ended up on my ass a couple times."

Vaughn's face grew serious, and he glanced back to Braden. "I don't know if it's something you'd be interested in, but I wanted to mention we have several self-defense classes at the gym. If you're at all interested, let me know, and we can work something out."

Surprised, Braden glanced up at Cade and then back at Vaughn. "I... Yeah, maybe. Let me think about it."

Vaughn smiled and shrugged. "Of course. Sometimes it just feels good to have a little more confidence, and these classes help with that. Ask Cade about it sometime. He teaches free self-defense classes at his headquarters and might even teach a few of mine for me while he's here."

Braden looked up at Cade in surprise. He'd had no idea that Cade did that, or even that he could fight well enough to take down a former MMA fighter and teach others how to defend themselves. His respect for Cade grew, and he put his arm around him and squeezed. "I'll make sure to ask him about it. Thank you."

Cade looked down at Braden and kissed his temple. "Do you think you're up to checking out your bedroom? I think you'll be pleased and hopefully feel comfortable there."

At Braden's nod, Vaughn, who had been watching the two of them with interest, smiled and lead the way. "So, I had Jackson take a few pictures of your room, to get an idea of what kind of bed you'd need. I kind of went a bit further than they asked, and you've now got all new furniture and bedding in there. We had the movers set everything up and remove all the old stuff. They said they'd keep it for a few days, in case you don't like what I bought, or your old pieces had sentimental value. I didn't know what he touched in there, so I figured why not start with a clean slate?"

Braden was speechless as he walked into his room, and even more so after he took in the details. The pieces were similar in style to his old ones, but the woodwork had a bit more detail and a darker stain. Where his old bedding had been blue, this bedding was olive green, very masculine and luxurious. There were new window treatments to match the bedding. All of his personal items were exactly where they'd been on his old pieces of furniture. He opened his drawers and found them filled just as they had been.

He couldn't believe the amount of work these men, these relative strangers, had put into fixing his home and making him feel secure. He sat on the bed and could tell just by sitting there the mattress was much nicer than the one he'd had. He took stock of how he felt, in that moment, in his room. He felt safe, and the room was warm and welcoming. He thought he might even be able to sleep on his new bed tonight.

He glanced up to see Cade, arms crossed over his huge chest, leaning against his doorjamb and watching him intently. Vaughn had left the room and given him some privacy to see how he felt being in the room that had, just hours ago, been violated by his stalker. However, he didn't feel like it was the same room, and he felt such overwhelming gratitude to Cade and his friends at that moment that the emotional dam broke, and he fell back on the bed, raising his hands to cover his face.

Cade was beside Braden on the bed almost immediately, lying down and pulling him into his arms. "Shhhh, shhhh, you're okay, baby. You're safe. I'm here. It's all right. I'm so sorry this happened, Braden, so fucking sorry."

Cade surrounded Braden with his bigger body, enveloped him, made him feel warm and safe and cared for. Braden wondered if he'd ever get the chance to repay Cade, if he'd ever get the chance to be the one taking care of Cade, rather than Cade always taking care of him. God, he sincerely hoped so and couldn't wait for that day to come. Braden purged his emotions, wrapped tight in Cade's arms. When he calmed, he wound his arms around Cade and squeezed him as hard as he could.

He pulled back and raised a hand to touch Cade's cheek as he looked into his sad eyes. "I'm just overwhelmed. A week ago, I was getting these notes and feeling so scared and alone with it. I didn't know where to turn or what to do. Now, you've come into my life and made me feel so many things. Things I didn't know I'd ever feel again, not the least of which is safe."

They looked into each other's eyes. Braden ran his hand over the back of Cade's head, scratching his blunt nails over Cade's short, thick hair. He smiled when he saw a blissful look pass over Cade's face. "You've literally taken something awful that happened today, erased it like it never occurred, and made things better. I get that it's Jackson and Sawyer's job to set up my security, but they went well beyond that today."

He scrubbed his hands over his face and shook his head. "And Vaughn. I've never met him before, and he went shopping for me personally and made sure, in less than three hours, I came home to not only a safe place, but a warm and comfortable one too."

Cade ran his fingers through Braden's hair. "They're a pretty great group of guys."

Braden cupped Cade's cheek in his palm and their eyes met. "You made it all happen. I can't even begin to figure out how to thank you all properly. I might have to make you coffee cake weekly for the next six months."

Cade chuckled, pulled Braden's hand from his face, and kissed it. "I'll take that coffee cake every week for as long as you'll make it for me. We're gonna get through this. We're gonna find this guy and put a stop to him. I'm going to keep you safe, Braden, and after that, you're gonna have a hard time getting rid of me."

Braden grinned and kissed Cade softly on the lips. "Is that a promise?"

"Yeah, it's a promise. Take a few minutes and come out when you're ready. I think I smell food, and if I know my guys at all, it's pizza. So I guess everyone's going to eat here now. You okay with that?"

"I'm more than okay with that. I'll be right out."

Cade

Cade walked towards the living room as Maya headed back to Braden's room. She stopped him, pulled down to her level, kissed him on the cheek, and hugged him. He hugged her back and whispered, "He's doing okay. He was upset, but mostly because it's been kind of an emotional rollercoaster in the last hour. He's checking his glucose and is coming out in a minute."

Maya took a shuddering breath and tightened her grip. "Thank you so much, Cade. You're taking such good care of my favorite person on the planet, and it means everything to me."

Cade rocked her back and forth, holding on just as tight. "He's really important to me. I'm doing my best to take care of him like he deserves. Once this guy is dealt with, I want to continue to take care of him, if he'll let me."

"I hope he will."

"Me too. Head on back there, I'm sure he'd love to see you." They pulled apart and Cade headed into the living room. He asked the room at large, "Did you save any for me?"

"We ordered enough for an army." This from Sawyer, who glanced at Jackson, who used sign language to speak to Sawyer, who translated, "Coop mentioned Braden was diabetic, so we also ordered a couple different types of salads for him if he doesn't want pizza."

Cade clapped Sawyer then Jackson on the back and thanked them. He looked around the room and realized some of the most important friends in his life were there, men he considered brothers, helping him, helping Braden. "Guys, thank you all for your help today. It means a lot that you dropped what you were doing to deal with this situation. Braden's become very important to me, and his safety is everything. Because of you guys, he's feeling comfortable in his home tonight."

The men merely nodded, except for Cooper, who spoke for them all. "You've done the same for all of us. Everyone in this room has had their life, or the life of a loved one, saved by you and your actions. You're family, and we can see how important Braden is to you, so that makes him family too. With us, it's as simple as that."

Vaughn lifted his beer in salute as did the other guys, followed by Cade. Nothing more was spoken.

Braden

Braden stood back at the end of the hall by his bedroom door composing himself, getting himself psyched up to have more company than he was used to, when the voices in the family room filtered through his own thoughts. He stepped a bit closer and watched as Vaughn got up so that Maya could sit down. Braden grinned when he saw her telltale blush as they chatted. He had no idea what they were saying but he could tell by their body language that Vaughn had turned on the charm and Maya had turned her flirt on and was fidgeting with her food, a sure sign she was nervous. She looked immensely relieved when they were both drawn into the bigger conversation.

He turned his gaze to Cade and stepped closer still, wanting to hear what the men were saying. He'd been with Cade mostly one on one, so it was interesting seeing his interactions with his friends. He watched as Cade shook his head and started to deny something someone said. Braden focused on the conversation and realized the men were telling war stories.

The two men talking the most were Sawyer and Cooper. He was still very curious about Jackson. The only thing that Cade had offered as an explanation for the fact that Jackson didn't speak much was that he had permanent damage to his vocal cords. Not that it mattered to him, the guy had dropped everything to come out and help him, so in his eyes, it didn't matter what any of their stories were, they had his undying gratitude. Maya and Vaughn asked a few questions, but most of the time, Cade kept his mouth shut, or contributed by downplaying his own actions.

What he was hearing was just so far removed from his reality, he stood there stunned. It became immediately obvious that the person he was getting to know so well was someone altogether different when he worked. He realized he would have to do his best to get to know Cade better in all ways. He had a feeling it would be difficult since Cade seemed reticent to speak of his life and his work. Braden knew he'd been standing there too long, so he took a deep breath and joined them.

He looked at everyone in his living room then saw everything they'd had delivered; pizza boxes, breadstick boxes, salad containers, drinks, and more covered every flat surface. He couldn't think of a time that he'd had this many people over with this much food. He smiled and decided he really liked it. Cade scooted over and patted the seat next to his. He sat with an exhausted sigh.

Cade handed him a plate with a slice of pepperoni on it and offered him a beer, which he refused. "I don't usually drink because of the diabetes. It's possible to drink low amounts of alcohol, but the effects are pretty unpredictable. It can drop my blood sugar levels for a day or two, and I could risk getting hypoglycemia, so I just avoid it."

Cade looked concerned. "Would you rather I didn't drink around you? I can take it or leave it, but if it makes you feel uncomfortable, I won't do it."

Braden squeezed Cade's hand and gave him a grateful smile. "It doesn't bother me at all. I promise, it's not a big deal to me."

Cade relaxed and smiled in response, keeping hold of Braden's hand, entwining their fingers and pulling them over onto his lap. They both managed to eat one handed with plates on their laps. Braden finished his first piece, and Cade handed him a veggie slice. Braden grinned, realizing Cade had a knack for knowing what he needed and wanted.

He was halfway through that piece when Cade reached over and grabbed a fork then the salad with Italian dressing on the side and set it in front of Braden on the table. He got up and grabbed a glass of ice water for him as well. Cade sat, stretched his long legs out, and leaned back against the sofa cushions, draping an arm around Braden's shoulders, and playing with the ends of Braden's hair.

Braden laughed. "How do you do that?"

"Do what?"

"Anticipate what I might want."

"Did I get it right?"

Braden blushed. "Well, I was wavering between taking a veggie piece or a sausage piece."

Cade argued, "But, you had sausage for breakfast."

At the same exact time, Braden said, "But, I had sausage for breakfast."

Braden burst out laughing, and Cade winked. "I'm getting to know what you like."

They looked at each other and grinned. He realized the room had gotten quiet and everyone was watching them. He didn't turn to look, he could just feel their curious eyes. He grabbed the salad, needing to do something with his hands so he wasn't focusing on the scrutiny. He turned back to Cade and smiled when he wrapped his arm more firmly around Braden, dragging him closer.

Cade leaned in and whispered, "I think *they* think they're being sly, but give it a second and they're gonna start talking about us like we're not sitting in the same room."

Braden snickered and forced himself to avoid looking at the sea of eyes that were watching their every move. Out of the corner of his eye he saw Maya tug her brother close and heard her whisper, "This makes me so happy. I haven't seen Braden smile and laugh like this in years."

Braden blushed when he heard that and Cade grinned at his reaction and winked again. "Wait for it…"

A couple beats of silence then Cooper responded, "Cade hasn't been this happy in a long time either. They're great together, and I don't even think they fully realize it yet."

Cade leaned in again and whispered, "I realize it."

Braden couldn't help but duck his head and blush, focusing on his salad. When he finally had the guts to look at Cade again, the big man chuckled, shook his head, and leaned in to kiss his temple, whispering, "God, you're gorgeous when you blush."

Braden covered his face with his free hand and shook his head in frustration. "You can't keep saying stuff like that! It makes me all flustered!"

Cade threw back his head and laughed. "I dunno. I like you all flustered."

Braden gasped and looked away, entirely too embarrassed to respond. He stuffed salad in his mouth as a diversion and ignored Cade's chuckle. After he'd put a dent in the salad and the conversations had lulled, he realized he needed to thank everyone again.

"I just wanted to thank all of you for being here to help. I can't explain how much it means to me. If you guys hadn't done what you did, I probably wouldn't even be sleeping in my place tonight, let alone in my own room, so thank you for your help. It's not much, but if you all let me know what your favorite dessert is, I'll bake it for you."

Cooper spoke up, "Braden, I'm sure I speak for all of us when I say we were happy to do it. We take care of our own. I'm sure the guys will agree that you don't have to bake us anything, though I for one won't be turning the offer down."

Braden grinned. "There's a notepad on the kitchen counter. Write down your name and your favorite, and it's yours."

Everyone laughed their asses off as Jackson silently got up and went into the kitchen, wrote on the notepad, and came back, wearing a satisfied grin. After that, they continued to eat and chat for another hour. Braden rested against Cade and closed his eyes as Cade played with his hair.

He was half asleep when the group started telling stories again, and though they were not all centered around Cade, a lot of them were. He supposed it made sense as he was the commanding officer of their unit. He was learning things about the serious and heroic man he didn't think he'd learn by asking him. He had a feeling Cade didn't put a stop to it because he thought Braden was asleep, so he kept quiet and still and tried to learn all he could.

Cade had been through so damn much, and you wouldn't know it from looking at him. He seemed so unaffected, but that was obviously not the case. Cade tensed several times during the conversation and even broke in and tried to deflect the storyline, quietly though, as if to avoid waking him. His men, however, were undeterred and continued to talk about some of their hardest deployments.

As Braden sat, cuddled up against Cade, he barely registered that he wasn't pretending any longer and was tuning in and out as exhaustion took over. He'd been running on fumes ever since he'd learned of the break-in. Braden woke when Cade removed his arm from behind him, telling him to stay put as he began to clean up the mess. He didn't put up much of a fight and was fading in and out again as everyone joined in to help Cade.

The living room was spotless in less than ten minutes and people were filing out the door by way of the kitchen notepad. Braden smiled tiredly, glad he'd have a way to thank them in the best way he knew how. Cade kissed him on the forehead and went to let them all out. Sawyer had a whispered conversation with Cade at the door while Maya hugged Braden goodnight before heading to the door herself. When everyone was gone, Cade set the new alarm system.

Braden sighed, finally forcing himself off the couch. "It's only eight-thirty. Why do I feel like it's midnight?"

Cade approached Braden, slid his hand into his hair, and hugged him close. "Because, it's been an emotional week, let alone the emotional clusterfuck that was this evening. It was bound to catch up with you. Do you want to go to bed early?"

Braden smiled and looked up into Cade's eyes. "How about we watch a movie?"

"That sounds great. You've got a TV in your room, do you want to watch it in there, see how you feel about being in your new space?"

Braden nodded and pulled slowly out of Cade's arms. "Yeah, I was thinking the same thing. Why don't we get ready for bed and meet in my room in a few minutes?"

Braden could feel Cade's eyes on him as he walked toward his room. "Sounds good. Tomorrow morning, I can explain your new security system."

Braden turned back with a smirk. "Okay, good, cause that thing looks like it could pilot an airplane."

Chapter 10

CADE

Cade was chuckling as he headed to the guest room. He got ready for bed and checked his email. He'd gotten the file on Eric and would look at it later. He wanted to spend time with Braden, ensuring he was feeling comfortable and safe in his bedroom. They picked out a movie and began to watch it, cuddled together with Cade's arm around Braden. Less than thirty minutes in to the movie, Braden was asleep. Cade took the remotes and turned everything off.

He stayed for a while, enjoying the feeling of Braden sleeping against him, but eventually got up, moving carefully so he wouldn't wake Braden. Cade sat down on the couch in the living room and turned on his iPad then downloaded and read the file on Eric. His teeth clenched and his muscles bunched. His gut was telling him they'd found their stalker.

The file on Eric was long and extremely thorough, and it left Cade feeling uneasy. Within minutes, he sent Cooper the file with a note, "Our guy?" Apparently, Eric no longer worked as CEO for the local non-profit Homeless Youth Support Coalition (HYSC), the job Braden said meant everything to Eric. That did not bode well for Braden's insurance policy being as meaningful as it had been in the beginning.

Eric had sold his condo and cashed out a savings account. Brody couldn't find a trace of him anywhere in the continental US since. It wasn't irrefutable proof Eric was their guy, but it was pretty damning. Cade knew the information would upset Braden, so he wanted to do what he could to get more info locally before he had to break the news.

He called Cooper and asked him to make a stop at HYSC early the next morning and ask around to try to find out what the scoop was from the workers there. The file stated that he resigned, but upon further digging, Brody had found several company emails hinting he'd been asked to leave because of a possible sexual harassment claim. Brody had stated there was nothing more he could find digitally as they'd kept mention of it out of further emails and digital files.

Cade also asked Cooper to talk to Sawyer and Jackson about staying and helping out with some legwork to gather more data on Eric as fast as possible. Apparently, Vaughn had offered up his house as a place for them to crash instead of continuing to stay in a hotel room. He'd told Sawyer and Jackson to head over there for the night after they were done wiring the system. Cameras and outdoor work could wait until the next day.

Cade had been working for about two hours when he started getting tired. On his way to bed, he checked in on Braden, who was still sound asleep. He got ready for bed, turned out the light, and was asleep in minutes.

He was woken from a dead sleep by a cry of alarm coming from Braden's room. He was up and armed in seconds, running down the hall. When he got to Braden's room, he heard Braden cry out again and realized he was having a nightmare and wasn't in any danger.

Adrenaline pumping, Cade set down his SIG on Braden's dresser, took a deep calming breath, and walked toward him. Braden began thrashing around, and Cade sat beside him, placed a hand gently on his chest, and whispered that he was okay. When Braden calmed and continued to sleep, Cade got up and went back to his room.

Less than an hour later, Braden's nightmare returned, and again, Cade's soft touch and voice calmed him and kept him sleeping. This time, instead of heading back to his room, he got into bed with Braden so he would be close if he had further nightmares. Braden must have sensed he was near because he turned toward Cade and laid his head on his chest. Cade hugged him closer and drifted off to sleep himself.

He woke around five the next morning and realized Braden was still curled up next to him, fast asleep. He thought about waking him but decided to let him get as much sleep as his body needed, and if they had to take an extra-long run in the evening to make up for it, they would. Cade loved how Braden felt, snuggled up next to him, fitting perfectly, like he was made for him. Cade pulled him a little closer and dozed off and on for another hour.

Around 6:30 a.m., Braden began to stir. He blinked bleary eyes, realized his head was lying on Cade's chest and blushed. "Hey, I must have fallen asleep during the movie. Sorry about that."

Braden glanced towards the clock on the nightstand on the other side of Cade and saw the gun. He sat up with wide eyes, fear etched over his face. "What happened?"

Cade sat up as well and touched Braden lightly to reassure him everything was all right. He explained what happened the night before, and Braden put a hand on Cade's and caressed it softly. "I guess I was affected by the break-in more than I thought I was. It's weird, because I didn't even see any of it, you guys had it cleaned up so fast."

"You didn't see it, but that doesn't mean you weren't affected. Having someone break into your home is such a violation I think I would have been more surprised had you not reacted in some way."

Cade watched as Braden lifted his hand, turned it over, and kissed his palm. He turned it back over and looked at it. When Braden kept staring at his hand, Cade asked, "You all right, Bray?"

Braden glanced up and nodded, smiling the sweetest smile Cade had ever seen. "They're so much bigger than mine. They could…" Cade watched Braden struggle, take a deep breath, and finally continue, "They could do a lot of damage."

His heart plummeted and he opened his mouth to respond, but Braden looked up at him, shook his head, and put his own hand on top of Cade's. "You only ever use them to sooth me and take care of me, but I can see by the scars they haven't always been used for that."

Fuck. "Does that scare you?"

Braden gazed up at him and Cade's heart thrummed at his intense gaze. "No. It should. Hands smaller than yours nearly destroyed me, so yeah, it should scare the hell out of me. But it doesn't, and I don't know why." Braden's smile wobbled and he gave Cade a sideways glance. "Isn't that funny?"

He had a nearly impossible time keeping himself calm. Hearing Braden talk about nearly getting destroyed by Eric made him want to track the motherfucker down and kill him. If he was lucky, it could still happen. But Braden didn't need to see his anger, he needed to see that he was right, he'd never in a million years hurt Braden. "I would sooner die than ever hurt you, Braden."

"If someone else said that to me, I'd know they were exaggerating at the very least. I don't think you are."

Cade shook his head. "I'm not."

Braden nodded and caressed the back of his hand. "I know that. I do. I'm not afraid of you, Zavier. You make me feel safer than I've ever felt in my life."

"I'm so glad."

"I didn't know if I'd ever feel comfortable with another man's touch, but I like it when you touch me."

Cade wrapped his arm around Braden and pulled him closer, kissing him gently on the lips. "You're killing me, baby."

Braden blushed again, smiled, and looked up at Cade. "I'm sorry."

Cade chuckled, trailed a finger down Braden's nose, over his lips, and under his chin, tilting his head up to steal another kiss. "Never be sorry for that."

Braden chuckled and shrugged, "Okay, I won't."

"What are your plans for today?"

"Um, I gotta get ready to go to the café. I have lots to keep me busy and quite a few thank you desserts to get started on."

"Sounds good, let's get our lazy butts up then."

Braden stopped him with a squeeze to his hand. "Thank you for last night, for staying with me and making sure I was able to sleep somewhat peacefully."

"You're welcome." Cade lifted their hands and kissed the back of Braden's.

His boy's smile was a bit wicked, and Cade watched as he bit his lip. "I like your hands, Zavier. One day, I'm gonna want them all over me. I'm gonna jump in the shower."

Just like that, he was out of bed in a flash, and Cade was left in a state of yearning arousal he felt deep in his core. He scrubbed his hands over his face and collapsed back on the bed with a groan. He'd seen the look in Braden's eyes as he made his escape. It was at that moment he decided to make a call to Maya.

She answered after one ring. "Everything okay?"

"Yes, he had a rough night with a couple nightmares, but he seems to be doing well. I wanted to talk to you about this Saturday. Does Braden usually work weekends?"

"He usually comes in on both Saturday and Sunday for a few hours to get us through the weekend business, but he does the bulk of his weekend baking, and subsequent freezing, on Friday so that his hours on the weekend don't have to be too long."

"Would you be all right without him on Saturday?"

"I'll make sure we are. What's up?"

"I just think he needs a day off, a day to do some fun things and not worry about all this stalker bullshit. I want to spend some time with him, take him out."

"That sounds great, Cade. With everything going on, he hasn't had time to replenish the backup stash we used when he had his migraine, so I'll tell him we got a special order for mixed pastries for Friday night pick up. That way, we'll be okay both Saturday and Sunday and you get to surprise him. He could use the time, he never takes any for himself and refuses to get someone to help him in the kitchen."

If Cade had anything to do with it that would change. They said their goodbyes, and Cade went to his room to take a quick shower and change then to the kitchen to cook some breakfast. Braden came out of his bedroom ready for the day and sat down with Cade to eat. When they were both ready to leave, Cade grabbed his iPad and iPhone and went to the front door where he explained the security system to Braden, and how it could be managed from their secure website.

Cade knew he was being overly enthusiastic about the security system, he could see the amusement in Braden's eyes as he tried not to laugh at him, but he was just so relieved Braden's home would be properly secured for the future. Braden stopped him with a hand in the air and a grin on his face. "Just tell me how to turn the thing on and off; all the other bells and whistles will have to come later."

Cade chuckled and asked for Braden's hand. He helped Braden place his thumb and ring finger to the screen when it prompted them, and Cade finished the rest of the set up so the system could only be turned off and on by either his finger and thumbprint or Braden's. He walked Braden through the short process of turning the system on and off, and they left the row house together. Cade held Braden's hand in his bigger one and walked them across the street to the café's back door, where Cade noticed a camera was already installed. He locked the back door behind them.

Glancing around, he noticed the cameras and sensors in the kitchen and was happy to see them in the office and break room as well. He got Braden's promise not to leave the kitchen and went up front to look for Sawyer and Jackson. He caught Layla making some coffee. "Hey beautiful, mind if I have a cup?"

Blushing and stammering just a little, she was finally able to pour him one. Murmuring his thanks, he took his cup of black coffee and walked towards Sawyer and Jackson then smiled when he saw Jackson being hit on by a very flirtatious Zoe on her way to unlock the café doors.

"Hey Boop, you giving my guys a hard time?"

She flashed a megawatt smile at him over her shoulder. "Well, according to Maya, you're off the market, so I decided to try my hand at this tall, dark, and handsome fella. I just love the strong, silent type."

Cade shook his head and chuckled; if she only knew. She sauntered forward, unlocked the front doors, and winked suggestively at Jackson. Cade grinned when he saw the slight blush on Jackson's bearded face. To give his friend credit, he merely gave her a crooked half smile and kept packing up their tools. Jackson tapped the security monitor screen with a few commands, and it went dark. Cade went behind the counter and got the attention of Zoe and Layla.

Once the ladies were both standing in front of him, he spoke softly to them both. "I'm sure Maya has made you both aware of why we are all here and some of what is going on with Braden. Did Sawyer explain the security alarms we placed back here for you to use in case anyone tries to get to the back from up here or anything else happens?"

When both of the ladies verified that they had gotten directions on how to sound the alarms, Cade let them get back to work and walked into the back after Sawyer and Jackson. In the kitchen, Cade told the men to contact Cooper for next steps, as he might want them to start on Maya's system or he might have some more info to go on after his appointment that morning.

Both Sawyer and Jackson were aware that Cooper was at HYSC and knew from the look on Cade's face not to say anything about it around Braden, even though he had his buds in, as always. Jackson went towards the back door to run the final diagnostics on the security system. Sawyer didn't move to help, however, but looked at Cade with a burning intensity that got his blood racing. Cade immediately turned and walked towards the office, Sawyer followed.

"Talk to me."

Cade's gaze narrowed at Sawyer's accusatory tone, "Have you placed any of your tracers on him or added Brody's app onto his phone?"

Cade tilted his head, studying Sawyer with eyes that had gone glacier in warning, and waited. Sawyer raised his hands palm up. "Cap, I'm not questioning your management of this job, you know me better than that. I've got a feeling that the security systems will help, but more is needed."

He waited, not in the mood for guessing games.

Sawyer cleared his throat. "My skin crawls every single time I work on one of the systems we've installed. We brought you two tracers."

Still waiting.

He watched Sawyer rub the back of his neck. "Cap, use them, both of them."

He raised a brow. "You think I need to use *both* tracers?"

"Yes, sir, and install Brody's app on his phone. Tell Braden about one of them."

Hold up, what now? He narrowed his eyes, incredulous. "You want me to use two of my tracers and the app and tell Braden about only one of them? Do you have any idea what this man has come to mean to me and what lying to him could do to our relationship?"

Cade could see his tone made Sawyer uneasy. "Yes, cap, I know what he means to you, which is why I'm pushing on this in the first place. From my body's reaction to working on the systems and to having this conversation, it's the best advice I can give at this point, sir."

Cade released a pent up breath. He knew that Sawyer was doing his best to look out for Braden. "Fuck's sake, Sawyer, stop calling me cap and sir."

Sawyer seemed to exhale in relief at the irritated, yet much calmer tone of voice from Cade. "I'm usually pretty successful at doing so, captain, but not when you use *the look* and the waiting. When you do that, sir, it's nearly impossible not to call you by rank."

Aware that his unit had always talked about the look he gave his men when he didn't like what was being said and wasn't hearing what he wanted to hear, not to mention his ability to wait them all out no matter how long it took, Cade jerked his head towards the door and muttered, "Get outta here before I toss you out."

Sawyer made tracks, apparently not needing him to say it twice. He was going to do exactly what Sawyer had asked him to do. He would tell Braden about one tracer but place another on him that he didn't know about. He'd also put the app on his phone. He hated, absolutely hated, not being completely honest with Braden. He hoped like hell Sawyer knew what he was talking about because he could completely fuck up everything they had going if Braden thought he couldn't trust him.

Cade entered the kitchen and slid his hand up Braden's back. Braden pulled out one of his buds, glanced back at Cade, and smiled gently. Cade squeezed his neck. "Hey, I know you're listening to your music, but can I borrow your phone for a minute or two to download the security app on it?"

Braden tugged the phone out of his back pocket, plugged in his passcode, and handed it over to Cade. There were two versions of the same security app that Brody had created, one with a tracer attached and one without. He pulled up the app with the tracer and downloaded it. Cade felt a little sick to his stomach at having to keep this from Braden. He handed Braden his phone back and kissed him on the temple. "I'm gonna try to get some work done in the office. Please stay in the kitchen, and if you need to go anywhere, including the front of the café, come get me first."

Braden smiled and nodded while plugging the jack back in and turning the music back on. Cade walked to the office and called Brody, who answered on the first ring. "Hey Cade, I got a tracer that was just activated from Braden's phone. I'm assuming you downloaded that for him? Does he know about it?"

"Yeah, it was me, and no, he doesn't."

"Okay, well, I've got him live so you're good to go. I checked the other tracers I sent up with Sawyer this morning, and they all seem to be at Maya's."

"Yeah, I wasn't sure if we'd need them, but Sawyer's sixth sense was making his skin crawl, so later today I'll be putting those on him."

"Sounds good, I'll text you when I see them moving to verify they're all active and on him."

"Thanks. Cooper is at the non-profit today, trying to get more info on Eric. I need you to continue trying to find him, Brody, and if you need help with anything, call in Landon. Actually, let me call him to see if he'd be interested in helping us out with this. I've been meaning to offer him a full time position with us, anyway."

"Great, he was a huge help with the Meyers' case and we could use the extra man power with our caseload. Your current case is my number one priority though. I haven't found any further trace of Eric since I sent you the file, but I'll keep looking. I'm running facial recognition software and hacking into a lot of digital camera feeds around the city. This could take days as more and more camera signals are coming up that I can check against. I hope something'll pop. When it does, you'll be the first to know."

After talking to Brody, Cade checked the camera feeds in the kitchen and saw Braden pulling something out of the ovens. He pulled up Landon's contact info and file on his iPad and called. Landon was going to be a great asset to them. He was from another unit under the same Special Forces command as his unit had been. Landon was a computer whiz, a lot like Brody, but with less hacking under his belt.

Landon lost his leg, just under his knee socket, while in Afghanistan and was still dealing with a lot of doctors' visits and physical therapy, not to mention getting fitted for a new prosthetic. However, before someone else snapped him up, Cade needed to be sure to extend him a formal offer. He let him know that they'd like to work with him on a part time basis around his PT and doctors' visits, but that as soon as he felt ready to work full time, they would be extending him an offer.

Landon seemed pretty damn happy with the news and said he'd be in touch with Brody to help on this case and get back to Cade about his full time availability as soon as possible. Cade felt much better after talking to Landon and hearing how pleased he was to get started with them again. He double checked the camera feeds and when he saw everything was good, he got online to review the file on Eric. He read and reread the file, over and over, to learn all he could about Braden's ex.

He spent some time checking his email and responded directly to requests for new security detail. A number of requests had slipped through to him, rather than being rerouted to Micah, so he took the time to respond personally to each request, copying Micah who he knew would take it from there. He wasn't going to be able to focus on anything else until everything with Braden's stalker was cleared up, and he knew that Micah would disperse the jobs to the proper guardians. After responding to those few communications, he put them out of his mind.

Glancing at the clock, he was surprised to see it was close to noon, and he'd been working for hours. Anxious to check on Braden, he walked toward the kitchen to find him exactly where he'd left him earlier. He drew up beside Braden, who smiled his way while he stretched his neck. Cade began to massage his shoulders and asked him what he'd like for lunch.

He saw Layla head to the break room and called her over while he kept massaging Braden's shoulders. He smiled flirtatiously at her and asked if she'd be willing to pick lunch up for everyone if he called it in. She blushed but agreed, and he called the deli and ordered lunch for everyone. He handed her enough cash to get their sandwiches and for her to pick up some drinks for everyone as well. When he finished, he went back to Braden and continued his massage.

"I can't figure out why she can barely speak around you, why she blushes and stammers. I mean, yeah, you're gorgeous as hell, not to mention gigantic, but I'd figure she'd be over it by now."

"Well, considering that the first time she saw me and Cooper she looked at us both and said, 'threesome,' I figure she'll be blushing for a long time."

"She said *what*? You're shitting me!"

"No shitting involved."

"Well, hell, now it makes so much more sense. Little LaLa, having dirty thoughts; I think I just might like the girl after all."

"The only person I want having dirty thoughts about me is you."

"Oh, I've had several, but I can't say any of them had anything to do with a threesome."

"Fuck, they better not. Just me and you Bray, got it?"

Braden seemed surprised by such a forceful and serious response, but Cade couldn't help letting his desire and possessiveness show. Cade wanted to devour him when he nodded and leaned into Cade's caress and whispered, "I got it."

After lunch, Cade went back to the office to check his phone, shutting the door behind him. He'd missed a call from Cooper, so he gave him a call back, being sure to wake up the monitor to see live footage of Braden while they spoke. Cooper was over at Maya's and said he had just been on his way over to talk to him, but since he called, he'd stay there and continue working.

He warned Cade that he wasn't going to like what he had to say and proceeded to tell Cade what he'd gleaned from his visit. Cade watched while Maya came from the front, chatted with Braden for a couple minutes then headed out the back door. Cooper kept talking, and the more he did, the more pissed off Cade got.

He watched, confused when Maya came back in not a minute later and stood by the back door, staring at Braden who went to her immediately. Both of them looked tense and Cade was on his feet before hearing Braden call his name. He ran out to the kitchen, took one look at Maya's pale, frightened face, told Cooper to get his ass over to the café, and hung up his phone.

"What happened?"

"I don't know, she just shook her head and said your name, so I called you. She left to get a change of clothes because she spilled coffee on herself. She came back a minute later, looking like this."

Cade approached them, saw that Braden was holding both of her hands, figured that was good, and ran his own hand over her blond curls. "Sweetheart, can you talk to us?"

Just then the back door slammed open, causing Braden and Maya to jump. Cooper came in looking pissed off, holding his phone to his ear, into which he muttered, "Take care of it," and hung up the phone. He folded Maya in his arms. "You found it. Did you touch anything?"

Maya shook her head. "I know better than that, Coop."

Braden tensed and Cade put his hand on the back of Braden's neck, settling him. Maya looked at Braden who made a sound in the back of his throat but managed, "Tell me. I can handle it you guys, just tell me."

Cooper answered, looking directly at Braden, "Your car is the black Ford Edge parked across the street, right?"

Braden's shoulders slumped and he nodded. "Yeah, what did he do?"

"Slashed all the tires, keyed it, and left a note under your windshield wiper. Jackson went to get some gloves out of the van, and Sawyer's calling Detective Miller. We'll deal with this."

Cade's hand tightened on Braden's neck when he turned to him. He was holding it together and for the most part, looking more pissed off than anything. Cade had to tell him about Eric. He didn't want to wait much longer.

"You okay to leave for the day? I need to talk to you about some information we've found."

"Maya's got a big order needed for tomorrow evening pick up. I'm backed up and need to get at least a couple more hours of work done. Do I need to deal with Detective Miller?"

"No, Sawyer and Jackson will deal with Miller."

"Is it bad, what you've found?"

"It's not good, but we'll deal with it, Braden. Get what you need to get done here, take the time you need, then we'll talk."

Braden gazed up at him, looking thoroughly exhausted from all the shit going on. He leaned his forehead on Cade's chest, took a deep breath then nodded. "Okay, yeah. I need to make a few more batches of scones and muffins, finish the pain au chocolat, and make some sea salt and caramel brownies. Three hours, probably."

"Take whatever time you need. Coop, stay here for a minute, let me go talk to Jackson and Sawyer."

Maya settled in next to Braden and they talked quietly as Braden continued to work. Cooper stood next to the back door and took a call while Cade stepped outside. He walked over to Braden's car and asked Jackson to see the note that was left there. Sawyer seemed to be on the phone with Braden's insurance company dealing with the claim and promising to provide the police case number when it was available. Cade realized not only were the tires slashed, but the knife was left in the front tire which is probably what had been used to leave slashes in the paint all over the front and sides of the car. The note was clear. "You don't want to make me angry, Braden, who the FUCK is he?"

Cade wanted to hit something and had to pace for several minutes while taking deep breaths to calm down. He didn't want to upset Braden any more than he already was. Sawyer glanced over at him as he got off the phone. "Detective Miller should be here any minute and the insurance company is sending out a tow truck to haul it into a body shop within the next hour or so. Will Braden be working for a while, or will he have to see this shit?"

"He needs to work for at least a few more hours, so get this thing outta here before then. Thanks for handling this. I need you to stay here for as long as Cooper and I can make use of you. Is that going to be an issue?"

Both men shook their heads and Sawyer spoke for them both when he said it wouldn't be a problem. "Good, I'll make sure you're comped some lengthy time off after this. I don't want Braden brought into this mess with his car. Get it fixed and back to him, and if you have to tell the insurance company that you are Braden to get it dealt with, do so. And, while you're getting his car repainted and new tires put on, have them install the best security system out there. Let me know the outcome of your conversation with Miller."

Cade asked them where the tracers were and detoured over to Maya's, grabbed her a shirt and the tracers then walked back over to the café. When he walked in the door, Cooper walked out. He handed the shirt to Maya and received a hug and kiss on the cheek for the effort as she went off to change. He took the stool she had been sitting on by Braden and watched him until he was done mixing some batter.

Braden

When Braden finished mixing together the ingredients for his scones, he turned to Cade, leaned his hip on the counter, and crossed his arms. He knew he was putting up a defensive wall but he couldn't help it. Cade leaned forward, grabbed Braden's waist, and pulled him between his legs, putting both hands on Braden's hips and looking him in the eye. "You doing okay?"

Braden shook his head, and Cade nodded. "All right, that was a dumbass question. Are you hanging in?"

Braden released his crossed arms and rubbed his face in frustration but muttered an affirmative. He absolutely hated feeling out of control, but he'd deal.

Cade took something out of his pocket, opened the little case, and showed him what was inside. "This is what we call a tracer. I created it with one of my guys. Each of us, the core team anyway, has a similar one embedded in our skin. Should anything happen to one of us, we will always be able to be found. I think it's very important that you wear this. I don't think it will be needed, but better safe than sorry."

Braden pulled in a deep breath and let it out with a woosh, suddenly nervous. "All right."

Cade, sounding trepidatious, said, "If you're okay with being traced, I'm going to place it on the inside of the ring you always wear on your right hand. You won't feel it and it's waterproof. Are you good with tracers being on you? I don't want to take any chances with your safety, Braden."

Braden looked at the tracer, surprised anything that tiny could be more than just a little black sticker. He pointed to his ring on the counter adjacent to him where he kept it and his watch to avoid getting them covered in flour and dough. "Go ahead, I'm fine with it." He crossed his arms over his chest and watched Cade put the tracer on the inside of the ring and said, "I need to call my insurance company. Fuck, I didn't even think about the house break in. I need to call about both."

"It's being handled, Braden."

What the fuck? Braden put his hands on his hips and asked, "What do you mean it's being handled? I'm the one who needs to call."

"And you have, so don't worry about it."

Braden, shocked and suddenly angry, crossed his arms over his chest again. "So, someone called pretending to be me?"

"Yeah."

He bit off an angry sound of frustration and practically growled, "Are you managing me? Because, I'll tell you what's gonna send me over the fucking edge right now is you trying to control me and tell me what the fuck to do. You don't own me, Zavier! Nobody fucking owns me. Got it? I was with someone who thought they owned me, and I got the fuck out, so don't think you can come in and take his place, you hear me? Never again, Zavier!"

His outburst didn't seem to upset Cade as his hands remained steady on Braden's hips and his voice was gentle, his eyebrow winging up, when he asked, "You done?"

Braden's eyes narrowed, but he admitted, "Yeah."

Cade smirked. "Feel better?"

One side of Braden's mouth quirked up, despite his best efforts. "Yeah."

Cade nodded. "Good, because I have a few things to say. First, if anyone owns anyone at this point, it's you who owns me, Braden. Second, I'm not trying to manage you or tell you what to do. Do you want to spend at least an hour of your day today answering questions from your insurance company? Is that how you want to spend your day?"

Pfft. He threw up his hands. "No, of course not. Nobody wants to spend their day doing that, but life is full of shit we don't wanna do."

"You've got enough on your plate right now, and if getting someone to deal with your insurance company because of this clown's bullshit is going to help you, then I'm damn well going to do it. I haven't found this guy; I haven't been able to keep these fucking things from happening to you, which fucking kills me. So, you're gonna have to deal with my need to fix things."

"But–"

Cade squeezed his hips and pulled him closer, between his legs. "If I see a problem that I can tell you wouldn't want to have to deal with, I'm going to take care of it. That doesn't mean I'm trying to tell you what to do, it just means I'm trying my fucking best to keep you from stressing on the stuff that I can easily manage. You had several hours of work to do, and I just wanted to make sure you didn't have to focus on anything else except getting through your workday."

Braden drew in a deep calming breath, let it out in a whoosh, and nodded. He leaned forward, laying his forehead against Cade's, and closed his eyes. "I'm sorry for being such an asshat. I'm stressing about him and taking it out on you."

Cade stood up, pulling Braden tight against him. Braden inhaled sharply as Cade clasped the back of Braden's neck to hold him in place while he leaned down, bit Braden's earlobe, licked away the sting then whispered in Braden's ear, sending a shiver up his spine. "Next time you do that, keep in mind the consequences."

Braden swallowed audibly. *When did the kitchen get so hot? Why was there ringing in his ears?* His voice shook when he finally choked out, "Consequences?"

Cade continued his sexy whispering, his lips brushing Braden's ear, making him tremble and break out in goosebumps all over his body. "Consequences, baby. You standing up for yourself? The next time you do that, I'm gonna have you naked and under me so fast your head will spin."

Cade nudged Braden with his hard on and growled again. "You feel that? You feel what you're doing to me? Your strength turns me the fuck on. My mouth is watering; I want to taste you so bad. So keep that in mind for next time."

Cade abruptly let go of Braden. His body looked so tense Braden wasn't sure if he was going to walk away or pounce on him. Wide eyed, heart beating up a storm, Braden watched Cade adjust himself, turn away, and leave the kitchen. What. The. Ever. Loving. Fuck. Was that? He looked down at his own cock, which was hard as a rock, and managed a laugh while shaking his head in disbelief and adjusting his own dick in his pants. He got back to work, thinking to himself that he might just have to make a habit of raising his voice and sticking up for himself. He'd never been so turned on by the thought of consequences in his life.

Chapter 11

CADE

It actually took Braden more than three hours to finish for the day. They went over to his place and sat on the couch together. Cade sat close so he could touch him and do his best to keep him calm. Facing each other, Cade reached out to hold Braden's hand gently in his. Braden let out a shaky breath. "Before you start, can you tell me what the note on the car said?"

"I don't think…"

Braden squeezed his hand. "Please don't keep things from me."

Cade sighed. "Okay, you're right, I just don't want it to touch you. It pisses me off."

"You're keeping an amazing amount of it from touching me, Zavier, and I'm glad, but I need to know what he's saying."

"He said, 'You don't want to make me angry, Braden. Who the FUCK is he?'"

Braden's pupils dilated and he sucked in a startled breath, shaking his head. "No, no, no, no, no, no, no…." Cade watched as he slapped a hand over his mouth to cease the runaway chatter of denial, but his poor boy's body took over and started rocking back and forth instead.

Cade tugged Braden closer, practically into his lap, and held him tight. Braden's whole body shook violently, and he was having a hard time catching his breath. Cade folded him over so that his head was between his knees.

"Breathe. Take a deep breath. No, don't sit up. You're having a panic attack; take a deep breath, baby. Come on, you can do it. Okay, good, take another. Another, that's it. Just stay there until you feel like you can breathe regularly."

Braden stayed bent over for several minutes, his hands gripping the hair at the back of his neck. Cade rubbed his back and talked to him until he was breathing more easily. He sat up but stared straight ahead, almost talking to himself. "It can't be him. It can't. I have insurance. I have fucking evidence!"

"Braden, how do you know it's Eric?"

"That's what he'd always say to me. He'd text me, he'd yell at me, he'd call me, and that's what he'd always say: you don't want to make me angry, Braden, be home on time; you don't want to make me angry, Braden, wear the clothes I bought for you; you don't want to make me angry, Braden, keep your mouth shut; or my personal favorite, you don't want to make me angry, Braden, get on your hands and knees."

Cade shot up out of his seat. Muttering expletives under his breath, he paced back and forth, clenching and unclenching his fists. Goddamn he wanted to wrap his hands around Eric's neck and slowly choke the life out of him. His chest was heaving with anger until he looked into the wary eyes of his boy. *Fuck.* He shook his head clear of the angry red haze and dropped down to his knees in front of him.

"I don't know what to say or do for you right now. How do I fix this? I want to punch my hand through the wall right now I'm so angry, but I won't have you looking at me like I'm a loose cannon. I don't ever want you to look at me like you're scared of me. Tell me what you need from me because I need to do something."

Braden was still shaking, and he could kick himself for letting his anger pull him away from his boy when he needed his strength. He heard Braden's shaky breath before he whispered, "Can you just hold me for a few minutes?"

Cade pulled Braden forward and into his arms, drawing him in tight. He exhaled a relieved breath when Braden held on just as tightly. They both clung to each other like lifelines, the cadence of their breaths syncing. Cade kissed him on the neck, his smell so sweet. Cade wished they didn't have to continue their conversation, but they couldn't avoid it any longer.

Braden pulled back, gazing at him intently. "Thank you."

Cade sat back down next to Braden. "Don't thank me yet. We still have a ton of shit to talk about, and none of it is gonna make you feel any better. Just know that I'm here, and I'm not going anywhere. We're going to handle this together."

He watched as Braden seemed to take a fortifying breath. "Okay, go ahead. Let's get this over with. I'm assuming it all comes down to the fact that even before the car damage today, you knew it was Eric?"

"We were pretty sure he was the one, but you confirming it from the note took care of any questions we may have had."

Cade proceeded to tell him about the file that was put together on Eric. When Braden learned he no longer worked at HYSC, he lost what was left of the color in his face and the rocking began again. The more Cade explained, the more Braden pulled away. Finally, Cade couldn't take it anymore. He pulled Braden's legs over his so Braden could curl into the corner of the couch. Cade ran a hand up and down Braden's legs and used the other to massage his scalp.

He hated needing to have the conversation at all, but it had to be done. He made Braden as comfortable as possible, reassuring him with words and comforting touches and finally told Braden about Cooper's visit to HYSC where he'd learned the reason for Eric's resignation. Cooper hadn't gotten much out of the management staff, but as he was leaving, a young lady walked out with him and explained that Eric had gotten caught sexually harassing a co-worker. It had all been caught on tape and he'd been given the choice to resign or be fired the very next day which was four months prior.

Braden scoffed, angrily. "Fucking asshole thinks he's infallible. Cameras seem to be his downfall. Too bad that one basically rendered mine useless. I'm so fucked."

"You're not fucked. We're in this together. We'll figure it out."

Braden's shoulders slumped and he shook his head. "How? He's hiding. We'll never find him now, and I have *no clue* where he could be."

Braden turned and put his feet on the ground, hanging his head with his elbows on his knees. "We would go out with his work acquaintances occasionally, you know? But there wasn't anyone he was close with. No family. He's smart, though. Really smart."

"He'll make a mistake, Braden, and when he does, we'll find him."

Braden rubbed his hands over his face and sighed. "I just... I can't believe it's him. I shouldn't be surprised, but somehow I am. I convinced myself I outsmarted him and was free and clear. But I'll never be free and clear of him."

"Yes, you will. I'll personally make sure of it. I'm not saying it's going to be easy, but I'll make sure you're safe from him, for good. I think, with all the new information we have, we need to call Detective Miller and let him know that we know who it is now, without a doubt. Do you want to do this before or after your run?"

"Before. I want to be able to run and then crash."

"Okay, let me get him over here."

Cade called Detective Miller and asked him to come right away. He also called Cooper, letting him know what was going on. He arrived within minutes with Maya in tow. Maya took one look at Braden with his head hanging over hands that were now fisted and shaking and made a noise in her throat. Braden looked up at her, his expression utterly defeated. He spread his hands wide in a "what the fuck am I supposed to do now" gesture, and she sat right down on his lap and hugged him fiercely.

Her voice was muffled against his hair, but Cade could make out, "He'll keep you safe. It's gonna be okay."

At the knock on the door, Cooper let the cop in. Cade and Cooper took over from there and informed him of what they'd been able to find and what Braden had explained about the note received on the car. Detective Miller had inquiries for everyone there. He was thorough and asked all the right questions, so Cade felt somewhat at ease knowing he was taking things seriously.

More than once, the thought he was very close family friends with the Chief of Police had occurred to him. He was glad that he wasn't going to have to utilize that particular relationship for this situation; not yet anyway. When they were done, Braden went to the kitchen and grabbed a snack then went to his room to change and stretch. Closing the door behind the cop, Cooper asked what the plan was.

"Braden's gonna need to run. I'll take first leg, you can take second. If Jackson and Sawyer can help, we can be on him two deep, which would make me much more comfortable. With Eric escalating, I have no idea what his next move will be."

"They're next door finishing Maya's system up right now, so they can split up and run with us."

"Okay, sounds good. I'm gonna get changed and stretch. Get ready to have your ass handed to you."

"Maybe he'll take it easy on us."

Cade shook his head. "He needs to run, so he'll get to run for as long as he wants. I don't give a fuck if he wants to Forrest Gump his ass across the country, we cover him, are we clear?"

"Crystal, Cade. You know I've got him. You don't need to worry about him with me."

Cade's shoulders relaxed, some of the stress leaving him. "I know. Thanks."

Cade was on his second leg of five miles, a bit drained and running behind Braden, with Jackson right beside him. Jackson looked over at him and raised an eyebrow, looking a little tired himself, but true to form, not saying a word. Cade's lips twitched, but he shook his head. Braden was on mile fourteen, which meant, with the five miles that Sawyer and Cooper took in the middle, Jackson and Cade were on mile nine. Braden could run another ten without an issue, Cade knew, but he was hoping it wouldn't come to that. Cooper was calling, so he tugged his phone out and answered.

"We're four miles in on this leg, so we've got another mile in us then you and Sawyer can come and relieve us, wherever the next mile takes us."

"So, he's still going strong? I'm mapping your location and using the route he's been taking us on. It looks like he's doing a big loop and will be done at around twenty miles if he keeps going where I think he's going. He's most likely done this run before. I have Brody keeping an eye on our tracers. I realized when I got back here he can look at live footage of cameras along the run and when we're done, continue to look at recorded feeds."

"Fuck, we should have gotten him going at the beginning. Keep your eye on my location and meet us in a mile. I want to let him run for as long as he needs, so we'll keep an eye on your location during your next leg and get in touch with you towards the end if it doesn't look like he's bringing you in."

"Sounds good. Hopefully Brody will find something we can use."

Cade huffed. "We could use a break. See you in a bit."

Cade needed to think, and strangely enough, he was beginning to see how the distance running got Braden through a lot of stress. From the set of Braden's shoulders and his gait, he looked like he was more relaxed now than when they'd started. He'd hated the haunted look in Braden's eyes when he'd come out of his room dressed in running gear with his phone already strapped on his arm, buds in. The message not to talk to him was clear, so he'd let Braden take the lead. He'd remained silent the entire run.

Cade knew deep down it was a good thing they now knew who the stalker was. Having a target was much better than flying blind. However, the damage it was doing to Braden was hard for him to watch. The look of horror on Braden's face when he'd told him about what the note had said would be forever etched in his mind.

Not running beside Braden now was killing him. He wanted to be able to glance over and gauge how he was really holding up, but he knew Braden needed this run, this solitude, more than he needed Cade's presence at the moment. He'd be lying to himself if he said that didn't sting, just a little bit. Even so, he was proud as hell of Braden.

So many people, after a blow like this, wouldn't take the situation nearly as well. Not that he could blame those people, but he was so damn proud Braden knew enough about himself to know this was the healthiest way for him to push through this latest setback.

Cade, eyes ahead, saw their rental SUV pull up and park. Sawyer and

Cooper stepped out, ready to run. Braden gave a small nod to them as he passed by, but otherwise didn't stop or slow down. Cooper looked Cade in the eye and tossed the keys to him. "We've got him from here. Rest up, in case he needs more than twenty miles."

Cade, hands on his head, walked towards the SUV with his chest heaving in great lungfuls of air. Watching them jog away was harder than it had been on the first leg. He wanted to be with Braden every second while this nut job was loose, but he knew that wasn't feasible, especially when Braden could run twenty miles without getting winded.

He trusted Cooper and Sawyer with his life, and obviously Braden's life as well, but suddenly it hit him that was exactly what he was doing, trusting them with his life. How in the hell it had happened so damn fast, he hadn't a clue, but the men he considered his brothers were jogging after and protecting the man that had, quite literally, become his whole life.

He had the sudden urge to run after them and let them know how important Braden was to him. Make sure they understood that nothing was more important than his safety, but he knew it was ridiculous, not to mention he had a feeling they already knew. Still, he made a move to do just that and was stopped by an arm around his chest from behind, holding him in place, and a voice he hardly ever heard growled out, almost indecipherably, "They've got him. Rest, now."

Stopping in his tracks, in shock that he'd been about to take off after them and because he so very rarely heard Jackson talk, he looked back at his friend and saw a wealth of understanding in his eyes. He nodded, letting him know he wasn't going to hightail it after them, and only then did his arm release him. Jackson clapped him on the back, and they both resumed walking for a few more minutes before getting into the SUV and heading back to Braden and Maya's place.

Cade followed Jackson into Maya's when they returned. He asked her what Braden would need from a food or drink standpoint after a twenty-mile run. He also grabbed Cooper's iPad which already showed the first fifteen miles of the run. He took it back with him to Braden's and adjusted it to reflect where he now saw Cooper's tracer. He showered and rested for a while then got on the horn to Brody who was watching their route along with several others in the office and would let them know if anything popped.

From the current location of Cooper's tracer, he had been correct that Braden was looping back home and they'd arrive in just a little while. Cade went to the kitchen and made Braden a protein shake with fruit and yogurt and grabbed a bottle of water as well.

Cade heard when Braden finally unlocked the front door. He came out of the kitchen with the smoothie and water bottle. Handing Braden the water, which he drank in a few big gulps, Cade waited for him to catch his breath, knowing he needed a bit to recover. Cade reached for the now empty water bottle and handed Braden the glass. Braden looked at it then at Cade in inquiry.

Cade smiled at him sadly. "Protein shake with berries and Greek yogurt. Is that going to help get your levels under control or do you want something else?"

Braden set the glass down on the hall table, turned back to Cade, and walked into his arms. Cade's heart clenched in his chest as his boy wrapped his arms around him and held on as tight as he could. He gripped Braden back just as tightly, Braden's heaving breaths slowing as they stood in each other's arms.

He bent down, whispering, "I'm so sorry, Braden. I'd give anything for it to be someone different, for this not to be haunting you right now. I'm going to keep you safe, baby. I swear on my life; I'll do anything it takes to keep you safe."

"I know, Zavier, I know."

"What can I do for you right now? Do you want the smoothie or something else? Do you want to shower and rest, or I can cook us dinner?"

"Just this, right now, just this."

They stood in Braden's entryway, holding each other tightly, each soaking up comfort from the other. Five minutes turned to ten, and finally Braden pulled away, reached up and pulled Cade's face down and kissed him lightly on the lips. "I'm gonna take my smoothie, which is perfect by the way, and go take a shower. Give me twenty minutes, and I'll be out."

"Take your time."

After Braden's shower, they had a light dinner. Braden asked him if they could avoid discussing Eric anymore that evening, and they chatted about completely unrelated topics, Cade doing his best to avoid anything that caused Braden anxiety. They sat on the couch for a couple hours, talking and relaxing.

Cade massaged Braden's feet and calves; Braden in turn had Cade sit on the floor between his legs and massaged his shoulders and head. When it was time for bed Cade suggested Braden take a sleeping pill to avoid nightmares. He was happy Braden agreed and when he went in to check on Braden, he was out like a light.

He detoured to Braden's bathroom feeling uneasy but knowing he needed to get it over with. He found Braden's McCade Watch on the countertop. Hoping fervently that doing this wasn't going to fuck up their relationship, he put the last tracer on Braden's watch and thought if it did fuck it up, at least Braden would be alive and safe, and in the end, that's all that really mattered.

Friday morning, Braden and Cade arrived at the café by five-thirty. Braden began his normal routine, and Cade went to the office to see what they'd gotten back from Brody. His heart rate sped up as soon as he saw a couple emails from Brody including attachments, one with the subject, "Gotcha!" He opened the first email which showed Cade a map with the location of all the cameras on their route he was able to hack, and after that, a link was provided. Cade read the email under it.

I think we've got him. I'm running the plates and everything else I can think of throughout the city to see what pops. The link above will show you footage from every camera I was able to get in case you want to see everything that I saw. I'll send another email with the clips I found.

The next email was the one with the "Gotcha!" subject and contained five clips, all showing a sand colored, non-descript, older model Toyota Camry. There were multiple still shots attached reflecting pictures of the driver, but the resolution was poor. However, the fact that they had a lead at all was fantastic. Cade went to the kitchen, waiting until Braden noticed him and took out his buds.

"We have a lead on him, Braden. Do you have a minute to look at some photos?"

Braden sucked in an audible breath and let it out slowly. Cade realized Braden was running on fumes and didn't know how much longer he was going to be able to function before hitting a wall. His gut clenched, wishing he could do more to help his boy.

Cade approached slowly, took Braden's hand in his, and looked into his eyes. "You can do this. I'm right here. You can handle the rest of today as well, and then you'll have the weekend to take some time and regroup."

Braden shook his head and his shoulders drooped. "I'm working this weekend. I work most weekends."

Cade tilted his head, scrutinizing Braden. After a few seconds he used his thumb to smooth out the stress lines between Braden's brows. "Not this weekend. I already talked to Maya. That's what your special order for pick up is tonight, just enough to get you guys through the weekend, so you don't have to work at all."

Braden snapped his head up, an incredulous look on his face. "Are you serious?"

Cade nodded. "You're wearing yourself out with all that's going on. I wanted you to have some time to rest. Tomorrow I have the whole day planned and Sunday we can do whatever you want. I swear, I'm not trying to manage you, I just wanted…"

Braden raised his hand and laid his fingers over Cade's lips. "You planned the whole day Saturday?"

With Braden's hand still covering his lips, all Cade could do was nod his head.

Braden continued, "So, like, a real date?"

Cade nodded his head again and a smile like none he'd ever seen spread slowly across Braden's face. "Where are we going? Are you going to tell me?"

Cade shook his head no, and Braden smiled wider if that were even possible. "A secret surprise first date all day Saturday?"

Cade's eyes crinkled at the sides as he nodded again, his smile emerging around the edges of Braden's fingers.

Braden's face grew serious again. "Are you taking care of me again, Zavier?"

Cade's eyes lost their crinkle as he stopped smiling, his eyes intense as he nodded slowly, unsure how Braden would react.

Braden's face relaxed, and he regarded Cade closely as he pulled his hand away from Cade's mouth. "You always seem to know what I need when I need it. Are you always gonna look after me so well?"

Cade nodded again even though Braden no longer covered his mouth. Cade looked at Braden, really looked at him, and saw there what he needed to see: acceptance. The walls Braden had built around himself were coming down, and he was no longer fighting it. In fact, it seemed he was welcoming it, welcoming him. It was a big step. Cade lifted Braden's hand to his lips and kissed the back of it. He tugged on it and walked them to the office, still holding his hand. He had Braden sit in the chair and he stood behind him and leaned over, waking the screen so that it reflected the best picture that Brody had been able to get from all of his footage.

Braden looked at that picture for several minutes without saying a word. Cade showed him the footage from the cameras as well, but then went back to the same picture.

Braden shrugged his shoulder. "It could be him. I can't be sure. He's got a beard, and his hair is darker than it was when I was with him. He's also got the hat and sunglasses. I can't be sure, Zavier. I'm sorry."

"Don't be sorry. I knew it was a long shot. I've seen pics of him from around the time when you guys were together, so I knew it wasn't going to be one-hundred percent, but I needed to ask."

"I guess we just go with the thought that it's him and try to track down the car, right?"

"Right. Brody's already on it, but I just thought I'd check with you as well. He's made a mistake, and he'll make others. We'll find him."

Nodding his head, Braden got up and smiled at him. "Well, let me get back to it. Apparently, I've got a hot date on Saturday. I've got a lot to do to make sure they have everything they need for the weekend. Can you have lunch brought in again? Whatever is fine; you know what I like."

Cade agreed but stipulated Braden grab some ibuprofen for the headache he had brewing. All he got in response was a wide-eyed Braden who nodded before leaving the office, most likely shocked that he'd seen the strain on his face. Sunday he'd make sure Braden got the rest he needed, and Saturday, he'd ensure Braden had a great time and didn't think about work or Eric all day.

The rest of the day went off without a hitch, and Braden seemed happy with a short run in the evening, Cade running beside him. They ate dinner in the living room with a movie going and relaxed the rest of the night, talking and telling funny stories from their pasts. Braden asked Cade, just as they were going to bed, if he'd still be able to go to his Pilates class in the morning. He assured Braden he could go to Pilates, but he had several things planned that would be active, so if it was a workout he wanted, he'd get one and he could sleep in. Turned out Braden thought sleeping in was a great idea.

Chapter 12

BRADEN

Braden woke up the next morning around eight and couldn't believe he'd slept so late. Cade, having some kind of internal Braden alarm, walked in with a fresh cup of coffee and asked him to get ready so they could go out for breakfast. He hopped in the shower after testing his blood, dosing himself then tucking his kit in his backpack. Per Cade's request, he also packed two sets of workout clothes. He was ready in twenty minutes and felt good about his choice of outfit when he saw the look of desire in Cade's eyes.

Cade asked, "Can you do me a favor?"

"Sure."

"Can you go get your glasses? I want you to be able to wear them all day because you're rubbing your eyes again. But, I have plans that require your contacts, so can you pack them in your backpack to put on later?"

Braden grinned and turned back around to get his glasses and his contacts stuff. He knew better than to ask what they'd be doing that would require contacts, but he couldn't help being excited for the day. Once he was ready to go, Cade ushered him out the door and down the steps, stopping in front of his Ford Edge which looked like new with fresh paint and brand new, high performance tires.

He looked at Cade, eyebrows raised. "How?"

"Doesn't matter. What matters is that it's done and upgraded with a better security system and a few other safety measures. It won't stop something like that from happening completely, but it will emit two loud horn blasts which usually sends the perp running, and it'll signal your phone as well. Mind if I drive?"

Braden narrowed his eyes at Cade. "Are you the type that won't let me drive my own car when you're with me?"

Cade admitted, "I prefer to drive, but if you really want to drive, it's your car, so of course it's your choice."

"I'm happy for you to drive. In fact, I'd prefer it." Braden's face scrunched up. "But hold on, upgraded security? Is that really necessary, and what did it put me back?"

Cade opened the passenger door and helped Braden into the car. "Yes, it's necessary, and not a dime."

"Zavier…"

"Braden, maybe we can chat about this later? Right now, I'd like to get started on our date, and I don't want it to begin with you in a bad mood. Please."

Sighing in resignation, Braden agreed with one stipulation. "We'll discuss this tomorrow. Deal?"

"Deal."

The rest of the day was like no other date Braden had ever been on. Cade was such a gentleman the whole day. He opened doors for him, including the car door, every single time. He either held Braden's hand, fingers entwined, or guided him where he wanted him to go using a gentle hand on Braden's lower back.

Braden had never been treated with such respect. It almost felt like Cade was courting him. He felt silly for even thinking something so fanciful and old fashioned, but every time he caught Cade's eyes, he realized Cade was doing everything he could to show Braden a good time but also ensure he felt safe.

He couldn't believe everything Cade had planned. Their breakfast, one of the best he'd ever had, was at Hollywood Café down on the wharf. From there, Cade took him to the House of Air, a trampoline park in an old airplane hangar, which he apparently rented out for them because they were the only two people there.

They bounced, flipped, and played dodgeball until they were laughing like crazy and sweating like pigs, and Braden realized about halfway through that this was why he needed to keep his contacts in. When they were both exhausted and getting hungry, they showered quickly and got ready for lunch. Braden wore his glasses, which he was happy to notice pleased Cade to no end.

From there, they gorged at The Italian Homemade Company, and Braden had the best lasagna he'd ever eaten. They gave each other bites of their meals. He felt cherished and cared for; it was such a wonderful feeling, one he didn't think he'd actually ever felt in a relationship.

"Cade, so far this day has been so wonderful. I just want to thank you; I've had so much fun and felt so relaxed and at ease with you all day."

"You're welcome. The day isn't even close to being over."

After lunch, they ventured to the California Academy of Sciences, where they checked out the planetarium and the aquarium along with the earthquake simulator. Then they stopped in at a local coffee shop. In addition to Cade's own coffee, he ordered two more cups and several pastries, and picking up some creamers and sugars, he put everything in a carton. As they walked out of the shop, Braden was about to ask what was going on when Cade whispered to him, "Can you stand where I can see you just up a few feet by the newspaper dispensers?"

Braden tilted his head in question but saw the seriousness of Cade's face, so he decided the questions could wait. He walked over to where Cade asked him to stand and turned back to see Cade squatting down by a couple of homeless guys he was ashamed to say he hadn't even noticed. Braden realized Cade kept him in his sights while he set the carton down, shook each of their hands, and handed them the coffees and the bag of pastries while having a short conversation with them.

Cade dug into one of his cargo pants pockets, pulled out a roll of quarters, broke it, and handed both men some of them. Pulling out his wallet, he extracted what looked to Braden like two Walmart gift cards and handed them to the men, one of which Braden could see was close to tears, his hand shaking as he took the proffered gift card. He also handed the men what looked like business cards and pointed to a number he had written on the back.

Braden watched as Cade stuffed the remainder of the quarters in his cargo pocket, grabbed his own coffee, and made to get up. He was surprised when both of the men got up as well, one of them struggling and receiving help from his friend. He shook hands with them both, and Braden could hear Cade say, "Thank you both for your service."

At that point, Braden felt a few of his own tears fall as he watched both of the men salute Cade, and Cade in turn saluted them. He headed back towards Braden who wiped his tears away just in time to hide the fact he'd been crying. Braden turned as he approached and felt Cade's hand on his lower back, guiding him. Braden's mind was spinning, but in that whirling dervish of thoughts, one thing was clear–he'd just tripped and fallen head over heels in love with Zavier McCade.

Neither of them said anything at all as they climbed into Braden's car and drove to their next destination. Cade reached across the middle console and clasped Braden's hand in his. Braden squeezed Cade's hand, pulled it to his mouth, and kissed it before returning their hands to his lap. They remained there until they pulled into the parking lot of Planet Granite, and Braden smiled over at Cade. "Our second set of workout clothes?"

Cade grinned a devilish grin, nodded his head, and grabbed their backpacks from the back of the car. Cade went to the front counter and asked for the manager, letting the young lady know he had an appointment. They waited several minutes, during which time the woman handed both of them waivers, and Cade explained, "We can't climb unless we sign the waivers."

As they were signing, a man approached Cade. "Zavier McCade?"

Cade shook hands with the man who introduced himself as well. Cade turned to Braden. "This is Braden, I'll be giving him the training myself after you test me."

Braden, a bit confused, shook hands with the manager who then walked to the desk and asked the young lady for a different set of forms which only Cade signed. Walking them to the locker room, he let them know he'd meet them right outside of the door when they were ready. Braden looked up at Cade as they were going in. "What was that about?"

"Well, if you've never climbed before, they make you take a beginner's class, but if you're a good climber, you have to test yourself out of that beginner's class. I called ahead to make an appointment with the manager so I could essentially teach the beginner's class to you, once he tested me on their hardest climb, so that's what we're doing first before we climb together."

They both changed into their workout gear and went out to meet the manager. Walking through a maze of climbing apparatus, they ended up in front of an extremely tall wall with multicolored small handholds and footholds attached all the way to the top in a haphazard way. He watched Cade suit up in what he explained was called belaying gear. Cade nodded at the manager who'd been scrutinizing his actions, and then he was up.

Braden had no other way to describe Cade's ascent to the top except to call him a spider monkey. He was on the ground then he leaped up, grabbed onto one of those tiny bumps on the wall, and proceeded to climb quickly to the top. He was already impressed, but then he heard the manager mutter, "Holy shit," under his breath, and he went from impressed to awestruck.

Once Cade was back on the ground, the manager asked, "So Mr. McCade, do you do this for a living?"

Cade answered evasively. "I used to do quite a bit of it as part of my job."

The manager nodded. "Well, you're definitely skilled enough to teach your friend. If you ever need a job, let me know."

Cade laughed and nodded, telling him thanks but turned his attention to Braden. Cade got him situated in his own gear, gave him the lesson he needed, and they spent several hours climbing and bouldering. It was exhilarating to Braden, learning more about Cade, but also learning something new and physical he could enjoy. At the end of their time at the gym, Braden's hands and fingers hurt and his arms and legs were shaky and rubbery with fatigue. He knew in the morning he'd be sore.

They got showered and changed again, and by the time they got outside to the car, it was getting dark and he was hungry again. When they got to their next destination, The Mission's Foreign Cinema Restaurant, Braden got so excited he turned in his seat to face Cade. "I've wanted to come to this place forever, I've just never made it here."

"How does The Maltese Falcon and dinner in the private mezzanine sound?"

"It sounds perfect, Zavier, like everything else today."

They ate amazing food in the cozy mezzanine with the movie playing on a wall across the courtyard. Braden sat in the curve of Cade's arm, and they held hands and whispered to each other. More than once, Braden felt Cade's lips on his hair and sighed in contentment, enjoying the gentle caresses.

He'd never in his life had a day like it. Even if the day was broken up into individual dates, he could honestly say each and every separate event was special in its own way. They'd laughed, Braden had cried, they'd gotten sweaty and acted like kids, they'd held hands and hugged each other, and they'd whispered to each other and shared intense gazes.

He knew Cade was doing all he could to show he cared for him. He also knew Cade was making use of what precious little free time they had while in the midst of chaos and stress, and for that and everything else today, Braden was so grateful. Blushing at his own thoughts, he realized he hoped he'd be able to thank Cade properly later that night for everything he did and would continue to do.

At the end of the night, they held hands walking up the short flight of steps to the front of Braden and Maya's house. Braden was reaching into his hip pocket to draw out his keys when Cade turned Braden to face him. He leaned down, gazed intently into Braden's eyes then looked at his lips before he leaned in and kissed him.

That kiss.... Oh god, that kiss was like none he'd ever experienced. Cade nipped lightly, pulled back a bit, looked searchingly into Braden's eyes again then devoured him with his lips. There was no other way to describe it. It was an all-consuming, sensual onslaught that had Braden swaying in Cade's arms, which banded tightly around him, molding them together.

Braden moaned softly and opened his mouth to let Cade inside. Cade's tongue delved in slowly, as if asking permission, his head tilting to the side to gain better access. Cade swept his tongue in then retreated; he sucked lightly on Braden's bottom lip and nipped at it with his teeth. He changed the angle again, and when Braden shyly slid his tongue along Cade's, he groaned loudly and yanked himself away from Braden. He placed his forehead to Braden's temple, whispering in his ear. "You're killing me, baby. Give me your keys so we can get inside."

Breathing deeply, trying to gain some amount of composure, he dug into his pocket again and found his keys. Cade unlocked the front door then proceeded to unlock Braden's side of the house and was ushering Braden inside when he glanced up above Braden's head.

Braden watched an immediate change came over Cade. It was as if a mask slid over Cade's face and Braden could no longer read him. One minute, he was burning up in Cade's arms and the next, it was like a bucket of ice water was tossed on him. Cade became a completely different person, nothing like the man he'd been with all day, and it chilled Braden to the bone.

Cade finally glanced down at him and his demeanor changed completely, like he was an actor who just took the stage. Suddenly, he smiled at Braden and it was like the last eerie seconds had never happened, though Braden knew they had and was immediately very worried that the whole day had just been an act. Jesus, the thought made him sick. Was he so easily duped? Was Cade playing a part, acting out a scene, making Braden into what Cade said he'd never be; bait for Eric in some kind of twisted game he wanted to win?

Now, Braden wondered, truly wondered, if that kiss, along with all of Cade's other romantic gestures, had been for the stalker's benefit. He'd begun to take Cade's behavior at face value early in the day when Cade started showing him a softer romantic side he'd only seen glimpses of prior to today.

God, he was so stupid, Cade had even warned Braden several days ago he was going to be touching him in public. Yet, as soon as Cade had started touching him and holding his hand, he'd been a sucker and fallen for it all.

Braden toed off his shoes by the front door while Cade woke up the security panel display and adjusted it to reflect their return.

Braden turned to Cade, his voice shaky. "It's been a long day. I'm going to go to bed."

"Wait, what just happened here, Braden? We just shared the best kiss I've ever had in my life after the best date I've ever had. I had to force myself to stop so I could get us inside where we could feel more comfortable and not be on display for the world to see. Did I do something wrong?"

Braden turned, facing Cade, but he couldn't keep the tears from his eyes. Cade confusion was evident when he asked, "Baby, what is it? Don't cry, talk to me." Cade stepped into his space, placed both hands on either side of his face and brushed away the tears that had just fallen with his thumbs. "Please come talk to me, Braden. Let me fix it, whatever I did."

Shaking his head, Braden pulled out of Cade's grasp. "It's nothing. Forget it. I just want to go to bed."

Cade wasn't going to let him go that easily though. He grabbed Braden's hand in his and tugged him to the couch. Braden reluctantly followed and wondered what game Cade was playing when he sat down and patted his lap. "Sit down, please. Let me talk to you, let's figure this out. Please, don't go to bed before we have a chance to talk."

Braden met Cade's eyes and blushed. Despite what he'd just seen, something he recognized as yearning unfurled warm in his belly. "You want me to sit on your lap? You know I'm a grown man, right?"

Cade reached out to clasp his hand and tugged. "Believe me, I know you're a grown man, but right now, *this* grown man needs to feel you, to be grounded by the weight of you. Something happened just now, and I'm at a complete loss. I have no idea what I did, but I'm going to fix it, and I need you to give me that chance. Please, sit. I need you near me."

Sighing in resignation and feeling rather silly, though strangely pleased, Braden straddled Cade's lap but sat slumped and as far away on Cade's knees as he could with his hands in his own lap, not knowing what else to do with them. Cade apparently wasn't having that because he slipped his hands under Braden's thighs, just behind his knees, and pulled him closer so their zippers were touching and Cade, in his relaxed and very slouched pose, was actually looking up into Braden's eyes, seemingly as puzzled as Braden felt.

It was a rather strange sensation, looking down at Cade rather than looking up at him. For some reason, it made him feel calm and a bit more in control. He had a sneaking suspicion Cade knew that's how he would feel and had done it to make him feel at ease; just one more reason he'd lost his heart to this man, but now was scared to death he was alone in those feelings.

In a nervous gesture, Braden turned his sweaty palms over onto his jeans and rubbed them up and down his thighs. Cade placed his hands on top of Braden's, stilling them, and waited patiently for Braden to speak.

Cade always seemed so refreshingly honest which was what had Braden so freaked out. And regardless of what happened, Braden could do nothing but be completely honest himself. He took a deep breath and spoke directly to Cade's chest. He was going to tell Cade the truth, but he couldn't seem to look him in the eyes.

Braden's voice was low and tentative. "You warned me the other day you'd be touching me in public, holding hands with me, maybe kissing me, to convince people that we are together. I forgot, until after that kiss."

"Braden, no, that's not..." Cade cut himself off and groaned, his anguished voice soothed something in Braden. "You think that's why I did everything I did today?"

Braden shrugged his shoulders and nodded, determined to get everything out in the open. "A mask came down over your face. You completely changed, or maybe you became yourself and today was just an act. I don't know. You got really upset, then like magic you weren't, and I remembered your warning. Today confused me and I obviously made more of it than it was. It's embarrassing to admit how long it took me to realize you don't have the same feelings for me as I do for you. I'm sorry."

"Baby, please don't apologize. And don't, for one second, think that you're feeling things that I'm not." Cade sat up a bit and sighed. "I saw our rental SUV drive by and remembered I'd asked Coop and the guys to follow us all day."

"What?!" Braden moved back on Cade's knees again, shocked and embarrassed they'd been watched all day by Maya's brother, not to mention Sawyer and Jackson. Fucking hell.

Cade shook his head. "I did exactly what you did...got so wrapped up in you I completely forgot about them. Which is why I did it in the first place. Your safety is my number one priority."

Braden nodded, believing that was true. "I know."

Cade tipped his head up with a finger under his chin. "I asked you out on a date because I needed to spend time with you, to see you happy and smiling and laughing. I needed to get your mind off of him, not to mention off work, off running, off of everything that puts stress on you."

Cade rubbed his hands softly up and down Braden's arms. "I knew I'd never be able to focus on your safety one-hundred percent, so I asked them to follow us to protect you. The warning a couple days ago was only so you wouldn't pull away if someone was watching and didn't even enter my mind today; I'd forgotten I'd even given it to you."

Braden took a deep breath and tried to get his emotions under control. "The look on your face was like none I'd ever seen before. I felt like it was all lies and I really *was* just bait, like the whole day was meant to piss him off and I was a worm on a hook to catch the big fish."

Cade's face looked pained as he shook his head. "Braden, no. You mean too much to me to use you like that with no regard for your safety. Baby, look at me. I've *never* treated *anyone* like I treat you."

Cade looked down at their laps and sighed. He tugged the back of Braden's knees toward him again, as if the few inches Braden had moved back didn't sit right with him. "When I'm working, I'm nothing like the person you see. Being with you, it's separate, and it's wonderful and what I didn't even know I needed. What you saw wasn't an act; it was me switching gears. I compartmentalize, become a different person. That's what you saw, and I'm sorry it scared you or caused doubt."

Cade sat up, eyes level and intense on Braden's. He slid his hand to Braden's nape and gripped his hair. "How can you doubt my attraction to you? It consumes me." Cade took Braden's hand with his free one, pressing it to his protruding fly. "This is what you do to me whenever I'm near you. This is real."

Braden's emotions made his body tremble and his voice shaky. "Are you sure? Oh god, please be sure. Because I'm falling for you, Zavier, and if you're not being serious, it will kill me."

Cade looked at Braden beseechingly, clasped his head softly in his hands, and brought their foreheads together. "Yes, I'm sure, baby. I've already fallen for you, can't breathe for wanting you. And I want to spend the rest of the night making love to you. Can you give control over to me tonight? Let your walls down enough to give in to your pleasure, with me?"

Something about the way Cade asked him if he could take control had him panicking. Just when he thought everything was going to be fine. He knew what it was like, being controlled by someone. He knew it started small then snowballed out of control. He pulled back, stiffened on Cade's lap, and began to shake his head. He tried to pull away and became panicked when Cade held him on his lap, unwilling to let him go. He couldn't move, he couldn't….

"Breathe, Braden. Dammit, breathe! Look at me." Cade shook Braden lightly, enough to jar him back into the here and now. "That's it. No, don't struggle. I'm not hurting you, I'd never hurt you. I'm removing my hands from your shoulders so you don't feel trapped. I need you to take a deep breath and stay where you are. Breathe with me, Braden, deep breath in, that's it; now out. In again, now out. Good. Please, don't allow him to come between us. I would never hurt you. It would kill me to see you harmed in any way, don't you know that by now?"

Braden grimaced and looked away. "But, you want to control me. You said it yourself. I can never let that happen again. I'm sorry, I just can't. I didn't know that's what you wanted. I know how it feels, and I won't ever allow myself to be in that type of relationship again."

Cade placed his hands lightly on Braden's thighs and drew nearer. "Tell me how it feels. Tell me what it was like. And not just the big things, but the little ones, too. Sometimes it's the little things that hurt the most. I don't think you've told anyone, Braden, and that's got to be a huge burden to bear on your own."

When Braden couldn't seem to force any words out past the lump in his throat, Cade asked him, "In this moment, right now, do you trust me not to hurt you?"

"I..." Braden glanced down at his hands gathered in his lap. "Yes, I do."

"Do you trust me enough to share your story? The worst bits. The ones you held back?"

A pained look crossed Braden's features. "How did you know?"

"Oh, baby." His heart hurt for Braden. "I heard it in your voice, saw it on your face. Let me shoulder the burden for you. Talk to me."

His boy took in a ragged breath, swiped a lone tear away, and nodded. "Okay."

Cade gently swept his hand over Braden's hair, holding it away from his face. "Why don't we take a few minutes and get ready for bed? I promise not to do anything more than hold you, but I'd like us to be in your bed where I can feel you next to me. Afterward, I'll hold you all night or if you want to be on your own, I'll leave you alone. It'll kill me, but I'll do it if it's what you need."

Chapter 13

BRADEN

Braden finally looked into Cade's eyes and saw the raw emotion there. He was feeling defeated and exhausted, but the thought of unburdening himself didn't seem so daunting anymore. He saw no judgment in Cade's eyes and it gave him the strength he needed. He'd never felt like he could talk to anyone about it, except Maya, and he didn't want her to know about all the little things still weighing him down.

Cade sat under him, patiently waiting for his response. He finally nodded and made to get off of Cade's lap, but Cade stilled him when he put his big hand over Braden's heart. "I'll take care of this. Always. You just have to give it to me."

Braden's breath hitched, his heart melting at Cade's words and the emotion reflected in his eyes. He leaned forward and kissed Cade's lips softly. He pressed his forehead lightly to Cade's then got up to head to his room and get ready for bed.

He tested his blood, brushed his teeth, pulled on a pair of pajama pants and a fresh t-shirt, and was just climbing into bed when Cade walked in wearing a tight, ribbed tank top that was so thin he could see through it and a pair of loose fitting basketball shorts that highlighted the muscular V cut abs arrowing down into his shorts.

God, he was a work of art. His muscular arms bulged under all of that gorgeous ink and Braden discovered, seeing the outlines through the tank, that the ink made its way across parts of his chest and abs as well. He was entranced and his eyes traveled slowly up Cade's six...*oh good lord, was that an eight pack and pierced nipples? Does it ever end?*

Braden huffed out an incredulous breath. "Seriously? What is with that body? How can it be real? And how can you be attracted to me? I'm nothing like you."

Cade sat in front of him as he tried to cover his body with the blanket. Cade grabbed it and gently tugged it away. "First of all, we dressed in front of each other a couple times today. Didn't you see me naked, or nearly so, when we changed or went to shower in the locker room stalls?"

"Um no, I avoided looking at you because I didn't want to bounce on a trampoline with a boner. You realize your attraction to me makes *no* sense, right?"

"You have no concept of how beautiful you are, do you? Your tight little body, all lean muscle; gorgeous, long hair; soft, flawless skin; beautiful deep green eyes; and those soft full lips. Oh Jesus, those lips are the stuff dreams are made of."

Braden scrunched his nose, still unable to believe Cade's words. "But, we're complete opposites. Wouldn't you prefer someone your size? I'm not strong and tough like you and your friends."

Cade shook his head. "You're stronger than a lot of the men I served with, I can promise you that. And I can't wait to learn every inch of you."

Braden watched as Cade shifted his weight, obviously irritated he couldn't get his point across. "I'm sorry, I just don't get it."

Cade clasped his hand. "I'm extremely protective of you, and I think that's pretty significant. Your size brings that out in me, and I never knew that was something I needed in a partner. There isn't a thing about you that I would change, especially your size."

He glanced quickly up into Cade's eyes. "It's just hard to believe."

Cade's brow furrowed. "Believe it, Braden."

Braden glanced back down at his lap and nodded, wanting more than anything to believe him. He sighed and let it go. "All right."

They sat in silence for a moment or two. Cade reached out and placed both of his large hands on Braden's knees. The gesture had him glancing at

Cade's forearms. Braden stopped fiddling with his ring and reached a hand out to trace one of Cade's tattoos, looking up into his eyes, he bit his lip and asked, "Can I ask you something?"

Cade ran his thumb across his lip, and Braden couldn't keep himself from letting his tongue lick it. He smiled a little and looked back down to his lap when Cade's breath grew ragged as a result, his voice rough when he said, "Anything."

He glanced back up, shyly. "Do your tattoos mean anything? You have so many and they're all over. I thought at first they were just on your arms, but you have them everywhere, don't you?"

Cade's face looked concerned, and something else Braden couldn't grasp. "Do they bother you?"

"No. Umm, I've never cared one way or another about tattoos before, but I love yours. Really, really love yours."

Cade's face relaxed at that news, a knowing grin slipping across his lips. "Most of them are just beautiful designs created by my tattoo artist who I've been friends with for years. I told him I really liked the look of Maori tribal tattoos, where each design builds on top of the next, so he incorporated a lot of that."

"They're beautiful."

"He's an amazing artist. Some of them have specific meaning, but they're usually embedded in such a way that I'd need to point them out. One day I'll tell you about them, but tonight is about you, okay?"

Braden blushed, but nodded and whispered, "Okay."

"Good, let's get under the covers. Which side of the bed do you prefer?"

Braden shrugged. "Uh, it doesn't matter. You can choose."

Cade shook his head. "This isn't about my comfort, it's about yours. You pick your side. I can sleep anywhere, so don't worry about me."

"Okay, I like this side."

Cade slid over to the opposite side of the bed and got under the covers with Braden. He stacked a few pillows behind him so he was reclining and patted his chest. "Put your back to my chest."

Braden narrowed his eyes. "I get the feeling you're positioning us in ways that make me feel more at ease."

Cade reached out a hand and brushed Braden's hair back over his shoulder. "This is new between us, but I feel that a big part of my job in our relationship is to take care of your needs, to put them before my own. I want you to trust me, to feel safe with me. So, yes, I'll do anything I can do to help with that."

Braden pulled Cade's hand into his lap. "Thank you. It helps. Can I ask you a favor?"

Cade squeezed Braden's hand. "Anything."

Braden glanced a Cade, his gaze imploring. "Can you promise not to go beat the shit out of a punching bag until your hands are bruised and bloody? I think I'm really going to need you here with me."

Cade pulled Braden closer and kissed his palm. "I promise. I'm sorry about that."

Cade gently took Braden's face in his hands and drew him into a soft kiss. He got up, dimmed the lights, and got back in bed. As he helped Braden get situated, he pulled the blanket over them and settled his arms around him. Then he kissed the top of his head and whispered, "You feel so good in my arms. You're safe here, Braden. Talk to me."

Taking a deep breath, Braden started at the beginning. His relationship with Eric had begun like most of his relationships. He'd been attracted to Eric immediately and had made the first move. They'd dated and gotten to know each other. Eric was older than Braden by ten years. He was in awe of Eric at the beginning of their relationship. He was so self-assured, so strong and commanding. Braden easily began to lose himself in Eric, but he thought he was in love, so he didn't think anything of it. He found himself moving in with Eric after only dating him for three months.

Braden blushed, but he knew he needed to say this next bit, before he lost his nerve. He needed Cade to understand why he couldn't give someone else control. "I don't even want to tell you this. But before Eric, I had fantasies about being dominated in the bedroom. I wanted to let go, to trust someone with my body and push my limits sexually. I kept it to myself because I was embarrassed. Hell, I'm still embarrassed."

Braden cleared his throat and shifted in Cade's arms. "In the early days with my rose-colored glasses, I thought his domineering ways were sexy. That he was just *that* into me. Thinking back on it now, I'm ashamed to admit I enjoyed feeling like he'd fallen in love with me so quickly. I had never been with someone so intense, and it felt good because he was purely focused on me, and I'd never had that. I wish now I hadn't been that naïve, and I hadn't convinced myself it was love when it was really more like an unhealthy obsession. I'm angry I didn't see him for what he was."

He couldn't remember when it started to change. It wasn't like one day, out of the blue, Eric beat the shit out of him. It was small things at first. Things that, if looked at individually, weren't a huge deal but lump them together with the whole, and there was a definite pattern. At first, he would act sad when Braden came home late or disappointed if Braden spent a lot of time with Maya. Braden hated seeing him upset, so he started to make an effort to be punctual and reserve his free time for Eric. Then Eric had issues with the way he dressed and the things he would say. Eric had started to buy Braden clothes, and though Braden didn't like them, he wore them so he wouldn't hurt Eric's feelings.

Pretty soon the relationship was taking a toll on Braden. He was having more migraines than usual and generally just not feeling well physically. He took a good look at what was going on, the way he'd begun to change who he was completely. Eric's sad and disappointed expressions had long since been replaced by irate looks and angry words. They were fighting all the time, and Eric would push him around and make it look like an accident. It happened often enough that when Eric eventually moved on to hitting Braden, he wasn't even surprised and didn't believe Eric's promises that he would never do it again. At that point, he felt trapped.

He was in an abusive relationship with a man who was known in the area as a do-gooder, the CEO of HYSC, a foundation doing amazing things for the community's homeless youth. He didn't trust anyone would believe him, and in the end, he knew Eric would go ballistic if he ever reported him. That was when he made the decision to leave, and he began planning.

He went and bought another phone from a different carrier with a new number. He didn't know if Eric had somehow cloned his old phone or had a tracking app on it because he always seemed to know every step Braden took. After that, he maintained both phones, hiding his new one from Eric and giving everyone else in his life his new number.

He asked Maya if he could move in with her for a while. Over the course of several weeks, he gradually moved all of his own things out of Eric's house, with Eric none the wiser. It was unexpectedly easy to do. Most of his stuff, including his clothes, were in boxes in the basement as Eric had said he didn't have a lot of room for Braden's stuff in the house. Braden had nearly an entire wardrobe full of stuff Eric had bought him, his own clothes had been moved to the basement months prior so they weren't in the way of what Eric called his "new look".

Once he had all of his stuff moved out of Eric's house and over to Maya's, he created a new email account he would use going forward and a dummy email account for backup. He went about changing his passwords for everything else he could think of. He even went so far as to open several new bank accounts. Anything that Eric could tamper with or use to keep tabs on him was changed or shut down.

He set up a draft of an email on his old email account with Eric as the main recipient and his dummy email address under the BCC line with the subject: Video. He typed up a letter to Eric, one he would leave on the countertop for Eric to find when he got home after Braden had made his final escape. He drove back over to Eric's and set up a camera in their bedroom, knowing that Eric would hurt him, but not seeing another way to guarantee his safe escape.

From past experience, Braden counted on being knocked around and Eric storming out of the house for hours. That evening, when Eric got home from work, Braden told him that he was going to leave. Things went according to plan, only much worse than Braden had expected. Eric beat him until he was nearly unconscious then viciously raped him. Eric screamed and railed at Braden, telling him he would never let him leave, even threatened to kill him. All of it was caught on camera. Eric left after that, assuming Braden was too hurt to move and would stay, like he always had in the past.

Eric was gone for at least an hour, as it took that long for Braden to be able to get himself off the bed, complete his plan, and leave. When he'd finally made his way over to his phone, he saved the video to his new Dropbox account, attached the video to the email draft he'd created earlier, and sent a copy to Eric and the dummy email account. He found Eric's iPad, logged in, checked that the email came through and the video worked, and marked it as unread. He left the letter he'd printed at Maya's on the kitchen counter, walked out the door to his car, and left.

The letter said he was leaving, and he never wanted to see or hear from him again. It asked Eric to check his email and view the video he received. It stated there were two more copies of the video and one of them was sent to a lawyer who would remain nameless. If anything were to happen to him, Maya, or Nana, Eric's board of directors would receive a copy along with all the local news channels and the police department.

Braden drove to the closest supermarket and tossed his old phone into the dumpster out back. He drove himself to the hospital where he had a rape kit done so he'd have the evidence later in case he needed it. He was urged to contact the police, but he refused at that point and was treated for the rest of his injuries. He had a concussion and possible internal bleeding, so they kept him overnight for further observation and testing.

He was released the next day and went home to Maya's place. He got in bed, let her know he was there but feeling like shit and just needed a few days off. He assured her he was fine and would see her when she got home. Later when she arrived, she came to talk to him, and he convinced her that the breakup was dealt with and he just had a really bad migraine and needed to stay home for a few days.

Thankfully she didn't have much help available in the café at the time and couldn't take time off to help him, which worked out perfectly. He was able to recuperate without her knowing he'd been beaten so badly, and three days after getting home, he was back at work. He'd never heard from Eric after that and had hoped he never would.

Finally done telling the story, he sat in Cade's strong embrace for a while, coming back into himself and taking stock. He hadn't realized he had been shaking the whole time he'd been telling Cade about the abuse. Nor had he known he had tears running down his face which he rubbed away. Neither of them said anything for several minutes. He could feel how tense Cade was. Sometime during his walk back through his relationship with his ex, he'd ended up on Cade's lap again and was being held so tightly it was just shy of being hard to breathe, yet somehow it was perfect. At that point, he had nothing to lose, so he asked Cade exactly what was on his mind. "Do you think I'm weak?"

Cade's body shook with emotion. "God, how can you ask me that? Braden, look at me."

Taking a deep fortifying breath, not knowing what was to come, Braden turned his head and looked at Cade. He had tears in his eyes and such sorrow in them it nearly broke Braden in two.

Cade gently swept away Braden's remaining tears. "I think you're the strongest man I know. You did what you had to do, and you were so fucking smart about it. As pissed off as I was to learn about that video when you first told me, I know you did the only thing you could think of to get the hell away from him. You protected yourself, Maya, and Nana which in itself makes me so damned proud of you. I would give anything to have been there, to have been able to protect you myself. I feel so useless right now. I want to kill him, Braden. I want to kill him for laying a hand on you. The only thing that will keep me from it is knowing it would end up hurting you in the end."

Braden was stunned by Cade's words. He reached up and trailed his fingers gently down Cade's face, leaned in, and kissed him with every ounce of emotion he had in him. Cade drew away slowly. "Can I stay with you tonight? We won't talk about the other stuff right now, but please, don't ask me to leave. I need to hold you in my arms."

Braden managed a tremulous smile. "Yes, stay. I've never told anyone what I told you. It feels good to finally say it, to get it out, like a weight has been lifted. Thank you for listening."

"I'd do just about anything for you." After a few beats of silence in which they gazed at each other, Cade tilted his head. "Can I ask you something?"

Braden nodded. "Sure."

"When I was asking questions to help us learn more about who could be stalking you, you said you've been single for over a year but have you had any dates since that time? Been with anyone else?"

After a deep breath and a small tremor that shook his slight frame, he whispered, "No. I've been too scared to trust anyone enough." After a long pause, Braden's voice grew stronger, "Until you."

Cade tightened his hold in a reassuring squeeze. "Oh god, baby, I promise you, I'll never make you regret it."

Braden glanced away. "I want so badly to believe that. Actually what scares me most is that I do believe it. That's the worst part. Isn't that fucked up? I obviously can't trust my instincts. They've always steered me wrong. Last time, they steered me to someone that beat and raped me. How can I ever trust myself again?"

Cade grasped Braden's shoulders and pushed him back so he could look in his eyes. "Braden, men like Eric are predators. They know how to act to draw people in, to make them feel secure and cared for, loved. Eventually, their true colors show, which is exactly what happened. It kills me that you blame yourself for being beaten, for being raped…"

Indignant, Braden recoiled. "I don't!"

Squeezing Braden's shoulders, Cade raised his voice, sounding frustrated. "You do, Braden. When you say you can't trust yourself, you're blaming yourself. You need to stop the negative self-talk. You're making yourself out to be a victim, not a survivor. You can damn well trust your instincts, Braden. Your instincts told you something wasn't right, he wouldn't stop beating you, and you had to get away from him. Your instincts told you to pack your shit and find a safe place to go. Your instincts got you out, Braden. Trust your damned instincts."

Cade was so upset he was shaking and sometime during his tirade, he'd cupped Braden's cheeks and was brushing away his tears. He leaned in and kissed the tears away, kissed Braden softly on the lips, and again repeated his plea, his voice guttural with emotion. "Trust yourself, Braden. Don't let him win."

Sobs suddenly wracked Braden's smaller frame, and Cade held him tightly and rocked him, murmuring softly that everything would be okay. He rocked him and kissed his temple, his hair, his cheeks. He rubbed his stubbled face against Braden's soft hair, caressed his back until Braden's sobs diminished and he began to calm, and he continued to murmur until Braden pulled back.

They looked into each other's eyes for what seemed forever, until Braden raised his own hands to clasp Cade's face, and whispered, "Okay", and began to kiss him in return. He kissed Cade's forehead, his eyes, his cheeks, his nose, his chin, and finally, his lips.

He glanced at Cade anxiously. "Do you still want to stay with me tonight, after all that?"

Cade nodded and squeezed him tighter. "More than ever."

They snuggled down in bed, spooning, their clasped hands held over his heart. Cade's other hand caressed over him in leisurely strokes. Emotionally exhausted, Braden fell asleep immediately, feeling completely safe and protected.

Chapter 14

CADE

Cade woke with Braden still asleep in his arms. They had both slept in, and he was glad Braden had slept soundly through the night. Braden's head was lying on his chest and his arm was tight around his waist as if not wanting to let go, even in sleep. Braden's leg was also tossed over one of Cade's which was currently wreaking havoc on his ability to control his libido, and the more he thought about it, the harder the situation became.

Cade felt the moment Braden woke and took stock of his position, nearly on top of Cade. He waited to see how Braden would react and though his first reaction was tension at waking up in a strange situation, he immediately relaxed and melted into Cade. He flexed his hand under Cade's, laced their fingers together, looked up into Cade's eyes, and smiled sleepily. "Hi."

"Morning, baby."

Braden smiled as if he liked the endearment. "I think this is my new favorite place to wake up."

"What, your new bed or in my arms?"

"Yes."

Cade chuckled. "It's my new favorite as well. You gonna kick me back into the guest room tonight?"

"I don't know. I'm getting kinda used to waking up like this; it might become an addiction."

Cade growled, reached down and tugged Braden's leg over his hip, bringing Braden to rest on top of him where he could have no doubts as to Cade's aroused state. He watched Braden's eyes go wide and his lips part in surprise. That surprise turned to desire, and Cade could feel Braden's body react to his. Braden brought both of his hands up and stacked them on Cade's chest, resting his chin on them with a seductive gleam in his eyes. "Well, now that you've got me where you want me, what are you going to do with me?"

Cade reached up with both hands and ran them through Braden's hair, tugging it back from his face and holding him in place. He pulled Braden forward, but instead of kissing his lips, he nipped along his jawline to his ear, tugged Braden's earlobe into his mouth and bit it, loving the moan it elicited. He teased the lobe with his tongue, causing Braden's whole body to shiver.

Cade felt Braden get even harder between them and smiled to himself, apparently he found one of Braden's hot spots. He'd file that away for future use. He nipped one more time, again soothing the bite with his tongue, and answered in a whisper. "I want to strip you of every piece of your clothing and kiss every inch of your body; suck on your neck, your chest, your stomach and inner thighs, branding you, marking you as mine."

Cade heard Braden's sharp intake of breath and pulled back to look into eyes that had turned to a dark jade and looked glassy with longing, pupils blown. He let go of Braden's hair and slid his hands down Braden's sides, past his hips, down his thighs that had split and were lying on the outside of Cade's. He ran his hands over the back of those thighs and pulled them farther apart then up towards his hips so Braden was on his knees.

Braden reached out with one hand and traced Cade's bottom lip with his fingers, his eyes heavy lidded. Cade focused solely on Braden's gorgeous green eyes. Their stare was so heated that Braden's breathing quickened, and Cade's voice was a low growl. "I want to bury myself so deep inside of you that you can't tell where I end and you begin."

He trailed his hands up Braden's thighs again, cupping his ass cheeks in his hands, squeezing and massaging them. Keeping one hand on his ass, he trailed the other up under Braden's shirt, using his blunt nails to lightly graze his back.

As Cade lightly caressed Braden's back, he could feel the shivers move through his lean frame and marveled at his boy's response to his touch. He seemed starved for it, probably as starved as Cade was to give it to him. Their eyes met and Cade found himself shivering when Braden leaned in and whispered, "I can't wait to have you there, deep inside of me, where I can't tell where you end and I begin."

Braden traced the outline of Cade's ear with his tongue, continuing down until he reached his neck where he pressed the softest, lightest kisses down the side. Cade tilted his head back, allowing Braden to continue his kisses across his throat and up the other side of his neck. Reaching Cade's earlobe, Braden switched back to licking and traced his other ear with his tongue before he whispered, "I want to lick, nip, and kiss every tattoo and tug on those piercings with my lips and teeth, sucking them into my mouth so I can flick them with my tongue."

Cade groaned, more turned on than he could ever remember being. He delved his fingers deep in Braden's hair and drew him down for a kiss. It was a soft meeting of lips that gradually grew heated as he caught Braden's luscious, full lower lip with his teeth, nibbling and tugging on it, licking it, and then letting it go. He did this several times until Braden surrendered and opened up to Cade's plundering tongue.

He delved deep, reveling in the tastes and textures. He heard Braden let out a tiny whimper and kissed him deeper, releasing his hair and grabbing Braden's ass. Sitting up quickly, he tugged Braden against his rock hard erection, and their cocks rubbed against each other. He pulled Braden in harder, grinding their cocks together while he delved into his mouth again and again.

Gripping Braden's hips, he felt the flex of Braden's muscles as his boy undulated against him. As they looked deep into each other's eyes, moving together, Cade's hands pulled him in faster, harder until they were both breathing heavily and those sexy little whimpers continued to fall from Braden's lips, music to his ears. Braden wrapped his arms around his neck as he rode him, the feeling more intense than Cade could have imagined.

Tilting his head back, Braden let out a groan and Cade growled. "That's it, baby. Just like that."

With Braden's throat exposed, Cade wasn't going to miss the opportunity to mark him. He nipped down his jawline, down his throat to where Braden's neck met his shoulder, and it was there that Cade opened his mouth wide, sucked hard then bit Braden with enough force to make the smaller man grunt and start moving faster on Cade's lap. Again, Cade's mouth began a strong suction on that same spot.

He felt Braden shudder over him and moaned. When he knew Braden would be wearing his mark for days to come, he stopped and was about to kiss him when Braden's phone rang. Braden jumped, but they continued, trying their best to ignore it. When it finally stopped, Cade made a move to take his mouth again, but it rang a second time.

Cade ground out a frustrated, "Fuck me."

Braden laughed a little. "I was doing my best."

Reaching over to grab his phone, Braden glanced at the screen appearing puzzled. Still sitting astride Cade, he mouthed an, "I'm sorry," to Cade as he answered it.

"Nana? Are you okay?"

Cade could hear Braden's grandmother's voice on the other end. "Am *I* okay? Braden, I haven't heard from you in well over two weeks which isn't like you. Either something's wrong, or you've met someone. Which is it? And don't even think of lying to me; you've never been good at it."

Cade smiled, liking the woman already, even though she had interrupted the hottest make-out, grinding session he'd ever had. He leaned back against the pillows while Braden sat astride him talking on the phone. The blush suffusing his cheeks was utterly adorable. "Nana, I've just been really busy. I'm sorry I haven't called."

"You bring your new man over here. I want to meet him and make sure he's good enough for you. Today, Braden, or I'm calling my car service, and I'll be there within a few hours."

"How do you always know?"

"Because I raised you. Let me show you both off then you can take me to lunch. I want a big steak, none of this sissy food they have here. I'm wasting away in this prison you keep me holed up in. Poor Ethel took a dirt nap two weeks back, probably starved to death."

Horrified, Braden chastised, "Oh my god, Nana! That's awful. Don't say that kinda stuff. Is Ethel really dead?"

"As a doornail."

Cade snickered, and Braden slapped his chest playfully in exasperation as he scolded his grandmother, "Nana, stop! I'm sorry your friend is dead."

"Well, you youngsters keep putting us geriatrics in lockup, what do you expect?"

Braden rubbed his face, and Cade grinned. "Lockup? Really? You're the one that wanted to move there and you love it. Besides, how else would you be able to find enough men to entertain you?"

"Well, there is that. In fact, a nice man moved into Ethel's old place. Name's George, and we've got a date this week. He's a charmer that one. We'll probably end up schtupping sooner or later. In fact, just last night..."

Cade's body shook with quiet laughter at the turn the conversation had taken and got his nipple twisted hard as a result. He watched Braden heave a sigh and cover his eyes in exasperation as Nana went on about the new man in her life. Still blushing, he glanced down at Cade and raised his eyebrows and mouthed, "Lunch with Nana?" Cade grinned widely, put his hands behind his head, and nodded.

"Nana, no more, my ears are bleeding. We'll come by and see you around eleven."

"Good boy. See you soon!" And just that fast, she hung up.

Braden groaned and all but collapsed on Cade's chest. He laughed and hugged Braden to him. "So, that was Nana, huh? Can't wait to meet her."

Not looking up, Braden covered his face with his hands and kept it buried in Cade's chest. He whispered, "Oh god, the two of you together. Just... God."

Cade laughed and held onto Braden even tighter then rubbed his hands up and down Braden's back in reassurance. "Come on, you're gonna give me a complex. Are you embarrassed to bring me to meet her?"

Braden bolted upright with a horrified expression and practically yelled, "No!" before he realized Cade was pulling his leg. Braden narrowed his eyes and grabbed one of Cade's nipple rings through his shirt and tugged. He didn't react but looked intensely at his boy, suddenly wanting to be reassured. "You sure?"

Braden's brows drew together, as if confused. "Are you serious, Zavier?"

Cade shrugged. "I can feel your reticence to get too close to me. And, we've established we're together, but we never discussed meeting each other's families. I want you to meet mine, but if it's too early for you to introduce us, I can wait."

Insecurity was somewhat of a foreign concept to Cade. There weren't many things he tried and failed at doing, at least not after some practice, but this was a whole new ballgame, and though he knew Braden was beginning to care for him just as deeply as he cared for Braden, he wasn't as surefooted as he'd like to be. Everything was still so new. He didn't want to push Braden too far too fast. But when he gazed into Braden's eyes, any insecurities he may have had drifted away with his boy's beautiful smile.

"Zavier, I'm gonna be so proud today, taking you to meet Nana. You're everything I've ever wanted, all rolled into the perfect package. You treat me like I'm everything to you, and god, I've never, ever felt that bef–" Cade couldn't stop himself from interrupting Braden with a kiss. After several intense moments, he pulled back and rested their foreheads together.

Braden sighed, and Cade pulled away to see a dreamy smile on his face. "She's just such a handful, and you can be quite a handful yourself, so the two of you together, I just can't imagine what this day will bring. But Z, I can't think of anything I want more than for you to meet her."

The buzzing in Cade's head stopped as soon as Braden reassured him. Then he realized Braden had finally called him by a term of endearment, and he smiled a mile wide. "Z?"

Braden blushed and looked down. "Yeah, it's how I think of you. I don't know why. It just sounds right in my head. If you hate it, I don't have to call you that."

Cade drew Braden in for a hug, pulled back, and looked into Braden's eyes. "It's perfect; I love it. No one has ever called me that, so I like it even more because it's only your name for me. I promise, I'll be on my best behavior."

Braden grew serious. "I don't want to worry her about Eric. Can we just not mention that?"

Cade's brows drew down in consternation. "I don't know, Braden. She's your only family. Are you sure you don't want to talk to her about it?"

Braden sighed. "I'm sure. As funny and lighthearted as she seems, she'll worry herself to death. I just don't want to do that to her."

Cade shook his head. "Okay. It's your call."

Braden rubbed his chest and looked into his eyes. "As sad as I am not to be able to get back to our make-out session, we should get ready to go out there. It's about an hour drive, and I need to check my blood and eat something."

"Why don't you take your time getting ready? I'll take a quick shower and fix us some breakfast."

"Sounds good."

Cade took a cold shower. After Nana's cock-blocking routine, it was either that or jerk off, and he didn't want to get off without Braden, so his options were severely limited. He brushed his teeth then pulled on a ribbed tank top and one of his many pairs of tactical pants. He carried his button-up shirt into the kitchen to put on as they were leaving and fixed a quick breakfast, eating his while fixing Braden's food. He called Cooper and let him know about their plans. He was uneasy about not having backup while having to look out for both Braden and his grandmother. Cooper agreed and said he'd follow them. He also let Cade know there was no sign of Eric the day before.

He mentioned that he'd gotten copied in an email from Brody to both of them stating that he'd been able to locate the Camry as it was driven into a mall parking lot on Thursday night, and it hadn't been driven back out. Cooper said he sent Sawyer and Jackson there that morning to try to locate it and put a tracer on it to make things easier should he use it again. Leaving it someplace like a mall parking lot, however, didn't bode well for them being able to track him that way. It reeked of final drop off location, even though Cade hoped it wasn't the case, since it was the one lead they had on the fucker.

He didn't want to keep this info from Braden, and he also wanted to tell him about Cooper following them today, so he went into Braden's room with his breakfast to let him know. Braden was standing in the bathroom in his boxer briefs and Cade's body reacted immediately. He was also wearing his glasses, Cade had never seen a sexier sight in his life. He set the breakfast on Braden's dresser, walked into the bathroom, and moved behind Braden, who had shaving cream in his hand and a bit already on his face. Braden, hair still wet and dripping down his back, met his eyes in the mirror then blushed when he saw the look in Cade's eyes.

Cade finally, *finally* got to look at Braden without a shirt. He'd had the chance yesterday, but exactly like Braden, avoided looking, knowing he'd be walking around with a permanent hard on, not to mention he hadn't wanted to make Braden uncomfortable. He looked at Braden's neck and was immediately turned on even more by the mark he'd left on Braden's skin. He reached up and lightly touched him there, crowding up flush against Braden's back, looking his fill, and letting Braden feel what seeing him like that was doing to him. Braden was thin, but god, he was amazingly muscular for someone so lean. His muscle definition was perfect and his skin flawless.

Cade reached around to Braden's chest and gently caressed him there then on down to his stomach where Cade could just see the little red mark on the skin from his latest injection. He gently rubbed that spot, looking into Braden's eyes in the mirror. Braden's eyes had turned molten with desire, and Cade clasped him by the hips and turned him around so they were facing each other. He pressed himself against Braden, putting his hand under Braden's chin to make him meet his gaze. "You're so fucking gorgeous."

Braden blushed, saying nothing. Realizing Braden was holding his hand out to the side to avoid getting shaving cream on him, he lifted Braden up and deposited him gently on the bathroom countertop. He kept his eyes on Braden's as he spread his knees so he could stand between them. He swiped all the shaving cream off of Braden's hand onto his, and grabbing the wet washcloth on the counter, he slowly and gently cleaned up Braden's hand and placed it on his own chest, wanting Braden's hands on him. Cade gently spread the shaving cream on Braden's face, feeling like this was one of the most intimate acts he'd ever taken part in and loving it.

Once all the shaving cream was lathered on, he stepped aside, ran some hot water in the sink, rinsed off his hands, and found Braden's razor. Stepping back into Braden's space, he pulled him closer to the edge of the countertop. Braden hooked his legs behind Cade's, drawing him even closer and leaving them there. He gave a quick jerk of his head, and Braden responded immediately, lifting his chin and exposing his throat to Cade. Holy fuck, the trust in that one small action from Braden made Cade hard as a rock.

Braden splayed both hands on the sides of Cade's chest and lightly rubbed his thumbs in circles, driving Cade crazy. He focused on the task at hand and began to shave Braden's neck, slowly and methodically, watching the blade slide over Braden's perfect, flawless skin. Each pull on the razor revealed a throat Cade wanted to lick and bite and suck. When he was done with his neck, Braden brought his head back down, and Cade proceeded to shave the rest of his face, rinsing off the blade every once in a while in the hot water in the sink.

When he was done, he took the washcloth, ran it under the hot water, and thoroughly cleaned off all remnants of the cream from Braden's skin. Braden turned to the counter and grabbed a bottle of aftershave cream, handing it to Cade without a word. Cade pumped some of the cream in his hand, and Braden kept his eyes on Cade's as he slowly applied the cream onto Braden's neck. He knew Braden was just as affected as he was when he felt Braden's fingers dig ever so slightly into his sides. He applied the cream to the rest of Braden's face then rubbed his hands together and looked deeply into Braden's eyes.

He gripped Braden's ass with one hand and the back of his neck with the other, kissing him deeply as he walked out of the bathroom with Braden in his arms. When he was by the bed, he tapped both of Braden's legs. As Braden released his hold on Cade's waist, Cade helped ease him down to his feet and had him sit on the bed while he grabbed the breakfast plate. Joining him on the bed, Cade proceeded to feed Braden slowly and silently.

Braden

Braden had never been a part of such incredibly intimate moments in his life. As soon as Cade had stepped into his bathroom, the room itself seemed to shrink and the air seemed to get thicker. Cade had taken control of Braden in every sense of the word and created a moment in his life that Braden would never forget. The intensity with which Cade regarded him was nothing short of breathtaking.

He hadn't spoken the whole time, not sure he could even find his voice. When Cade eased him back down to his own two feet, they looked at each other for long moments before Cade got the food and fed him. When he was done eating, Cade kissed him, handed him his coffee then took the plate and fork and left the room.

Braden sipped on the coffee while he finished getting ready, meeting Cade in the kitchen where he was finishing cleaning up after breakfast. Braden put his coffee mug in the dishwasher and turned to see Cade shrugging into his button-up shirt. When Cade reached to button his cuffs, Braden brushed his hand away and began to button up his cuff for him, and when he moved on to the other cuff, Cade reached out with his other hand and tugged Braden closer to him by a belt loop. Braden moved on to buttoning the rest of the shirt, slowly and methodically, and when he got close to the top, he noticed Cade's Adam's apple bob when he swallowed. *How is it that the act of dressing Cade felt as sexy as the act of undressing him would be?*

Inordinately pleased that Cade was reacting to him just as he'd reacted to his shave, Braden smoothed his hands down Cade's broad chest, and when he got to the edge of the shirt, he looked up at Cade questioningly. Cade widened his stance and Braden lifted the hem of the shirt enough to get to Cade's belt, which he slowly loosened, then he undid the button and pulled the zipper down. Once he had everything undone, he grabbed both sides of the pants and slowly tugged until they bunched just below Cade's hips. He looked Cade in his eyes as he reached around behind him and tucked the shirt into his pants, molding the shirt to Cade's ass and squeezing gently. He continued to tuck in the shirt around the sides and around to the front where he reached his hands in with the shirt and brushed Cade's hard length while finishing the job.

Cade reached his hand up and raised Braden's chin, forcing their eyes to meet. Cade raised a brow and Braden couldn't help it, his lips twitched. He glanced back down and began the torturous task of ever so very slowly pulling up Cade's zipper, again letting the back of his hand graze Cade's solid length on the way back up.

He buttoned him up, slid the belt back into place, and threaded the belt's needle through the hole. Cade adjusted himself then grabbed Braden's hand. He raised it to his mouth and kissed the palm then nipped his fingers and threaded their fingers together as they walked toward the front door. A secret little thrill raced through him knowing Cade was still hard because of him.

After setting the alarm, Cade cleared his throat. "So, I wanted to let you know a few things. First, there were no signs of Eric following us yesterday. Second, it looks like the Camry was dropped at a mall close to here, so Cooper is sending the guys out to search for it there to see what they can find. And third, I wanted you to know from the beginning today Coop is going to tail us in the rental. I don't want to be that far away from here and not have some backup."

Braden looked up at Cade. "Thanks for telling me everything."

Cooper met them at the front door where Braden gave him the address, and Cade proceeded to lead Braden down to his car, help him into his seat, and buckle him in before shutting the door and heading over to the driver's side. Both SUVs pulled into traffic. They listened to music for a while, holding hands, then Braden remembered a discussion they never finished yesterday.

Braden bit the inside of his cheek. "Zavier, can we talk about the cost of my new bedroom furniture and my new car security system?"

Cade lifted his hand and squeezed the bridge of his nose. "Braden…"

Turning sideways in his seat, Braden placed a hand on Cade's knee. "Just listen, please. I have money. I have more money than I need, so I don't want you to feel like these are things I can't afford."

Cade squeezed Braden's hand gently, keeping it firmly planted there on his knee. "Baby, I wouldn't care if you had millions or only hundreds, I wouldn't allow you to pay me back, regardless. You're not the only one with money to spare. I bought those things for you because I want to take care of your needs. It's not about the money, it's about me providing what you need, whether it costs me a lot of money or no money at all."

Braden shook his head. "But Zavier…"

Cade raised a brow and quickly glanced over at Braden. "Remember the talk we had about me taking care of you? I asked you if it felt good when I take care of your needs, and you said it felt great. This is just an extension of that. You need to understand this type of thing will continue. In this relationship, I need to know that I am meeting all of your needs."

Braden tried to extricate his hand from Cade's knee, but Cade was having none of it. Braden let out a little growl, tugged, and got nowhere. "But, what about your needs? I need to take care of you, too. This can't be all about me taking and you giving. I want to be on equal footing with you. I can't always feel indebted to you."

Cade pulled Braden's hand up to his mouth and nipped at his knuckles, making Braden gasp. He gave Braden an exasperated glance. "Indebted? Do you *really* care about the money? Let's say something happened to my car and I was busy with work or away on assignment, so you took care of it. And I needed a better security system in it, so you paid to get it done. Would you care about the money? Would you expect me to repay you for doing that for me?"

Braden sighed because he knew he wouldn't, and he was just proving Cade's point. "You know I wouldn't care about that. But, that's not the point."

Cade scoffed. "Bray, that's *exactly* the point."

Braden growled again. "Not when you're always meeting my needs, and I'm never meeting yours."

Braden's frustration grew. He'd never feel like an equal with Cade if he continued to do this. Cade entwined their fingers and caressed Braden's hand with his thumb and briefly met his gaze before focusing back on the road. "But, you *are* meeting my needs. I know this sounds backasswards, but you're fulfilling my needs by allowing me to fulfill your needs. I'm protective of you, you're quickly becoming everything to me, and I'm a fixer."

Braden shook his head. "It's not that simple."

"It is. I take care of what's mine, and Braden, as far as I'm concerned, *you* are mine. We've got *major* extenuating circumstances going on right now. When we catch this asshole and you no longer need protection twenty-four-seven, I won't be installing security systems and buying new bedroom furniture because some fuckwit is after you."

The GPS interrupted them to give directions, and they sat in silence for several minutes. Braden's stomach was churning. How could he forget this was all temporary? Why were they even talking about this? When Eric was caught, it would become a non-issue. Cade would go home and that would be that. He turned so he was facing forward, suddenly defeated.

Cade reached over to run his hand over the top of his head. "Hey, Braden, look at me a second."

Braden lifted his eyes, unable to hide the sadness he was feeling. "What's going on? What just happened?"

Braden glanced down to his lap, his hands clasped tightly together. "I just.... I know that when you're done here, you'll be leaving and going back to Colorado Springs. I just don't know how we'll work long distance. Not to mention, what if it's not me that you're falling for?"

Cade recoiled at that. "What in the fuck are you talking about, not you? Who else could it possibly be?"

Looking down at his hands again, Braden realized this, this right here, was one of his biggest fears with Cade. He felt sick to his stomach, but he had to say it or it would become all-consuming and he wouldn't be able to function. "What if it's the situation and not me? You said you're a fixer. What happens when you fix things? You'll grow bored."

"Braden–"

"No, really, Zavier. I'm a pastry chef for fuck's sake, not one of your military buddies that you have so much in common with. You're going to go back to Custos after this job, I'm no longer going to need things fixed, and that will be that."

Cade quickly pulled off the highway and Braden's eyes widened in surprise. He watched as their rental SUV pulled up right in front of them. Cade's phone rang, but it was already in his hand. "Give us ten," he said and hung up, tossing the phone in a cup holder.

Braden unlatched his seatbelt, turning in his seat. Cade's gaze was intense as he unlatched his own belt and moved his seat back. He leaned over and scooped Braden onto his lap to straddle him before Braden could even react.

"Zavier, what are you doing?"

"Z."

Braden tilted his head in confusion. "What?"

Cade scowled. "You call me Z from now on, that's what you call me."

Braden softened, feeling timid. "Z, what are you doing?"

Cade heaved an aggrieved sigh. "I can't have this conversation with you so far away."

Braden's brow rose. "Far away?"

Cade grunted. "For this type of conversation, I need you right here, where I can feel you."

Braden reached up and cupped Cade's cheeks. "I didn't mean to make you mad. I'm just scared that you're such a fixer once I'm fixed, there's nothing tying you to me."

Cade grabbed Braden's shoulders and shook him gently. "There is nothing about you that needs fixing. That's not why I'm here. I fix situations, not people. I'll deal with this Eric situation, you can count on it, but that's completely unrelated to my feelings for you. You think Eric's what is tying us together?"

Confused and defensive, Braden pulled back. "No. I don't... I don't know."

Cade growled. "It's you, Braden. You are tying us together. Eric has *nothing* to do with *us*. I want you. I want your smiles, your laughter, your eyes to turn liquid jade when I turn you on, your coffee cake, and your shoulder rubs. I want to see the smile on your face when you're hugging Maya. I want to rub your stomach after you give yourself an injection."

Braden blushed and looked down at his lap. Cade kissed his forehead and continued. "I want to take care of you when you get a migraine. I want you to run circles around me while we're running together."

He looked up and smiled at that. Cade captured his face and pulled him in for a kiss. "I want you to call or text to see how my day is going, and I wanna do the same for you. I want to leave notes for you on your pillow when I leave earlier than you. I want to take care of your needs, every single one of them. I told you once if you wanted to keep me around, all you had to do is say the words. Do you remember that?"

Cade's words melted Braden, but he still shook his head. "I can't ask you to give up your business, and I'm so sorry, but I don't want to give up mine either."

Cade's eyes met Braden's, beseeching. "Baby, I would never ask that of you, you have to know that by now. But, I guess the question is, do you want to keep me around? If my business was no issue, would you say those words? Or do you only want something temporary with me?"

Braden gripped onto Cade's shirt and tugged. "God, yes, Z. *Yes*, I would say those words. I wouldn't be bringing you to meet Nana today if I wasn't thinking of a future with you. I don't understand how it can work, but it doesn't mean I don't want it to."

Cade let out a breath, his shoulders finally relaxing. "That's for me to worry about. I'm the fixer, so let me figure it out. Regardless, I need you to actually say it, Bray. Say the words."

"Z…"

Cade gently caressed Braden's cheek. "Baby, do you trust me?"

"With my life."

"Then trust me with this."

Braden realized it really was as simple as that and relented. "Okay. Yes. Please, stay with me. I don't want you to go. I never want you to go."

Cade smiled wide. "I'll stay with you, Bray. I'll stay with you forever."

Chapter 15

BRADEN

Cade pulled Braden in for a kiss then suddenly, Braden found himself back in his seat and Cade was pulling the seatbelt across his lap. A bit dazed and a lot bemused, he watched Cade latch his own belt and pull quickly back onto the road. "You realize I reserve the right to call you Zavier as well as Z, right?"

"No, only Z."

Braden laughed and poked Cade in the ribs. "So, following your logic, you will only ever call me Bray and never Braden."

"That's not the same."

Braden's jaw dropped and he huffed. "It's exactly the same!"

Cade shook his head. "Nope, Z is like when I call you baby. It's not just a nickname, it's an endearment."

Braden softened, but not by much. "Okay, that was sweet, but I'm still going to call you Zavier sometimes, especially when I'm mad at you."

Cade, eyes on the road, shook his head, his face serious. "Never gonna happen."

Braden laughed. "Never? I'll never, ever get mad at you?"

"Nope."

Braden chuckled and shook his head. Cade grinned, obviously happy that he put a smile on Braden's face. Less than twenty minutes later, they arrived at the community where his grandmother lived. Cooper parked beside them, got out, opened Braden's door, and leaned down to look at both of them. "How good is the security in this snazzy place? I figure someplace this fancy has got to have *some* security."

Braden was taken aback by the question then suddenly felt sick. "Fuck, I didn't… I was only thinking you needed backup while we were out with her, I didn't even think about when we leave here. Oh god, oh god…"

"Breathe, Braden. Don't panic. Just breathe."

He felt Cade's grip on his left hand, and Cooper's on his right. He opened his eyes and saw Cooper squatting down beside him, looking concerned.

Braden gulped in a breath. "Did we put her in danger coming here today? Of course we did. What the fuck was I thinking? We should go. Let's just go. I can call her and tell her something came up."

Cade put a hand on Braden's chin. "Bray, look at me. Everything is fine. How long has she lived here?"

Braden looked into Cade's eyes and relaxed when he saw how calm he was. "About four years."

Cade clasped his hand and squeezed gently. "Didn't Eric meet her? I thought you said he met both Maya and your grandmother when I was asking you all those questions about him."

Braden nodded. "Yes, we came here once right after I moved in with him, before he started…."

Cade squeezed his hand again. "Right, so he knows about her and where she lives and hasn't mentioned her. So far, it's only been about you, and maybe me, because I'm living with you which is what pisses him off. He's obsessed with you, Braden, and I think his focus is pretty narrow at this point. Coop was just asking as a precaution."

Braden nodded. It made sense. "Okay. If you're sure."

"I am, but I think that we should show the security team pictures of him, current and past, and let them know to be on the lookout. I also think you should tell your grandmother about him, again, just as a precaution, but that's up to you. I know you said you don't want to worry her, but in the end, warning her to be on the lookout might be wise."

Braden wanted to argue, but he knew Cade was right. He sighed and his shoulders fell in defeat. "You're right. If we don't warn her and something happens, I'd hate myself."

Braden pulled his phone from his pocket and dialed. "Nana, we're here. Sorry we're a few minutes late. Where are you right now?"

"The Commons, dear."

Braden sighed and rubbed his forehead. "Of course you are. Okay, we'll be there in a few."

Braden hung up and looked at both Cade and Cooper in resignation. "She's in The Commons which is the area where everyone socializes, plays games, and watches TV. Basically, she's having us come into the lion's den where she'll be holding court, waiting to show us off."

Cade laughed. "Lion's den?"

Braden shook his head. "You think I'm joking, but you'll see. She draws people in because she makes people laugh, includes everyone, and makes everyone feel important, but it also means she's always the center of attention."

Cooper stood and waited by Braden's door. Cade leaned over, pulled Braden's chin towards him, and laid a quick kiss on his lips. "Coop will come in with us, but he'll check out security, talk to them, and give them the pictures."

Braden shrugged. "Okay, let's head in then, no sense in delaying the inevitable."

Cade

Cade, fingers entwined with Braden's, laughed and thought it couldn't be that bad. Then they walked into The Commons, and he realized Braden had been spot on. The Commons was a huge room with areas designated for different activities. There had to be at least thirty people, all busy doing different things. A tiny little spitfire of a woman stood and walked toward Braden with arms outstretched. "Braden! My boy! Give me some sugar!"

All eyes turned towards them, and several people stopped what they were doing to wander closer while Braden pulled his hand from Cade's and walked forward to greet his grandmother. Braden, looking strangely tall beside this little bit of a woman, gathered her in a fierce embrace and actually lifted her right off her feet, causing her to giggle like a young girl. Cade heard him murmur, "Nana, you're looking beautiful as ever."

She blushed like a schoolgirl. "Oh, you!"

Braden put her back on her feet, and she cupped his cheeks in her hands and looked at him for long moments while more of her friends drew near. She narrowed her eyes at him. "There's something going on that you don't want to tell me about. I can see the strain on your face. We'll discuss it at lunch. In the meantime, introduce me to your handsome new man. My, he's rather big, isn't he?"

Braden shook his head. "I can never get anything past you." Cade watched as Braden turned around and held a hand out to him. He stepped up next to Braden, clasped his hand, and entwined their fingers. Braden smiled. "Nana, this is Zavier McCade, Zavier, this is my Nana, Clara Cross."

Cade reached for her left hand before she could raise her right one to shake his. She lifted her left hand, looking surprised, and blushed as Cade kissed the back of her hand. "Mrs. Cross, it's an honor to meet you, ma'am."

"Oh, none of that Mrs. and ma'am stuff. Call me Nana!"

Cade winked. "Yes ma'am, Nana it is."

Nana smiled. "You're a cheeky one, aren't you?"

Cade gave her a devilish grin. "Guilty, ma'am."

Nana harrumphed. Before she could lead them deeper into The Commons to become fodder for the old gossips, Braden caught her. "Nana, as much as we'd love to stay and chat with all of your friends, I'm getting hungry and need to check my blood and eat fairly soon."

Nana narrowed her eyes. "Never was one to be the center of attention, more like my Ronald that way. I guess we can go now, let me just get my bag and my coat."

She walked off and grabbed both and brought them back over. Cade helped her into her coat, causing another blush, then Braden held his left arm out for her to hold on to. Cade guided them, his left hand at Braden's lower back, and led them both out to the car where Braden did his best to get her to sit in the front, but she refused. Braden opened the back door for her, helped her into her seat, and handed her the seatbelt. He shut the door and almost bumped into Cade who had been waiting there to do the same for him. Braden smiled at him, and Cade helped him into his seat, belted him in, shut the door, and walked around to the driver's side. As Cade passed by Cooper's car, he shot a glance inside to be certain he was ready to go.

He reached into the compartment between their seats and pulled out Braden's testing kit. While he started the engine, he asked Braden's grandmother something about the retirement community and her friends, and they sat in the idling car until Braden had given himself his injection. During the drive, Braden's grandmother continued to regale them with funny stories about her friends. Cade enjoyed her, seeing some of her in Braden, endearing her more to him.

He pulled Braden's hand back over to his side of the car, squeezed it, and rested his hand on his lap. It didn't take long to get to the steakhouse Nana had requested. As they were getting out of the car to walk into the restaurant, Nana shocked them. "You might as well invite your friend in. The one who's been following us. That way you can all fill me in on what's really going on."

Cade rarely found himself surprised, but Nana had done it. Braden grinned up at him. "Yeah, she's a noticer. She probably saw you share a look with Cooper in the parking lot."

Cade sighed and gave a jerk of his head to Cooper who followed them in, and they all settled down at the table the maître d' brought them to. After they all placed their orders, Nana gave Cooper a thorough once over. "Are you Cooper, Maya's brother?"

Cooper raised a brow and smiled. "Yes, ma'am."

"Well, you look just like her, it's not that hard to figure things out, if you pay attention. And, if I remember correctly, you're ex-military and co-owner of a security business. I'm assuming Cade is the other owner?" At their nods, she continued, "Now that that's out of the way, I think I deserve an explanation for what is going on with my grandson."

Cade clasped Braden's hand as he explained about the notes he'd been getting and everything that had happened since. He was proud of Braden for laying it all out there on the table and telling her it was Eric. When he was done, they all sat in silence as their food arrived.

Barely glancing at her meal, Nana admitted, "I always hated that nasty piece of work."

"Nana."

"Well, I did. He was always trying too hard, so smarmy and fake."

Braden gaped. "Why didn't you say anything?"

"I did, after the first time I met him, before you even moved in with him. I told you I didn't like him that he was too charming."

He watched as Braden flopped back in his chair in defeat. "I guess you did. At the time, I just thought he was trying to make a good impression and was nervous. I should have listened to you. I'm sorry now that I didn't."

They continued to discuss the steps Cade and Cooper were taking to ensure Braden's safety, and Cooper showed her the same pictures of Eric that he'd shown the security personnel at her retirement community. Throughout all of this, Cade could see Nana was taking stock of him, glancing at his arm draped over Braden's chair, and when they made eye contact, she narrowed her eyes at him.

"What is your interest in my grandson? I don't want you to take advantage of him while he's dealing with this. It doesn't seem like the best time for a new relationship. Do you want him to feel indebted to you? And exactly how old are you?"

He was about to answer when Braden jumped in. "Jesus, Nana, what's with the inquisition? We're together and will remain together after Eric has been caught. You don't know him and shouldn't be judging him. Don't be rude."

Cade reached over and grabbed Braden's hand in his, leaned down to Braden and spoke softly, though not so quietly that Nana couldn't hear him. "She's not being rude, Bray, she's being protective, and I'd think much less of her if she wasn't asking some of these questions. She can ask me anything she likes. I want to set her mind at ease."

Nana apparently took that as a challenge. "Are you after my grandson's money?"

Cooper had been drinking some water and choked on it when she asked that question. He felt Braden stiffen. "Nana, that's enough!"

Nana ignored everything else but him. Cade grinned. Damn but he liked this woman. "Ma'am, to answer one of your first questions, I'm thirty-eight, so ten years older than Braden. And to be quite honest, I wasn't aware he had any money until he told me himself today."

Nana raised an elegant eyebrow and continued to wait. Cade smiled again. "I assure you, ma'am, I am not after your grandson's money. His money is actually the furthest thing from my mind. Foremost on my mind is keeping him safe."

"Why should I believe you?"

Cade saw Cooper stiffen, and before he could stop him, Cooper demanded, "Tell them, Cade."

"Cooper, stay out of this."

Cooper leaned closer to Braden. "Can you hand me your watch?"

Cade gave him a warning stare. "Cooper."

Braden was obviously confused, and from the look of it, had a headache brewing, but he handed his watch over. Cooper took it and removed his own, handing them both over to Braden's grandmother who took them but didn't look at them. He gritted his teeth when Cooper spoke to Braden's grandmother.

"It's pretty hard not to be protective of Braden. I get it. You raised a really good man, but Cade's a really good man as well. He was my commanding officer, and he's saved my life more times than I can count. He'll save your grandson's as well if it's necessary."

Cooper leaned back, ignoring Cade's glare, and focusing his attention on Nana. "Cade's not after your grandson's money. He has more money than he'll ever need. Turn the watch over that's all metal, that's mine."

Cade turned and watched reality dawn on Braden's face. He turned to Cade, mouth agape. "Are you serious?"

Cade let out a gentle huff of air, still frustrated with Cooper. He'd have told Braden in his own time, it didn't need to be done like that. "It's not really something that comes up in everyday conversation."

Cade dug into one of his cargo pockets and pulled out a tiny metal rectangle case that he opened up and removed something from. He took Braden's hand and dropped a couple of Ibuprofen into it, leaned forward for Braden's water and handed that over as well.

Braden just stared at the pills then back up at him for several moments before he took them. Nana finally looked at the back of Cooper's watch, where the McCade family seal was stamped.

Cooper explained about the seal. "Cade's great grandfather and grandfather were watchmakers, his father as well. They did okay for themselves, but it wasn't a household name. Cade's father was in the military and took over the watch business when he retired and basically got the whole family involved in remaking the brand and creating McCade Military Watches–"

His voice held an edge when he interrupted, "Cooper, that's enough. She doesn't need the whole story."

Nana raised a brow. "Might as well let him tell it. He's on a roll now."

Cade rubbed his face as Cooper continued. "To make a long story short, they started selling them to the military as specialized watches then moved on to civilians. So, if Cade never wanted to work another day in his life, he'd still have enough money for their children and probably their children's children to live on."

Cade shook his head in exasperation. "Are you done?"

Braden's eyes popped wide. "Our *children*?"

Cade's focus went from Cooper to Braden and saw the shocked look in his eyes. Cade's face softened, looking at his boy, who had been overwhelmed by everything since they'd walked into the restaurant. He leaned over and tipped Braden's chin up. He smiled gently and teased. "What? You don't want to have children with me?"

Braden's mouth dropped open and he sputtered, "I... What?"

He laughed, leaned in, and kissed Braden. "I'm teasing you. That's getting a little ahead of ourselves, even for me. Cooper was just trying to make his point, against my wishes, I might add." That last bit he said much louder, and Cooper just shrugged.

Cade glanced at Nana who had been watching them. Her demeanor had softened, and he realized something must have changed. "Did that set your mind at ease?"

Her smile was tentative as she handed Cooper and Braden their watches and met Cade's eyes again when she answered. "No. Not really. Your behavior towards him did. I'm sorry if I offended you. I'm scared for him. He's the only thing I have left, and he means everything to me."

Cade smiled. "I completely understand, Mrs. Cross. He means the same to me. I'd never hurt him. Mind if I ask what changed your mind?"

"You did."

Cade raised a brow, confused, but she continued, "I should have paid closer attention before reacting. You're gentle with him, you're attentive, and you take care of his needs. All I had to do was watch you interact to see what you both have is real. You could tell before I could that he wasn't feeling great, and I can read him pretty well."

Cade rubbed his thumb between Braden's eyebrows. "He's overwhelmed and stressed out, having to tell you everything. When a headache is starting, he gets these tension lines between his brows."

Nana gave Cade a sweet smile, one that lit up her face. He blinked at the unexpected acceptance in her eyes. "I really am sorry for being so rude. I hope you can forgive me because I have a feeling that you're going to be in his life for a long time to come."

Cade smiled widely. "There's nothing to forgive. Your grandson means everything to me."

Tears came to Nana's eyes, her voice watery as she managed a tremulous smile. "Well, now, that makes me incredibly happy for you both."

The rest of the lunch went smoothly. Nana told stories of Braden when he was younger and had them all in stitches. Cooper left several minutes before the check arrived to scope the outside before they left. They constantly had to check the cars for any sign of electronic location devices in case Eric was tracking their movements, or worse. While that was highly doubtful, it *was* a possibility they had to take seriously and remain constantly vigilant.

Braden and Cade brought Nana inside her building to ensure she got home safely. Cade went to move back and give them some private time for a couple minutes, but she placed her hand on his arm to stop him. She reached her arms up and damned if he didn't feel like a giant next to her tiny frame as he bent down for her proffered hug. "Please, keep him safe for me."

"You can count on it, Nana. I'll guard him with my life."

She patted him gently on the cheek. "Take care of yourself too. He'll need you after this is all said and done."

Cade grinned and kissed the back of her hand again. "I need him too. It was so nice to meet you."

Nana blushed and smiled. "You too, Zavier."

Braden hugged her as well, and they said their goodbyes. Cade led Braden back to the car and they were on their way. It wasn't long before Braden asked, "Will you tell me more about the watches?"

Cade told him of that night, years ago, when his family was all sitting around their big kitchen table on some holiday or other between deployments which was so very rare. They'd been taught about McCade watches from the time they were young. Cade had just begun his career as Special Forces and his unit had gone on a few missions, and he'd realized he wanted some kind of watch that would help him on assignment. He mentioned it to his family and a discussion ensued about what everyone thought was needed in a watch from a military and technical standpoint.

Pretty soon his grandfather and father were talking about how they could try to come up with something then his mom joined in. She was a retired electrical engineer, and he had followed in her footsteps when he went to West Point to study micro-electrical engineering. He knew he wanted to be in the Army from a young age, but his parents had rules about getting an education. They could join the military, but it was understood that they would not delay their college education to do it. So he killed two birds with one stone, knowing when he graduated, he'd be required to be on active duty.

His sister was a computer engineer, so she started discussing making it a sort of "smart watch." That dinner lasted hours, everyone had input and wrote down ideas, requirements, made drawings. He smiled remembering it, the excitement was palpable sitting there discussing this new idea. They'd always been a close family, but there was something magical about that night, something that drew them even closer together.

One of his younger brothers, studying to be a doctor at the time, mentioned it would be good to be able to have the watch monitor your heart rate and temperature and also be fully waterproof. His older brother decided it should be secure with thumbprint technology in case they were stolen or lost. His youngest brother said that the data from the watches should have the option to be monitored from another location, meaning base ops could keep track of the information real time. Cade wanted there to be a location device so troops wearing one could be located which was actually the impetus for his development of the tracers that Custos Securities used and would soon be selling, now that all the legal patent issues were dealt with. He also wanted a way to communicate with his unit using code while on missions via their satellite uplink.

After everyone had given their input and they'd mapped out how each of their ideas could be placed into the hardware or software of the watch, they began the tough work of actually creating multiple prototypes. Their family was large, and they all took to working on it. Even while on deployments, they were able to keep up with communications and further development.

Once they had their prototypes, they tested them within their own military units to see how they held up and if they had included everything they needed to. There were several iterations of the prototypes as a result of the testing, and they finally were able to come up with their final military watch prototype. His father, who was a retired colonel, had enough clout to get their final prototype seen by the upper echelons in the Army. They offered steep discounts to the military to get their foot in the door, and the rest was history.

Braden's watch was a Militis watch, also known as the soldier's watch, which was sold to civilians. The watch Cooper had was the Bellator watch, also known as the warrior's watch, which was sold to the military. The watch he wore was called the Imperator watch, also known as the emperor's watch, which was the type only his family wore. Like the military, they had used the Latin language to name each of their different watch types. He'd carried that naming convention through to their security company.

Braden, having listened raptly to the whole fascinating story, asked, "I can understand not retiring on the money from McCade Watches. But, why go into security at all? You're an engineer; why not do that?"

"I became an engineer because I had an aptitude for it; I became a soldier because I had a passion for it. My parents required us to get a college education even if we were joining the military, so I wanted to get it all done as quickly as possible. Choosing West Point was an easy decision. I was getting education and training at the same time. Being in the military is about serving your country, but to me, being a soldier was about protecting our country's civilians. Our security business is a continuation of that.

"I didn't want to continue in a capacity where there was more red tape and politics, I didn't want to be in the FBI, CIA, or be a cop of some kind. That gets old regardless of my willingness to serve. There came a time, after I'd served for years, when I felt I wanted to make my own decisions regarding missions and what I wanted to take on. When I began to feel that way, I knew it was time to move on."

Cade could see an openness on Braden's face that hadn't been there even a day ago. He knew Braden's walls were coming down and he wasn't feeling such a strong impulse to protect himself from Cade. There were still some issues they needed to talk about, mainly the conversation he wanted to have with Braden regarding control, but things were falling into place and he was feeling really positive about where they were headed.

Chapter 16

BRADEN

The remainder of their day consisted of a lot of resting and watching a couple of movies. Cade knew the stress of the last several weeks was wearing Braden down, and he had no qualms with spending the rest of the day doing a whole lot of nothing if it helped his boy get some much needed rest. During the second movie, Braden had fallen asleep, so he'd gone to make them dinner while he rested, waking him afterwards with a soft kiss.

Braden licked his lips as if tasting Cade's kiss. "Mmmm, I like waking up like that."

He grinned. "I'll keep that in mind."

Braden sat up and Cade handed him his testing kit, watching while he gave himself insulin. Afterwards, Cade reached out to rub his stomach where he'd given himself the shot. They sat down to a dinner of chicken salads with lots of veggies. After their lunch of steak and potatoes, Cade knew they needed something light.

Once they finished eating, Cade broached the topic they'd put on the back burner. "Braden, I know this might be an uncomfortable discussion, but I think before we go any further into this relationship, we should have the conversation that worried you so much last night."

Braden rubbed his hands back and forth on his thighs, looking nervous.

"You're probably right. As much as I don't want to talk about it, we have to. Can I say something first?"

He nodded his head and encouraged Braden to continue. "I've been thinking a lot today about what you said last night about not blaming myself and I think you're right. I have to make a conscious decision to trust myself, to put that behind me and move on. Thank you for helping me see that."

Cade smiled and gathered Braden close, carded his fingers through Braden's hair, and kissed him softly. Braden's arms slipped around his waist, and they hugged each other tight.

Cade kissed the top of Braden's hair and whispered, "You're so strong and you *are* worth so much more than that."

They pulled apart, and he clasped Braden's hand and gave it a gentle tug. "Let's get comfortable in the other room so we can talk."

Cade led him into the living room, taking a seat and allowing Braden to choose where to sit. As much as he was happy Braden hadn't chosen one of the seats across the room, he *had* chosen to sit at the opposite side of the couch, too far away to touch.

Cade sighed inwardly. He knew he'd have to be happy with the seating arrangement for now. "Can I ask you a few questions?"

Braden bit his lip. "Okay"

"When you think of someone taking control, what do you think about?"

Braden tensed and crossed his arms over his chest. "I think of Eric telling me what to do, and what to wear, of being kept away from family and friends and being forced to have sex. I think about how miserable I was."

Cade ached to be able to touch Braden. "That sounds more like abuse. Did you have fun yesterday?"

Cade saw he'd surprised Braden with that question. "I had so much fun. It was the best date I've ever had and being able to talk to you last night was nice."

"What made you enjoy it so much?"

A peaceful smile came over Braden's face as he explained himself. "You took care of me all day and planned everything out, putting so much thought into it. And I think last night's conversation helped me turn a corner. I told you everything and you didn't blame me or judge me. I'm still a little scared about my own instincts, but I feel more like I can begin to trust myself again."

Cade relaxed into the couch, some of the stress leaving him. "I'm glad. I had such a great day with you. Did Eric take you somewhere special that you liked?"

Braden scrunched up his nose. "No, not really. He used to take me to this really nice restaurant in town. He was trying to impress me at first then he just wanted to be seen. It was pretentious and I hated it."

Cade frowned. "Did he ever pay attention to your wants and needs? It sounds like he manipulated you into doing everything his way, becoming someone you weren't."

Braden's hands fell to his lap and he picked at the hem of his pants. "No. I mean I think back on it now and even when we were just starting out, he'd manipulate everything so it *felt* like we were doing what I wanted, but we never did. It's embarrassing it took so long for me to realize it."

Cade nearly got up to pull Braden over into his lap, but restrained himself. He wanted Braden to come to him, needed it. "There's no reason for you to be embarrassed. Men like Eric are master manipulators and very adept at making it hard for people to see their true motives."

"Yeah, that's it exactly. I was never looking for signs, so I never saw them."

Cade nodded his head, glad that Braden could see the truth. "Do I do that to you? Think about it before you answer. Look for the signs. Have I been manipulating you?"

Braden sat staring at Cade, his brows drawn together. "No, not at all. You've always had my best interests at heart, even from that first night with my migraine. I just don't want someone taking control of my choices and telling me what to do, what to wear, and who to spend time with."

Cade's brow rose. "Are any of those things in your best interest?"

Braden scowled. "No, they're not."

Cade's expression softened, knowing Braden was frustrated with the conversation. "So keeping that in mind, with my track record with you, do you think that I would ever do those things?"

A pained look crossed Braden's features. "I don't know. I don't think so, but you said you wanted to control me, and I don't like that."

Cade's heart ached for his boy. "I don't blame you. I think our definitions of control are very different. When I asked you if you'd allow me some measure of control over you and your pleasure, I meant that I wanted to control the pace, ensure your needs were met so you could let go and trust that I would give you pleasure."

Cade shrugged and tried to make sure Braden understood how he felt. "You mentioned you'd always wanted to trust someone to dominate you in the bedroom. You've never had your needs met in that way. I have those same desires, Braden, and when you admitted that last night, it made perfect sense to me. I have the desire to dominate while you have the desire to submit."

Cade tilted his head, his gaze penetrating. He knew if he said the wrong thing right now, he could lose Braden completely. "Once we're able to trust each other implicitly, I think we'll be able to explore that together. I would love nothing more than to show you how a real Dominant and submissive relationship can be. Eric was an abusive manipulator. A true D/s relationship, if done properly, is fully controlled by the sub."

"But it's the Dom that makes the decisions."

"The Dom only has the amount of control the submissive allows. The submissive sets their limits and the Dom has to work within those agreed upon boundaries. I want to try that with you, Braden. But, if you never want to explore with me in that way, it's okay with me. I will respect that it's a hard limit, and it won't be brought up again. Do you understand what I'm saying?"

Braden looked down at his hands in his lap and nodded.

"Please look at me." Cade waited patiently and Braden finally met his gaze. "I need to hear the words."

"Y..." Braden cleared his throat and tried again. "Yes. I understand. I just don't know if that's something I'll ever be interested in after what I went through."

Cade smiled sadly. "I understand that. That's your decision to make. Let's chat about me taking responsibility for you. All right?"

Braden nodded again then realized what he'd done and looked Cade in the eye. "Yes."

Cade was happy that Braden understood his need for a direct answer. He was itching to pull him into his arms and hold him tight, but again he kept his hands to himself, for Braden's sake. "I don't want to take your choices away. I want to get to know you well enough to anticipate what you need and want and provide it without you having to worry about it or stress about it. I want to take care of you in that way because I think that's the kind of relationship you'd thrive in."

"That doesn't make sense to me. How would that even work?"

"We're still in the beginning of our relationship, so I don't know you as well as I want to. Because of that, I asked Maya what you like to do and I picked things to do I thought you'd like based on what she said."

Braden looked shocked. "What did she tell you?"

Cade chuckled. "Well, she said you weren't a fan of driving, she told me some of your favorite foods, she said you were adventurous, active, and you love old movies. Between that and what you've told me about yourself, I planned out the day with the hopes you'd have fun."

Braden bit his lip. "Why?"

"Why what?"

"Why'd you do all that?"

God, his boy was killing him. "Because I want you to be happy. Maya said that you stress internally about everything, even making small decisions sometimes. With work and your health, you've got so much on your plate, and the rest of it gets overwhelming and sometimes it makes you sick. Is that true?"

Braden nodded but looked up to meet his eyes and said, "Yes."

"I want to take on those responsibilities that stress you out, cause the anxiety attacks, and give you migraines."

Braden sat there in silence, as if trying to take all of this in and finally asked, "Why would you want to take that on? It makes no sense to me. You have your own burdens, your own stress."

Knowing it was probably too soon but needing Braden to understand, Cade told him the truth. "There are a lot of reasons, but the biggest of them, Braden, is because I love you."

Braden's eyes widened in disbelief. "You... What?"

Cade let out a soft sigh and repeated himself so Braden was left with no doubts. "I love you, Braden. It happened ridiculously fast, and I'm still wrapping my head around it, but that doesn't change the truth of it. I've fallen in love with you, so I want the best for you."

Cade watched a tear slip down Braden's cheek, but his boy didn't say a word. Braden looked so utterly shocked Cade was a little afraid of what he saw in his eyes. Cade hurried on to say, "I want you to always feel as good as you felt yesterday. Some people are made to take stressors and manage them. It's where I thrive, it makes me stronger and it's how I tick. You struggle with it because your body needs you to be on an even keel, or it backfires on you and makes you sick."

Braden was shaking his head. "You're serious about this."

He nodded. "Dead serious. Maybe if I take on those responsibilities, you won't have to run 10-15 miles a day just to get by. Or maybe it will allow you to fucking breathe, help you to thrive. It's not a magic pill, it won't fix everything, but it will make me happy and hopefully do the same for you. That's all I want. For you to be...."

Cade cut himself off when Braden abruptly got up from his side of the couch, a glazed look in his eyes, pupils blown, and took jerky steps towards him. Cade reached for him, panicked that he'd said the wrong thing. "Baby, what's... oomph."

Braden practically leaped onto his lap in a rush, kissing him so hard their teeth clashed. Cade gently pulled Braden back, hands cupping his face. Braden whimpered, and it was nearly his undoing. "What's this? Shhh, it's all right. I'll give you what you need; you have to know that by now."

Cade brought Braden close again with one hand in his hair, guiding him to his lips, and the other on Braden's ass, pulling him in. They kissed for several minutes; deep, passionate, voracious kisses. Braden finally pulled away and whispered, "Take control."

CADE

Cade was afraid he heard Braden wrong. His head was in a hazy fog of horny bliss that had his blood pumping and his heart beating out of his chest. "What?"

"Take control of me and my pleasure, just like you said. Do what you wanted to do last night."

"But…"

"No, no buts, please. I need it, I need you."

Braden met his eyes and what Cade saw in them had his hands gripping Braden's thighs and his cock leaping to attention. He stood, reaching around and grabbing Braden's ass with both hands. "Wrap your legs around me."

Once Braden had latched on, Cade headed towards Braden's bedroom before the other man could say another word. Braden looked like he was going to laugh, but then met Cade's eyes and the amusement faded away, a look of smoldering desire replacing it, nearly bringing Cade to his knees. Cade kneaded Braden's ass and when he heard the little groan coming from his boy, he pulled Braden's head back by his hair to expose his throat and began to kiss and suck that gorgeous column of skin. Braden moaned and squeezed his legs tighter around Cade's hips, he stopped in his tracks, unable to go any further, and pushed Braden's back against the wall, grinding their hips together.

Sliding his fingers into Braden's hair at the nape of his neck, he began a slow journey of licks and kisses from his neck to his lips. Braden's hands gripped his arms, fingers digging into his triceps, as if grasping for purchase. Braden rolled his hips, creating such delicious friction, Cade couldn't help but growl deep in his throat.

Using the wall to keep Braden in place, he released Braden's long hair and made quick work of unbuttoning Braden's shirt. Braden yanked the shirt over his head, taking his undershirt with it, and tossed them both on the floor. Cade grunted in satisfaction, pure need flashed through him at lightning speed. Gripping Braden's ass again, he walked them into Braden's room and lowered his boy to his feet beside the bed.

Braden surprised him and took a step back from him. "Z, wait."

Afraid he'd fucked everything up, he scrubbed his hands over his face, angry at himself. "Was I too rough? Am I moving too fast? The last thing I want to do is scare you. Jesus, it's the first time you've been with anyone since... Fuck... I'm sorry, baby."

Braden smiled, covering Cade's lips. "Shhh. Look at me. It was perfect. You were perfect."

When Braden lowered his hand, Cade sighed, grateful he hadn't completely fucked everything up. "Then wha–"

"I want to say it before we start. You need to know something."

Cade reached for Braden and pulled him closer. "What is it? You can tell me anything."

Braden took a deep breath, a look of such tenderness in his eyes that Cade's heart melted. "I love you, Zavier McCade. I'm in love with you."

Cade stopped moving, stopped breathing, and just looked down at Braden for several heartbeats, wanting to remember this moment, have it etched in his memory. "Say it again."

Braden's smile had never looked so sweet. "I love you, Z."

Cade crushed Braden to him, desperate to feel him, desperate to hold him. He clasped Braden's face, looking deep into his eyes as he bent down to kiss him softly. Brushing his lips back and forth over those beautiful, pouty lips set his heart racing again, but he kept it slow, kissing him languidly, tasting and learning his beautiful mouth as if it was the first time.

Trailing his hands down Braden's smooth, defined chest, he ran the backs of his fingers over his stomach, reveling in Braden's soft whimper. Slipping his hands around Braden's back, he slowly inched his way down over Braden's luscious ass cheeks to the backs of his thighs, taking his weight, and inch by deliberate inch slid Braden's body up along his until Braden's thighs were once again gripping his hips.

Cade got down on his knees on the bed, legs spread wide, and began a sensual assault on Braden's skin, caressing every inch of his body. Skimming his hand down Braden's lower back, he eased Braden onto the bed. Leaning over him, Cade saw his hunger reflected in Braden's eyes. Braden reached up to Cade's sides and began to pull his shirt up his torso, his enjoyment more evident with each slow inch of flesh he revealed. Cade sat back on his heels, unbuttoned his shirt, and reached behind his head to grip his shirt and undershirt, pulling them off and tossing them aside.

He reached for Braden again when his boy's soft sound of dismay stopped him, those gorgeous green eyes scanning over his scarred chest and arms. Finally close enough to see the damage to his body his clothes and most of his tattoos usually covered at first glance, Braden—somewhat frantically—began to unbuckle Cade's belt. With his help, Braden pulled off his pants, looking at the scars and tattoos on his thighs and lower legs.

A tear slipped down his cheek, and the tortured look in his eyes nearly broke Cade's heart. This wasn't what he'd wanted their first time to be like. He tipped Braden's face up. "I'm all right. It's done, over. This is just what comes from the type of life I've lived."

"So many tattoos. Are they all covering scars?" Braden's hands shook as they traced some of the scars on Cade's chest.

Cade reached for Braden and pulled him gently into his arms. "No. I do have a lot of scars. Shrapnel and other things associated with wartime wreak havoc on a body. It's why I started tattooing at first then I became addicted, and I wanted the art to tell a story, not my scars. I promise I'll tell you about everything. But please don't let this stop what we were doing. I need to be with you."

Braden nodded, took a deep breath, and let it out, his eyes refocused on

Cade's body, not the tattoos and scars. Cade saw the change in Braden, the flushing of his cheeks and the blown pupils reflecting his own arousal. He bent down to kiss Braden's lips, his cheek, his jawline, his neck, and inched down his sculpted chest to lick the flat disk of his nipple. Braden let out a hiss as Cade continued until both of Braden's nipples were hard points Cade took, one at a time, between his lips and teeth, causing Braden to squirm. Cade chuckled darkly. "So fucking sensitive."

Braden's hips shot off the bed nudging Cade's, a gasp falling from Braden's lips caused a satisfied growl to rumble through Cade's chest. "That's it. Don't hold anything back."

Braden moaned as Cade continued down his ribs to his stomach. He swirled his tongue around his belly button, eliciting another gasp from his boy. He did it again then a third time, causing Braden to whimper and writhe. "Mmm. Squirm for me."

Nipping down Braden's happy trail, he reached the button of his pants and popped it with a flick of a thumb. He pulled at the zipper, his eyes on Braden, who had tilted himself up to watch Cade. Grasping Braden's pants at his hips, he slowly slid them down his legs, kissing each inch of skin as it was revealed. He tossed them aside and took a slow meandering glance up Braden's body. He was slim, but he was well built and was filling out his boxer briefs to perfection. Meeting Braden's eyes and seeing his own lust reflected back at him, he leaned over and spoke in a hushed tone. "My mouth is watering for you."

At that, Braden groaned, raised his hands to cover his face, falling back on the bed. "You're gonna kill me with all this dirty talk. I've never been so fucking turned on."

Cade leaned down and laved at Braden's cock through his boxers. He breathed in deeply and groaned. "Gotta get these off of you so I can lick what smells so good."

He pulled Braden's boxers over his erection, watched it pop free and practically land on his lips. He grunted. "Fuck, look at you. So beautiful. So ready for me."

He grasped Braden's fat cock in his hand and tightened his grip on the upstroke as he licked his well-groomed sac, causing Braden's hips to arch off the bed. Hearing Braden moan softly, he encouraged him. "Let me hear you."

He kissed up Braden's cock to his cockhead and licked his slit, tasting his pre-cum. "You taste better than I imagined."

He couldn't wait any longer. He opened his mouth wide and took Braden's cock deep into his mouth, and when Braden groaned loudly and jutted his hips up to meet him, Cade moaned deep in his throat and tightened his hold. Braden shouted. "Oh fuck! Fuck yes!"

Braden moved his hips like pistons, his cock slamming in and out of Cade's mouth, and Cade loved every second of it, opening his mouth wider, relaxing his throat, taking him deep. He allowed Braden to fuck his mouth for several more strokes, but not wanting it to end too quickly, he stilled Braden's hips with his hands, pulled off of him, and chuckled as Braden groaned in frustration. "Not yet. I'm not letting you finish that quickly. Christ look at you, so greedy. Where's your slick?"

Braden pointed to his nightstand, his breath heaving in and out of his chest. He reached down to stroke his own cock, but Cade stopped him. "Mm-mmm, don't even think about it. That's mine. Look at me."

Braden didn't immediately comply. Cade grinned, realizing Braden's brain wasn't sending messages quite as quickly as it normally did. Cade let a few more beats pass, enjoying watching his man come back into his own head. "Braden, look at me."

When Braden finally came out of his haze enough to comply, he met Cade's eyes and smiled. Cade chuckled. "No touching yourself, baby. It'll end too soon, and I need to be inside of you when you come."

Braden sighed and watched as Cade pulled down his boxer briefs. Braden lost his smile and sucked in a breath as his eyes popped wide, clearly shocked at what he saw. "Fucking hell, Z! There's no way that monster cock is going to fit!"

Cade let out a deep laugh but Braden's jaw stayed lax and his eyes reflected a fear Cade didn't want his boy to feel. He crawled back towards Braden, lying on top of him, goosebumps skittering up his spine when he heard Braden's groan and felt him hook a leg behind one of Cade's, pulling him closer. Holding himself up on his forearms to avoid crushing Braden,

Cade tried to explain it away. "Bray, I'm six foot six and I weigh about two-hundred and sixty-five pounds. I'm proportionate."

Braden laughed and covered his face with his hands. "He's proportionate, he says... Jesus H... Okay, well let's put it this way, my asshole is proportionate, which means we are gonna have issues."

He nuzzled Braden's throat, making him shiver. Lifting his head from Braden's neck, he said, "Bray, look at me. We don't have to do a damned thing tonight, other than give each other hand jobs, blow jobs, or just have a hot frotting session. I can even bottom if you don't want me inside of you yet."

Braden was obviously completely shocked by that last bit. "You'd bottom for me?"

"I've only done it a couple times, but let me ask you something, my size aside. Do you want to feel me inside of you?"

Braden's eyes popped wide, again. "Are you kidding me? Of course I do! I couldn't wait until I saw that monster you're packing!"

Cade swept his fingers into Braden's hair and massaged his scalp, trying to ease Braden's sudden tension. "So why would I be any different? I haven't bottomed since I was learning what sex was all about in my teens, but you can bet your sexy ass that I want to feel you inside of me, eventually. How could I not? We can take some time to prepare you for me if you still want to try some other time."

Braden's brows drew together in concern. "Zavier, I've never topped, and I wanted you inside of me tonight. I still do. I ache for you, I just don't know how it will work, and I'm not even joking. You're huge. It scares me."

Cade smoothed out the lines of worry between Braden's brows. "Do you trust me?"

"With my life, you know that."

"Then trust me with your body. I won't hurt you, and I'll stop the second you tell me to. Let go and allow me to own your pleasure tonight."

Cade saw when Braden had made up his mind, but the timid, "okay," still hit him square in the chest.

Cade smiled wide. "Now, stop topping from the bottom. *I'm* in control of *you*, remember?"

Braden chuckled, his voice filled with snark. "Yes, Master Z. Do I need a safeword?"

Cade laughed. "Not yet, smartass." He dug his fingers into Braden's sides, hitting him in just the right spot to make him yell out and laugh as he tried to squirm away from his tickling fingers.

Out of breath, Braden wriggled. "Okay, okay! Shit, no more!"

Cade stopped his movements and brought himself flush with Braden again, rubbing his hard cock against Braden's flagging erection, waking him back up. He sobered when he earned a groan and felt Braden's hips flex and whispered softly in Braden's ear. "I'm gonna make you come so hard you'll see stars."

Braden moaned. "Please."

"Do you have any condoms? If not, I have some in my bag somewhere. It's been awhile for me, but I was tested three months ago and haven't been with anyone since. I can show you the test results."

Braden let out a soft gasp and shook his head. "I'm sorry, I wasn't expecting.... I don't have any, but I got tested right after I ended it with Eric and then again six months later. I'm disease free, and I can show you my results as well. Tomorrow?"

"Baby, I need you to feel safe. I'm happy to grab a condom or my test results."

Braden looked deep into his eyes, his expression earnest. "I feel safe. You wouldn't hurt me and I need you right now. I want to feel you deep inside of me. We can share our results tomorrow, right?" Cade leaned into his hand when Braden cupped his cheek and continued, "Please don't make me wait."

Cade sighed and nuzzled Braden's neck again. "Tomorrow. Don't let me forget." He watched Braden until he nodded and bit his lip. Shaking his head he whispered, "God, I can't resist you."

Braden raised his hips to rub against him and he groaned at the feeling of his fevered skin. He reached over to get the lube out of the drawer and as soon as he did, Braden flicked his nipple ring with his tongue. Cade grunted and thrust his hips against Braden's. He cursed under his breath, his voice a low rumble. "You little tease, do that again, but take it into your mouth this time and suck it like you mean it."

Braden's eyes closed at his words and Cade felt him shiver. Following orders, Braden pulled in that nipple ring with enough suction that he knew he'd have begged for mercy, and then his sexy boy flicked it at the same time and Cade dropped his weight down on Braden, curling his hips against Braden's, their cocks hard against one another, dripping pre-cum and becoming slippery.

He kept up his suction and flick routine and Cade groaned, nearly out of his mind with lust. He grabbed Braden's cock in his hand, aligning his own with it and squeezed their cocks together, fisting them both tightly as he whispered, "You wanna come like this? Keep doing what you're doing and we'll both come, just like this, all over each other. Bite me there, and I'll shoot off like a rocket right now. Oh, fuck, baby, you're so good at that."

He wasn't fucking joking. Much more and he'd embarrass himself. But if Braden wanted to come like this, he wasn't about to complain. His suction finally lightened up, and Braden gave him a quick flick at the ring and lay there panting, looking up at Cade. Breathing just as hard, Cade slowed the movements of his hips and eased off with his fist. They both looked into each other's eyes while they recovered, and Cade nuzzled his nose into Braden's hair. "Didn't want to come like that?"

Braden shook his head and one of Cade's big hands grabbed Braden's ass, his fingers dipping in the crease, eliciting a shiver from his boy. "You wanna come with me buried deep inside of you, pumping you full of my seed?"

Braden's breath hitched. He moaned, but managed to nod his head, yes. Cade smiled. "Good. That's how I want to come, deep inside of you, with you clenching your ass around my cock when you come."

Cade inched his way down Braden's body, kissing and licking his way down to Braden's cock and wedging himself between Braden's thighs, pushing them up and out to make room for his broad shoulders. Cade gripped Braden's thick cock in his hand and pumped it several times. He licked the tip and took the head in his mouth, then swallowed him deeper. He cupped Braden's sac in his hand, squeezed and massaged it softly and drew Braden all the way in. He began a slow rhythm, took Braden all the way in and pulled back until the head was at his lips, sucking on him and loving the sweet flavor of his pre-cum.

Braden's hips began to pump in a steady rhythm, and he moaned and reached down to run his fingers over Cade's hair. Cade continued on like that while he reached for the tube of slick and lubed up his fingers. With his other hand, he gripped Braden's cock at the base and twisted on the upstroke while continuing suction. He eased a slick finger gently to Braden's hole, pressing softly, repeatedly until he heard Braden moan. He pressed on the ring of muscle and felt a small amount of resistance before he was let in.

He pressed in and out, in and out of Braden's ass, mimicking what his cock would soon be doing. He kept sucking Braden's cock as he slowly added a second finger and spent some time moving them in and out, pleasuring Braden slowly with his fingers as he sucked his cock deep. His slow pumping movements with those fingers gave way to scissoring them to prepare Braden for his size. Keeping a slow pace, he finally added a third finger and he heard Braden shout out when he nudged his prostate at that angle. "Listen to you. You love this."

He nudged it just enough to hear Braden cry out, but backed off before his boy lost control and came. Again and again he built Braden up, only to back him off, using orgasm control and denial to get Braden ready, his boy moving with him, so eager, whimpering and panting. "Your ass is so greedy for more. I'm gonna give you what you need."

He finally deemed Braden ready for him. He brought him almost to the brink one final time, but before he edged him back again, he got himself in place, slicked up, and slid the head of his cock inside of Braden before he knew what had happened. He pressed still deeper and Braden moaned and bucked underneath him. He leaned down to Braden, whose eyes were closed tight, breath heaving. "Fuck, you feel good. Tell me if it hurts, baby."

Braden's eyes popped wide open with a gasp, and he clamped down on Cade in response. Cade groaned at the tight heat surrounding his cock head. He wasn't even halfway in but his breath came faster, and he met Braden's eyes. He knew immediately Braden was starting to worry, and he soothed him by gripping his long hair and holding him in place while he talked to him. "You're doing so good. Don't tense up. Feel me inside of you. Make room for me inside of you. Relax your muscles and bear down a little bit for me."

Cade pulled out a fraction and eased in a bit more. "That's it. So good. Relax your whole body for me. Breathe in and out slowly. You've got me. Oh, fuck, Braden, you feel so amazing. You're so tight. So fucking tight."

Cade repeated the process, pulling out incrementally and easing in even further. He was more than halfway in, and Braden had finally started to push back against him for more. He still gripped Braden's hair but reached between them with his other hand and gripped Braden's swollen, hard cock and began to stroke him, slowly at first then a bit faster. Using that pleasure as a catalyst, he eased himself in even further, laid his forehead to Braden's and ground out, "Almost there. Almost. God, baby, you're doing so good. Taking me so deep."

Braden hooked his legs around the back of Cade's thighs, his heels digging into Cade's ass. Cade inched himself just a small bit further into his boy, so proud that he was taking him so well. But suddenly he felt Braden use his heels to impale himself on Cade's cock and Cade went still, scared to death Braden had hurt himself and feeling sick when Braden's breath caught in obvious pain.

His boy yelled out, "Oh, fuck!" And Cade watched as he went completely still, tears building in his eyes, breathing fast and hard. He stopped moving completely and cursed under his breath. "Baby, why? I was taking my time. Tell me when you're ready and I'll ease out. Dammit, I didn't want to hurt you."

Mad at himself for pushing too far, too fast and at Braden for forcing the issue, Cade's heart hammered in his chest, his muscles locked up tight. He lowered his head down beside Braden's, and he felt Braden clasp the back of his head lightly, skimming his hands over his hair, and bringing a hand down to cup his face. At the slight pressure, he lifted his head up to look at Braden and was surprised by the gentle smile there. Braden brought Cade down for a slow kiss, one that he drew out with slow easy movements, both of them careful not to move any other part of their bodies.

He was about to apologize again, but at the shake of Braden's head, he kept quiet and just waited him out. Finally, Braden took a deep breath. "I couldn't wait. It only hurt for a few seconds, and now I just feel so fucking full. Don't you dare pull out after all this work!"

Cade huffed out a soft laugh and pressed his forehead against Braden's. "God, I love you, but you're going to be the death of me." He sucked in a breath and kissed Braden's neck, his heart so full. "Tell me when you're ready for me to move."

"Oh, god, yes, please move."

Cade didn't ask twice, he slowly slid himself part of the way out and then slowly back in. They both groaned. Again Cade pulled out, this time pushing back in a bit faster, and again, all the while whispering to Braden. "You feel so good. So tight."

He leaned back a bit to get a better angle for Braden and from his hoarse moan, Cade knew he'd hit Braden's prostate. He pushed in again at that angle and pulled back out, reached down and fisted Braden's hard cock and began thrusting in at the same time he was on his upward stroke. Braden's hips were moving faster now and he whimpered. "Oh god. So good, Z. That feels so good!"

Cade kept up a punishing pace. The tight grip he had on Braden's cock turning his words to moans. Braden reached down and grabbed onto his pistoning hips and met Cade's hard, fast thrusts. Cade had never felt anything like it. He'd never been in such a tight, hot sheath, and he was getting close to losing it completely, but wouldn't even think of it until Braden had come. When he knew Braden was close, he tipped his pelvis just a bit further upwards, grasped Braden's cock harder, twisted on the upstroke and ordered, "Look at me, baby. That's it. You're ready. I want you to let go. Let go and come for me."

That's all Braden had needed, permission to let go. Cade watched as the words released a hold Braden had kept on himself. His boy lost it, his cum shooting out onto his stomach, his chest, even his neck and Cade had never seen anything so beautiful. Braden threw his head back in pleasure as he shouted out his release, his body a paroxysm of ecstasy.

Each of his boy's spasms resulted in a tighter rhythmic grip of Braden's ass on his cock and had Cade's own orgasm tingling in his spine, zinging down through his body, and erupting from his dick, pulse after pulse, deep into Braden's hot sheath. He released Braden's spent cock and let out a deep growl of his own and caught himself on his forearms before he let his full weight fall on Braden.

Braden was apparently having none of that and tugged at Cade's elbows until his body fully rested upon his lover. Cade sighed in contentment as Braden's arms and legs both curled around him, and his whole body shook in satisfied spasms that he couldn't have stopped if he'd wanted to.

Cade wrapped his arm under Braden's lower back, his other hand tangling in the long hair at his nape, and was just about to turn them both over when Braden shook his head and whispered, "Please, don't."

Cade gripped Braden's neck. "Don't what, baby?"

Braden let out a whimper and tightened his legs around Cade's hips. "Don't pull out. Not yet. Not ready yet. Need you still." The words were muffled by Cade's shoulder and he could feel Braden shake his head and grip him harder to keep him from pulling away.

Feeling such tenderness for his boy, Cade clasped him tighter as well and whispered sweetly, "I'm not, Bray, I'm just going to roll us over so that you're on top. I don't want to suffocate you. I'll stay inside of you as long as you want me there."

He pulled Braden into him, holding him tightly so they wouldn't be pulled apart as he flipped them over, realizing only then he was close to the foot of the bed. He reached up towards the pillows and pulled the comforter over them both as Braden's spasms had morphed into shivers.

Braden rested his head on Cade's chest. "You're still hard. How is that even possible?"

Cade's fingers shifted through Braden's soft hair. "Only half hard, which is normal for me for a while. You still feel so good, so tight and hot around me. I've never come so hard in my life."

Braden hummed in agreement. "Me, either. I didn't see stars, like you promised, but my vision completely blacked out on me for a few seconds."

Cade chuckled. "Well, I guess I have a goal for next time."

Braden burrowed in. "Next time will have to wait. I can barely move."

"Good. I don't want you to." Cade ran his hands up and down Braden's replete form, unable to stop touching what was his.

They both lay there for some time, half dozing, half caressing and kissing tenderly until Cade softened fully. He rolled Braden back over and went to the bathroom to get a warm washcloth and cleaned Braden making sure he was comfortable for the night. Walking back into the bathroom as he cleaned himself off, he noticed Braden's testing kit and nudged Braden awake. "Baby, you need to test before we go to sleep."

Braden sat up, tested, and gave himself a shot as Cade went into the hallway to get Braden's shirt and picked up the other clothes that were strewn about the floor. He was about to lay back down when Braden mentioned brushing their teeth. Cade headed into the guest room to brush his and was surprised when Braden ended up following him a minute later. He walked into the bathroom and Cade glanced over in surprise as he was lifting up the toilet lid to take a piss. Braden turned bright red and stammered, "Shit, I'm sorry. I should have knocked."

He tried to hightail it out of there, but Cade caught his arm before he could leave and pressed his boy's naked ass up against the cold bathroom counter, the little "eep" making him chuckle. He kissed the stew out of him before he pulled slowly away. "It won't be the last time you walk in on me taking a piss. What were you going to say?"

After that kiss, Braden looked like could barely remember his name so Cade gave him a minute to respond chuckling again at how adorable a discombobulated Braden was. He saw Braden's eyes focus and smiled as he said, "Oh, I was just going to see, um, you know…."

Cade slid a finger down Braden's chest. He was cute as fuck, and he was loving this shy side of his lover. He nudged himself closer and crowded into Braden. "What, baby?"

Braden spoke in a rush, like he needed to get it out or he'd lose his nerve. "Um, do you want to move your bags and toiletries into my room while you're here, so you don't have to keep going back and forth?"

Cade knew his grin reached epic proportions by the dazed look in Braden's eyes. He bent down to kiss Braden's sexy neck and murmured, "Bray, are you asking me to move in with you?"

He lifted his head in time to see Braden's shocked look, all wide eyes and stammering mumbles, Cade laughed and pulled Braden into a tight embrace. "I'm teasing you, baby. And the answer is yes, to anything, to everything."

Braden softened against him and hugged him back fiercely before darting shyly back to his room to get ready for bed. Cade took a piss, brushed his teeth, and gathered his toiletries. He walked into Braden's bathroom and put his dopp kit on the bathroom countertop, kissed Braden on the back of the head, and went back to the guest room to get the rest of his stuff. He returned five minutes later carrying his roughed up, army issue duffle bag on his shoulder and looked at Braden questioningly. Braden walked into his closet and cleared a space on the floor. "Do you want me to clear out some space; a drawer, some hangers, or something?"

Cade glanced up from the spot where he'd kneeled as he unzipped his bag, and couldn't help but smile at Braden's blush. "No. I hung up a few things in your closet in the other room. I'll bring them over and hang them in here. Everything else can stay in the bag. I'm used to living out of this thing."

Braden nodded and walked back into the bedroom as Cade brought in a few items to hang up in Braden's closet. Cade tugged Braden's shirt from his hand just as he was about to pull it over his head. "Don't. I want to feel your chest against mine tonight."

They both crawled into bed, wearing only their boxer briefs. Braden turned off the nightstand lamp, and Cade gathered Braden close. "I'm assuming you'd like to run, since we haven't all weekend."

"Yeah, I wanna get three to five miles in tomorrow morning, after I get some stuff baked."

Cade grabbed his watch from the nightstand where it sat beside his handgun and set the alarm to five a.m. Braden tossed one of his legs across Cade's hip, and Cade grabbed him behind the knee and dragged Braden on top of him until their hips were aligned, and yanked the duvet up over Braden. Braden's head popped up with his eyebrows raised, in a silent, WTF? Cade grinned and pecked Braden on the lips. "You feel good as a blanket. I want you on top of me tonight. Love you."

Braden sighed as if in resignation, but Cade saw the secretly pleased little grin he couldn't hide as he tucked his head under his chin. Braden wiggled around a bit until he got comfortable, and was just about to nod off when Cade heard him mumble sleepily, "I love you too. Don't blame me if I drool all over you."

Cade chuckled and reached his hand up to cup the back of Braden's head then ran his fingers through his hair and left them there. "Wouldn't dream of it. Sleep now, baby. I've got you."

As easy as that, Braden was out like a light and Cade didn't take much longer to pass out himself, looking forward to waking up with Braden in his arms again.

Chapter 18

BRADEN

The following morning Braden woke to the feeling of calloused fingers running softly up and down his naked back. He breathed in deeply and realized he was still lying on top of a very aroused Cade, so he squirmed a bit to tease him. At the deep groan that came as a result, Braden lifted his head to look into Cade's gorgeous blue eyes and was a bit spellbound by the intense look he saw there.

His own cock began to stir, and he couldn't help but move his hips again, causing Cade to grip his ass cheeks, massage them in his large hands, and grind Braden's cock against his own. Braden leaned over Cade, who reached up and threaded his fingers through Braden's hair and brought him down for a kiss.

Trailing his lips down Cade's neck, nipping along his collarbone and licking down to a nipple ring, Braden took the ring in his mouth and sucked. Cade moaned, and his hips pumped up against Braden's. Braden gave the other ring equal attention and reached between their bodies, lightly stroking Cade's cock through his boxers.

Cade sat up so Braden was sitting astride him, his cock straining against his boxers. Braden gazed at Cade's gorgeous, stubbled face and traced the contours, leaning in to claim his lips. Cade scooped Braden off his lap and onto the bed beside him, glancing down at his boxer briefs. "Take them off."

Braden immediately removed them. Cade's eyes, at half-mast and so filled with sexual promise, met his. "Now mine."

He made quick work of Cade's boxers and was flipped over on the bed. Braden had never had his neck so thoroughly kissed, licked, bit, and sucked. His arms and legs were covered in goosebumps, and he squirmed as shivers wracked his frame. Cade whispered in Braden's ear, "Did I feel good last night, deep inside of you?"

Braden's breath hitched, and he moaned. "Yes, god yes."

"Do you want me there again?"

Braden's grip on Cade's sides tightened. "Yes, right now. Please."

Cade's sucked in a breath, his hips pressing down on Braden's. "Oh, baby, you don't know how much I want that, but I don't think you're ready. I don't want to make you too sore."

"I want it. It felt so good."

"I know, but I'm not gonna chance it." Cade met Braden's eyes. "I'll make you feel good though. Would you like that?"

Braden closed his eyes, pushed his head back into the pillow, and nodded as Cade gently took his earlobe in his mouth and sucked. He let out a gasp and gripped Cade's sides again, not knowing if he was trying to push him away from sensory overload or pull him closer for more. Their hips aligned, and when Cade nudged his pelvis into Braden's, Braden opened up his legs to make more room for Cade to nestle between them. Cade began a rhythmic pulsing of his hips into Braden's. To Braden it felt like a dance, so intense the cadence caused his breath to hitch. The feeling of Cade's cock aligned with his, rubbing up and down against it, was almost enough to drive him over the edge. He heard little moans come out of his own mouth and clamped it down, embarrassed to be mewling and whimpering.

"Don't stop."

Braden opened his eyes, dazed. "What?"

Cade leaned over him, his gaze intense. "Do you know how fucking sexy those noises were? Fuck, Braden, I need to hear them. I want to know how my touch affects you."

Embarrassed, but wanting to please him, Braden stopped trying to control his reactions and relaxed, letting himself go. After several minutes of sweet torture, Cade reached over for the slick and lubed up his palm. Looking directly at Braden, he reached down, clasped both of their cocks together, and began to massage the lube onto both of them, squeezing them together from root to tip, up and down, using a tight grip as he moved his body in counterpoint to his massaging hand. After they were both thoroughly slicked up, he maintained the grip on them both, keeping them together, but lay back down on Braden, kissing him and talking to him.

"That's it. Listen to you. So fucking hot, those little moans."

Cade's hips were undulating against Braden's, faster now, his grip ever tighter. Braden was close. Everything about Cade was making it harder for him to keep himself under control. Cade was always so intense, so laser focused on his needs that Braden felt overwhelmed with that much concentrated attention. He'd always found himself shying away from such close scrutiny, but there was no shying away from Cade, he wouldn't allow it and that was a thrill in itself.

Cade's eyes became heavy lidded. "You like it when I talk to you, don't you?"

Braden moaned and nodded. He bit his lip and shuddered under Cade's weight, reveling in the firm grip he had on his cock.

"Uh uh, don't bite that pouty lip. Don't hold anything back. You trying to keep yourself from coming?"

Braden's breath hitched, and he moaned. "Yes."

Cade shook his head. "Don't. Let go if you're ready. Look at me. That's it. Feel me, squeezing you. Are you ready?"

Braden closed his eyes and whimpered. "Fuck, yes!"

Cade gripped Braden's hair tighter at his nape to keep him in place. "Keep your eyes on mine and come for me, Braden."

Braden met his eyes and as soon as he did, he let go. He felt such intense pleasure he gasped and cried out. Cade grunted and moved his hips faster, calling out, "Fuck, yes. I'm coming. Oh, fuck, fuck, fuck."

They came together, staring into each other's eyes, the orgasm lasting far longer than Braden expected. They were both breathing heavy, Cade kissed his lips, and when he spoke, his voice was low and guttural. "God, you're beautiful. That was so intense, baby."

Braden loosed his grip on the comforter and brought both of his arms up to hold on to Cade tightly, barely able to catch his breath and loving his man with an intensity that he couldn't put into words, so he didn't try. They lay there, just like that, for a good ten minutes before Cade pulled away enough to look down at Braden. "Take a shower with me?"

Braden smirked. "Okay, but no funny business."

Cade laughed, rolling off of Braden. "I need to work on my technique if you thought that was funny."

"The fuck you do." Braden mumbled as he moved to get up. "Don't change a damn thing."

They showered, washing each other and getting themselves ready for the day, dressed in running gear. They ate a small breakfast and dug out their test results, sharing them with each other as promised. After they cleaned up the kitchen, they went over to the café where Braden began his prep and baking. It felt good to get back into his routine. He enjoyed having a weekend off, but baking was something he absolutely loved, and he felt energized from his days with Cade. He set about getting as much done before his run as possible.

Cade

Cade went to the office and got some work done. He placed a call to Olivia to check in. Their office manager was a gem, and he knew damn well they were lucky to have her. She kept them running and organized, which was a feat in itself as Custos was becoming larger than Cade and Cooper had ever hoped it would be. He asked her for the real estate report he'd requested from her and several other things that were pending. She had a number of people below her that she managed in order to keep things running smoothly, and she caught Cade up on anything that needed tending to.

He checked his email for any new cases needing to be sent on to Micah to be assigned to the appropriate personnel and was happy no more had slipped through the cracks. He emailed Micah as well, asking him to call if he needed anything and telling him he would continue working the case here with Cooper, Sawyer, and Jackson until further notice.

He sent a message to his local crew and asked them to look into some of the reports he'd gotten from Olivia and get back to him with their findings. He searched his inbox and found the email from Landon he was hoping for with his full time availability beginning in three months along with a note saying he would be available part time to support Brody in the meantime. He would be an enormous help, even at part time. He'd proven that his twenty hours a week was more like an average man's forty hours a week, so he was well worth the wait and the healthy salary they would be offering him.

Having worked for a couple of hours, he stepped out to check on Braden, who was wrapping up his baking and ready to run. They were able to get four miles in and he could tell that Braden was not only happy about getting back into his kitchen but also to be running again. He loved seeing that happiness on his face and would do anything to keep it there. This situation with Eric needed to come to a head. He needed to provide Braden with closure on that part of his life before they could move forward together.

After their run, they went back to Braden's to shower and change for the day. Heading back over to the café, he got the feeling that they were being watched. He hurried Braden into the café, set the alarms, and was just about to talk to Braden about it, when he got a text from Sawyer. Making sure Braden was back at work, he took a seat at one of the counter stools in the kitchen to stay near Braden, and checked his phone.

Sawyer: Stick to him like glue. Something's off.

Cade: I'm feeling it too. Where are you?

Sawyer: Other side of town with J, but after my spidey senses hit, we got in the car and we're on the way back. ETA 30 minutes.

Cade: Good. See you soon.

He texted Cooper to get him to come to the café and went over to talk to Braden. "Hey, something's going on. Felt watched on the way over here from your place. I need you to promise me you won't leave the kitchen without one of us going with you."

The fear in Braden's eyes was palpable. "It'll be all right. Follow my instructions and you'll be fine. Sawyer and Jackson should be back in thirty minutes, and I'm giving Cooper a call. I'll put Cooper up front, to keep an eye out, and Sawyer and Jackson on perimeter search once they get here."

He finally got a nod from Braden. "I promise, Z. I'll stay right here."

Reassured that Braden would be safe with the security alarm set, Cade went to the office for a few minutes to call Cooper.

Braden

As soon as Cade left, Braden received a text. He removed his earbuds and pulled his phone out of his back pocket. The phone number was listed as unknown, and a sense of dread settled in the pit of Braden's stomach. A picture of Maya, wearing the same clothes she had on when she came into the café that morning, popped up. A second picture came through, this one of Nana that looked very recent as well. His heart started a fast beat, and his stomach lurched.

Unknown: Maya, Nana, and your new boyfriend can't be protected 24/7. Keep your mouth shut and do as I say.

Braden: What do you want, Eric? Why can't you just leave me the fuck alone?

Unknown: Did you think your little video would save you from me forever? What do I want? I want you. You're mine. And unless you want your precious Maya or little old Nana, or even your latest dick, to end up dead, you'll fucking do what I say. Tell me we understand each other. You don't want to piss me off, Braden...

Braden: What do you want from me?

Unknown: I want you alone, outside of the café in the next 10 minutes and leave your phone there. I've got my eye on the back door, so I'll know if anyone else is with you, and I'm armed, so don't fuck this up or one of them will have to go.

Braden: I've got someone in the back with me, I can't just leave without them wondering what I'm doing.

Unknown: It's either now, or I change my target from you to any one of them at any time. Their death would be on you. What will it be?

Braden: I'm coming. But I have to figure out how to leave without arousing suspicion. Give me more time.

Unknown: You have 10 minutes from now. Figure it out.

Tears flooded Braden's eyes as he tried to find a way out of it, knowing all the while it was impossible. He was on the edge of a panic attack, all the old feelings Eric stirred up in him dulled his vision. His hands were shaking and he started to sweat. And that all too familiar feeling of dread and inevitability took hold. If he told Cade, Eric might not get him now, but he could get Nana anytime, same with Maya. Eric was a patient man, he'd wait until they felt they were safe and then he'd make his move. The only thing that would ensure their safety was to go. They wouldn't be in danger if Eric had what he wanted. He had no other choice. He knew what he had to do.

His heart jackhammered in his chest, his hands shook, and his body had broken out into a cold sweat. Cade was just down the hall, could he go now? He just wanted to see him one last time, but if he did, he wasn't sure if he'd be able to get away again. He heard the door from the front of the café swing open, and he turned so that his back was to whoever was coming through. He made himself out to be busy and hoped whoever it was didn't try to talk to him because they'd know something horrible was happening the second they saw him.

He glanced quickly over his shoulder and spotted Maya heading past him. She must have thought he had his buds in because she kept going. He glanced back down to the countertop and tried to look involved in what he was doing.

Knowing very well he might never see Nana, Maya, and Cade again, he at least wanted them to know he loved them. He wanted to leave some kind of message, some way to let them know he was sorry. Not giving himself time to question his idea, he started a text to Maya that he would send when he walked out the door: "I'm so sorry to you both, and I love you both so much! Tell Nana I love her too and tell Z I'm sorry I lied. I couldn't let him hurt you guys. This is the only way I could guarantee everyone's safety."

He felt sick to his stomach as he looked at the time on his phone. He hardly had any time left. He was just about ready to leave when Cade came back from the way Maya had just gone. Surreptitiously watching him out of the corner of his eye, he realized that Cade was focused on his phone. He stuffed his hands into the dough that was rising in front of him and saw Cade tuck his phone in his pocket. He was careful to keep his voice neutral so Cade didn't become suspicious. "Hey, I'm really worried about Maya. She just headed into the office. Did you talk to her?"

"No, I was trying to get Cooper on the phone, and she passed me as I was coming out of there. What's wrong?"

"I don't know. But, my hands are covered with dough. Can you please go check on her? I'll wash my hands and head back there in a second, but she looked pretty upset."

"Yeah, I'll check in with her, but if she's upset, she'll want you, not me."

"I know. Be there in a couple minutes."

Cade went back to the office, and Braden knew he had seconds to get out of there successfully. He ripped off his apron and wiped his hands on it, grabbed his phone and ran to the back door. He turned off the alarm system to avoid bringing them out any faster and unlocked the door. He looked down at his phone, keyed in the code, and sent the text. He set the phone on the counter by the door, opened it, and left.

Once he was outside, he looked around frantically, not knowing what to do, until an old Honda Civic pulled up and the passenger door was flung open.

There sat Eric, a crazed gleam in his eyes. He quickly made his way over to the car and slipped in just as he heard his name being called. He looked through the driver's side window as he pulled his door shut and saw Cooper standing at the front door to their house, drawing his gun. He watched the look of horror slide over Cooper's face as Eric slammed his foot on the gas and they sped off.

Chapter 19

CADE

Cade lifted his phone from his pocket and saw that he'd missed Cooper's text.

Cooper: Sorry, was in the shower. Getting dressed and coming over immediately.

He breathed a sigh of relief and knocked on the now closed office door. Maya called out that he could come in and when he did, she held up a finger for him to wait, the phone sandwiched between her shoulder and ear. She started writing something down on an order form. "Okay, Mrs. Newton, I'll give your order to Braden, and he'll be in touch soon about pickup or delivery. If he hasn't seen you in a while, I'm sure he'd love to stop by and bring your order with him. He could even bring his handsome new boyfriend."

Cade raised his eyebrow at that and wondered what Braden meant when he said she seemed upset. She seemed fine.

"Nope, sorry, Mrs. Newton, that's all the info I can share at the moment, I have to get back up to the front! Talk to you soon!"

Maya hung up the office phone and grinned up at Cade. "Hi! Now you'll get to meet one of Braden's little old ladies in the neighborhood when you help him deliver an order for her little tea party."

"Sounds fun. Listen, Braden said he thought you looked really upset earlier, so he sent me in here to check on you and said he'd be back here in a couple minutes. Everything okay?"

Puzzled, Maya's brows rose. "That's weird. Yeah, I'm perfectly fine. Let's go see what he was talking about."

She picked up her phone from the desk, and Cade was just about to open the door for her when she sucked in a breath. "No, no, Braden."

Turning around to face her, he saw she was looking at a text on her phone. He grabbed it and read it then cussed, wrenching the door open, his heart seizing and his stomach twisting in knots. He ran out to the kitchen but knew he'd be too late.

He grabbed the back of his head with his hands, bent at the waist and roared. "FUCK! Goddamned mother fucker has Braden!"

Just then, Cooper ran in the back door and yelled, "I saw him get in the fucking car! I couldn't shoot, too many people around and he was sitting in the passenger seat. I could have easily hit Eric and hit Braden as well. I ran to the SUV to follow him, but the tires were all slashed. What the fuck happened?"

Maya walked over to Cooper and showed him the text from Braden then she noticed Braden's cell on the counter. While Cooper read the text and cussed another blue streak, Maya's hands shook as she handed the phone over to Cade. "He must have heard from Eric. His code is 9951." She took a deep shaky breath and went up front to close the café, herd any customers out, and send the girls home.

Cade grabbed Braden's phone and thumbed through the texts, seeing the conversation immediately. He set the phone down before he threw the thing and broke it into a million pieces. God, he should have had this conversation with Braden, warned him that Eric might try this, and promise Braden that they could protect Maya and Nana. He'd fucked everything up, he'd become too complacent, too wrapped up in their new relationship to pay attention. If Braden got hurt, or worse, it was on him.

Cade wanted to throw something, hit something, hurt someone, but he knew if he was going to get Braden back, he needed to get his fucking act together and start thinking. Sinking down into a crouch, looking at the floor between his knees, he placed his folded hands behind his head and took deep breaths to calm his heart rate. That's where he was when Jackson and

Sawyer came through the back door. He met both their eyes and he could see in their expressions they knew Braden was gone.

He watched them turn to Cooper, and he showed them Maya's phone and Braden's phone as well so everyone was up to speed. Maya came back from the front, looking dazed and wiping several tears away. Cooper opened his arms, and she ran into them. He murmured to her as he rocked her back and forth, "We're gonna get him back." And louder, "You hear me, McCade? We're gonna get your boy back, so take a minute to get yourself under control then get your game face on. We need our leader right now."

When Cade stood up, he was all business, the CO they'd served under. He had to lock all traces of Braden's lover away. All three of his men stood taller, more rigid, and Cade saw the change in them and was grateful.

He watched as Maya moved to Braden's workstation to clear the countertops of anything Braden had been working on. She probably needed to keep busy. He was just about to turn back to his men when he saw her pick up a few things and place them by Braden's phone. When he looked closer and realized what they were, his heart plummeted and any control he thought he had vanished as he saw his only chance of finding Braden slip away. There, sitting by Braden's phone, were his ring and his watch that he never wore when he was baking.

Goddammit. Why couldn't he have chosen something else to put a tracer on?

He leaned over and gripped the edge of the countertop and yelled at the top of his lungs until he had no breath. He heard some movement behind him then felt a hand clamping down on the back of his neck, exerting enough pressure there that he couldn't ignore it. He growled, "Get the fuck off me, Cooper."

Cade brought his left elbow up and easily got himself out of Cooper's hold. He stood up, breathing heavily, glaring at his friend. The wrecked look on Cooper's face did what nothing else could do, it calmed him down enough to focus on him. Cooper very quietly grated out, "Are you with me? You're all up in your head. I need you present, cap. Braden needs you present."

Taking a few deep breaths, he stepped back several paces, hands on his hips. He surveyed the kitchen, saw the worried faces, and cursed himself for losing it. Cooper was right, he needed to get his shit together. He turned back to Cooper, nodded his thanks, "Hand me his phone."

His men all approached him, ready to get to work. Cooper handed over Braden's phone and Cade spoke quietly to his men, giving instructions. He heard Layla and Zoe come into the kitchen after presumably cleaning up the front. They approached Maya and Zoe wrapped an arm around her while Layla held her hand. He looked in her eyes and saw her fear but also her strength as she swiped angrily at a tear that fell, jaw clenched. In control now, and ready to admit he'd fucked up, he approached Maya who looked up at him, more pissed off than he'd ever seen her. The other ladies moved aside, whispered that they'd wait in the break room, and he stood in front of her and apologized. She stood on her tiptoes and slowly wrapped her arms around him, her whole body trembling, "He's going to hurt him. I don't know if he can go through it all again. I'm so scared for him."

Fear pierced his heart, and he worried what she said was true but also knew Braden was far stronger than anyone ever gave him credit for. But he wasn't about to minimize his culpability "Me too, but remember how strong he is." He pulled away and looked down at her. "I'm sorry. I failed him. All I can say is that I'll find him. You have my word that I won't rest until I do. He's my life. He's my whole fucking world, Maya."

She nodded and they hugged again. When they broke apart, she crossed her arms over her chest, and whispered, "You didn't fail him. In his mind, he was protecting us. You aren't to blame for that."

Cade refused solace and shook his head. "I am. He didn't trust me to take care of him and to ensure your safety and his grandmother's safety. I should have had the conversation with him, explained that Eric might try this tactic, explained we could handle it if he did. Instead I got complacent and just let Braden get taken."

Maya shrugged. "Or maybe I'm to blame because Eric threatened me. Or maybe it's Nana. Yes, that's it, let's blame Nana. Makes just as much sense as you blaming yourself. No one is to blame except Eric. Don't do that to yourself."

Cade looked at her, so fierce and loyal. He loved her for how much she loved Braden. He sighed and nodded. "Yes, ma'am."

"That's better. Okay, so, you gave instructions to the guys, now give instructions to me. What do I need to do?"

Knowing she needed to stay busy, he said, "Call Nana. She'll be pissed if we don't tell her what happened, immediately. She'll want to be involved in some way. In order to keep her occupied and to help you out, I think it's best to keep the café open after today."

Maya looked at him, incredulous. "What? No, we can't, not without Braden. The café doesn't matter right now."

Cade clasped her shoulders in his hands. "Maya, think for a minute. It's what Braden would want, and I have a feeling it's what Nana will want. He said he learned everything he knows from her. She'll want to be here anyway, this way she has something to do."

She narrowed her eyes at him, but he continued, "She can take over Braden's duties. She can stay at Braden's place tonight. I won't be there until he's back with me anyway, but if I need a catnap later, I can do it in Braden's bed. I moved my stuff in there, anyway."

Maya's breath hitched and she sighed. "Okay, I'll call her right now. I'll ask the girls to help me get his place ready for her, so you don't have to worry about that. We'll help her settle in, and if she doesn't want to take her usual car service, I can go pick her up."

"If it comes to that, I'll send one of the guys with you as a precaution. I'll be working out of the office here, or the kitchen if we need more space, so let me know."

"I will." Maya threw the words over her shoulder as she was walking towards the bathroom. He followed and kept going down the hall toward the office and was just opening his laptop when he heard her shouting his name less than a minute later. He immediately jumped up from his seat and ran down the hall to get to her. When he spotted what she held in her hands, he was dealt another blow that he didn't know how to come back from.

He pulled Braden's testing kit out of her hands and stared at it. He looked up and saw tears filling Maya's eyes. He knew he should comfort her but didn't know how. He could see in her eyes how much worse this made things, and if his mind went down that road, he didn't think he'd be able to come back from it. But he had no choice. He couldn't be blind to all the repercussions of what could happen.

He took several deep breaths and kept control of himself by the skin of his teeth. He looked at her and made sure she saw confidence in his eyes before he spoke. "I'm going to find him, and he's going to be okay."

His body was a solid mass of tension and his hands shook, his anger palpable. Taking the kit with him as a reminder that he'd keep in sight until he had Braden back with him, he pulled his phone out of his pocket and called his younger brother Finn who answered on the second ring, "Zavier?"

"Yes."

A beat of silence. "What's happened?"

Cade clenched his teeth. "I need your help."

"You have it, tell me."

Keeping his voice calm and even was impossible. "I need to know what happens to a type 1 diabetic when he doesn't get his insulin."

"How many doses has he missed?"

Cade rubbed his palm back and forth over his head in frustration. "Let's say he had a dose this morning at five-thirty, ate a healthy breakfast, and ran four miles, but hasn't had another one and might not get another one."

"Ever?" Finn waited a few seconds, probably hoping that wasn't what he meant. "Diabetic coma, brain damage then death."

Cade squeezed his eyes shut against the truth and choked out, "Timeline?"

Finn's voice was strained. "What the hell is going on, Zavier?"

Cade's voice wobbled when he repeated more firmly, "Timeline, Finnegan?"

"I would have to check to be sure, and I will do so and get back to you with an answer as soon as I can get it, but my best guess is less than 48 hours. Zavier, do you need us?"

Knowing that by "us", his brother meant the whole family, he responded, "Possibly."

"Where are you?"

Cade winced. "San Francisco."

Finn sucked in a breath. "You're in town? Where?"

Cade ended the call after he told his brother where he was. He knew he'd essentially just called in the cavalry. His family would be arriving very soon and he knew, at that point, he'd welcome just about any help he could get. He stepped into the kitchen to find Detective Miller there with Cooper. He let Cooper handle it and walked back to the office. He was just about to put a call through to Brody to get an update on what his team had been working on so far when Finn called back.

Cade skipped the hello's. "What did you find?"

Finn cleared his throat, obviously not happy with the answer he had to give. "You're looking at around thirty-six hours, give or take a few, depending on extenuating circumstances."

Fucking hell, Braden couldn't catch a break. "What types of circumstances?"

"Has he had any recent surgery, illness, or trauma?"

Cade pinched the bridge of his nose. "What type of trauma?"

Finn sighed. "Extremely high levels of stress or any acute injuries."

Cade gripped the desk, knuckles white. "Both are possible, at this point. Stress for sure, possible injuries. If so, what does that mean for the timeline?"

Silence. Cade growled.

"It means that it could shorten that timeline, but there's no telling by how much. It's different for everyone. Zavier, what's going on?"

Cade's voice was guttural when he was finally able to answer. "I think it's best if I tell the story only once when everyone is here. Did you send out the SOS or do I need to?"

"I will, it sounds like you have enough on your plate. Now you won't have to do it alone. Everyone that is in town will be there within the hour."

"Thanks, Finn. I need to get going."

He put in a call to Brody.

"What information do you have for me, Brody?"

Cade could hear computer keys clicking in the background. "Nothing yet. I've watched the camera feeds from outside of the café and their house. He got into a dark blue Honda Civic. I'm still working on getting the picture clear enough to see if I can get a license plate. I've got Braden's phone number, and I'm having Sawyer hook it up to his laptop to see if I can clone it and back-trace the unknown caller."

"We've got a countdown hanging over our heads, Brody. I don't care what it takes, how many people you have to pay, call in favors from, or bribe in order to help you, but in less than thirty-six hours, and I can't even tell you how many hours less, Braden will lapse into a diabetic coma. We just found his insulin here. If he is subjected to undue stress and any injuries, which is precisely the situation he's in right now, his body will shorten that countdown, and we'll be looking at even less time."

"Fuck. Okay, then let me get the hell off the phone and start working with Landon and anyone else we can get on it, so we can track him down. I'll do everything in my power to find him, cap."

He hung up, not feeling much better, but knowing Brody was doing everything he could do at that point. He felt like his hands were tied. He knew his best bet was Brody. His hacking and computer skills would, hopefully, be what found Braden in the end, because he'd left all the tracers behind. He headed into the kitchen to see if there were any further status updates. He found his men, along with Detective Miller, discussing the situation. He tossed Braden's testing kit on the countertop in front of them and the men all looked at it then looked up.

"That, gentlemen, is a ticking time bomb. Braden didn't take his diabetic testing kit and insulin with him. According to my brother, a doctor, if circumstances are perfect, Braden has thirty-six hours until he lapses into a diabetic coma. If circumstances aren't perfect, if say, Braden is under an excessive amount of stress, or perhaps, finds himself injured in any way, that timeline lessens, but we aren't sure exactly how much time we have."

Jackson's hands started moving and Sawyer translated, *"When was the last time he took it?"*

Cade shook his head, "His first, and possibly only, dose today was at five-thirty in the morning. He had a healthy breakfast and ran four miles, which are both things that could impact this timeline. He might have dosed himself again after his run, but I didn't see him do so. At this point, we need to operate under the assumption that he dosed himself at five-thirty and hasn't had any insulin since."

Cooper spoke up, "That means we'd need to find Braden before five-thirty tomorrow evening, worst case."

"Keep in mind, nothing about this fucked up situation is ideal, so the reality is that we need to find him as soon as possible, within twenty-four hours would be ideal in order to have any hope of him avoiding a coma, and that might not even be early enough. But with the information I have that's what we'll be using as our goal. Set your watches."

Just then, his cell phone pinged the arrival of a new text. His family had arrived. He walked to the front of the café to let them in. The smell of coffee drifted through the swinging door as he pushed his way through. He saw Layla putting a tray together with coffee and some of Braden's scones and muffins. Zoe was walking to the front door, but he stopped her. "That's my family. I'll let them in. Thank you, ladies, for staying and making coffee, it will help. If you could take it to the kitchen that's where we'll all most likely be working."

He realized with some surprise that the only person that wasn't there was his youngest brother, Aiden, who was most likely on a mission with his SEAL team. He opened the door and received hugs from everyone, but there were no questions and there was no chatter. His family knew from talking to Finn and from the look on his face that something bad had happened and he would tell them about it as soon as he was able to. He assumed Aiden was out of the country but wanted to make sure he didn't need to wait on him. "Is Aiden OCONUS?"

His dad answered, "Yes, he's been overseas for several weeks."

Nodding, he led his family back to the kitchen where the ladies had joined the men and Detective Miller was still present. He began introductions, "Detective Miller, Layla, Zoe, Maya, Sawyer, Jackson, and you all know Cooper. Everyone, meet my family; my mother, Siobhan; my father, Duncan; my younger sister, Rowan; my older brother, Gideon; and my younger brother, Finn. I've invited them here to help out. Let me explain to them what's going on, and we can go from there."

Cade took a deep breath, faced his family, and got straight to the point. "We came here, Cooper and I, just shy of two weeks ago. We were here for work, obviously, but we were going to surprise our families. When we got here, Maya's business partner, Braden, had some trouble with a stalker, and we decided to take on his case. Since then, even in so short a time, a lot has happened. Braden has become… Well, he's become my everything."

At his mother's gasp, he smiled sadly at her. "We discovered that his stalker was his abusive ex-boyfriend, Eric, and have been protecting him ever since we arrived. He started escalating by breaking and entering and destroying Braden's property. This morning, he threatened Braden with recent pictures of Maya and his grandmother, threatened me as well, saying that if Braden didn't cooperate and go with him, he'd kill one of us. Braden is very protective of those he loves, so he left of his own accord. That was just shy of nine this morning."

Cade crossed his arms over his chest and continued to explain as much as he could. "In addition to that, Braden has a couple health concerns, the biggest being that he is a Type 1 diabetic, and we discovered that he left without his insulin, which means, according to Finn, we have less than thirty-six hours to find him before he lapses into a diabetic coma. I believe we have much less than that, however, because that timeline shortens when there are high levels of stress and possible injuries. Let me walk you through what has already been done and what is being done currently."

After explaining what he could about the video cameras catching the car and the phone being cloned, he glanced at Detective Miller who let them know that he had put out an APB when Eric had slashed Braden's tires the first time, but he just updated all information to reflect the navy blue Honda Civic and the pictures they had. Maya spoke up, reminding him that Braden's grandmother would arrive any minute. She also talked to Zoe and Layla, letting them know they could stay if they wanted, but it was okay if they wanted to leave. Both girls elected to stay and try to help in any way they could.

Cade met Braden's grandmother in the front when she arrived so that he could tell her what had happened without an audience. She walked in the door looking rather regal and extremely pissed off. As soon as Cade recounted the events of the morning, he could see the fight leave her body and her shoulders slumped as she took a seat at one of the café tables.

He apologized to her, took responsibility, but just as Maya had done, she put him in his place, reassuring him it wasn't his fault. She admitted she arrived feeling as if he was to blame because he was supposed to be protecting him, but after being told what happened, she believed Braden would have found a way to leave no matter what, as long as he thought he was protecting people he loved. She asked several questions then seemed to get herself together and stood up, prepared to meet everyone who had come to help find her grandson.

Chapter 20

BRADEN

Braden woke, his head pounding, completely disoriented. His vision was blurry, his thoughts fuzzy, and he didn't know where he was. He tried to turn over and realized he was caught somehow. He tried to extricate his arm from whatever was holding it and had to squint to look at what was on his wrist. He panicked when he realized it was a pair of handcuffs. He used his free hand to try unsuccessfully to remove the cuffs which were connected to a chain and attached to something under the bed that he was lying on. His breathing became erratic as his panic grew.

The cuffs allowed for enough movement to change into any position on the bed, but didn't allow enough slack to move more than a couple steps away from it. His vision cleared just enough to make out familiar shapes and colors, and he realized with horror that he was back in the old bedroom he used to share with Eric, only it was different. He recognized that it was painted the same, had the same pieces of furniture, but the layout was wrong. He was in a different room, a different house, but everything, down to their pictures they'd had done together professionally, were all put where they'd been in their old bedroom.

He remembered everything now. He remembered leaving the café and getting into Eric's car. He remembered regretting his decision the second he climbed in and saw the disbelief and shock on Cooper's face as they drove away, knowing Cade would feel so betrayed and disappointed. He remembered a sudden feeling of hope when he thought about the tracers, but one look down and he remembered he'd taken them off first thing that morning to knead dough. He'd been a shaking, panicked mess with tears streaming down his face. And finally, he remembered the gleam in Eric's eyes when he glanced his way for the first time since getting in the car. It was that look that did it, the one thing keeping him silent.

As soon as he'd seen that look in Eric's eyes, he'd remembered the way Eric used to look at him when they argued, as if it made him perversely happy. He remembered the look of utter satisfaction on his face after he would beat Braden. The more Braden talked back, yelled, cried, or begged, especially begged, the happier Eric seemed to get. But Braden wasn't the same man any longer. He was in love with someone else, someone who was worthy of his love and in that love, he'd gained strength and insight into what had been. The second he saw the look in Eric's eyes, Braden decided he was no longer going to play Eric's games.

Yes, he'd left of his own free will. He'd been stupid and scared for the people he loved. All he could think about was them and–he was ashamed to admit–the all too familiar instinct to do whatever Eric said to avoid making him mad had kicked in, making him feel like he had no other options. As soon as he got into that car, however, he'd realized the mistake he'd made, and he vowed then and there he was done making mistakes where Eric was concerned.

Braden was determined to wipe out the maniacal gleam in Eric's eyes. No matter how hard Eric beat him, he wouldn't give Eric the satisfaction of begging, talking, crying, or reacting the way Eric wanted. He'd made that decision in the car and it felt like he'd flipped a switch. Calm indifference took over, and he felt as if he was taking some of his power back. He was determined not to break, and he'd be strong until Cade found him or Eric killed him. He would show nothing of his fears, his feelings, his anger, or his sadness, as those emotions no longer belonged to Eric.

Eric realized almost immediately that things were different. He began trying to fill the silence and get a reaction from him. He talked about their relationship and how they were finally together again. He got no reaction. He mentioned Cade and laughed when he asked Braden if he thought he'd really be man enough to keep someone like him. He got no reaction. Eric continued trying to put doubts in his mind about Cade, doubts that wormed their way into Braden's psyche as much as he wanted to deny it, but outwardly, he did not react. Eric talked about what he'd been doing and how he'd left his job in order to find something more challenging. He got no reaction. He'd talked about how he'd been watching Braden while he ran, while he hung out with Maya, when he saw Nana, and while he was making deliveries. He got no reaction. He raised his voice to Braden, told him he'd be sorry for the way he'd left him, sorry for the way he was acting now. He got no fucking reaction.

It didn't take long for Eric's composure to crack then he lost control completely. He'd slammed Braden's head into the glass in the passenger door; not once, not twice, but three times and knocked him out. His vision was still blurry, and he was very thirsty. He glanced around and saw a bottle of water on the nightstand. He opened it and drank the bottle empty in a matter of seconds. As much as he didn't want to see Eric, he had to use the bathroom. He had no idea what time it was, or how long he'd been out. He felt his head and found a rather large lump where his head had slammed into the window and realized his hair was matted with what must have been dried blood.

He rolled over as much as he could and saw a digital clock on the nightstand table that read two fifty three p.m. He thought he had left the café around nine in the morning, so it had almost been six hours. His head felt like shit, but he didn't know if he would have been knocked out for that long because of it, so he began to worry about being drugged, and what might have been in the water he just gulped down. He wanted more, felt like he could drink a gallon of the stuff.

He didn't know how long he'd have to wait for Eric, and he had to urinate, badly. No longer able to wait, he stood up on wobbly legs, made to unzip his fly, planning to pee into the water bottle he'd emptied, when Eric strode in, a gun in his hand, and spoke angrily. "I'll unlock you to take you to the restroom if you promise not to try anything. I'm not afraid to use this, so don't fuck with me."

Braden stood there, made no attempt to answer and waited until Eric unlocked the cuffs, only he didn't. He got down low in front of Braden's face and glared into his eyes and grated out, "This silent treatment bullshit isn't going to work! You need to promise me you won't try anything when I unlock you." Braden didn't respond. Eric yelled, "Answer me, goddammit!" Still Braden didn't say a word and avoided eye contact completely.

When he saw the backhand coming, he tried to move out of the way, but he still felt dizzy from hitting his head earlier and possibly being drugged, so his movements were sluggish. Not to mention, he was surprised Eric was aiming for his face. In the past, he'd always avoided it so others wouldn't know he was being beaten. The backhand missed a direct hit to his upper cheek and eye, but he caught the hit on his upper eyelid and eyebrow and felt it split open immediately.

His backward momentum had him reaching back to try to avoid a fall. His hand landed on the edge of the nightstand table, which tipped over under his weight, sending everything that was on it sailing. Braden lost his balance completely and fell at an awkward angle. His left hand took all of his weight, wrenching his wrist back into an impossible position. Braden felt the crack of a bone breaking and shooting pain flew up his arm from his wrist. He screamed out in agony and grabbed his arm to his chest. He gritted his teeth and breathed in deeply, trying to dispel the nausea that resurfaced with the pain. His whole body shuddered in agony.

Eric stood above him, his face an angry mask. "Now look what you did! You're always fucking everything up! Get up!"

Braden knew from experience if he didn't get up as quickly as possible he was risking a kick or two to the ribs, and he didn't need any more broken bones than he already had. But, even knowing this, he was too slow and as soon as Eric's foot made contact with the ribs on his left side, he fell down again, clutching his chest, gasping in pain. He lay there shaking, his body wrecked, and was close to just giving up but didn't want to give Eric the satisfaction, so he struggled to his knees then slowly got to his feet, still cradling his arm and protecting his ribs.

He knew he was fucked when Eric tucked the gun into the small of his back and reached aggressively for the same arm, preparing to remove the cuffs. Nothing about Eric was gentle, and he knew getting the cuffs off of him was going to be excruciating. Braden was careful to move his arm closer to Eric to try to avoid any rough handling, but Eric grabbed onto his forearm and yanked his arm closer, nearly causing Braden to black out with the pain. He twisted the cuffs until the lock was on top and used a key to unlock them. Eric tossed them on the bed and dug his fingers into Braden's upper arm, dragging him to the bathroom and practically shoving him inside.

Braden kept his back turned towards Eric to avoid giving him the pleasure of seeing his tears. He struggled to breathe in and out slowly to avoid more pain in his chest. He used his right hand to lower his fly and proceeded to urinate as quickly as he could. He struggled to get himself back into his pants and zipped back up, but in the end, he knew he didn't have a choice.

He wasn't going to show that weakness to Eric. Not to mention, all he needed was that sick fuck's hands anywhere near his dick. He did his best to wash his hand and glancing at himself in the mirror, he cringed inwardly. He looked awful. His hair was matted at his temple from his introduction to the car's passenger window; his eyebrow was split open and still oozing blood. His wrist was canted at a strange angle, held gently to his chest, and he looked pale as hell.

He was so damn exhausted and felt so sick to his stomach that he walked by Eric without a glance in his direction. He struggled to climb onto the bed, but when he finally managed it, he lay down and held out his right wrist for the cuff this time. He wasn't about to put that damn thing back on his broken one. He heard Eric stomp out of the room and just lay there for a couple minutes, thinking his pain was too great and his stomach too upset to fall asleep. He was wrong. He was out only minutes later.

Cade

Cade realized he was pacing when he looked up and caught Gideon's eyes, seeing the raised eyebrow. It wasn't like him to pace, but he was used to taking action and felt like a caged animal. It was nearly four in the afternoon, and they were no further in their search than they had been six hours ago. He wanted to get in his car and drive around town searching, but he knew that would be a waste of time and probably make him lose whatever sliver of control he had on his temper

Everyone was scattered around the café. They were using the office, the front to make coffee, and the break room, but mostly, everyone was using the kitchen as the home base. His mother had immediately gravitated towards Braden's grandmother and he'd seen them having more than one whispered conversation. He was sad they'd met under these circumstances. His family had all let him know they were here for him, and everyone was keeping themselves busy in some way or another.

Detective Miller had asked them if they wanted to get Braden's story on the news so people could be on the lookout for Braden. Both Cade and Maya immediately rejected the idea, and Cade had warned the Detective, in no uncertain terms, who he would blame if it leaked. He knew Braden would hate his life splashed in public that way. As much as they needed to find Braden, there was no guarantee that a media blitz would help in the cause, especially since Eric seemed like such a loner, but there was a guarantee that Braden would feel completely violated by that type of intrusion into his personal life. Not to mention, they had no idea how angry it might make Eric if he saw it, or what would happen if he proceeded to take it out on Braden.

Brody had gotten the license plate number from the stolen Honda, and Detective Miller had added it to the search the police were doing. Now it was just a waiting game as they scoured the city looking for the car, the same way he'd done with the other one. However, this time Brody had solicited help from Cade, Sawyer, Jackson, Cade's sister, and older brother. Brody had gotten them all hooked up to Brody's intranet on their own laptops and had walked them all through how to search throughout the city for camera footage.

So far Brody had been unable to get a location from the unknown phone number. He'd successfully cloned Braden's phone but had been unable to get anything through a backtrace. It was a prepaid burner phone and, unless it was actively being used, it was very hard to locate.

Actively being used. Shit. He looked up, caught Sawyer's eye. "Braden's phone?"

Sawyer turned, unplugged it, and handed it over to Cade. He yanked his own phone from his pocket and dialed Brody. He looked up when he realized the kitchen had immediately become silent. Everyone was hyper aware of him, as if they were walking on eggshells, and perhaps they were. Apparently, not only did he feel like a caged animal, he probably looked like one, which was making some of the natives restless. Brody answered the phone without a greeting. "I caught him on a Wells Fargo Bank camera in the Castro neighborhood, but lost him again after that. We'll find him, Cade. I've got several computers constantly running the search function automatically. I've got Landon working on it and my tech guys and the help of everyone there will definitely make a difference. The more eyes we have on the cameras, the better."

"I know you're doing everything you can. I'll see if I can get my Dad and one of my brothers to head over to the Castro district and drive around in the neighborhood on the off chance they find the car, so let me know if you have any more random sightings. I thought about what you said regarding back tracing the unknown number from Braden's phone. You said that if it's not actively being used, it's nearly impossible to trace. What if I called it or texted it?"

The silence on the other end didn't bode well, but then he heard Brody suck in a deep breath. "Okay, yeah, that's a possibility, but if you call and he doesn't answer, we won't get anything. If you text and he eventually answers, it will be hit or miss. I'd have to edit my program to ping that phone every second after you send your texts, so when a text is sent back to you from his phone, my program can ping it as it's being received then trace it back. Let me start working on that. It shouldn't take long for me to edit my program, maybe an hour or two. Don't take any action yet. Let me get working on this and I'll get back to you as soon as I can."

Braden

Braden woke up with a jolt when he felt someone slapping his face. He was completely confused, felt sick, and his wrist hurt like a son of a bitch. He heard Eric's voice. Wait, Eric's voice? What the fuck was… Then, it came back to him, this time in pieces, or more accurately, in snapshots of what had happened since he'd gotten in that damned car, and he groaned from pain, frustration, and anger at what he'd gotten himself into. "Wake up! You didn't hit your head that hard in the car, there's no reason for you to be fucking sleeping right now!"

Braden groggily turned to look at the clock and realized it was after five in the evening. He saw another water bottle on the nightstand table that apparently had been righted. He reached to grab it, putting weight on his left arm and realized his mistake when daggers of pain lanced his whole arm from fingers to shoulder. He wrenched himself back and lay there, hoping the pain would subside, but it didn't feel like it was going anywhere any time soon. He gave up on the idea of water even though he was extremely thirsty, and he moved to get more comfortable, maybe get some more sleep. He couldn't understand why Eric was so confused about how tired he was. He was sure he'd been drugged. He felt so sick to his stomach it seemed like the only explanation unless he hit his head harder than he thought and had a concussion which seemed possible and might explain a lot of his symptoms.

Eric shoved a tray next to Braden's pillow on the bed. "I made you a microwave dinner. You need to eat. You need to stay awake. We need to talk."

Braden took one whiff of the meal and promptly lost whatever had been in his stomach all over the dinner tray. Eric screamed at him in disgust and shoved a trash can into his face; he grabbed it and continued to be sick into the can. Eventually, between bouts of nausea, Eric brought him into the bathroom and left him there, muttering under his breath that he wasn't a fucking nursemaid and Braden better get his shit together.

He lay on the cool tile of the bathroom floor, feeling stabbing pain in his stomach and his wrist. His skin felt tight, dry and hot, like he had a sunburn. Maybe he had the flu. His stomach revolted again, and he was barely able to get himself positioned over the toilet in time. He felt short of breath and disoriented.

Eric came into the bathroom and kicked his calf. "What's wrong with you? If you're faking this shit, I'm gonna beat the hell out of you!"

He didn't have the energy to move, let alone react to Eric's anger and accusations. He heard Eric muttering in the bedroom then it was quiet again. He knew something wasn't right, but he couldn't concentrate long enough to think about what was going on. Most likely it was a concussion. He'd had them before and most of his symptoms fit. He felt as if he could doze off again, lying on his side on the cold tile floor. He just couldn't seem to keep himself awake and didn't really know why he should try. Hell, if he did, he might find himself getting beaten again, and he didn't think his body could take much more.

Cade

In the confines of the café's little office, Cade was afforded a small bit of isolation. He felt uneasy, and it was such a rare feeling for him that he needed to sequester himself for the possible conversation to come. As private as he'd like this to be, he had an audience of one in Brody, who had been able to update his program to hopefully catch Eric's location if he responded to any of Cade's attempts to communicate. His first try at communication was going to be a direct call to Eric's phone. If he didn't get a response, he'd leave a message on the off chance Eric would listen to it. Brody had given him the go ahead. He was monitoring Braden's phone and his computer was pinging it for return signals.

Cade dialed the number and listened to the phone ring, and ring, and ring. Finally, a computer modulated female voice repeated the phone number and a beep sounded. He took a quiet, deep breath, and began. "Hello, Eric, we haven't been formally introduced. My name is Zavier McCade. I'm Braden's partner, and I guess you could also call me his personal guard. It seems you felt comfortable taking something that doesn't belong to you which is going to be the biggest mistake you have ever made. Right about now, Braden is probably experiencing insulin withdrawals, as you've kidnapped him without ensuring he has access to his basic medical needs. The longer he goes without insulin, the worse his symptoms will get, until he lapses into a diabetic coma which may cause brain damage and if left untreated, death."

Cade's hand curled into a tight fist, his anger palpable. "Let me be perfectly clear, Mr. Pollard, if he lapses into a coma and he does not receive immediate medical attention; if he suffers brain damage or if he dies, there is no place you can go, nowhere you can hide that I cannot find you. Google my name and understand me fully when I say that you will be hunted down, and you will be killed viciously and painfully. Heed this warning and take this threat very seriously. Return Braden to me alive, or you'll be looking over your shoulder for the rest of your short life."

He hung up the phone, expelling a heavy breath, his body tense. He turned quickly when he heard a shoe scuff behind him. He found himself looking into the eyes of his horrified mother and immediately regretted not locking the door. He opened his mouth to apologize for what she had to overhear, but she looked down, not meeting his eyes. "I'm sorry to interrupt. I didn't know you were on the phone. I was coming in to see if you'd like us to pick you up some dinner. No one really wants to cook right now, everyone seems too anxious, I guess. I'm not even sure anyone is hungry, but "

Cade interrupted her rambling. "Mom, sit down and look at me. I'm still your son. I'm still the same one you came to help today. The same one who sends you flowers on your birthday, Valentine's day, and Mother's day."

"I know. I know you are."

"No, you don't. You're trying to reconcile the child you raised with the man who just threatened to viciously kill a man. Maybe, after we talk, you'll understand. Let me show you my Braden and tell you a bit about him."

Cade sat next to his mom and put his arm around her to pull her close for a kiss on her head. She leaned into him, and he handed her his iPad and manipulated it for her, signing in to pull up Braden's Facebook page. He smiled when her breath caught at the first picture of Braden, which was a close up of him and Maya, both with huge smiles, him hugging her from behind. He flipped to another one of him sitting next to his grandmother, holding her hand and tilting his head towards hers. He moved on to many others, Braden in his running gear, Braden in his pastry chef apron, Braden dressed to kill, sitting on the countertop of his kitchen island.

His mom had her hand over her heart, and he knew she was thinking how beautiful Braden was, and hopefully, she could see exactly what he saw in Braden. She looked up into Cade's eyes. "How tall is he?"

Cade chuckled at that. "He's shorter than you are. He's five foot nine, and he's extremely fit, slim, but very muscular. His diabetes keeps him very disciplined with his eating, but it's his running, coupled with his stretching, yoga, and Pilates, that really keep him so healthy. He's just as beautiful inside as he is outside, maybe more so."

His mom gazed up at him, teary, a smile on her face. "Was it love at first sight?"

He shrugged. "I don't know. It was attraction and desire at first sight, at the very least. The first time I saw him, everything in the background went fuzzy and all I could see was him. Something in me recognized something in him, Mom. It's the only way I can explain it. All I do know for sure is that he's the love of my life, and I'd do absolutely anything for him."

He went on to tell her all about Braden's accomplishments with his business, his life growing up, his friendship with Maya, and his diabetes and migraines. He told her how hard he worked, how much he stressed, and initially, how hard it was for Braden to trust him and accept help from him, how he finally let down his walls and let Cade in.

He shared with his mother all the things he'd kept to himself since he'd met Braden. He knew one day he'd be having this conversation with her, he'd just had no idea it would be under such dire circumstances. He set the iPad aside, faced his mom, and took one of her hands in his. He hated to put the thought in her head, but he didn't see another way. Looking into her eyes, he took a deep breath and did what he felt he needed to do, in order for her to hopefully understand, if only just a little bit.

"What if Rowan found herself in an abusive relationship and wanted to get out of it? What if she told him she was leaving and he beat her and raped her? Let's say she even went to the hospital alone for her injuries and a rape kit, but never told anyone about it. And what if, over a year later, her ex decided to stalk her and kidnap her, and quite possibly kill her? How would you and dad react?"

His mom had gripped his hand hard with hers as soon as he mentioned rape, and her free hand flew up to her lips, while tears rolled down her cheeks. It killed him, seeing her pain and regret coursed through him. "I'm so sorry. I shouldn't have used Ro as my example, that was inexcusable, putting those thoughts in your head. I just didn't know how else to explain everything that's going on and where my heart is. If I lose him… Mom, if I lose Braden, I lose myself."

"Oh, honey. That poor boy." His mom drew him into her and hugged him tight. After a moment, she pulled back, fury in her eyes, her body full of angry tension. "You get him back, Zavier. Whatever it takes, you bring your boy home and you destroy the man that took him."

Cade hugged her tight and sighed. "That's my plan."

It felt good, her support and love. He felt like the phone call and voicemail he'd left and his conversation with his mom were steps forward, and he just hoped he'd get a response from Eric. His mom left the room with his food order, and he placed a call to Brody. Brody let Cade know it was okay to send whatever texts he wanted to send, so he sent several succinct texts making sure to mention insulin withdrawals and diabetic comas. He'd rattled that cage, and hopefully, it would prove fruitful. He went back into the kitchen to resume his search for the stolen Honda.

Chapter 21

ERIC

Eric couldn't believe the bullshit he was dealing with. He finally had Braden back where he belonged and what the fuck did he have to show for it? Braden wasn't reacting to *anything* he said, he wasn't speaking to him, he wasn't looking at him, he wasn't even responding when he was being shown the proper way to act. He'd always counted on Braden's reactions to his discipline because he loved the way he could mold Braden's behavior into what he wanted it to be.

He'd planned for this day for so goddamned long, and instead of making sure Braden understood why he'd been so wrong to leave, so wrong to threaten him with that silly video of their heated exchange followed by their lovemaking, here Braden was, lying on the bathroom floor vomiting more than anyone he'd ever seen vomit. He was so pissed off he wanted to beat Braden's ass, and he would, but he wasn't going to get himself covered in vomit. He'd wait him out, wait for him to be done being sick then he'd fucking teach him a lesson.

As much as he didn't like the timing, he could be understanding enough about Braden getting sick, but when he was well, they'd be having a conversation about how their future would go, and Braden would realize the mistakes he'd made. Eric would be damned sure to force Braden to make up for his poor choices.

He'd been so angry when he'd found that video and Braden's letter. He'd practically ripped his townhouse apart and broken every breakable thing within reach. However, that was also the day he'd vowed to himself that he'd figure out a way, a way to get past the barrier of the video and what it could mean for his future if it got out; a way to get Braden back into his life permanently, no matter what it took; and a way to punish him for thinking he could ever leave him.

He'd gotten fired from his job because of that fucking piss-ant Intake Advocate. He almost decided to teach that little shit a lesson he wouldn't forget, but that would have to come later. He realized after he was let go it might be a blessing in disguise. They said he'd be allowed to leave with the official story a secret because he'd put in so many years, they figured they were doing him a solid.

The real story was the little fucker had manipulated events to reflect poorly on him. In the end, they let him know they wouldn't provide him with a recommendation, but they wouldn't let anyone know he had been fired either. He could very easily settle in another city and use his position there on a resume, excusing his missing time as a family emergency. All he needed before he moved away was Braden by his side where he belonged.

He'd wanted to slowly ease himself back into Braden's life. He'd decided he was going to keep an eye on him, make sure he was free and wasn't fucking some schmuck he'd have to take care of and get through in order to have Braden back. When he'd started watching him, he'd finally felt right. He'd finally felt like he was doing what needed to be done. Pretty soon, he couldn't help himself; he started leaving little notes and love letters for him. He'd done it for months then the day came when he saw a man carry Braden from right outside of the café over to his house, and he'd seen red.

Braden had been sick, in the fucking gutter of all places, with his little twit friend Maya trailing along. That giant of a man had picked him up, as if he had every right to do so, and he could have sworn the man had kissed him on the forehead and nuzzled him while whispering to him. He'd almost lost it then and there. Who the fuck was this guy? Where had he come from? Who the fuck did he think he was, touching Braden like only

Eric was allowed to? He'd decided his waiting was over, and he'd begun to make plans.

That little motherfucker had finally gotten into a relationship, and of course, the asshole had to be some huge jock type. Not that it scared Eric, muscle bound idiots were just that, stupid caveman that didn't know their dicks from their brains, and Eric knew he wouldn't be a problem. What pissed him off is that he was *never* away from Braden. It seemed like the huge fucker had literally popped into Braden's life and taken residence, and he didn't look like he was budging.

Eric had even seen them start to hold hands. However, maybe, just maybe, it was all an act, because suddenly, there were three other men around, going in and out of Braden's home and café and wasn't that just so interesting? Maybe Braden was getting a little scared and had hired some two bit bodyguards to protect him.

Once he'd figured that out, he'd been thrilled, and he'd begun to make some noise. He wanted to be heard, and he wanted to shake up the status quo. Oh yes, he was going to have everyone on their toes then he was gonna do what he did best, manipulate Braden using his biggest weaknesses, his love for his family and friends and his fear of him. If those muscle bound jokers thought they were a match for him, they'd be surprised how quick and painless his checkmate was going to be, whisking Braden away from them all with barely any effort on his part.

It had worked too, but again, he hadn't been counting on Braden developing the fucking flu or god knows what. He'd given him some soup that had stayed down for all of twenty minutes. He'd tried to give him crackers and some fruit and it had come up too. He was drinking a lot of water, but when Braden did try to eat, it wasn't much, and it all came back up. Now it was just a matter of bile and mostly dry retching, so fucking disgusting. He'd had to check on him and move him from bed to bathroom four times in so many hours.

Finally, he'd just left him there, and he'd been in there on the floor for hours now. Jesus, he could still hear him retching through the walls of this ugly fucking cheap ass house he was renting. Not that he was really complaining. He knew he was damn lucky to have found this place. He'd been driving along, in one of his stolen cars, going through some of the rental listings, when he'd come upon one of the locations and knocked on the door of the owner. It had been some little old lady who had been more than happy to accept six months rent under the table, in cash.

He'd grown a beard then dyed all of his hair a dark brown and added a bit of weight to his middle by stuffing a very small pillow under his t-shirt and covering both with a hoodie. He'd made himself look like a hairy, chubby, trustworthy guy who just moved into the city to find a new job. He'd even offered to take care of the yard work himself so no one would disturb him. The old broad had eaten his story up, said he looked like her grandson, and even offered him coffee and cookies of all things. Stupid bitch served her purpose though. And it all worked out because he had a place to hide that was off the books and a place to bring Braden before they made their move out of town together.

It was close to midnight, and after about thirty minutes of silence, he went into the bathroom and was horrified to find vomit and bile all over the bathroom floor and also on Braden's shirt. Braden seemed to be asleep. Disgusted, he dragged Braden out of the bathroom by his feet. Realizing he was just dragging him through his vomit, he yelled and kicked Braden's thigh. When he did that, Braden's body rolled so he was on his back, and he realized that sometime during his vomit fest, he'd fucking peed himself. Just great, he didn't want to deal with this bullshit right now!

Finally, he yanked Braden's clothes off, picked him up and dropped him into the tub and turned on the shower to rid him of most of the filth stuck to his skin. He wasn't about to actually clean him with soap, the water would have to do. After several minutes, he realized Braden hadn't even reacted to the cold water like he'd hoped he would and his lips were turning blue, so he dragged him out of the shower, dried him off as much as his patience would allow, picked him up under his arms, and dragged him back to the bed.

Normally, he'd be taking advantage of a naked Braden, but he looked pathetic and still smelled like a goddamned sewer. He didn't want to spend too much time thinking about what was going on with Braden because if he did, he'd freak the fuck out. He'd done all of that and Braden hadn't reacted at all, almost like he was not just sleeping but passed out or something.

He was about to crawl into bed next to Braden when he realized he wanted to check his email for any responses to his inquiries in Seattle regarding rentals and jobs as he'd decided that was far enough to get himself and Braden away from their California lives. He went searching for his phone and couldn't find it.

He smirked when he realized the last time he'd used it, went out to his latest stolen piece of shit car, and grabbed his phone, which of course was dead. He plugged it in and managed to clean up the rest of Braden's mess in the bathroom before getting himself ready for bed. He got in beside Braden, but instead of getting close to him, he kept his distance, wary of being vomited on during the night.

Cade

Their SUV rental with the slashed tires had been picked up and replaced with another. Braden's SUV would be returned with new tires the next day. It was after midnight, and Cade was driving around town looking for the blue Honda with Cooper. He'd wanted to go out alone, but Cooper had insisted on tagging along, and he honestly didn't have the energy to fight him.

He knew Brody was doing his best; hell, everyone was doing their best, searching all available cameras. They'd been lucky several times and had gone out each time to search in the areas where the car had been spotted. At that moment, they were once again passing through the three areas where the cameras had spotted the car to be sure no one had missed anything.

Frankly, he couldn't sit at the damned computer any longer without taking some sort of action even if they were just chasing pavement for a second time around. He was going stir crazy and everyone tiptoeing around him like he was either fragile or a ticking time bomb was making him wanna punch something.

He glanced over at Cooper and saw he was texting someone. "Any updates?"

"No. Nothing new from Brody or the others."

Cade saw in Cooper's eyes that the situation wasn't just fucking him up, it was messing with Cooper as well. Cooper had finally gotten Maya to agree to Finn's suggestion of taking an Ambien to help her sleep right before they'd left. Braden's grandmother had told Maya in no uncertain terms that they were opening the café in the morning, and she was going to do the baking.

After that assertion, she'd turned to Finn. "You're the doctor, right? Good. I need an Ambien, young man, or something of the like. I couldn't sleep now if I tried, but I'm too damn old to stay up all night then work all day tomorrow. So you're just gonna have to give me a prescription for something tonight."

Finn had raised an eyebrow but answered promptly, "Yes, ma'am," while digging out his prescription pad. He'd asked his mom and sister to go pick up the prescription, and he'd gotten enough for several people for several nights. Both Nana and Maya were out cold, along with Cade's mom, which was good.

Cade, and of course, Cooper, had rejected the offer and instead, drove out in their new rental. They'd ordered Sawyer and Jackson to get some rack time as well while they went out to do some more searching, but his men wouldn't need Ambien to sleep. They'd all been trained in the Army to get sleep when and where they could, so falling asleep and waking immediately to be ready to go at a moment's notice was second nature to all of them.

Hopefully, those that could rest, would. Cade was wide awake and had a feeling he wouldn't be able to sleep if he tried, but he knew he wouldn't allow himself that luxury, not when Braden was out there probably being beaten to shit and dealing with insulin withdrawals. He was getting frustrated that he'd moved from sitting on his ass in the kitchen to sitting on his ass in the SUV. He'd been feeling claustrophobic at the café and had just swapped locations to get the same feeling.

They were leaving no stone unturned, but it felt like they were just spinning their wheels. He needed to keep his mind and his body occupied instead of sitting and waiting for their luck to change. He needed stress relief in the form of something physical. They were doing everything they could do, and it wasn't enough and the out-of-control feeling was going to take its toll if he wasn't careful.

Fuck, he couldn't take it anymore and pulled his phone from his pocket, dialed. "I'm sorry it's so late... No, Braden was taken... Yes, Cooper and I both do... Yeah, ten minutes. Thanks."

Pulling a U-turn, Cade headed back the other way. It took Cooper less than a minute. "Vaughn's?"

Cade nodded his head, and they both settled more comfortably into their seats, a bit more relaxed, knowing they were going to be able to work off some of the stress at the gym. They got there quickly and didn't have to wait. Vaughn was already there. Cade stepped out of the SUV, approached Vaughn with his hand outstretched to clasp the fighter's. "I didn't even think to ask if you had Mikayla. Sorry, man."

"I'd have spoken up, no need to worry about that. She's with her mom this weekend. Talk to me," he demanded as he turned towards his gym and took them inside. Cade explained everything that had happened so far while he and Cooper changed into some of the gym gear Vaughn sold there to get ready to work off some of the tension that weighed him down.

"Fuck man, that's awful. Look, I know it's not much, but I've called a couple of my guys. I've got them managing the gym for me tomorrow so I can be available for you. I'll just plan on following you back to the café tonight. Another set of eyes for the computer, a driver to check the places that the camera caught the car, a tester for some pastries, a distraction for Coop's sister or Braden's grandmother, whatever you need from me."

Cade felt humbled by the offer though he wasn't the least bit surprised by it. He was incredibly lucky to have generous and supportive friends and family. Everyone was dropping everything to help him and Braden, and he knew he'd do the same for them in return. He got himself psyched up for a beat down. Both Vaughn and Cooper knew he needed to get out his anger, frustration, and stress, so they'd both be coming at him hard.

They all warmed up on both the speed bags and the heavy bags before going at it. Cade sparred with Vaughn first while Cooper lifted some weights. Neither of them pulled any punches, and the match was fairly even. Cade had size and strength on his side and some tricky Krav Maga moves that he pulled out in the end, but even so, if they were being ref'd, he wasn't sure who would have won.

He was tired, but nowhere near exhausted. He needed to feel dead on his feet in order to release the kind of stress he was storing. He took a small break, got some water, walked it off, and then met Cooper in the ring. Cooper was a dirty fighter, and he was stressed for Braden and Maya as well, so that match was pretty even as well. In the end, they'd both worn him out, and that's exactly what he'd needed.

After showering and putting their street clothes back on, they left for the café–Cooper behind the wheel of their SUV and Vaughn in his own car. By the time they got back, they'd been gone for nearly four hours. Cade's dad and older brother were out checking in another neighborhood where a 7-Eleven's camera had caught a glimpse of Eric's car. No other updates of note had occurred.

Finn approached both Cade and Cooper after they'd checked in with the rest of the crew that was still working in the kitchen of the café. "Zavier, Cooper, can I ask you both to get some rest?"

"Finn, I'm not going to sleep when Braden is out there, possibly being beaten to death, if a diabetic coma doesn't do it first."

"Zavier, listen to me and listen good, we're gonna find Braden. I'd be willing to place a bet on that, but when we do, he's gonna be in bad shape. There's no avoiding it, as too much time has passed for him to have avoided insulin withdrawals. Everyone is doing everything they can and none of us would let you down."

"I know that, but–"

"If anything happens, you know one of us will wake you. But right now, for your health, you need to get some sleep. I'm asking for at least four hours, preferably six. I can tell you now that you'll be operating on all cylinders only if you get some sleep right now, and Braden's going to need you the second he's found. You can't help him if you've gotten yourself too tired to do what needs to be done."

Cade was getting pissed at Finn's suggestion that he wouldn't be there for Braden, and he was about to say as much when Cooper interrupted him, obviously knowing exactly what he was thinking. "Cade, he's not trying to insult you, he's trying to ensure that when Braden needs you, you're at your best. Why don't you get some rack time; I'll stay up. I can sleep once we've got Braden back and into the hospital, but Finn's right, you won't be able to sleep when most of us will. Once Braden is found, you're on deck, and I know you, you'll stay on until he's home and no longer in danger, which means you'll need this sleep because you may not get any for days."

He wanted to argue. The thought of heading to bed and getting some sleep when Braden was hurting and needing him almost killed him. However, he also knew that if situations were reversed and this was happening to one of his guys, he'd be saying the same damn thing to them. He knew Braden was going to need him at his best, and it was the only thing that got him nodding, heading across the street, and climbing into Braden's side of the bed.

He plugged both his phone and Braden's phone into their chargers and left their volumes set to high. After he set his watch to wake him in six hours, knowing he'd probably wake automatically in four, he pulled one of Braden's pillows into his arms, forced himself to turn his mind off, and was out in less than two minutes.

Eric

NO! Just. Fucking. No! This wasn't fucking happening. It wasn't. After all the planning, all the bullshit, living in this goddamned sty, driving pathetic ten-year-old stolen cars, being fired from his job, left by an ungrateful son of a bitch who threatened him with exposure, and *this* was how it all panned out?

There was no fucking way this was his reality. Eric stared at his phone in disbelief. He'd had five texts when he'd turned on his freshly charged phone that morning, a fact that rattled him more than he cared to admit, because absolutely no one knew the number.

He'd read all the texts, each one bringing with it more information than the next, information he didn't want, information that filled him with an insane anger he hadn't had since the day he'd come home to find Braden really had gone, a video left in his place. How in the fuck had he forgotten about his goddamned diabetes? The laundry list of the shit he was in was long: insulin withdrawals, coma, brain damage, death, a long ass list of other symptoms, every one of which Braden had already suffered, all over the fucking bathroom floor.

He went back to his home screen, and his heart stuttered in his chest. He had a voicemail. There could be nothing good in it, nothing. His thumb hovered over the delete icon, but he couldn't bring himself to do it. Taking several deep breaths, he pushed the speaker icon then the play icon. The voice that came through those speakers was one he never wanted to hear face to face.

When he imagined the man Braden was with, he did not imagine that just hearing his guttural, angry voice would make his stomach twist. His heart was beating ten times its normal speed. He'd never been threatened like that before, he'd always been the one to do the threatening. His mouth grew dry, and his hands began to shake.

He listened again, in complete disbelief. The instructions to Google his name nagged at him, almost daring him to do it, so he did, to his utter regret. He searched for Xavier McKade, but even his misspelling wasn't a deterrent to seeing a nightmare spread before him. What came back made his skin crawl. "Showing results for *Zavier McCade*," of which there were many links, including pictures to verify his identity, and, of all things, a Wikipedia page. Wiki-fucking-pedia, for fuck's sake!

The more he read the more he felt like he was going to have a vomit fest of his own. His whole body broke out in a cold sweat as he read. The information got worse and worse, and words popped out at him like little daggers: West Point, micro-electrical engineer, US Army, Green Beret, Special Forces, Army Distinguished Service Medal, two Silver Star Medals, two Bronze Star Medals, Millionaire, McCade Watches, Co-Owner Custos Securities, specialist and ranked in Jiu Jitsu, Krav Maga, and Muay Thai.

He turned back towards the bed and glared at the person who, in the last twenty minutes, had rapidly become the bane of his existence. It was well after nine in the morning, and suddenly he felt time ticking away. He needed to get rid of Braden, and he needed to do it in a way that ensured McCade would know in order to avoid more of a man hunt for him than was already in effect. He grabbed some sweats and a t-shirt and struggled to get a comatose Braden into the clothing. Dragging him out to the garage, Eric stuffed him in the back seat and covered him from head to toe with a blanket.

In a full on panic, he drove faster than was wise through the streets of San Francisco, back towards the café. Two streets west of the café, he pulled into a parking spot on a side street under the shadow of some trees lining the sidewalk. He pulled up his hoodie, covering his ball cap, stepped out of the car, and walked away. Only after he had walked ten blocks from the car and hopped a bus to the opposite side of town did he pull out his cell phone and send a text.

Chapter 22

CADE

Cade was in the office the next morning when his phone pinged with a new text. He pulled it out of his pocket to see a black screen and immediately his heart started hammering in his chest. He reached into his other pocket and pulled out Braden's phone and saw there was a text just before the screen turned black. He swiped it open, put in Braden's passcode, and opened his messages. He'd finally gotten a response, it was only two words: Lapidge Street, but those two words made him weak with relief.

He burst out of the office and ran to the kitchen, surprising those that were in there working. Everyone stood when they saw his face. He looked Cooper in the eye. "Get Detective Miller on the line. Have him send an ambulance to Lapidge Street. I don't know where that is, or how long it will take us to get there, but get Finn, and I'll find it on GPS."

Cooper was already on the phone and headed out to grab Finn from Maya's place. On his way out the door, Cade turned to Nana. "I don't know what we'll find, or even if he's physically there. We'll call here and tell you and Maya which hospital to come to when we find him."

The strain of the last twenty-four hours was reflected in her scared, wide-eyed gaze. "This was my old neighborhood. Lapidge is just a few streets over from here. Please, find our boy."

Cade nodded solemnly at her before he ran out the door toward their

SUV, hopped into the passenger side and pulled out his phone. He had a text.

Brody: I've got him. You worry about getting to Braden, I'll worry about tracking Eric. I'll be in touch.

Feeling a bit relieved that Brody was on Eric's trail, he got to work and searched for Lapidge on Google Maps. Nana was right; it wasn't far. He glanced up when he heard Cooper open the driver's door and climb in. Finn got into the back seat with his medical bag. Cooper cranked the engine on and hauled ass out onto the street. Cade gave him directions, and less than five minutes later, they were turning onto a tree-lined street, moving slowly, searching for Braden or signs of the car.

Cade shot out of the still moving SUV when he saw a blue Honda up ahead. He almost fell to his knees when he recognized the license plate. He heard a siren in the distance and wondered if he'd have to break into the car. He didn't see anyone in the front seats. When he glanced in the back and saw what he thought was a bundle of blankets, he took a second look and saw Braden's barefoot peeking out from under the bundle of cloth on the opposite side of the car.

He yanked frantically at the back door, not really expecting it to be unlocked, but relieved when it was. In seconds, he'd removed the blanket and was kneeling down, breath sawing in and out of his lungs. He leaned over Braden's inert form, feeling for a pulse with shaky fingers and kissing his forehead, tears in his eyes, his voice a shaky whisper. "I'm here, you're gonna be alright, baby. I love you. Oh god, Braden, I love you. Don't give up, baby."

His skin was hot to the touch, and he didn't move or react at all to Cade's words. Cade almost passed out from relief when he felt Braden's pulse then nearly took Finn's head off when he tugged on his shoulder to pull him away from Braden.

"Zavier, move back. The EMTs are here and they need to help him."

Reluctantly, Cade moved back and allowed the EMTs access to Braden. He heard his brother talking to the EMTs in medical jargon, but only some words made it into his head before he moved aside: diabetic ketoacidosis, coma, and physical trauma. Another EMT followed with a wheeled stretcher, and he hung back, watching the two men and a woman treat

Braden. When they slowly began to remove him from the car and place him on the stretcher, he rushed to Braden's side.

He ignored the medical speak and anything else going on around him. He followed them to the ambulance and when one of the male EMTs tried to stop him from getting in the ambulance, he took an aggressive step forward into the EMT's personal space, and used his size to intimidate the smaller man, who backpedaled in panic. Cooper and Finn held him back as they both tried to talk him down.

He heard Detective Miller speak over the din. "Let him go with you. Mr. Cross is under protective custody. Mr. McCade must stay with him at all times, as his kidnapper is still at large. Pass this information along to the hospital as well. They are not to be separated, understood?"

The male EMT gave Cade a cautiously curious look. "Sure thing, Detective."

Cade stared at the detective, incredulous that he had essentially stepped in and fixed any further issues that Cade would have as merely Braden's partner with no legal right to stay by his side. He glanced over and nodded his head at the detective in gratitude and got the same nod back in return.

He climbed into the ambulance and sat at the back of the vehicle by Braden's head and did his best to keep his large frame from getting in the way. Once they were on the move, he pulled his phone out of his pocket and dialed Cooper.

He spoke in Dari so the EMTs wouldn't have anything to report to the cop. He hadn't wanted to speak directly in front of the detective, even if he was speaking in another language, as the guy would immediately be suspicious and know Cade was keeping information from him regarding the case. Not to mention, the cop had just done him a solid, and he didn't want to insult him.

"Call Maya and Nana, let them know we found him and what hospital we're going to. Brody is tracking Eric; check in with him for progress reports and get back to me, but I expect to be in on taking that fucker down. It doesn't happen without me. If he looks like a flight risk, call me."

Cooper responded in the same language, agreeing to keep him apprised of the situation with Eric and letting him know they'd be at the hospital soon. Cade ignored the curious looks from the EMTs and placed his hand on Braden's head, keeping a connection with him the whole way to the hospital.

When they got there, they immediately took Braden into a trauma room in the ER where several doctors and nurses got to work. Cade stood off to the side at parade rest, not saying a word, staying out of the way, but letting everyone know he was there and wasn't about to go anywhere. When he'd talked to Braden about his size being intimidating and the fact that he occasionally used that to his advantage, he was talking about situations like this. He wanted them to know they'd be having a fight on their hands if they asked him to leave.

Several of the hospital personnel that came in and out of the room sent him alarmed looks, but the EMTs cleared his presence with the doctor that met them when they arrived. One of the other doctors glanced at him and recognition seemed to flit over his face before he turned back to Braden. He heard his brother's name bandied about by the doctors there and realized his brother must have called in and gotten the right people on the job. They were taking blood for tests, putting in an IV to start fluids, and injecting something into the bag that was being hung from the IV stand. A small bit of the stress he'd been carrying around left him when everyone seemed to be taking action to help Braden as quickly as possible.

That stress immediately came back tenfold when they began to cut Braden out of his clothes to search for any and all injuries. The first thing he realized, and wondered why it hadn't occurred to him already, was that Braden wasn't wearing his own clothes. It made him sick to his stomach, and he stepped forward, without thinking, and was immediately held back by Cooper and his brother. He'd had no clue they'd even arrived. He shook with anger and meeting Finn's eyes, ground out, "Those aren't his clothes, Finn. He could have... He could have been..." His breath came out in a shaky whoosh as he let it out and gulped air back in. "They need to bag those clothes. They need to..."

"Stand down, Zavier. I understand what you're saying, and I promise you that I will see to it that this is handled properly. Do you want me directly involved in his care down here before they take him to ICU?"

"Yes. Make sure everything that can be done for him is done, whether you supervise it because there's someone better suited or do it yourself, I don't care. But he gets only the best working on him. Please, Finn."

Finn nodded. "Give me a minute."

Finn intercepted one of the doctors, and they had a whispered conversation. Cade heard rape kit, DNA swabs, physical and sexual trauma, and then he tuned out, unable to listen anymore to the reality that was stretching out before him. He took another step forward and was held back again by Cooper. He turned towards his best friend, a man he considered a brother, and the anguished look on Cooper's face about did him in, knowing that if Cooper looked that devastated, he wasn't faring any better.

Time seemed to stand still for him as he watched them cut away all the clothing and put it in brown paper bags marked EVIDENCE. Plastic bags were brought out of a box, along with swabs and glass slides. His knees grew weak, and he had to lock them in place to stay standing, as hospital personnel went about the task of treating Braden and gathering evidence.

When they'd done the invasive tests on Braden, he and Cooper turned their backs to give Braden privacy, regardless of his state of consciousness. His brother had long since donned doctor's scrubs and helped with the evidence gathering, but unbeknownst to Cade, had also turned his back when his colleagues had done the invasive tests checking for any signs of sexual assault.

One of the nurses let them know it was safe for them to turn around, and it was then he saw Finn turning back around as well. Jesus, he'd never been so grateful for his brother in his life. Finn had a whispered conversation with another doctor and glanced over and him.

He saw the look in his brother's eyes and wasn't sure how to read his expression. There was a small bit of relief, but there was also a lot of tension remaining, and he stayed silent waiting for an explanation, his fists clenching and unclenching the only outward sign of stress he'd allow himself. Finn led him to a chair that had been brought into the trauma room next to Braden's bed, and he pushed Cade down onto it, pulled a rolling chair forward and sat as he began to talk.

"The good news is there's no evidence showing sexual assault. However, I'm afraid the good news stops there. I know you're aware by now that Braden is in a diabetic coma. For Type 1 diabetics, what causes the coma is diabetic ketoacidosis, or DKA. Knowing you, you researched DKA and I don't have to explain it, correct?"

When Cade nodded, Finn continued, "He's being treated right now with isotonic IV fluids, electrolytes with supplements, and insulin. He will be very carefully monitored to ensure that these methods are working to bring his body back from being insulin deprived. Once his body has stabilized from the treatment, we'll hopefully see him pull out of the coma, but it may take some time."

At Finn's pause he opened his mouth to speak but Finn raised his hand, letting him know he wasn't done. "Hopefully, we caught it early enough that there will not be any brain damage as a result of the coma. I know you need information because it helps you function in high-stress situations, but I have to ask you to think about this question before answering. Do you want me to walk you through all the physical trauma he's sustained?"

Cade rested his elbows on his knees, his head falling low. He rubbed his face with his hands and clasped them behind his head. He sat for several minutes, just breathing, trying to calm the inner turmoil of hearing all of that information, still not knowing if Braden was going to come out of this without long-lasting effects. He looked at his brother imploringly. "Yes. You know I need to hear it, Finn. I have to know."

Finn took a deep breath and nodded his acknowledgement. "Why don't you pull your chair up to Braden right now and hold his hand. It will help you feel grounded and close to him, and my own opinion is that coma patients are sometimes aware of the world around them, including the senses of touch, smell, and hearing, so this can help him as well."

Grateful for his brother's understanding, he nodded and stood to pick up the chair and move it closer to Braden's side. He sat again, clasping Braden's hand gently in his. He teared up when he saw how pale Braden's skin was, how small his hand looked in his own, much bigger one. Noticing the bruises on his wrist, he took in a shaky breath to keep himself under control. He leaned down and rested his forehead on their clasped hands, waiting for his brother to start.

"Braden sustained head injuries—three distinct bumps on his temple—that caused a concussion. He received a contusion to the upper eyelid and eyebrow, causing his brow to split open, he was given several stitches there. His right wrist has some bruising and his left was broken and has been placed in a cast. He sustained contusions on his lower chest on the left side around his ribs, however, after they brought in the portable X-ray, they ruled out any fractures there. He also has several contusions on his legs. That's where it ends, but you know these injuries will take some time to heal, so it's really just the beginning for him. He's gotten excellent care here and will continue to receive it under my direct supervision. I asked them to give us a bit of time for me to explain this to you, but we need to move Braden to the ICU so we can free this trauma room. The staff there has been prepped to care for him, and his room will be private, allowing you to stay with him at all times. They've been made aware of the situation with Eric and will not try to keep you from him, for any reason."

Cade looked at his brother and nodded his understanding. Finn opened the door and spoke quietly to someone on the other side. A few nursing assistants came in and prepped Braden for his move and minutes later, they rolled him into the elevator to take him to the ICU several floors up. Cade stayed with him during the transition to his room, and Braden was transferred gently to the big hospital bed, which dwarfed him and seemed to emphasize his vulnerability. The bright, fluorescent lights amplified the paleness of Braden's skin and Cade felt reality bear down on him, almost crippling in its weight. Taking a deep breath, he did his best to set his worries aside for now. He dimmed the overhead lights in the room, letting the natural light take over.

The room was rather large, the bed on the left side, and the back wall was mostly windows, under which was a long built-in couch that ran the width of the room. There was a fairly comfortable looking padded, reclining chair that looked as if it might lay flat for another sleeping surface in addition to the sofa. He wasn't sure if Cooper would be able to talk Maya out of spending the night here with Braden, so at least there was a place for both of them to rest if need be. There were already flowers on the windowsill behind the sofa. The artwork was fairly modern, and the room was painted a sage green.

He turned when there was a knock on the door and saw Cooper opening the door for Maya and Nana. Nana looked like she'd aged five years since yesterday, and Maya looked pale, circles ringing her eyes. Both women gasped as they saw Braden and rushed to his side. They clasped each other's hands tightly to share their combined strength as they cried together for Braden. He saw Finn by the room entrance and told him he wanted another recliner brought in and perhaps a couple smaller chairs if they'd fit.

Cade approached the women and put his arms around them. He made a mental note to have a sweater brought for Nana, her skin was like ice. He kissed them both on the head and continued to hold on to them, needing the contact for himself and knowing they needed his strength as well. "How much have you been told?"

Maya looked up at him with tears in her eyes and spoke quietly, almost as if Braden was just sleeping and she didn't want to wake him. "Finn told us he's in a coma but he's been treated with the meds he needs to come out of it, and now, we're just waiting. He also said Braden was beaten up a bit and to be prepared for that."

Looking down at Braden, her tears spilled over and she swiped them away with one hand as she lowered her other hand toward his bandaged head, fingers shaking, and gently moved a stray lock of hair caught in the gauze. "But how can we prepare for this?"

Her breath hitched. "I can't prepare myself for seeing Braden beaten and comatose. Oh, god… Was he… Tell us the truth, how bad is it, Cade? What can't we see?"

Cade hugged her tighter and took a deep breath. "The things you can't see are the bruises around his ribs and a few on his lower legs. We won't know until he wakes if he's sustained brain damage, and it's doubtful that he'll come out of this without any emotional trauma."

At that news, it seemed like the fight went out of her, and she grabbed him around the waist to hold herself up. He could feel her shoulders shaking and knew she was crying. Soothing her the best he could, he worked to distract her with information. "Finn says it's important to talk to him, that he might be able to hear us. He told me earlier to hold his hand because he might be able to feel it. We can also bring things in that we know he likes the scent of so he can smell things he loves. Those are the senses we have to work with to help him come around."

Maya looked up at him with hope and a tiny smile on her face. "He loves the smell of vanilla and baking sugar cookies. He loves the way you smell, like sandalwood and cedar. I can bring in some of the scents he likes."

Maya moved forward, sat gently on the bed by Braden. She touched his chest, his arm, and pulling his hand into her lap, she held it. Leaning over and kissing his forehead, Nana whispered in Braden's ear while she touched his face. Cade stood back and let them have time with Braden uninterrupted.

He wanted more than anything to be touching him, talking to him, but he wasn't going to get in the way of the two most important women in Braden's life doing their best to help him heal. He slid his hand up Maya's upper arm to her shoulder and squeezed. He smiled down at her. "I'm just gonna make a call, have some things brought here for Braden and a sweater for Nana. I'll be just outside the door, if you need me. Can I have anything brought here for you?"

She shook her head. "Don't bother with her bags, just have someone go into my room and get a couple of sweaters and pillows for the chairs. At the foot of Braden's bed is a navy blue fleece blanket that he loves. Whenever he's sick, he curls up with it. Oh and have them bring his pillow. If he's allowed his own clothes, he has a pair of ratty old flannel PJ bottoms that are blue and green plaid and a long sleeved Phish t-shirt that I always threaten to steal from him because it's so soft and comfortable. That's his go to clothing when he's sick. His feet are also cold all the time, so have them bring some fleece socks for him, if they can."

She looked up at him after giving her list, turned red and looked away. "Sorry. You can have them bring whatever you want for him. I just thought…"

Cade brought her in for a tight hug and rocked her back and forth. "It's perfect, you're perfect. I didn't know all of that, and those are the exact types of things I want brought for him, so thank you. Let me step outside in the hall and make a call to my family to check in and give them the list of things to bring. Take care of him while I'm away."

Nodding, she went back to Braden's side and sat back down on the bed and held his hand. He stepped out into the hall and saw a nurse pushing one of the reclining chairs towards his room. He opened the door to let her in, thanking her. Finn and Cooper approached him, and he told them everything that he needed from home for the ladies, himself, and Braden. Cooper said he'd call the order into Sawyer and Jackson, while Cade called his family to update them.

He spoke to his mom, who was busy baking cookies for the café with his sister to help Layla and Zoe keep the café open while everyone was at the hospital. They assured him they had it covered and would be at the hospital as soon as the café closed. His dad and brother had been gone for some time, running an errand that they'd kept from everyone else, which surprised Cade, but he let it go and figured they'd tell him when they came to the hospital.

He hung up just as he saw the same nurse struggling with a couple of stacked chairs. He relieved her of them as he thanked her again for her help and carried them into the room, placing them against the wall on the opposite side of the bed, out of the way but there for when they'd be needed.

He saw that Nana was standing next to Braden, so he moved the recliner directly next to the bed so she could sit and still talk to him and touch him. He did the same on the other side for Maya. He backed away and sat down on the long sofa in front of the windows, leaned back and rubbed his face. Cooper came in and nodded at him, silently letting him know that he'd relayed the message to Jackson and Sawyer. He walked towards the couch and sat by Cade, asked if he could bring anything from the café downstairs.

Cade figured they'd be there for the long haul so he might as well have Cooper go outside of the hospital and get some good food for everyone so they didn't have to eat the hospital food. Cooper left to head to a local deli, and Finn came in carrying some hospital blankets for the ladies then joined him on the couch. They sat there for the next thirty minutes or so, watching Braden's women tend to him, Finn, silently supportive, and Cade, itching to be close to Braden again.

As much as he wanted to be checking in with Brody, he knew now wasn't the time for him to be thinking about Eric and how much he wanted to get his hands on the man and wring the life out of him. He knew that he couldn't bring that anger, that need for revenge, into this room. There was already enough trauma Braden had to wade through; he didn't need bad energy in the room as well.

Cade took some deep breaths and stood up slowly to pace, which seemed to be a new habit he'd formed. He looked up and saw Cooper come into the room carrying a rather large Styrofoam cooler with a large paper bag sitting on top of it. He placed them on the countertop that housed cabinets and a sink.

When he approached Cade, the look in his eyes was one of understanding, and he put his hand on Cade's shoulder and said exactly what Cade needed to hear. "Listen, you don't need to be worrying about Eric right now. I'll stay in contact with Brody, Sawyer, and Jackson. If it's possible to wait on going after him until Braden is safe and well at home, that's what we'll do. If it looks like he's a flight risk, we'll be in contact with you immediately."

He nodded and his voice was rough when he replied, "Thanks, Coop."

Cooper squeezed his shoulder and continued, "I'll be in and out of here today, checking in. There are a ton of sandwiches and salads in there, all different types, and cold drinks as well, all on ice. The bag is full of other items like chips and some fruit. That should keep everyone that visits in food until tomorrow."

He gave his best friend an appreciative look and nodded. He relaxed his shoulders and felt himself let go of the rage and terror that had held him captive for the last thirty some odd hours. Braden needed him and damned if he was going to let him down.

He walked over to Braden's bed. "Cooper brought food for us and anyone else who visits. There's snacks, fruit, sandwiches, salads, and drinks. I know you're probably not that hungry at a time like this, but what we need to do is take care of ourselves so we're all able to take care of him. What can I bring you ladies?"

They gave their orders and he pulled the rolling tray over to the counter and loaded it up with their meals. He pulled up one of the smaller chairs and they all sat and ate, chatting with each other, telling Braden stories, making sure they were loud enough for him to hear so he knew he wasn't alone.

Several nurses had come in since he'd been in the ICU, one of which had drawn some blood. Cade was happy to see that the medical staff seemed to be doting on Braden, checking on him and making sure everyone visiting him got what they needed. Cade was even more relieved when his ICU doctor came to introduce himself. Dr. Eduard Himmel was of average height, sported wire-rimmed glasses, and had curly hair sprinkled liberally with gray. He smiled kindly at them.

"So, let's see how Braden is doing, shall we? I'm not very familiar with his case yet, as I just came on shift, but I've gotten a few tidbits. He's our most popular patient right now, which is rather ironic, as he's in a coma, but all the nurses seem quite protective of him already."

He glanced down at the iPad he had in his hands, tapped a few buttons and swiped through a few of the screens in Braden's medical file. He frowned at something he read and looked up at Cade. "There's mention here of a personal guard. I'm assuming that would be you?"

"Yes, among other things."

Dr. Himmel raised his eyebrows at that and smiled good naturedly, but tilted his head to look at Cade a bit closer. "You're a McCade. I should have seen the resemblance right away. Are you Finn's brother?"

"Yes."

The doctor smiled. "A man of few words. Another similarity, I see." Seeming to move on, he looked at Nana. "And you're his mother?"

Nana blushed a bit. "Grandmother."

Dr. Himmel smiled wide. "I don't see how that's possible, but I'll take your word for it. Miss?"

"I'm Maya, Braden's best friend and business partner."

Cade was slightly bemused that the doctor wanted everyone's story, and his lips twitched when the doctor continued. "And what is your business, if I may ask?"

"We own the Sugar n' Spice Café together."

The doctor stared at Maya for several beats and then snapped his finger and pointed in her general direction. "A couple blocks over from Dolores Park?"

Maya nodded. "That's us."

The doctor closed his eyes and sighed as if in bliss. "Oh, your coffee and those scones! My wife told me about it. Found it one day and dragged me there the next. She's a fan of your teas, too. We've made it a habit to come round for your English Tea Tray, I'm a sucker for the traditional scones with clotted cream and preserves."

Maya smiled, genuinely pleased. "We're so happy that you enjoy it so much. I run the front so the coffee and tea portion is mine. Braden is our pastry chef."

"Well then, let's hurry and get him well, so he can get back to doing what he's best at, shall we? So, you're all Braden's core team, as it were. He's going to need you. Right now, I'm going to take a look at his injuries. If any of you would like to leave, for his privacy or yours, it will only take a couple minutes."

Maya looked at Nana. "I don't think I can take seeing more of the damage that bastard did to him. I'll be in the hallway for a few minutes." Nana must have agreed as she nodded and followed her out.

Dr. Himmel set down his iPad, washed his hands, and proceeded to turn down the blanket from Braden's chest to his waist. Cade's muscles bunched in his torso and arms as he crossed them over his chest and moved to stand closer to Braden. The doctor paused to look up at Cade. "I really am rather fond of those scones, Mr. McCade. I want nothing more than to get Braden well so I can continue to enjoy them. I'm also a very big fan of keeping all of my teeth, having working limbs, and undamaged fingers."

Cade smiled at the doctor and noticed him relax a bit at the gesture. "Just Cade, Doc. You have nothing to worry about, it's the guy that did this to him that needs to be worried."

"I would imagine he is if he knows you're his guard… among other things." This was said with a smile, as the doctor continued, "I'm going to pull up his gown, take a look at his ribs, and then take a look at his legs. I just want to check on the injuries so that I can monitor their progress while he's here."

At Cade's nod, the doctor gently tugged Braden's gown up above the blanket at his waist to reveal the dark bruising and slight swelling of the area on his lower chest, over his ribs. Being this close, Cade noticed the skin was actually broken there. His insides turned to ice when he thought of the amount of pain Braden had sustained.

The doctor gently touched the area around the bruising and told Cade that the bruises themselves would take a month or more to fade but the pain–as it didn't crack any ribs–shouldn't last more than a week or two. Though some tenderness would remain for several weeks, and Braden shouldn't overdo with strenuous activities. The fact he was talking about Braden being able to do strenuous activities gave Cade a bit more hope.

Dr. Himmel lowered the gown under the blanket, being very careful to respect Braden's modesty. After that was done, he lifted the blanket from the bottom of the bed to reveal Braden's bare legs and took a look at the bruising there.

When Cade realized Braden had tubes coming out of him, practically from head to toe, he felt reality hit him like a ton of bricks. A bit of that renewed hope, dashed. He rubbed his face and pushed his hands into his hair then realized the doctor had continued to talk about Braden's condition and here he was, in his own head, paying attention to his own issues.

He got his head back in the game and admitted to the doctor that he'd zoned out and asked him to repeat what he'd said about Braden's legs. The doctor gave him a sympathetic look and did just that. The doctor moved to Braden's face and pulled back the medical tape holding the gauze to his eyebrow.

After covering the stitched area back up, he moved over to Braden's right temple, removing the gauze from around his head. Cade couldn't keep a hiss from escaping his lips when he saw the damage to Braden's skin there. There were a couple large bumps, the skin had split, and he was bruised and swollen. The doctor once again covered up the damage, returned to the sink, and washed his hands again.

Cade frowned. "Did you doubt he'd been taken care of properly by the ER?"

Dr. Himmel shook his head. "Not for a second, but with the trauma his body has sustained, the more eyes on his open wounds the better. I want to check them every day to ensure there's no sign of infection, which would greatly impact his recovery time and possibly keep him comatose longer if his body isn't healing properly."

Cade nodded, and the doctor turned to write a few things in the iPad file with his stylus. When he was done, he swiped back a few screens and checked on something before turning it off. Dr. Himmel looked up at Cade.

"Braden's glucose numbers are slowly coming back in line. In another hour or so, a nurse will come in to administer an insulin injection and an hour or so after that, another one will come in to draw some more blood. This will continue to be the case until he's released and can do his own testing and injections, as he's always done."

"Thank you."

Dr. Himmel smiled warmly, "The nursing staff is wonderful in our ICU, and you'll all be treated well. If you need me while I'm on shift, please let one of them know, and I'll make my way back around to you. I'll be checking on him again prior to the end of my shift or if anything should happen that needs my attention."

Cade sat on the side of the bed closest to the window. "Thanks, Doc."

Dr. Himmel reached across Braden to shake Cade's hand. "It was a pleasure to meet you, Cade."

"You as well, Doc."

Dr. Himmel walked out, and Nana and Maya came back in, followed by Cooper, Finn, Vaughn, Sawyer, and Jackson. Several minutes later, the door opened again and his mom and dad, as well as sister and older brother walked in. He took it all in, the support in the room, and realized that nearly everyone he loved was there, not only to support him, but to support the man he loved, even if they hadn't even met him before.

Emotion and extreme gratitude, the likes of which Cade had rarely felt, swamped him in that moment and all he could do was watch, as his family and friends talked quietly together. His dad approached him, not saying a word, but placing his hand on his shoulder and squeezing there in quiet support and understanding that he was feeling overwhelmed.

Gideon drew near and they both looked like they had something on their minds. Feeling emotionally exhausted, he hoped they didn't have anything earth shattering to discuss, as he wasn't sure how much more he could take. He kept himself rooted to the spot, sitting on Braden's bed, holding his hand, but he did turn a bit to face his dad and brother and spoke in a low voice to keep the others from overhearing. "Okay, out with it. I know you two went off on your own today, so you might as well tell me what the cloak and dagger routine is all about."

His brother had his hands in his pockets, and Cade caught the smile which was a rarity for Gideon in recent years, before he looked at his feet, waiting for their dad to do the talking it appeared. Cade looked at his father and saw something there, pride maybe, but he wasn't sure. Tilting his head, he didn't say a word and waited for his dad to speak, and when he did, he couldn't have been more surprised.

"So, your mom and I never really talked about what would happen when one of you kids found the love of your life. It wasn't part of our family only plan, but I think it should have been, and that was an oversight on our part. We had a conversation with your brothers and your sister earlier today, and we know Aiden wouldn't have a problem with our decision. We want Braden to have this, but we think that it needs to come from you."

Cade looked down at the box his dad had in his hand and reached to take it, giving him a questioning look. Cade opened the box and looked at their family crest that was etched into the wide platinum frame around the face of the specialized Imperator watch that only their immediate family wore. His heart beat faster and he had to blink several times to clear the tears from his eyes. He took a deep breath and was about to try to say something, but his dad beat him to it.

"If Braden is going to be a part of our family, he's going to need an Imperator watch. We saw his Militis watch in the café, with its leather band, which we really like by the way, and we figured he'd need an upgrade. We want to welcome him to our family properly, but wanted to hand it off to you, to give to him as you see fit."

Cade wasn't talkative at the best of times, but at that moment, he couldn't think of a single thing he could say that would fully explain all that he was thinking and feeling, so he stood and gathered his brother and his dad in a hug and held on tight, and they gave as good as they got. His family didn't doubt for a second that Braden was it for him; his one, his only. They never would have brought Braden one of the Imperators had they not all fully believed in Cade's claim that Braden was his everything.

He sat back down next to Braden, reached for his right arm and placed the watch on his wrist. It was huge on him, so he'd remove it later when his family left, and set it aside for when he woke. He knew he'd need to remove the links on the watch and attach it to Braden's leather handmade band or have another made for him, if it didn't fit. However, right now he could think of nothing he wanted more than for Braden to wear it.

His dad put his hand on the back of Cade's neck and squeezed. "Why don't you take a nap. You've been put through the wringer. You won't get much sleep tonight because you'll be on guard. At least one of your men, or Gideon, will stay until you wake up, so take advantage of it and lie down."

Cade looked at the sofa and the reclining chairs. Every spot was taken, and he smiled up at his dad, about to say he was out of luck, when his dad nudged him. "Braden's small enough that there's plenty of room for you beside him. Just lie down and rest, Cade."

Finn lifted a brow. "Why do you think I asked for one of our bigger beds to be brought in here?"

He nodded and smiled as his mom walked over with Braden's pillow from his bed and his blue fleece blanket. He gently lifted Braden's head and replaced the pillow with his own, took the other, and lay down on Braden's left side, facing him. His mom covered them both with the fleece blanket, and Cade let himself relax to the rhythm of the conversations around him as his family and friends continued to talk and eat.

It felt so good to have Braden next to him. As much as he wanted to curl himself protectively around him, he knew Braden was too injured for that, but just being close enough for their bodies to touch was enough for him to let down his guard and will himself to sleep.

Later on, when Cade woke, he realized he had moved himself closer to Braden in his sleep. He had started out on his side, arms folded across his chest so he didn't hurt him while he slept. He woke with his hand lying lightly on the side of Braden's neck, like he was pulling him in for a kiss while he slept. His lips were a mere inch from Braden's forehead, so he leaned in and kissed him, nuzzling his hair and whispering that he loved him. He checked his watch and realized he'd let himself sleep for over four hours, and he felt much better.

He sat up and realized what had woken him when he saw Braden's nurse drawing blood. She smiled so sweetly at him that he was taken aback. "Even in sleep, I can tell how much you love him, and even in his coma, he turned his head towards you to be closer. I had your friend take a picture for you. One of us will be back in about an hour to give him some insulin."

She left the room, and he glanced to the sofa to see Maya sitting with Cooper, everyone else had left. He used the bathroom and when he came out, he remembered to take the watch from Braden's wrist to give to him later. He moved one of the recliners close to the bed again and sat.

Cooper walked to the counter at the front of the room, and from what looked like a warming bag, pulled out a small tray with a cover over the food. He brought it to the rolling table and lowered it in front of Cade, removing the cover. The steak on the plate was enormous and the roasted baby red potatoes and seared asparagus had his mouth watering. It was no longer hot, but it was warmer than he expected as he dug in while Cooper updated him.

"Nana went home with your mom and sister around eight. I think this day really did her in. I brought back some food for the three of us, and the guys just went out to eat. I think you'll probably have some visitors off and on during the night."

Cade looked up at him and didn't say a word. Cooper knew what he wanted to hear and he sighed, which clued Cade in to the fact that he wouldn't be happy with his next words. "After he abandoned the car with Braden in it, he hoofed it several blocks, and from what we can tell he caught a bus. From there, he got off at the mall and that's where the signal stayed. Jackson and Sawyer drove to the mall and found the phone had been dropped in one of the outside trash cans.

"We've done a number of things so far. We've contacted Detective Miller, who is searching for any and all cars reported stolen today, no matter where they went missing. Jackson and Sawyer went to all the stores in and around the mall that sell burner phones with a couple pictures of Eric. So far, no one has said he looks familiar, but he's changed his looks and the camera footage pictures are grainy, so that's no surprise. We've got Brody and Landon going through camera footage from any of the cell phone retailers in the area that have security feeds available."

Cade muttered several expletives under his breath. "So, he's in the wind, and we're back to square one."

Cooper sighed. "Basically, yeah, until Braden wakes, and we ask if he has anything he can tell us that might help. Take this time during his recovery to rest. Even if we're not in the room, one of us will be on the floor, keeping an eye on you both. He'll need you at your best when he wakes."

Cade nodded. He knew Cooper was right. His stress levels were already rising and he didn't want that to impact Braden, so he asked Cooper to take lead the investigation on Eric and to keep all updates to himself until he said otherwise. He trusted Cooper to do what needed to be done and set it all aside, vowing not to think about it until Braden was out of the woods.

For Cade, the next twenty-four hours passed in a blur of visitors, doctor and nurse check-ins, blood draws, insulin injections, and a lot more pacing. He'd been able to sleep off and on the night before, feeling more comfortable with the safety of the hospital after Cooper had assured him the staff was being very cautious and one of his men would remain on the premises at all times. However, the day had been long and his tension had been high. Some sleepwear and his dopp kit had been brought for him, and he was able to take a quick shower and brush his teeth in the en suite bathroom to freshen up which made him feel a bit better.

Coma patients were often in danger of getting pneumonia, so his medical staff was religious about checking his wounds, testing his blood and vitals, and administering treatments. Cade knew he was getting the best care possible and had to trust in that, or he'd drive himself crazy with worry. That anxiety was lessening by the hour, however, especially in light of his continued conversations with Braden's medical team. Dr. Himmel was very optimistic that Braden would have a full recovery and reassured Cade every chance he got without making any promises.

Earlier that evening, the doctor had ordered CAT and SPECT scans, as well as an MRI of Braden's brain. Though they couldn't be one-hundred percent certain until Braden woke up, the results were negative for brain damage, and it didn't appear he would have any permanent impairment.

Cade could tell by staff's demeanor they felt positive it was only a matter of time until he woke. They simply waited for Braden's mind to recognize that his body was ready. As a result, Cade felt more at ease and began to relax around the caring staff. He couldn't keep himself from softening toward them as they doted on his boy, and if he was being honest, they doted on him as well.

Braden had been in the hospital going on thirty-six hours. Feeling restless and craving the intimacy of touch, Cade lay down next to Braden, curling his body around him. He settled in to talk to him and touch him, making sure Braden could feel, hear, and smell him.

In lieu of his pillow, Cade snuggled an arm under Braden's head, his lips whisper close to Braden's temple. He snaked his other arm across Braden's lower abdomen–avoiding his bruised ribs–and clasped his boy's hand gently. Cade's tension fled as he held Braden in his arms. Weary beyond his imagination, he let down his guard and allowed himself the sleep his body needed to refuel.

Having finally succumbed to exhaustion, Cade dreamed of Braden, healthy and whole. He could see Braden's smile, hear his beautiful voice, and feel his boy's warm smooth skin against his own. They were in bed, talking and laughing, holding hands and snuggling. The absence of stress and anxiety in the tableau almost jarring in its peacefulness.

Even in the dream, Cade felt the happiness and tranquility of holding Braden in his arms was somehow symbolic of their future. He felt the tender clasp of fingers much smaller than his own, squeeze him gently, but failed to recognize it for what it was. Cade slept on as the man he loved more than life itself gripped his hand like a lifeline and struggled to pull himself out of the depths of an abyss.

The End, *for now.*

Protecting Braden: Custos Securities Series Book 2, out now.

Author's Note

Thank you for reading *Trusting Cade*. This is my debut novel and it's been a labor of love and angst from the beginning. If you enjoyed it, please take a moment to leave a review.

I welcome contact from readers. You can find me on Facebook; Twitter; Instagram, Pinterest, and Luna David.

⌘ **Luna David** ⌘

Acknowledgements

To my husband, I'd like to thank you for working tirelessly to allow me to pursue my dream. I approached you about it in December 2014 and you immediately took me seriously. You told me that I need to treat it like a job and be given the time to do it. Not only do you work every single weekday to allow me to be a stay at home mom for our little ones, but you then come home and watch them every night, so that I can take the time to write. You believe in me, sometimes more than I believe in myself, and for that, and so many other things, I'm grateful for you.

I'd like to thank my family for being so supportive and my friends as well. Liz, Lizard, my fellow wordsmith, I don't even know what to say. Thank you doesn't seem good enough. The list of things you've done for me is pretty much endless. You've supported my ideas, helped me flesh them out, and put me back on course when I've veered too far in the wrong direction. You've encouraged me, been my sounding board, and my editor and beta reader all wrapped up in one. You, lady, deserve some sort of award for putting up with my neediness! Thank you, sincerely.

To my wonderful beta readers, thank you so much! Elizabeth Coffey, Becky Ellsworth, Michael Edward McFee, Denise Dechene and Jen Barten. Each and every one of you provided unique and much needed feedback, corrections and ideas on what to do to make my book better, stronger. I appreciate each and every one of you and can't thank you enough, not only for all the work you did, but for being patient with my endless questions and first-time author jitters.

And last, but definitely not least, I'd like to thank my editor Miranda Vescio at V8 Editing and Proofreading and my proofreader, Allison Holzapfel at Allison's Author Services. My amazing cover artist, Kellie Dennis, at Book Cover by Design (www.bookcoverbydesign.co.uk). Your work is amazing. I was ridiculously demanding and you were ridiculously patient. I had a million requests and you handled them with ease. Thank you.

About the Author

Luna David is a true romantic at heart who was fortunate enough to find and marry her soul mate. Most of the time she considers herself lucky to have been blessed with having g/b twins, but they're giving her a run for her money. She's a stay at home mom and an author, so when she's not begging her little monsters to behave, you'll most likely find her writing.

She loves anything book, coffee or dark chocolate related and can't think of a better way to pass the time than to combine all three. She reads romance novels voraciously and while she prefers contemporary romance with strong Alpha males finding their soul mates, she's a sucker for any well-written, romantic story, regardless of genre.

She created the Custos Securities Series because she loves to write what she loves to read. Her books feature strong dominant males and the men they would die protecting. Toss in some BDSM and kink and you've got her Catharsis Novel Series and The Boys Club Series. She loves nothing more than making her readers feel a wide range of emotions with her words. And she hopes you enjoy her stories. Happy Reading!

Printed in Great Britain
by Amazon